HE WHO WOULD BE KING ...

Spinel-alpha was not the first Emperor to be roused out of bed at midnight by armed men, but perhaps he was one of the first to be mildly cynical about it. He had never cared for the throne, and had often tried to give it away. No one dared take it; he was one of the few Emperors genuinely loved by his subjects.

Though at the moment he did not care about being overthrown, he was very peeved about being awakened and handled roughly. His vocal organ was compressed against rough wood so that he could not beg, as he would not have done in any case, or offer the throne, as he had done many times. An alien laughed and said something in a rough voice. The aliens had never taught the inhabitants of Qsaprinel their language, and Spinel did not know that this one said, "Emperor Crawdad!" If he had understood he would have shrugged aside the unearned insult as he shrugged away flattery. . . .

Ace Science Fiction Books by Phyllis Gotlieb

A JUDGMENT OF DRAGONS
EMPEROR, SWORDS, PENTACLES
THE KINGDOM OF THE CATS *(coming in July '85)*

EMPEROR, SWORDS, PENTACLES

PHYLLIS GOTLIEB

ACE SCIENCE FICTION BOOKS
NEW YORK

EMPEROR, SWORDS, PENTACLES

An Ace Science Fiction Book / published by arrangement with
the author

PRINTING HISTORY
First Ace printing / April 1982
Third printing / May 1985

ISBN: 0-441-20547-X

Ace Science Fiction Books are published by
The Berkley Publishing Group,
200 Madison Avenue, New York, New York 10016.
PRINTED IN THE UNITED STATES OF AMERICA

*the hand of the Diviner takes the
cards from the carved ivory box
and offers them to the
Questioner, who shuffles
and returns
them*

the Emperor

Spinel-alpha was not the first Emperor to be rousted out of bed at midnight by armed men, but perhaps he was one of the first to be mildly cynical about it. He had never cared for the throne, and had often tried to give it away. No one dared take it: he was one of the few Emperors genuinely loved by his subjects, and his political value was enormous. His detractors claimed that he was a bit stupid. Spinel cheerfully agreed—but in strict terms he was only four years old, and his Maturing-Day was scheduled with his official Enthronement, six days away.

Though at the moment he did not care about being overthrown he was very peeved about being awakened and handled roughly. When the hard instrument slid beneath his body and pressed against the ganglion that controlled his intake, and his skin-water automatically began to decant, he was seized by equally uncontrollable anger and panic, and his bipolar arms rose at tremendous speed. There were restraints ready for those too: they were held down until the electric charges evaporated harmlessly. A thousand interdermal valves relaxed, his water store overflowed the rim of his basin and splashed across the floor in streams of phosphorescent green and purple from its algae and protozoa.

The instrument was removed from the ganglion, leaving

1

him twenty kilos lighter, but with enough water so that he would not dry out. He gulped air through his pouch opening and found voice. "Spinel-beta?" he croaked.

"Shut up." It was his sib's voice.

He popped his fore-eyes from their sockets, but their surrounding membranes were not moist enough to let him extend them fully; he saw only a wall and ceiling lit with flickering light. The primitive light-organs circling the back of his brain-case sensed moving flames and unmoving cold-light standards. Cold light meant that the aliens were here too, and that did not surprise him either.

He was dragged from his bed and dumped on a wooden trolley; first his electric arms were strapped down on crossbars, then his muscular rear legs. His vocal organ was compressed against the rough wood so that he could not beg, as he would not have done in any case, or offer the throne, as he had done many times. But he could not even ask now what was wanted, and why at this time.

An alien laughed and said something in a rough voice. The aliens had never taught the inhabitants of Qsaprinel their language, and Spinel did not know that this one had said, "Emperor Crawdad!" If he had understood he would have shrugged aside an unearned insult as he shrugged away flattery.

"Wouldn't want to try eating this one."

"Or the other. Especially the other."

He was dragged backward on the board. The wheels slid at first on the wet floor and then squeaked.

"Into the Room of State," said Spinel-beta.

These sibs were not called Alpha and Beta by Qsaprinli, but the terms were the nearest the aliens could find to express their relationship. They were the products of fissioning by the former Emperor Spinel, whom the aliens called Meta-Spinel.

The Room of State was much like all the other rooms in the Palace. It had a low table at which business was conducted, slanted wooden stands to support those who wished to emphasize or elaborate on a statement by signing with their forelimbs, and several sunken tubs for eating and replenishing oxygen by drawing water.

Spinel-alpha's outer skin was becoming slightly dry and darkening into crinkles like dead leaves; the sudden loss of water had sent him into mild shock, and he was beginning to feel rather suffocated. But his mind was still clear.

Oil lamps were bright in the wall-sconces, and the great windows looked on the sea in darkness. The walls were stone, the floor was wood coated with a lacquer so hard and clear it seemed to be made of amber. A wide archway led into the throne room, but there were no lights there, and all that could be seen were reflections from the facets of jewels that crusted the throne, an otherwise plain low pedestal.

Now the Emperor could see Spinel-beta, his First Minister and other self, before his eyes. That one was well-watered. Beyond the transparent container-skin laced with purple veins, and within the translucent true-skin, behind the brain-case, Spinel-alpha saw the blue heart beating at the same pace with triumph and determination as his own beat with terror and fury.

Spinel-beta gestured toward the end of the table. "Now free him and set him against that stand."

The aliens whose arms were fitted with so many fine clever digits lifted and placed him where men came to ask favors of the Emperor. The Emperor drew up moisture into his pseudo-mouth to loosen the flap, protecting the cradle-pouch and its organs, which served Qsaprinli for tongue and epiglottis. "Are you no longer afraid of my arms, sib?"

Beta, leaning against the Emperor's stand, said. "This man here—" the alien who stood beside him bearing the metal weapon called *gun* "—is an ESP who knows what is happening in your mind, and is not afraid to kill you, Emperor or not." Then Spinel understood for the first time how the aliens had learned so quickly the breathy click-ticking language of his people, when their own vocal arrangements were so different.

"Since you have now made me harmless perhaps you may

risk letting me have a little water."

"Later," said the First Minister. "We have business to do."

the Emperor reversed

It was said throughout the Empire that Spinel-alpha had been given the looks and Spinel-beta the brains. Even all those who loved their Emperor said this with lazy intolerance. Few asked whether Spinel-alpha had brains, but Beta could not hide his looks and did not try. He had known soon after fission that he could not rule and be accepted, except as his sibling's shadow. He was grossly deformed on the right side; his body curved around it. His bipolar arms functioned well, but his lower right limb was partially paralyzed and his right upper arm wasted and formed without its three fingers; he had had the tip removed to generate tentacles: there were four, and he made good use of them. It had been Alpha who urged on him the exercises that helped him move more easily.

Guilt, said Beta.

Sorrow, said Alpha.

But Spinel-beta had excellent eyes and brains, and these served him very well indeed.

They had not, however, let either him or his advisors learn why Meta-Spinel had decided to fission in the first place, particularly at such an advanced age.

Spinel's people had come from the sea and never let go of it. Each being carried it about on its back behind the brain in an external elastic skin; in an adult it took nearly a third of the body-weight, about thirty kilos in the usual two-meter Qsaprinil, and it cleansed the blood and fed the body with the sea's life forms. Gills, pores, inlet and outlet valves adjusted it. They had never needed to do so, but Qsaprinli could live in any atmosphere that had a little oxygen and some water, even if it contained moderate amounts of toxic matter. The system, tough as it was in some ways, was delicate in others, and the world's medical practice centered on it.

But the people had this in common with most of the

Galaxy's intelligent life-forms: they were diploid and two-sexed; they reproduced by egg and sperm, though their organs were situated where many other races had mouths. Their splitting function was an ancient and not quite vestigial inheritance of their sea-lives: when they were ravaged by predators the immature would fission when the colony population reached a critical point.

Meta-Spinel had been a normal healthy person. Although he had reached middle-age by the time he inherited the throne he promptly took an Empress and two concubines. The last of the three was very young, but by the first two he had had seventeen healthy children waiting in line, though the eldest was not even yet mature enough to take the throne. Then he had fissioned—into, so to speak, two young-old men, and there was no choice for it but to give one of them his Empire, for they were the oldest among his heirs.

Spinel-alpha said, "Must we discuss business before I have water? I will do as you wish, but I think you would wish me to be as alert as possible for—business."

"We will fill a tub for you in a moment!" Beta's voice was harsh and rattling. Anger was a medium he swam well in. "We are here to talk of the agreement!"

"Yes, yes, the agreement! My braincase has been well dented with it. We are to give these men from another world the stuff we have in our mines which we do not need and in return they will give us ships to fly—somewhere or other. Meta-Spinel's agreement must be honored, and in a six-day, if I am alive, I will announce it to the world. I, the Emperor, fit to use the amber seal, and thousands will cheer and say I am a grand fine fellow." The water-loss was now beginning to make him feel a little toxic, or perhaps intoxicated, as those otherworld people became when they drank their strange waters.

"You are speaking like the child you are!" Beta gestured. "Fill a tub for him. He is becoming irrational."

"Not too irrational to ask why all of this is happening," said Spinel-alpha quietly. "I have never refused to seal the pact. All of your—all of our advisors seem to agree it is a good one.''

Beta hissed: "They want it sealed *now!*"

Spinel-alpha was truly astonished. "But why?"

the King of Swords reversed

The man with the weapon stepped forward. "If I weren't an ESP I'd say you were putting on some kind of act. You may not know—you may think you don't know—but we're pretty sure your Meta-Spinel was avoiding the agreement for some reason. That was why he fissioned. We think whatever his plan was it would have left him with a lot and us with nothing.''

"*I* know nothing," Alpha said sharply, "but you are the mind-reader.''

"Oh now, not quite so simple. You share his short-term memories, but a lot of his deeper connections got broken and lost when his brain divided. I can't find anything in either of you—I'll say that much—but I'm not sure there isn't something there I can't reach. . ." Or perhaps he was not so powerful an ESP as he claimed. Spinel-alpha had had flashes of past memories, but none with such matter as might have been suppressed.

"I resent—" Spinel-beta began.

"You have nothing to resent. We said we found nothing—so far. But we have sources, and we've heard rumors—so we have come here to have the agreement sealed. Now.''

It had occurred to the Spinel-sibs more than once that their Progenitor might have fissioned to avoid completing the agreement, though they could not imagine why he was so afraid of it. They did not care for it either, but only because there was nothing they wanted. They had great stores of wealth: for use, wood and stone; for show, jewels. And their jewels were not all what others considered valuable. They loved zircon as well as diamond, and opal as well as emerald. Half the rocks in the Galaxy produced something of this sort.

They had been visited many times before by aliens, some who were members of Galactic Federation, and their commerce was modest: communications and medical technology, trovers' rights for XenoBi teams, methods of improving metal-refining that did not involve the extreme heats they feared. As for weapons, Qsaprinli did not need many; most of their battles were fought with bare arms, and were usually ideological.

Now these aliens from the nearest sun had come with weapons, threatening, and it seemed to the Spinels that keeping the agreement meant less harm than avoiding it. If trouble arose they were not entirely defenceless. . .

Spinel-alpha said, "If you are determined to have this treaty ratified now I will seal your personal copy. Then the other two will be sealed at the Festival, because that was to be part of it for all the people who will be here, and I am sure—if you care to keep our relationship reasonably amicable—that you will want to be a part of it too."

The armed ESP snarled something in his own language that expressed what he thought about amicable relationships, and added, with greater control, "We don't intend to stay here that long. We want the whole thing completed and we want it *now*."

The greatest fear of an Qsaprinli was of being smothered from lack of water. Once Spinel-alpha had gotten past this ridge of terror, the prospect of sudden death ran well behind it. And he was stubborn. "You admit you find us honest and we do not understand what you mean by rumors—"

Spinel-beta cried, "I promised it to them!"

Alpha looked into his sib's popping eyes and found a kind of fear he had never seen before.

I surely am stupid!

Nevertheless he said quietly, "That was not in your power."

"It will be if you die," said the ESP, and the weapon rose. It did not seem worth telling him that the people would not love Spinel-beta.

Qsaprinli could hardly tell one alien from another: they
were much of a size, stood upright on two limbs, had no
bipolar arms at their middles, were furnished with many
useful digits on the arms they did have, and their brain-cases
were moveable and set on top of their bodies. Moreover, they
were all flat-eyed, had nearly as much hair as land-mammals,
and breathed through pointed snouts which they often covered with masks or filters to adjust the air.

But there was one who was quite distinguishable, in part
because it spoke the local language only very haltingly,
mainly because it was female. She did not seem different in
character from the others, but in this mammalian class she
differed in having comparatively heavy breasts, soft pale skin
and little body hair. She was also the only female in the
group. This person held up her hands, weaponless, and said,
"Hartog, hold it."

"Keep out of it, Renny."

"Just wait a bit." She touched his shoulder to make him
stop a moment and think. A moment of life. "You confuse
these people by attacking when not needful. If you come
between them and custom you make shame and things will
not go well here for anyone."

"You aren't giving orders here. If you're afraid of a little
blood you should have stayed up in the ship's galley."

"Hartog, if you were afraid of women like me you could
have left me at base—and stayed out of my bed."

Two or three other aliens drew forward and Spinel-beta
was looking ever more fearful and pop-eyed. Hartog
growled, "I'll settle with you later. Now get out of here!"

She said through her teeth, "It is still better to *ask!*"

"What the hell for?"

"To make the ceremony earlier. Give them a little time to
think. We have some to spare, and they have good,"—
Spinel missed the next word because of poor pronunciation,
but he was sure it was *communications*—"they can gather
their crowd and hold it tomorrow."

"Tomorrow, yes, tomorrow!" Spinel-beta stammered.

The conversation went on in the language of the aliens, and Spinel could guess something of its meaning too.

"You're heating things up too much, Hartog," one of the other men said. "It was a mistake to threaten them. You could have thought of six other ways to persuade them to give it to us now. This way they're frightened and angry and we're pushed into giving them more time—" and as Hartog opened his mouth, "—don't bother telling us how important you are. If things keep going like this we'll all wind up being electrocuted in a dark place when our backs are turned."

Hartog gave his lieutenant a look that would have electrocuted him then if it had had the power, holstered his weapon, interlaced his fingers and turned to Spinel-alpha. "You have until tomorrow."

"I will be happy to consider that," said Spinel-alpha. He dropped from the stand without asking permission and hopped toward the bath. Binatrel, his one friend, advisor and servant, had drawn it for him, and was waiting beside it.

the Page of Wands

"Thank you, dear friend," said Spinel-alpha, and gave him a look. In Binatrel's eyes he saw the look reflected as he slid into the phosphorescent water, opening his valves and inlets, and sank to the bottom. He realized only at that moment that he had come to the unconscious decision that the treaty would never be sealed, not by the present Emperor, and that he was willing to die first. He did not know what was wrong with the document, or what it was really about, but when men were willing to behave in such an ugly manner to achieve it, it must be evil. His countrymen were telling themselves that they were honor-bound to seal it because it was Meta-Spinel's; in truth it was because they were afraid of men with guns. Perhaps Meta-Spinel also. . .

He too could fission, but that would be stupid: there were already too many Spinels, aside from the heirs-in-line. He had no escape. He could fight, and perhaps he would win, but he did not wish to kill or see his people killed. He would settle accounts and make his last bath a poisoned one.

And he had come to all these conclusions because of the despair he had seen in the eyes of Binatrel.

When he climbed out only Beta was left in the room. He did not look at his sib; he was afraid to show his feelings either about himself or the fear and shame he had witnessed in that other self.

Beta said awkwardly, "I am sorry we treated you so roughly."

"No matter."

"Truly, I don't know whether you are more impossibly noble or more impossibly stupid!"

Spinel-alpha preferred his sib in this mode of false bravado, because it masked the other terrible things. "Possibly foolish is the word you want. We *have* been one, and perhaps there is still a great deal we share . . ." He looked at Beta with farewell in his eyes.

"What do you mean?"

Oh, Beta! You are the stupid one if you have no regard for me at all! "I was only expressing one of my usual foolish thoughts—trying to do it gently and failing, always failing . . . I want to be alone now, sib."

"They will be guarding your room."

"As long as they stay out of it."

the Empress

Someone had cleaned the basin and floor—probably Binatrel, since the real servants were terrified of the aliens and Spinel would not force them. The lacquer on the floor was impervious to everything and translucent as amber, as beautiful, Spinel thought, as the amber rings of office he wore on his bipolar arms. He pulled the circlets off and set them rolling on the floor, but they ran crookedly because of the stones they were set with: diamond, emerald, opal, garnet. He did not know that his own name was the word for a jewel in one of the aliens' languages.

He climbed to the sill of his high arched window; he could crawl down the wall with the suckers running along the undersides of his electric arms, but the ramp below was patrolled, and if it had not been he could not outrun an alien, though he could move like lightning within his own circumference. No, there was nowhere to go and nothing else to do with dignity.

He heard a tapping in the wall and jumped from the sill to answer it. An ancient Empress with an appetite for paramours had built a secret passage to allow access to her favorites. By now it was the worst-kept secret of the Empire. Previous rulers had kept it up to maintain privacy and mitigate jealousy, Spinel on a whim, because there were not many he could indulge in during a troubled reign. The only person who used the passage was his own Empress, Aspartil. She had been the second concubine of Meta-Spinel, and Alpha had chosen her because she was childless, scarcely older than the eldest of heirs-in-line, and had agreed that any children they might have would not compete with the present claimants. And above all, because he loved her.

When he pressed the release to slide the panel she was squatting on hind limbs in the darkness of the passage and made no move to come in.

"Are you going to do that terrible thing?"

He asked fearfully, "What terrible thing, love?"

"Let your ugly sib and the evil men make you seal the treaty tomorrow."

"Ah, that. Gossip goes quickly around the walls. I said I would consider it. I didn't have much choice. But the treaty will not be sealed by me. And—"

"Don't tell me not to say it about him. He has an ugly soul. I would love you no matter how your body was twisted."

"I might also have had an ugly soul—"

"Never!" She beat the padded ends of her bipolar arms together so fiercely the vestigial claws clicked, and her hands signed thoughts that words were inadequate for. "What will you do then?"

"I don't know. I said I would consider. Why do you not come in, Aspartil?"

"I am afraid of what you *will* do."

He sank to his knees. His voice trembled. "Aspartil, come in!"

They had few embraces; their bellies were horn-plated and only their fore-openings and their delicate hands were sensitive to loving touch.

"There are your beautiful armlets on the floor," she whispered. "Who will wear them now?"

"They are not very comfortable. Why must you think—"

"Spinel, I am ripe. Give me children."

"In such a dangerous time? Aspartil . . . I don't know if I am capable."

"You will be capable. Come into the bath." She turned on the faucets of his basin. "Come . . ." He saw the flickering of the sconces reflected in her eyes and the beating, almost in time with the flames, of the pale lymphatic hearts below her bipolar arms.

A kiss.

They were headless and neckless; their rigid cartilaginous spines gave them no more movement of the torso than a slight bend in the front quarters to increase the arc of vision. On land as in sea they had no choice but to copulate in water, crosswise to each other, so that the hinged openings of their pseudo-mouths would fit and seal to allow the sperm to bathe the egg-sac.

He found the power she wanted, and did not remind her that none of their children would wear the armlets. There was no need.

They lay alongside for a few minutes on the pool's floor among the small currents of cold mineral water. Presently Aspartil climbed over the rim. "I'll leave you alone to make your plans." But she waited there, unmoving, as she had done in the doorway.

He raised his snout above the water. "Aspartil, I believe I

have more intelligence than I have been credited with, but I
do not know what to do. For my people.''

She said firmly, ''You must make better plans for yourself
than you have been thinking of. I want to be in them as well,
with our children.'' And left without another word.

He climbed from the water he had planned for his poison-
bath and crouched dripping on the floor, angry. She had
cheated him of farewell. Of drama. . .

Of foolishness.

And he still did not know what to do. He crawled slowly
across the floor to retrieve the royal armlets and replaced
them. Emperor Fool.

The disadvantage of the "secret" passage was that it did
not connect with the user's chamber, and once she emerged
from it Aspartil had an arc of ramp to travel until she reached
her quarters at a lower level. It was poorly lit by only one
flame, and she hurried. She was terribly afraid for the Emperor because of the double threat: of the dangerous aliens
and of the furor they had stimulated in his mind; but she was
content with the fertilized egg-sac, for the day when it would
quiver with twelves of lives.

On the way she discovered she must pass the man with the
gun, the one it was said who knew minds. She recognized
him, not only by the blast of heat that all aliens gave off but by
his sickly smell. These aliens continually ran with loathsome
streams of water to which many Qsaprinli were allergic, and
it took all their courtesy to control distaste for it. As she
passed abreast of him his wiry arm sprang out; lifted, pressed
and silenced her.

Hartog was fearfully angry, and his anger had a grain of
madness in it. He was frustrated; his esp was not strong
enough to control his men—and certainly not the woman,
Renny, who was impervious to it, and whose mind he did not
care about. There was discord all about him and the time
which had ripened so slowly was turning rotten. The Spinel
his earlier compatriots had dealt with was gone. The Spinel

he could manipulate by playing on his feelings about his
warped body was matched by the one with real power who
had the suspicious stubbornness of the dimwitted. That one
would turn in his own circumference like the slow hand of a
clock until he reached a time in which he could escape the
treaty.

If he had had Renny under his hand this moment he would
have slapped a couple of teeth from her head; and this one,
called an Empress, a concubine-whore, had been making
what the big slugs called love, and thought she controlled the
power's soul. He did not care, no, did not care any more.

Aspartil's eyes had sunk, she was supported against the
wall by his hand, half fainting. He grinned with clamped
teeth, forced his other hand into her mouth, reached beneath
the flap to wrench the egg-sac from its mooring on the pouch
wall, and fling it against the wall of stone.

Aspartil fainted.

He backed away a few steps to avoid her falling weight,
and watched the liquids running from her body until her
autonomous system stopped them. Among them was a thin
tongue of blood from her mouth opening.

Let them despise us now. Let them learn.

Justice

A dark figure emerged from beneath the ramp, and because he could not esp it he knew who it was.

The woman Renny had been guarding the Emperor's door.
It was thick and she had heard little of what went on inside,
but had recognized Aspartil's voice.

Because she was an Impervious and had no access to
Qsaprinli minds through Hartog's esp, she had learned nothing of the language except what was taught her by the crew
during the voyage. But in the few days they had spent here
she had explored the palace and enlarged her knowledge of
the language, by sign and tongue; she had met all the inhabitants and learned of their occupations. If Hartog knew of
the passage through his esp, she knew by exploration, and did

not believe there would be any harm in leaving the Emperor and Empress to their love. Knowing Hartog, she thought there might be harm to the Empress, afterward, and had followed—too late.

Hartog faced her. "What are you doing here?" Breathing fast now.

"You've gone too far."

His laughter was like icicles breaking. "The treaty's ruined. He was going to kill himself."

"Now they'll kill us." She knelt briefly to check the beating hearts of Aspartil. When she rose the weapon was in his hand, but she came closer until she was within two meters of him. "There'll be sixty Qsaprinli with charged arms."

He tossed and caught the weapon. "Water-filled balloons."

She took another step. She was at a disadvantage, down the ramp from him.

He nodded. "I never should have taken on an Impervious. Even though you were good in the—service . . . maybe you were just playing at being. . ."

She looked at the gaunt surly face with the blue jaw and thought that no matter what happened she would never have to see it again.

His voice was conversational. "Even from here I can kick you so your skull cracks on the wall. Tell everybody you did this."

She hissed, "No, no! Get back! I'll take care of it!"

Hartog's head jerked up but did not turn. "You fool! Think you can pull—" and his eyes widened as two charged bipolar arms came round his shoulders.

She screamed, "Let go! Let go!" and the arms drew back just in time: she leaped forward and with hands like hot steel grabbed the weapon and forced it upward, rammed down the trigger finger and a bar of flame blew Hartog's head in two.

Over the body she faced Binatrel who was crouching with eyes popping, hearts thudding.

If Hartog had been a better ESP instead of a mad head swarming with violent fantasies. She wanted to retch.

And Binatrel: loyal servant galloping to the rescue! "You idiot! They would have killed you." He scrambled back. "No! Come here! The Empress is safe. Help me pull her over the body. Tell everyone when she fainted she fell on him and the gun went off." Noise was growing from below. "There. Now get back to the Emperor and lock the door."

She wiped sweat off her face and took a drag of oxygen from her mask. While the noise came closer she freed her mouth, let out a piercing shriek that tailed off into genuine hysterics.

She told the truth up to the point of Hartog's violence against the Empress, and the story held. Ordinarily the men would have been mildly regretful at the loss of Hartog; now they were frightened of scores of rampaging Qsaprinli.

Renny snivelled, "I'm scared. I think we ought to get out."

The lieutenant, Jiminez, said, "We'd better get to the tower and see that the radio's safe. Call everybody in, gather the stores in case there's a siege, and bring the boats up to the roof."

None of them needed to be assigned. They all ran.

Except Renny. She backed to the wall and waited until the noises faded. Hartog's body lay with Aspartil beginning to stir feebly over it, but she was staring at the place on the wall where the running liquid of the egg-sac was drying, jelled. Miscarriages and abortions were common pains and sorrows, but this was obscene. She was about to leave when four Qsaprinli skittered upward with a trolley to bear the Empress away. Her hand rested on her stunner for a moment, but they ignored her, and, having caught breath, she ran upward toward the Emperor's quarters. But not before pulling the chronometer off Hartog's dead wrist.

Spinel-alpha was crouching in deadly silent rage. Binatrel watched him anxiously. There was a light knock on the door and the woman's soft voice said, "Let me in! Please let me in quickly!"

"Yes," said Spinel. Binatrel kept staring. "Go ahead."

Binatrel pulled the door aside. She was standing in the frame, her weapon aimed. Binatrel hopped back a few steps. Spinel did not move. He said in a rasping, almost stammering voice: "You have avenged the rape of my Empress. Why are you now going to kill me?"

"This gun does not kill. It makes people sleep. I never was hired to kill, not even that beast." She smiled grimly. "But I was afraid you would be angry enough to embrace me."

"I am angry, but not at you. I will not touch you." She kept her eyes on him, but could not read his, though they protruded and were dilated to the utmost: they were alien. Nevertheless, he had matched his vocabulary and speech pattern to hers. She tucked the stunner beneath the hem of her knitted parka. He said, "Now tell me what you were hired for when you came here with men like them."

She glanced at Binatrel. Spinel said, "He is my true other self. What is mine to know is his."

"There is not much time. I work for Galactic Federation, and I came to find out what those men wanted, and when I heard of the treaty I looked for it in that, but it is difficult to understand. Those other men think it is jewels or some new mineral that will make terrible weapons. I learned from Hartog what he knew—and that was little enough, but just enough. The bodies of Qsaprinli manufacture some substance that *may* be of very great value. I don't know if that means a medicine or a poison."

"That does not sound like enough to bring down such savagery upon us. There is nothing like that in the treaty."

"Oh yes, there is. The version in *lingua*, I mean, Galactic Language, uses words I can say only in that language: 'ecosystems', 'natural resources'. Those mean the matter and life-forms found on your world. Under the complicated language that pact—in your own tongue and by your laws, your very own laws—gives you the right to have your bodies cut, or drained, or punctured, or burnt, or boiled—alive or dead—so that others may discover what that substance is."

Spinel's eyes sucked in for a moment and popped out again. "Meta-Spinel studied carefully and he did understand. I did not bother to study and that is what being a fool is.''

"It is also hard to deal with men who have powerful weapons and bad tempers.''

"Yet they accused us of delaying in order to make a better treaty with others.''

"Hartog did. He was trying to turn away your attention. The others are mean tough men, but they are ignorant; they did not intend personal attack on you.''

"At least we know a little of why Meta-Spinel fissioned. Such helplessness is a sorry state. Binatrel says those men are shut up in the tower.''

"Yes, all fifteen, I think. You have no guards outside now. The ship in orbit has two men to maintain it, and they can't come down because there are no more shuttles.''

"We could kill them—but you say they are ignorant, and the other two would go away and bring more. And we are known to other worlds and peoples. I think we should warn these. . .''

The scratching on the door was frantic.

"Now what?''

"Your sib! your sib!'' A rattling, gasping voice.

"Maybe a trick—'' Renny began.

"No trick,'' said Spinel-alpha. "That sib does not perform very well.''

Spinel-beta dashed through the re-opened door, followed by two of his council, and immediately began whirling like a pinwheel, whimpering, "Sorry, sorry, terrible, fearful, so sorry!''

"Be still, Beta, and do not make yourself an exhibit. You really do seem more sensible when you are angry. The Empress is not badly hurt and I have a few matters to discuss with you.''

Renny said, "Please excuse me for breaking in, your Majesty, but those men will be missing me, and though I doubt they care much for my safety, they may want to know what I'm doing!''

"That's simple. You are our hostage."

"Well and good, but—" she held up her wrist, "I have the—" she struggled with equivalents for 'remote'—"I have the far-working switch for one of the boats, and I took it from Hartog's body."

"That will only take you back to the ship."

"Not this one. It's a between-world lifeboat, a really fine one, stolen from GalFed, and I need it to get home in."

"Good. Then *we* have stolen it, and they can get back to their ship only if they can crowd into one boat, or make two trips. Now let me speak for a few minutes and we will make some plans." Beta had stopped his dance and crouched trembling, with the others behind him in obeisance. "Now, sib, and Lady Petranyl and Lord Beletrel, I have decided that I want to live, but I hope I don't live long enough to want power as much as you do! This woman of the aliens declares that she works for Galactic Federation and that we were about to deliver away our rights to our bodies and lives with that treaty. I believe her, and I expect that you will study it until it becomes clearer to you why Meta-Spinel fissioned. I take it, my lady, that you do not wish us to make any kind of pact with you?"

"God, no!" said Renny, near dancing, but with impatience. "I've done my job and all I want is to get home."

"Yet . . . it is not such a bad idea. Will that fine boat hold room for one Qsaprinil?"

"Oh, your Majesty, are you asking—"

"I am. We have been sitting too long afraid of being attacked, and it is time to use our humility to ask for help. I may be killed. I may be ridiculed first. Then we will have to fight on our ground. If we are as important as these out-worlders would have us believe, then Galactic Federation will help protect us, at least with an Observer or Surveyor Force. If they are men of honor we will have friends, which we now lack, and if they are corrupt we are already used to enemies. But—Lord of the Sea! Do be quiet! Especially you, Binatrel. I would have thought—"

"My lord! I only wanted to beg you to send me!"

"No. When I am away no treaties can be enacted, and I will take the Seal with me to make sure."

Spinel-beta hissed. "You are trusting this person who was one of those who—who—"

"A very short time ago, Beta, you were also one of those who. I will have to trust you also, unfortunately. And I do trust her, because what she says explains everything rationally."

"There are hiding places here!"

"In our shore cities with our small populations? Ten good ESPs could find me quickly. Under the sea, or on dry land in thorny forests among the mountains? I would die of loneliness or starvation, and in either case be useless. I do not intend to be useless again."

"Emperor, please! I can't take you on the boat!"

"Why not, lady? Remember—I was not joking when I said you are a hostage."

"There is no equipment to fit you. The force of lifting from the world will crush your body like a fall of rocks. I don't have anything to feed you, our water—" She clenched her fists to keep her hands off the stunner: five big leapers with ten big pop-eyes beamed on her, ten electric arms—

"My water recycles very well for quite a long while, and I grow most of my own food in it. The rest I can bring dried in very small volume. That, with my seal and armlets, will be my baggage. You will consider a way to take me wherever you are going—safely, and stay here until you do. You may bring food from your boat, and we will certainly not kill you, but you will stay."

"I—"

"You will consider, lady."

the Chariot and the Tower

A radio message, designed to be repeated for a full day, went out—to the tower, the castle, the men and women of all cities on the Two Continents.

*Citizens of the World, this is Spinel of Qsaprinel speaking.
The Council and I have decided—unanimously—that we
will not seal the proposed treaty with the world Calidor. It
has been demonstrated to us that it is an agreement of
great disadvantage to every person here. I am going into
retreat to devise more beneficial ways of obtaining trade
goods. While I am gone, Aspartil and Spinel-sib will rule
in my place. With his intelligence and her wisdom you will
be governed well. If I am gone beyond twelve twelves of
days you will consider me to have abdicated, and your
ruler will be Dunenli, eldest daughter of Great Spinel,
with the two present rulers as regents until her maturity.
Rich water to you.*

The boat was hovering outside the window, and Renny
was waiting in it with her teeth clenched. She had collected
all the loose canisters of extinguisher foam, which was inert
and would firm, she hoped, into a safety-cushion big enough
for Spinel. And a vial of stasis pills for beings with copper
hemoglobin of which, she hoped, three would be enough for
Spinel and his water-content—if his inlets would accept
them. . .

Here I sit. Suppose he dies. Oh God. Hartog was bad
enough. What I have to do. Joan of Arc.

¿Sancho Panza? No. Rosinante.

Spinel alone spoke to the tower, over the babble of voices
at the other end of the connection: "No, I will not answer any
of your questions, but I can tell you that you are free to
go—and stay away—in the one shuttle you have, and will not
be harmed even if you have to make two trips. In the meantime I am ordering the sea-wall raised and the sluices opened,
and am sealing the doors and windows. The water will rise
quite slowly, and we down here will be perfectly comfortable
in it, but you have not only shut yourselves in, *you are now
locked in,* and if you are not gone by the time the water comes
through the vents it is your misfortune."

"I don't know what you think you are going to find," said
Aspartil, with a tinge of reproach. She was not quite sure she
liked the new Spinel.

"Dearest, I am happy to see you secure in your faith that I
am a fool."

"I didn't mean that!"

"But it is true, Aspartil! If I were wise I would know what
better to do before we have to fight against much harsher
weapons."

"Right now you are leaving Beta with so much power."

"I am leaving you to remind him of what he nearly did.
That will make him lose a little water! Dunenli has plenty of
sense, and her mother will be so happy to see her at the head
of the line that you will have good allies."

"I think you are beginning to enjoy *your* power."

"If I have enjoyed it for a few moments I will also never
forget that I got it because everyone was put off guard by the
terrible thing that happened to you. And by what that woman
did for us—for which I will thank her, when I come back.
Where I am going I doubt that I will have much power."

And that was as far as they dared discuss the dangerous
journey.

Renny set the boat down on the beach to prepare for takeoff
and held the Emperor's strange small hand while he descended into stasis on his foam cushion. Every once in a
while she looked up through the port at the tower: there was
nothing to see but its dark mass on the misty sky: the windows
were sealed; the shuttle had not yet lifted off the roof. She
thought they would lift soon enough when they heard her
departure. When Spinel was unconscious she foamed the
upper half of the cabin so that he was well cocooned. There
was no rest for her yet. She prayed a bit, first, to the rude gods
of her ancestors, set a crazy-work course that would be hard
to follow, and enciphered the messages to be sent on the way.
She looked up once more at the dark castle.

It was a tremendous cone of rock wound with balustraded

ramps along the great arched doors and windows. It reminded her of Brueghel's paintings of the Tower of Babel, though the folk within were much quieter and, she hoped, a little wiser.

the Star

The sun Fthel, around which Galactic Federation Central revolves, is not situated in the center of the Galaxy, where the cosmic climate is too exciting and erratic, but fitted loosely into one of the armpits. It is also disappointing for new GalFed members to discover that though the planets number twelve there are no more than six useful ones, even when this number would be remarkable in any solar system with a less inflated reputation. Fthel IV and V, the one a little too warm, the other rather cold, are civilizations of administrators, ambassadors, liaisons and various influentials, with all of their families. On VI, mainly underground, are Military with their vessels and armories, and the quieter forces and bases of Observers and Surveyors. VII is the world of Astronomy and Communications, tended by machines; VIII and IX are mines, dumps, and also scanners who eye the passers-by.

Fthel IV is the most beautiful of the twelve, with its gardens, farms, hydroponics and the shimmering warmth of gracious lives; the great burden of administrative drudgery is done on V.

the Knight of Wands

This is where the affair began for Kinnear, slowly, like the textbook description of an insidious disease.

He was surveying the territory and working his way through the administration backlog of his new position as Sector Co-ordinator. Sector 492 was grumbling along without any of the conflagrations in which GalFed would be expected to play a part. It covered 67 suns and 82 inhabitable worlds, not counting moons. He was supported by tremendous root-systems of staff, most of whom he would never

know; he was content with his Director, Narinder Singh, and
his sub-Director, Ptrilitititi. His greatest difficulty during that
time was his embarrassment that he could not pronounce her
name, nor that of the world she came from. In a thirtyday he
got used to the sight of her big glasstex bowl, with herself
half-submerged in cloudy liquid, all eyes and tentacles, and
looking like animated chowder. But she was a clear-minded
and cheerful ESP-one, a good counterweight to a rather
moody Singh and occasionally erratic Kinnear.

When he came back from vacation at the turn of the
Quarter-Year, Kinnear found Narinder Singh demoted, two
floors down, coordinating 374, a sector with a plurality of
reptilian forms whose previous incumbent, a reptilian, had
died of a stroke.

the King of Swords

His new Director, Thorndecker, did not call him or anyone
else to an interview. He, she, or it was sealed in an area with
new double whitewalls, and available only as a cloudy image
on his screen, a blob whose printed message was that he was
to continue working as he had been doing.

He stopped at Ptrilitititi's office, but before he could speak
she raised an eye and three tentacles in her *don't-ask-me-
it's-A-One-Security* gesture. The walls had too many ears and
eyes, even the white-noise ones that separated ESP from
ESP.

Prudently, he forced himself to work until break, and then
went two floors down without hurry, searched for a few
minutes and opened a door without buzzing, but slowly, to
give warning. The former Director's pale green turban was
bent over a flimsy on his desk, the set of his body full of
crackling intensity, like a lightning bolt about to strike.

:*Singh, you want to come down for a cup of tea, or shall I
bring it up to you?*:

Singh replied in the same silence, :*I will come down.*:

The Solthree Staff-Caff was a barn with worn grey carpeting, as welcome as a tomb at midnight. Most staff brought lunch and ate it there because the tea, grown on Fthel IV, was the only provision worth buying. No boiling, stewing or steeping could ruin it.

The two stood drinking tea, out of range of fixtures and potted plants, trying not to notice the avoidance space around them.

:Do you know why?:

:No, Dun. But I think it is political rather than personal.:

All who knew Dunbar Macpherson Kinnear knew that very few were welcome to call him by either of his first names. His parents and wife were dead; his brother, managing mines on a rim-world, called him Mac. Narinder Singh was a school friend of forty years' standing, and Kinnear had been delighted to be working for him.

:Who the hell is this Thorndecker?:

:From what little I am told, an otherwise ordinary Solthree with an exaggerated fear of bacteria—don't laugh! You know how strange ESPs can be.:

:I'd like to think Psych would hoick them out before they got to be Co-ordinating Directors!:

:I am not Psych.: His eyes flashed. *:See the way they pull away from us! I think fear is even more contagious than disease.:*

:It is disease, friend. Try not to catch it!:

Narinder Singh turned back to Kinnear and his eyes grew calm and earnest. *:And you, Dun, old Security man, do not become a research doctor. Take care!:*

Kinnear took care. He waited, and did the work he was paid for, without pleasure and in obedience to the blurred screen. Within a few days he finished the survey of his territory and began on the Appendix of Neutrals in the Sector, who did not belong to GalFed but did business with it.

He reached Pintrel II, locally Qsaprinel, three-world system of an aging but healthy yellow star, World I a lump of hot rock, World III a lump of cold rock, no moons, living world

with population under a million and a half; record of business
ten Standard years: exploration yielding samples, animal,
vegetable, mineral. Three years later, trade in ores, jewels
and lumber, half a million credits. Two years after, half that
amount, and nothing since. Five years of nothing-doing
should strike it off the Divisional roster.

He called Local Registry. It repeated the record in the
Appendix and added: Middle-aged planet mainly covered
with seas except for two great shield continents (called the
Two Continents), diameter about 13,000 km, gravity about
8.5 Newtons, many varieties of mineral, a great deal dissolved in oceans rich in life-forms. Continental sediment sparse
and supports little life except on shoreline and scrubby forest
bordering it; mammalian life-forms at one remove from reptile. Uncatalogued. Intelligent life-forms similar to
Cephalopoda, except for—

The screen went blank for a moment, flickered once, and
the Blur presented itself.

DO YOU HAVE PARTICULAR BUSINESS WITH THE
WORLD YOU ARE INVESTIGATING?

Kinnear picked up the mike. "Not particularly, Director,
but—"

USE THE PRINTER, PLEASE.

—BUT WE HAVE HAD NO BUSINESS OR COM-
MUNICATION WITH THEM FOR FIVE YEARS AND
WE USUALLY WIPE THEM AFTER THAT TIME.

I AM AWARE OF THAT. THIS MATTER IS HIGHEST
SECURITY AND YOU NEED NOT CONCERN YOUR-
SELF WITH IT.

YES, DIRECTOR.

Yessir, thank you sir, please sir!

Kinnear was A-3. He knew his place. And nearly left it. He
went home early to grouse. But came back the next day. He
did not know what kind of reference he would get from that
Director, or what kind of grotty corner he would be pushed
into. And Narinder Singh had a wife and six children, but not
many friends.

Neither did Kinnear.

A thirtyday went by, and another. Friendships and allegiances shifted, staff turned over, unease surfaced, sank, festered slowly. . .

One evening when he reached his apartment he found a special parcel waiting. He was thrilled; endless personal and business messages streamed through the terminal, but parcels were expensive and rare. And he could not afford to gather many material things in his spare quarters because the nature of his work had kept him moving. There was the rock-crystal collection sent by his brother, a small library of old books from friends on Sol III. . .

This, by shape and weight, was a picture-cube, and by labelling, from Anax II, locally Ungruwarkh. From the big cats. . .

Memories rushed, painful/joyful. He pushed them back, and like a child at Christmas, sat eating his supper and looking at the package. It was marked PERSONAL MESSAGE NO COMMERCIAL VALUE by Customs and, by Delivery, PACKAGING DAMAGED IN TRANSIT: RE-SEALED. He wondered why, when packages were so few, they still got mauled. He did not know the history of Communications.

He shoved the food-wrappings into the recycler and opened the package delicately. The cube was not scratched. He set it on his table, poured a finger of scotch, and sipped, and pressed the stud: the red plains of the world spread out before him, light-years away. A common fifteen-centimeter cube with small figures and whispering voices. . .

"Hello, Kinnear, it's Ekkart, hale and hearty." Jake, the Observer, stepped forward, still bearded, snub-nosed and cheerful, face almost clear of the scars from his long battle with parasitic disease. "Thought you'd like to see the landscape. It's changed a bit. Last season we actually got a crop, and we have some grain in the bin. We haven't had much luck with the seaweed and broadleaf plants for the wild cattle, so we're ripening a few domestic embryos and importing soy-

milk to feed them. Next year everybody who registers early
enough will get a bite of meat. I hope it doesn't intoxicate
them. I'll give you a look at Doctor Hsiu.''

Shift to interior of infirmary. Tiny Mei-lin Hsiu pinning
down hefty crimson cub in some kind of Oriental wrestling
hold. ''Sorry, Kinnear, can't look up.'' Sudden screech and
leap of cat, leaving Hsiu with needle in hand, brushing hair
from her eyes and grinning. ''It never gets easier, but I never
miss either.''

Jake again. ''I know you want the Big Reds, so I'll let them
talk. Oh, thought I'd tell you the great deed. I hijacked a
shipload of surgeons going to a conference, and among other
things we shamed Tengura into a cornea transplant so she
could see her great-grandson through her own eyes instead of
everybody else's. Her temper hasn't improved, but she says
he's the only thing she's found worth seeing in the last thirty
years. Here—'' he waved goodbye.

Plains again. Volcano in the distance with a wisp of
smoke. A big red cat running, running. . .

Kinnear broke into a sweat, pushed the glass aside and
rested chin on knuckles. Prandra running, black diagonal
stripe down her side curving and straightening as her muscles
stretched and bunched. Somewhat older, and rather slower,
perhaps because a cub was riding her, clutching the fur of her
back, the set of his body intense with fear and delight.

the King and Queen of Pentacles

''Hullo, Kinnear.'' The voice was Khreng's, and its roar
seemed to fill the room out of the little box. Partly in *lingua*,
partly in rumbling Ungru'akh: ''That is Prandra, of course,
with our grandson. She says she has no time to talk. I don't
know whether that is because she has a few white hairs on her
forehead, and is too vain, or . . . because she is not quite the
same as before our son dies. She is well enough generally. I
travel a great deal to bring tribal representatives who make
decisions about food management, so that we all argue as

much as ever, but fight a little less. Prandra comes with me at
times to see how our minds work, and maybe one day she
fulfills her ambition and builds her mind model. But I think if
it is possible to make the Tribes cooperate I reach my own
goal first—and that is just as well.'' Probably, because soon
afterward both those fierce red bodies would be the
windblown ash of funeral pyres, but the brain of Prandra,
ESP class-one, would be swimming in the dark glasstex
globe above the humming pump for centuries, like all those
others over the Galaxy, teaching the ignorant, as Ungrukh
had been taught, and learning as she went, the way Prandra
did. Fair exchange. Brain for grain, meat, ''civilization.''
Civilization, ha! snarls Prandra. *Civilization doesn't begin
yet!* The running figure stopped, the head turned to the
camera, a piggybacking heraldic cat, *passant regardant*.

The lens closed in. ''Hullo, big man!'' She grinned.
''Next time you visit you get roast beef.'' She casually
shouldered off the cub, turned and diminished into the distance.

''Hah. The old woman gives you a word.'' The massive
head of Khreng, now, white hairs filling up the black V on his
forehead a little more, not much. ''Now I go fast, before this
thing runs out. First you get the laugh. We have a Committee
on Language Reform, but nobody can agree on how to
conjugate tenses with the ten grunts and six growls that make
our language. Our Emerald, and Raanung, live with us now
and they are not much trouble, but it is not altogether good,
because Raanung's father Mundr, that damned proud fool
you may remember, decides to have one more battle before
law and order creep up on him, so he leads his Hillsmen into
an ambush of Westerners, and he is dead. This leaves his
woman Nga with a kink in her tail; she has no power base
with Hillsmen trying to pull themselves together, so they
have an excuse to kick her out at last. Naturally she comes to
live with us—not in my cave, by the Blue Pit!—and you have
one guess who she makes her best friend—''

''Tengura,'' Kinnear muttered.

"Tengura, you are right, they are thick as burrs, and on the Plains as welcome as a netful of polluted fish. Aarandru thinks he makes me and Prandra angry if he uses his authority to kick them out, but *I* know he is scared of them." The cub appeared on Khreng's back, then on his head, with one paw gliding over a big red eye. Khreng brushed it aside. "Prandra is glad that somebody actually likes her mother—yet, but for this one here and his parents we prefer staying away from the Tribe *all* the time. Believe me. And Raanung is of course unhappy because he is no longer the warrior and hunter son of the Tribesman of the Hills, and has no status when he takes a Plainswoman—and Emerald—but that is enough. The world is growing and learning and that is what we are here for. Goodbye, friend."

And blank. A transparent cube, faintly blue-grey, half a kilo in weight. Kinnear's hand reached for the stud again, drew back, picked up the whiskey and sipped.

And Emerald . . . left the Tribe of her fathers, got her Barbarian Prince. He is flung from the throne and doesn't know how to use a fork. Too bad.

He stood, picked up the packing to throw it away, and stopped.

DAMAGED IN TRANSIT.

As an old Security hand he had done a little damage in transit himself. He thought back over the last couple of thirtydays, and the personal packages he had received. The ones from offworld. A spool of wire-recordings from his daughter and her family. DAMAGED IN TRANSIT. An old leatherbound volume, *Macaulay's Essays* from a friend in Edinburgh, on Sol III. Again . . . Nothing spoiled inside, not so much as a scratch. Neat.

He looked at the ceiling, at the windowless walls, at the potted plant (part of the rented furniture): bugs?

No. The idea of conspiratorial planning in an apartment designed for civil service ESPs was laughable. The kitchen and bathroom were medium-sized closets, the closets rather small cupboards. Sex was an almost circumspect encounter

on a daybed with no room for dramatics, parties were held in
Common Rooms nearly as grim as the Staff-Caff; short-term
vacations were taken in tiny cabanas on narrow beaches
around little artificial lakes. Narinder Singh had a three-room
apartment, but had never been able to invite a guest; Kinnear
visualized it as a place where eight people sat on the floor
with their knees pulled up. The big salaries got banked or
spent foolishly in the pits of the City, and noisy fools got
picked off. Bugs for thousands of cells in a hive were inef-
ficient; DAMAGE IN TRANSIT was cheap and easy.

The phenomenon had been so recent he concluded that it
had been triggered by the query on Qsaprinel. His mind
returned to Narinder Singh, and he had a second's jolt of
terror. But he had not mentioned that query to his friend.
Singh may have known something before his demotion, but
Psych would have wiped it along with any other A-1 or A-2
material in his memory. And there had been no change in his
personality tone: he was still earnestly hard-working, a bit
moody, somewhat resentful, but harmlessly.

No danger to Singh, so far.

And no danger to Kinnear, if he did not mind being probed
and insulted. Kinnear was a very competent ESP class-two,
and would never rise higher, but behind the bland face and
under the mind's control there was a class-one temperament.
Six-toes, Prandra had called him mentally when first they
met. It was not name-calling, merely identification, but it had
struck hard. He had gone through childhood with six digits on
each limb, his own peculiar ESP wierdness. The toes looked
normal, but the fingers were warped and twisted like the little
tails children with abnormal spines were sometimes born
with. On the small outpost where he had been born no one
paid attention. A few months after a move to a crowded world
the attention was unbearable. The malformations were removed, a few months too late. He still scratched at the
long-gone scars when he was depressed or angry.

He was scratching them. He stopped, tipped the last drop
of liquor onto his tongue and put down the glass, found a

place for the cube on a shelf between the spool and the book.
Not a scratch. He threw away the damaged wrapping. What
was the use?

Qsaprinel. Whatever it meant to the locked-in man, the
blur on the screen, it meant nothing to him. He couldn't touch
it with a tongs. He stepped out of the apartment to look for a
game, a performance, an exhibition, something to keep him
from reaching deeper into the bottle.

The long ivory corridor branched off into incomprehen-
sible complexity. A tiny figure emerged from an elevator and
diminished. Another tiny figure boarded it. A Security guard
materialized around a corner in a tiny cart and addressed him
as "Mumble, sir," with an informal salute. Floors in the
hundreds, corridors in the thousands of kilometers, towers in
the hundreds and hundreds: this was the Terrarium, an unearthly box for Solthrees.

He paused at a crossing of ways a few meters from the
elevator. A slight unfamiliar tension urged him down the hall
to the left: a pull. He stood still and scanned briefly. ESPs had
whitewalled apartments, not for privacy but because some
had high Security ratings. Whether or not they did, almost
all, often working into the night, were completely unin-
terested in the privacies of others and kept their minds to
themselves. Kinnear esped the corridors with a small stab of
guilt, and under that a twinge of fear. No one, as far as he
could reach, was interested in him.

He obeyed the pull and took a few steps to the left. Thought
of the damaged cube, and Qsaprinel—and anger stopped
him. The tug stopped. He turned back toward the elevator. It
resumed, lightly. He swore and wiped his forehead, feeling
like a raw recruit in a courtyard on first manoeuvres. Drawing
and drawing at him gently, without urgency or threat, only a
sense of *please?* He turned once again and let himself be
reeled in, by a fisher of great skill. It was not Singh, not the
Director, who had only to order. No one he could imagine.

the Magician

At the next crossway the corridor widened to include a
moving walkway. He rode it for five minutes and debarked at
the main elevator bank. *Go down.* Ten floors down the pull
took him out at Social, Conference & Administration, and
led him to the pneumatic express along with weary
briefcase-carriers and harassed clerks. A long soft drop to
ground level: most departed for other parts of the Terrarium
and the City. Kinnear took a step outward. *No! Down.*

The pneumatic filled with maintenance workers, rough-
handed and self-conscious in their best clothes; junior de-
partmentals usually wan-faced, now a bit flushed with drink
or excitement, the wealthy or pretend-wealthy in glitter and
perfume, some already half-coked. Clothes and perfume did
not mean much; Kinnear knew without esping that the
glassy-eyed had the most credit. Slummers. Because the
pneumatic, dropping now past garages, hangars, computers,
maintenance machines, storage areas, supplies, heat engines, coolers, freezers, ventilators, did not stop at these
floors which were reached by service elevators, but ended, in
the depths, at Seventh Heaven. Poor man's paradise.

Here there were crowds, and the plain ivory corridors were
transformed by little stores with huge twinkling signs: cafes,
carnival games, markets for exotic foods and ancient drugs
reputed aphrodisiac, porn parlors for all sexual
orientations—everything for those driven half-crazy trying to
keep thousands of worlds sane. Kinnear wondered what
Ptrilititi's Heaven was like, and those of all the other sentient species he knew. All here were Solthree, and of every
variety. And every branch of Security. He would likely have
come to Seventh Heaven tonight of his own will, but not to
this section: his clothing was neutral, but his bland uncom-
mitted face belonged to Security, and he stepped gently
among the revellers, drawn by a fine thread.

Every few meters an impromptu group of musicians
played, loud and bad. He had a pocketful of standard tokens,

but he dispensed them sparingly because he did not know his
destination, and got for change a curse or the razz of some
ill-winded instrument. He kept his face straight and went on.

His destiny pulled him to a door in a wall, between a
contraband shop and a drukka-fizz stand. A door, nothing
else, but a beauty of deeply-grained wood that would never
scuff. What first seemed a small round window framed in
scroll-work was a mirror. One-way, probably. A silver bell
hung above the lintel; its pull ended in a much tinier bell. The
wrought-iron door handle was in the shape of a gryphon, and
gold lettering beside it said: OUT TO LUNCH.

Kinnear thought he was beginning to recognize the style.

He yanked the pull and wished he could hear the silver
ringing above the blasting music. After a few moments the
door opened inward, and a man so nondescript that he was
truly indescribable stood in the doorway.

Kinnear crossed his arms and looked him over. "Hello,
Locksmith."

A voice remarkably like his own said, "You were perhaps
expecting the Minotaur?"

"Maybe I was."

"Come in."

There were a lot of things Kinnear would have liked to say,
first that he did not care to be pulled at. But the Locksmith,
who had been wearing dark glasses, pulled them off with his
small translucent hand and added, "Please?"

Kinnear stepped into darkness, and the room lit.

"I like that door."

"It comes from Qsaprinel. They do fine wood and metal
work there."

Kinnear froze.

"Don't worry," said the little man. "You're under my
lock. Nobody knows you're here. You're drinking scotch
and reading Macaulay, away up there. Who is Macaulay?"

"A man who wrote essays. And poems."

"Ah. I have it. Your ancient Rome. Horatius, Defender of
the State."

Kinnear took another step forward to let the door close, and looked the Locksmith in the eye. The eyes glistened oddly in the light, like those on the painted beast of a carousel. They were genuine eyes, not mere light sensors, but Kinnear could not guess what exactly they saw. Perhaps the Locksmith had created them only a short time before, along with the black jumpsuit, image of Kinnear's, from which emerged only the hairless head and freeform hands. Kinnear had heard a lot about the Locksmith, but the only other time he had seen him, a few years before, he had been in the shape of a little old lady squalling helplessly in the grip of twelve high-powered telepaths. She had exuded so purely the aura of age, terror and weakness that Kinnear, the old hand, had had to turn away until it stopped, and he looked up to see the defeated tentacled thing shuffling sullenly toward exile. And that was not the Locksmith's shape either.

He was a Praximif. Praximfi were the only organic shape-changing species GalFed knew of, as opposed, for instance, to Qumedni, who were energy forms. Their planet was a world of mystics who changed into their native plant and animal forms in religious ritual, a kind of exotic freemasonry. They had nothing to do with anyone and were very jealous of their secrets, which were of value to no one but themselves, and of interest only to a few xenobiologists; they did not care for visitors and would not allow emigration. No one knew what any of them really looked like: a Praximif, pursued, would mind-block until he/she/it had changed into a tree, a cow, a rock, and it would not be caught dead, except as a water-puddle and a few swiftly-decaying lumps of ganglia.

"Take the chair," said the Locksmith.

Kinnear took it in trust. It was a chair. That and the desk were the only furniture in the room. The wall opposite the door had a curtained doorway; the wall opposite Kinnear was covered with mounted locks, a history of locks, Solthree and Galactic. The Locksmith made and mended physical locks, but dealt mainly in psychic ones, for petty criminals and deceiving lovers; he was, himself, a petty criminal.

"I'm here legally now." He was squatting in front of the mounted wall, arms crossed like Kinnear's. He had grown slightly larger, drawing water from the air, probably; his face was filling out a little, a thin layer of pale hair spreading over his head. He would become a person similar to Kinnear, rather smaller and older, unthreatening; it was his style.

The Locksmith was one of the very few Praximfi who had not wanted to spend life as the local equivalent of a tree, a cow, a rock. He had stowed away with a frustrated biological expedition, found that he preferred the Solthree form and the world called Seventh Heaven, and loved the field generated by power and activity. In his innocence he had chosen to sell his locks to mobsters of every stripe, and this had produced fearful gang wars. He had been trapped with great difficulty and expense and dropped back on his world by a passing freighter. But Praximf could not hold him. The world had begged GalFed to take him back. In its extremity, for exchange, it allowed XenoBi an expedition not exceeding three persons for a period not exceeding one thirtyday every five Standard years.

"You're here by permission," Kinnear said. "You just have lower-class custom now." His tone was very mild; he and the Locksmith had too much on each other.

"You also have friends in low places," the Locksmith said. His eyes had deepened enough to hold a glint of mischief. "But no games. I called you down here to do business. You want to do business?"

Please? the tone had said. It was still there under the words. Kinnear turned the cards face-up. "I don't care for Thorndecker—whatever he is—or the way he works. I want to stay with what I'm doing, partly because I'm stubborn, and mostly because I like the work, or would, if I weren't being treated like a suspect. And I'm very much afraid for Narinder Singh."

"Don't be. He knows very little and won't spill any. I've reinforced his locks. Your Psych department does a very sloppy job."

"You're working with—"

"I am working against your Director."

"There are very few things I don't want to know, but I'm beginning to think this is one." Praximfi were another of the few species who could esp but not be esped, and Kinnear was tired of being at a disadvantage.

"Kinnear, I want to live on this world, but I want to die on Praximf with my nestfellows."

"I can understand that."

"I know. I admit it to assure you that Narinder Singh is really safe. *He* has had no parcels opened and *he* is not rebuffed by a screen—"

"Corollary: I am not safe."

"That I am unsure of. The Director is wary of you."

"Then I am not here to be warned?"

"You had better be warned." The Locksmith flowed to his height and leaned against the wall of locks. "I said I wanted to die at home . . . Kinnear, if you knew your Index of Neutrals as well as you think you do you would have noticed that the sun nearest to Qsaprinel's is Praximf's. Qsaprinli don't leave their world either, so *they* aren't threatening anyone. But we have a large moon—here you call it Calidor. Your biologist team, whom I have become friends with, had been using it as their orbiting base—but a thirtyday ago they were driven off—with weapons—by a group of Solthrees who have built up quite a big installation in the last few years. . ."

"Were they attacked?"

"Only with warning shots. I am glad they are safe, but I confess . . . if it had been worse that gang would have been wiped off my moon. This way GalFed has no jurisdiction—so they say."

"The group could claim Praximf gave them permission."

"To use a GalFed lifeboat for one of their shuttles?"

"Nobody told me about it! God. Are you sure?"

"Those men are sure of themselves. My friends were quickwitted enough to get down the registry number. They reported it and were told the boat had been retired and sold, quite legitimately.''

"The number should have been removed, in that case."

"Yes, but it makes a good disguise."

"Was it that old?"

"Not according to the number. But the XenoBi team had come up against the wall of bureaucracy, and they were afraid to push because they depended on grants—''

"Why is this all so definitely in the past tense when it's so recent?"

The Locksmith sat on the floor with legs folded lotus-wise. "The team called on me. They were nervous about going back to Praximf and their work is blocked. It's unimaginable that my world would allow that kind of build-up on their moon, and we were afraid that if the strangers decided to settle for a while they would come to believe that Praximf was much more comfortable and convenient to live on. My people, for all their psi and self-righteousness, are physically weak: they can take care of invaders on land, but all their power is useless against an attack from space. I tried to contact them, but of course right now Praximf will have nothing to do with me. I got into the records, chasing that boat—a big risk when I'm here on such grudging sufferance—and a tight squeeze, too. The boat belonged to the first survey ship to land on Qsaprinel ten years ago. Its captain—unlike your friend Khreng I won't ask you to guess—was Thorndecker.''

"Um," said Kinnear. "I wouldn't have thought Germfree would go out into the void."

"He'd be quite comfortable in a good hermetic suit."

"What is he, actually?"

"What you have heard. A powerful ESP, I'm told, who is otherwise an ordinary Solthree—physically—except that as a child he was the only survivor in a colony wiped out by one of those fungus plagues that storm in from nowhere.''

"Furiously warped, in short."

"Whatever else there may be, I hardly dare meddle."

"What about your friends?"

"I didn't think it was too extreme a measure to convince them to leave their work temporarily and go into hiding with new identification and *very* strong blocks."

"That serious!"

"I didn't want them to be—damaged in transit. Now I no longer have friends. None to trust."

"Yes." Kinnear wiped away a hairline of sweat and tried to disregard the coating of ice on his spine. "I suppose you could force me to pledge undying friendship. You aren't doing that, and I don't think you did it with the bio team, so I believe you, and I also trust you. And you are going to let me take my feelings to their ugliest extreme and suggest you want to get back to Praximf and have stage-managed this whole affair to make me help you."

The Locksmith said nothing, and waited.

"But you could have done that earlier by hitching a ride with XenoBi, so I can dismiss that as a paranoid idea; I do get them. That aside, by picking me you have got yourself a civil servant who is only a fair ESP-two and also under suspicion."

"It's more accurate to say you are under control—not in mind or body but by authority, your Director . . . Kinnear! You seem to have decided to join me!"

"I don't especially want to control, but I hate like hell being controlled. What has Thorndecker actually achieved with all his juggling?"

"I'm sure he manipulated himself into Singh's position to get power over an area with two neutrals that seem to be important to him—and one of which is damned important to me. But I can't tell you what he'd want with them."

"You have no evidence Praximf was attacked."

"No. Neither from the team or . . . other contacts."

Kinnear glanced sideways. The mirror in the door was in fact a window, and occasionally a face appeared in it, but no one pulled the bell. "The ones who brought you that piece of art."

"They do a little running."

Kinnear grinned. "They're not in my territory."

The Locksmith said intensely, "Sector Co-ordinator Kinnear, I don't want your help out of revenge, spite or impulse. I spent quite a while deciding to ask, and it is an extreme act for me."

"Locksmith, when I act on impulse you'll know it before I do. Can you change records?"

"Can I change my shape?"

"Don't go near any material on Thorndecker or Qsaprinel. It's been kicked above my clearance and that'd mean my head. I want that boat put back on the theft list with just the first half of the number so it looks less like a plant. What's the name of that chief at the local base, with the sh-ch sounds in the middle?"

"Vereshchagin."

"And the fellow to get her onto it is van Heemstra. Gerrit van Heemstra, works under the Asst. Jun. Sec. of something, twenty-fourth floor, north-northeast. You can handle that."

"Child's play."

"Yes, it is child's play. It's a risk, but a modest risk for both of us. And those getting their heads turned round. But . . . for the one I'm thinking of sending out into the arena—who is a friend of mine—it may mean death and will certainly be an ugly experience for her."

"A woman? Among those men who seem so anxious to kill? Why not send a man who is not your friend?"

"Because I want the work done. And you came to me, remember."

"Yes. I truly believe my world is in danger."

"I want good locks for anybody who may need them. Especially me. Locks, blocks, and shields with reflectors. Memory intact. And oh, after that flurry of activity I may get picked up. If that happens I want enough people to know about it so I just don't get shunted into the converters."

"Agreed."

"And now I need your runners' radio." He growled suddenly, "If your bloody world was in GalFed we wouldn't have to do all this."

"They may be, one day," the Locksmith said calmly.

"I won't try to get in touch with you again . . . but . . . Locksmith, what makes you think your world will be ready to take you when you are ready to die?"

"It is a truism of yours that the young as they age begin to forgive the old . . . is it not?"

The radio room was nested in a hollow among redirected pipes between subfloors five and six. The place was filthy and neglected: that was why it had been chosen. Kinnear was nervous but rather happy, because he felt really at work again. The operator was a thin grimy young man wound in wires, running an unlit dopestick from one end of his mouth to the other.

Kinnear sent the message in a medium-security code, now obsolete but still used in places on Sol III.

"Fthel Four and Cinnabar Keys South I understand, but what the hell is Sign of the Tarot in The Refinery?"

"The place where I want it sent. They'll know what it means at the other end. Now get it on and forget it."

COUSIN IRENYI FROM 492: CAN YOU CHECK OUT POSSIBLE OUTBREAK BLACKBEARD SYNDROME AND LOOK FOR CARRIER ON MOON OF NEUTRAL PRAXIMF THIS SECTOR. OFFICIAL REQUEST COMING REGARD CARRIER. GREAT RISK INSULT AND INJURY YOU CAN REFUSE. REPLY OUT-COME.

"Insult and injury!" said Wires, who knew all the codes. "Insult's a funny thing to warn about."

"Not when it means rough treatment by killers."

"Good thing you said she could refuse."

"I don't think she will. She can take it," said Kinnear, "and she dearly loves to give it back."

Two thirtydays went by, and Kinnear kept plodding, yessing the blurred screen. He accepted one more damaged package, read Macaulay and thought about Horatius:

They gave him of the cornland,
That was of public right,
As much as two strong oxen
Could plough from morn till night. . .

So much for saving the State. He pushed the Locksmith from his mind.

When the pull came to descend to Seventh Heaven it took him straight down, far from the Qsaprinel door. After half an hour's wandering, Wires accosted him with a sales pitch on a bargain Tri-V, factory fresh. And under the shield:

:COUSIN 492, FROM IRENYI: RIGHT ALL COUNTS. INFECTION PINTREL II TEMPORARILY ARRESTED ONE BLACKBEARD FATALITY. HAVE CARRIER. GRANDFATHER DECIDED TO ACCOMPANY. WHERE PUT?:

So the infection had spread to Qsaprinel rather than Praximf. So far. One Blackbeard fatality—a dead pirate, in plain words. Hard work for Renny, as he had expected, and he had a pang of guilt. But Grandfather? The Big Qsaprinil? *Intelligent life-form similar to Cephalopoda, except for* says Register. Except for what? God knew what special conditions he needed. But Renny had been able to bring him. . .

"Hey, buddy, you made up your mind about this Trivvy?" :and for shit's sake how long you gonna keep me standing around here like a deadhead?:

"No thanks, I spend more on repairs with this kind of deal than I would on the full price outside." :And keep your snotty mind to yourself or you really will end up with a dead head. Reply to message, same address:

:MANY THANKS. LEAVE GRANDPA TO MAMA.:

Kinnear took next day off. He had been saving up his

holiday leave because he had been too strung up to do anything but work. A fellow-co-ordinator's slightly sarcastic remark about his extreme industry suggested he would be better maintaining a normal regimen. Now he thought about the accumulation of holiday time. He could get that in half a thirtyday, and Cinnabar Keys on Fthel IV was a pleasant place. There were a lot of questions he wanted to ask. And—this was a very hard nut to crack—Grandfather would need guarding. By a good, not merely competent ESP. Renny was an Impervious, and her Mama sensitive enough but not an ESP; and he had already overburdened them. But what ESP in GalFed would guard a Neutral whose situation was unacknowledged even if not, as he hoped, unknown? Nobody.

Except.

But the Ungrukh owed him nothing—or whatever they might owe him he did not want repaid. Yet he did not need repayment; he needed help. But they had worked and suffered, and they wanted to mind their own business and live in peace.

Renny had sent the message enroute. He did not know what would happen to her, or the Qsaprinil, or him. The infection had been only temporarily arrested. Many were on the move: the Director, the Locksmith, the GalFeds, the Qsaprinli, the Blackbeards—and even he, sitting still as he was.

He yawned, and wished he had a window, if only for a thicket of buildings and a bit of sky among the mist bellows under the dome. The thought of books, whiskey, recordings bored him; he was allergic to dopesticks. The Tri-V, much repaired, but legitimate, showed him a badlands in another Galaxy where Things were blasting each other. He snapped it off and turned to his terminal. He arranged for vacation time and pay in fifteen days, a flight to Fthel IV in seventeen.

He swallowed hard and checked supply routes to and from Anax II, locally Ungruwarkh. Ship landing five days Standard, taking off plus five local. He chewed his tongue and sent the message.

TO EKKART FROM KINNEAR. ASK THE BIG REDS
IF THEY CAN SHARE VACATION WITH ME ON
FTHEL IV IN CINNABAR KEYS BY NEXT
TAKEOFF. I HAVE SOME GOOD FRIENDS THERE
WHO NEED OUR ADVICE.

Ekkart knew his friends, and what advice meant. And
Khreng and Prandra might be older and slower, but they were
still the most quick and alive he knew.

But the disease was winding its slow malignant course.

Three nights later while Kinnear was cleaning up the
supper garbage he was visited by two large custodians in
crisp police uniforms.

"You are under custody, sir."

Kinnear's heart did a double-tick. "For what and by
whom?"

The policeman on the left produced a crumpled tissue of
hard copy. "Please read aloud and sign that sir, and we will
witness; otherwise maintain your rights by keeping silence."

" 'To Dunbar Macpherson Kinnear,' spelled it right,
'from the Public Custodian, Area 4285: You are charged with
Public Mischief in regard to a legally owned vehicle reported
stolen and illegally removed by your direct or indirect order,'
that sounds good and fuzzy, 'and you will be held in custody
by the Public Custodian until such time as etcetera.' Here."
He signed and they countersigned. "Can you wait a minute
while I file for false arrest?"

"We have already done that for you, sir."

Yes, and the System would provide him with a lawyer, and
clothing and toilet articles . . . just as the System pumped
waste-water of the proper temperature into his rented potted
plant.

Civil servants, whose crimes were rarely violent, did not
go to prison but to holding areas in their own vicinity.
Kinnear's holding area was not much smaller than his
apartment; the same kind of food came through the slot; he

had access to news printouts and plenty of time to worry. He did not expect visitors.

They had caught him, he supposed, by triangulation. Vereshchagin, van Heemstra and perhaps a few others would have revealed under probe that he was the one known in common by all. No one could find them guilty, but as for himself. . .

On the second day he had a visitor.

The door clicked and twitched, slid open only a little, and the Locksmith insinuated himself in. Kinnear stared. The Locksmith's right arm terminated in a most peculiar shape, like a piece of metal bent and folded in complicated pleats.

:*For God's sake, they've got spy-eyes here!*:

:*Spy-eyes don't pick me up,*: said the Locksmith calmly, :*and the guards are well under. Look, it's my fault. I had to relax some of the blocks or suspicion would have exploded.*:

:*You did right. I said myself I might be picked up.*:

:*You want out of here?*:

:*That'd really blow up suspicion! No, not unless there's plans to kill me. I should be out on appeal soon.*:

:*No immediate danger. I came because of the message.*:

:*Who from? What?*:

:*The red place. The Big Ones apologize that they are too busy and weary to come but Green and Company have volunteered to take their place.*:

:*Oh my God, what have I done? Emerald and Raanung! They have no experience! I don't even know if they're as much as eleven years old.*: He could not keep staring at what the spy-eyes assumed was empty space. He picked up a news flimsy but it trembled in his hand and he had to put it down.

:*I gather from your own past experience that they are a mature and competent pair.*:

:*They'd better be. You hear anything about Renny or the Qsaprinil?*:

:*No. But the boat was turned in—and so were you.*:

:*Yes, and you'd better get going. I don't want you taking any more risks. All debts cancelled.*:

:*My debt is not cancelled until everyone is safe.*:

:I don't believe there's any threat to Praximf right now. Nobody's made a serious attempt to disturb it in the hundred and fifty years since it was—Christ, why didn't I think of it? If there was a survey ship in the area they'd have had to make a pass at Qsaprinel when it was right next door—and my Local Registry only gives it a ten year history! There's probably a good hundred years' worth of evidence—and we can get it! The Archives, man, get to the Archives and hope Thorndecker's made a really stupid mistake once in his life. Any citizen can have access to material older than fifty years, and anything you find on Qsaprinel, even if they just name it and say it's neutral, will be useful. Get the Archives!:

The Locksmith slipped away without another thought, and Kinnear sat sweating over his news sheets, charges of minor theft and drug possession dancing before his blind eyes. All he could see were two big cranky innocent red cats running into snares and delusions on a strange world. And conspicuous as hell. But a good many people hanging around the area were conspicuous, not the least of them Renny's Mama.

the World

Fthel IV was the Golden Door to Galactic Federation. Its equatorial regions were spreads of dense jungle and burning desert; its subtropical temperate zones were paradise for people who could bear temperatures hovering at 30°C and gravity at 9.5 Newtons. Forcefields controlled atmosphere, pressure and humidity for particular groups. Tall eyries, deep caverns, and undersea installations were available for those who needed them.

New members were handled with the greatest delicacy while terms were arranged and agreements drawn up; after these were signed or sealed or marked with paw, claw, fingerprint or blood-drip the participants were shunted off to Number Five to do the real work. Many of them came back to Four for holidays. Galactic Federation depended on the skillful work done there.

Solthree country, Fthel IV's Terrarium, was Cinnabar
Keys, two upturned crescents of low islands that extended
from the east coast of the southernmost continent; in the
lower areas the over-rich oxygen was controlled by force-
fields, but the temperature was bearable, and the growth
luxuriant and beautiful.

The quarter million people of the Keys lived in two towns,
one per Key, and many modest estates. The smaller town, on
the South Key, was named Miramar, and called The Refinery
by its labor force because of the upper class ambassadorial
population. Travelers rode its gently curving avenues by
bicycle, moped, pedicab, ricksha and occasionally, pony-
cart. No building was higher than the tallest tree. Many of the
shops had bow windows with little panes, and creaky signs
with curly letters; here at great expense customers could buy
lace handkerchiefs, silver lockets, meerschaum pipes of ancient design, and metal boxes of tobacco with names like
Three Nuns and Baby's Bottom. Solthrees wore clothes in
fashions from all over the Galaxy, whatever their station, and
most looked strange and outlandish to each other.

All who were out in the long light of one slow pleasant
evening agreed that none looked quite so outlandish as the
two big red cats trotting up the center of the main street and
wearing nothing but their own thick crimson fur: garnished
with tagged neck-chains attesting that they were a) members
of Galactic Federation, b) decontaminated, c) deloused, and
d) vaccinated; and on the slightly smaller and darker of the
pair, a heavy necklace of cabochon emeralds.

the High Priestess

Mam'Anika Gurdja rode her moped across the bridge
toward the outskirts of Miramar. Some heavy event was
approaching and it would not tell her what. She hoped it was
not an ugly customer who would bait her into telling some
plain truths and then start a row. She had enough to worry
about.

A quarter km from the city limit she turned in along a fieldstone path past a creaking standard with *Sign of The Tarot* painted on it in the usual fancy letters. She swung around an octagonal gazebo enclosed in glasstex panes.

Once she was in the back door the light came on and machinery hummed; the air began to cool and dry out. Within a screened enclosure she shucked her zip to the waist, sat before the makeup mirror, dug her hands into cream, wrung them, wiped them, dug in again and spread cream on face and neck, rubbed it into her hairline, into every crease of her skin, wiped down with a damp cloth and repeated until her skin had changed from flesh-color to its normal blue.

Her face began to look sinister and she grinned. She got as much pleasure from this process as any actor making up. The blue took translucence from the light fat layer beneath her skin, and her lips were softly purple; she did not look at all sickly or cyanotic. She was one of the few dozen Solthrees alive who had methemoglobinemia, a hereditary blood disease that made people turn blue, and could have cured herself in a couple of weeks with a few cheap pills, but blue had become part of her stock-in-trade. She considered herself lucky to have grey eyes; sky-blue eyes would have clashed with her lake-colored skin. She put on a blue caftan that managed not to clash, and combed out her thick black hair; there were few white hairs except for one dramatic streak running from above her right ear like a lightning-bolt. She had very dark brows and strong classic features. People who saw her made up or on her rare vacations (when she took the pills) invariably thought to themselves that she must have been a great beauty in her youth. Like many who were the subject of such ideas she had been, except for the blue, quite ordinary looking; advancing age had brought her bone structure forward like an escarpment to sculpt her features.

She sat down at the table in the more softly-lit reading area, took the lid from the carved ivory box, and with her blue nails resting on the scrolled back of the deck she scanned for trouble and waited.

The man's face and bulging neck were red; his scalp was
red under the close-cropped hair. His mid-brown suit was
tight at the neck and arrayed down the middle with honest-
to-God button-holes filled with gold and diamond studs; his
fingers were heavily ringed and there was a small sapphire set
in one pierced nostril. She wondered if his teeth were inlaid
with diamonds too, but he had so far not opened his mouth
wide enough to tell. The walls beyond him were laminated
and soundproof; the white-noise field on; the three people he
had come with were lounging on the couch in the ante-room,
bored: the snow-queen of over-thin beauty, whitened hair
and even more diamonds, his wife; the other woman, by
resemblance a daughter who would become like her mother,
and Blankface the son-in-law who liked money. Somewhere,
invisible in the distance, a mistress.

Anika picked off the twenty-two Arcana and gave them to
Questioner to shuffle. He did this briefly and neatly with his
heavy-ringed stubby fingers, and put them down before her.

"Ask aloud or in silence?"

"In silence," barely opening his lips. *Will I double my
holdings next year? Keep my (personal, sexual, political)
power? Does she love me, or only the power?*

Anika turned over a card: The Emperor. His mouth
quirked at one corner. So did hers. Power.

"Covering." She crossed the Emperor with the Fool.
Some luck. His mouth turned down at both corners.

"Signifying choice, I suppose."

"A new start, perhaps," she said calmly.

"I don't need that."

"I can't read the cards properly until they are all down."
She turned the third card and placed it above the cross.
Justice: a reward.

Diamonds flashing, he looked up at her, unplacated. His
brown eyes were so light as to be almost yellow. Quite right,
my hearty. You are a bully and a fool, and if Justice got you
you'd be rewarded with filthy rags. Her blue fingers rested on
the fourth card. "I sense a doubt whether I should go on."

"Why not? We've hardly started, and I'm paying plenty."

Poor fool. He would burst a blood vessel and was probably trying to control an ulcer. "If you are not satisfied you pay nothing. If many left discontented soon no one would come. You bring your feelings to the cards and I try to help you understand them. I can't tell stupid lies about great fortunes and passions that last forever, but I do my best to show people where their best hopes lie so that they can work toward them." She lifted the fourth card and in a movement his eye could not follow flipped the corner and found herself facing the Devil. She slapped it face down and gathered the rest together swiftly. She was certainly not going to give him that for his past.

"Now *I* cannot go on." The sense of approach she had felt earlier was strengthening and it had nothing to do with this man. "My eyes are clouded and I don't think the cards are telling me exactly what they mean. If you would like to come back another day you will not have wasted much time."

He gripped the edge of the table and his teeth showed, now. They were unnaturally white, but not inlaid with jewels. "You mean that you can see no hope for me!"

Mam'Anika had a gaucho knife hooked in her boot for suitable occasions; this was not one. She said very gently, "You have a hope for a much longer life, just as much strength, and a great deal of dignity if you care properly for your body and your spirit. You certainly have more than enough intelligence to know how."

The corner of his mouth twitched once, and he got up. She was glad to see the back of that fat neck instead of the sulky mouth. In the anteroom he gathered the rest of his party with one imperious gesture and they left.

And of course he won't do one bloody thing about it. Blood. She saw the explosion of blood in his brain and shuddered. She went into the dressing room, rinsed her mouth and spat. When she was zipping her dayclothes she felt the presence and turned to see four red disks in the darkness of forest greenery.

She stood still.

Two big red cats came forward slowly.

The worry of having an Emperor in her bathtub, with her daughter on guard, led Anika to a train of thought that would ordinarily have been the last kind of thing to enter her mind.

Ashtray in one hand and knife in the other sharp edge up with her thumb steadying the base of the blade. Her hands were knotty and strong as old tree roots.

If the glass gave way, while they were struggling over its dagger-edges there would be time for a good thrust or two in the throat.

The darker of the cats moved its head back and forth as if to say *tsk,* came forward, rose and stood with paws on the glass, and she saw for the first time the green fire of the necklace below the burning red eyes. There were no whitewalls in this section, and she thought she heard a laugh, a bass viol played pizzicato.

:Madame, we are sent to this place by your friend Kinnear!:

the Queen of Swords and the Knight of Swords

"My God!" Anika set down the alabaster tray, put away the knife and shook sweat from her face. "Khreng and Prandra?" She opened the door; the first cat dropped to fours and both slipped in and crouched on the floor with paws before them, like sphinxes.

"No, Madame. I am their daughter Emerald, and this is Raanung." She spoke good *lingua* with the resonance usual in a big cat. "We are asked for help, but our parents are too busy to come, and it seems no one tells you about us. I am sorry we frighten you."

"Oh, it's nothing." Anika groped for the cigarette box and lit a Sobranie with cerise paper and a gold tip. "I just dropped a couple of years from my life figuring how far I could take you with me when I died." She sighed. "I've been nervous lately. What kind of help is this, and who asked?"

"Our Observer on Ungruwarkh, whom we trust, says: we and Kinnear are to meet here, where our advice is needed. I think Kinnear is afraid to say more."

"He seems to have been afraid to tell us about it. . . ."

Emerald pulled forward her medallion with the ESP lightning-bolt. "I don't know why that is so, but we are not pretend-cats, and I am certainly an ESP. I presume Kinnear needs one, just as—" she grinned, "he needs a blue lady to guard an Emperor—please forgive my prying."

Anika laughed. "I'll forgive that, and you won't be insulted if I tell you I'm going to trust you because you could have killed us all six times over if you'd meant to."

The Ungrukh were not insulted; they were cooler, Anika thought, than her own daughter. She stubbed the cigarette and lit another, wondering why beautiful Emerald needed that necklace. "I know how to block, but I'm not doing it. Take what you need."

And in return we give (for a moment she was dizzy) the red plains of Ungruwarkh, in light that was dim to her eyes, bright to Emerald's; the line of volcanoes, here and there spitting a red flame that was the tongue of the god Firemaster; Khreng and Prandra, caring for their grandson Engni: Emerald, not quite eleven years old, a mother! Her parents snarling and spitting at each other and making love the next moment . . . and faintly, a shadow of pain, the dead brother Tugrik, the great handsome one who was oddly sweet-natured. Odd for Ungrukh. . .

"Kinnear has much praise for Ungrukh, and my parents, whom he knows best," Emerald said. "I am sorry they are not here, because they are much easier to like than I." She presented this as a fact, without malice or sarcasm.

And Anika answered. "People who like me learn to know me first, and that will be the same for us."

"Now I am worried that we know so little. It is very difficult to protect an Emperor."

"Particularly when he can shock you to death. But he's not quite awake, so he's no bother. When he comes to himself

I'll try getting him out of the bathtub and into the fishpond
during the day.''

"I think—oh Madame! There is great trouble at your
house!''

The Ungrukh were out the door like flickerings of fire, and
Anika scrambled after them without bothering to close up,
and jumped on the moped. They were far away before she got
it started.

It was taking several days for Spinel to waken fully. He
alternated between dream and half-consciousness. Renny,
guarding him constantly except for a few hours of sleep when
she was spelled by Anika, alternated between anxiety and
boredom. She sat, gun in hand, less fearful of attack than of
the effects of the drug. An Emperor was an Emperor. He lay
half-submerged in the tub, and when he thrashed in spasms
she got drenched. She had cut down the cooling system in the
bathroom so she would not be chilled; after a while, from
sweat and splashing, she was nearly as wet as Spinel. She
kept the light off and left the door slightly open so that light
from outside would warn her.

Somehow, this night, she nodded, and the noise of splashing blended with a wave of sleep . . . and covered the slight
noise of careful steps—

—and the light went out, she heard the grind of the door
slamming back in its socket, the bathroom light turned up to
its brightest, she blinked, jumped up colliding with a body, a
hand gave her a push that whacked her head against the
corner of the tub enclosure and she dropped.

Killer did not have more time for her; he closed the door
behind him.

the Hanged Man

While Spinel slept his metabolism adjusted his water content to counter increased gravity and his autonomic system
freshened it. Renny had been afraid to subject him to

deepsleep during the journey, so he had been dreaming
continuously instead of at the edges of consciousness. Most
of his dreams had been vaguely unpleasant, but as he neared
wakefulness they sharpened into terrifying images: he saw
the attack on Aspartil and could not move to help her; he
imagined that he had had many children and that they, and the
children of Meta-Spinel, were being swept away into a black
whirlpool: he heard the despairing cry of each and every one.

The cries dissolved gradually into the ripplings of water,
the maelstrom became his own tortured thrashings; he raised
his snout until the nerves of his spine screamed, and could not
speak.

And the light went on.

The light of his world was soft and misty; he had never
known such brightness, it stabbed and savaged, it was mad-
dening.

He heard a bang and thump, and a shadow crossed him, a
half-instant of relief, and his eyes blinked open in nervous
tic, then popped out. He saw the stranger's upside-down
face, the gun aimed at his braincase. He was not quite
conscious, but his fury and terror were so great that his arms
rose twisting to pull that head against his charging areas. He
was weak; his arms were not fully charged; they held only for
a second and dropped as he sank away into the blackness.

He did not hear the shriek or the splash of the gun into the
water.

Killer was stunned, and if Spinel's charge had been complete, would have been dead then. His mind was whirling; he
staggered through the house and out the patio door he had
come in. His thoughts were in such turmoil he could not tell
where he was going, and the garden with its crazy paths
became vast and confusing in the dark. He heard distant
sounds and sensed vaguely that there were pursuers, and
began to run, stumbling wildly. The pain in his head made
him close his eyes for a moment and in that moment he was
stabbed a hundred times and died.

Five minutes later Anika was gripping Renny by the

shoulders and yelling in her ear. Renny was looking somewhat blue about the lips and nails but only because she had
inherited a less extreme coloration from her mother and did
not take the pills when she was home. Because of fright
Anika was looking very blue.

"It is better to put her down where she can lie quietly in
case there is an injury," Emerald said. She turned down the
light, because Spinel had begun thrashing again, and sat
nearby to calm him. Raanung and Anika awkwardly moved
Renny to a couch; her eyes opened and she moaned.

Emerald, still with Spinel, said, *:Her eyes are normal, and
likely she has only a few days of headache, but waken her
during the night in case of real injury.:*

"Yeah," Anika said. "Renny!"

Renny's eyes closed again. Emerald came in and looked at
her. "That is only weariness. Better she doesn't see us yet.
She needs no more surprises. But lady, there is a dead man in
your garden, and that surprises the neighbors and the police if
we do not get rid of him."

Anika smoothed Renny's tangled hair. "Screw them."

The CommUnit bleeped at her elbow. She jumped and
thumbed the onscreen button. POLICE HERE: WORKING
PREMISES OF ANIKA GURDJA STANDING OPEN
AND UNTENANTED WITH LIGHTS ON.

She grabbed the mike. "Anika Gurdja here: turn the goddam lights off and shut the goddam door!" She slammed the
mike down so hard the unit sputtered. She was shaking.
"You're right."

"I always hated that filthy thing." All premises in the
Keys were rented; renter was enjoined to maintain the property but permission for changes required a year of red tape.
And so the thorntree with its fifteen centimeter spikes had
stood growing slowly for many years. Now a man, knees
buckled, was hanging impaled from its thorns: one piercing
an eyeball, one in the heart, others it did not matter where.

Raanung and Emerald dragged him down. Anika turned
away.

"Look and see what you can identify."

"It's too dark."

"Not through my eyes."

Anika shuddered and complied. "No marks or labels. Clothes you could find anywhere. Gun's an old Service stunner, high-powered. It would have made a mess of . . ." she had to turn away again. "If we bury him here we'll make a mess."

"Are you strong enough to lift off a layer of this grass?"

"Of course I am!" Anika snarled. "But I don't see how *you're* going to handle a shovel!"

Emerald grinned. "At home we are now studying agriculture, and," she held up a paw with elongated digits, "for cats we very nearly have very good hands."

Anika would rather have died than admit she was not as capable as a couple of scrubworld cats, and this was exactly the attitude Emerald wanted.

The Ungrukh were as good as their word. The body was buried deep, neat, and in silence. They used the extra earth to hill up the other shrubs, so there was only the slightest mound left to allow for sinkage by rain or irrigation. Raanung then fought his own exhaustion long enough to lope back to the skimmer terminal and collect the supplies and equipment left in keeping.

When he returned, he and Emerald put on knife-harnesses and fed themselves from bowls of something awful that they referred to as dogfood.

"Of course you'll stay here," said Anika. "I don't have alarm systems, and I'll stand watch."

"No need," said Emerald. "Tonight I sleep but my esp stays awake. And you need only waken once or twice to rouse your daughter."

"I'll never sleep," said Anika.

But she did. With her beautiful daughter lying as one dead. With two weird cats in the spare room. With a man pierced on a thorn tree.

Renny wakened in the morning normally enough except for a rotten temper and a headache rating high on the Beaufort and Richter scales.

The Ungrukh did not dismay her; she had heard about them often from Kinnear. They in turn found a strong graceful young woman with her mother's fine features enhanced by youth in spite of their ravages.

"I should have had a look at the man. I'm not exactly sorry I didn't." she said. "But I'm really sorry I did so poorly by Spinel."

"Spinel is doing well by himself, and soon he wakes like a new man," said Emerald.

Anika grunted. Her skin had darkened to the shade of denim and the sky outside was surly with cloud. "The fellow was in his late thirties, about seventy kilos and a bit over a meter and a half—medium-sized, clean-shaven over heavy beard, black hair, eye—eyes brown. Wore a dark green zip with a hood, kind of lumpy nothing face you see on the newsflix wanted for something—"

"Most of the ones I was with looked like that," said Renny. "I should have seen him but he slammed in so fast I went out when the light came on."

"—and no i.d. or other metal except the old Service gun."

Raanung said, "Almost no claws—excuse me, nails—on his fingers."

Renny frowned. "Maybe Wardrop . . . he was jittery and bit his nails . . . but he didn't seem worse than the others."

"Jittery or not, they are well on your trail," said Emerald. "Now I think it is time to get the baby up."

Anika said, "Suppose there was more than one of them, last night?"

"I esp *one,*" said Emerald.

"And I *smell* one," said Raanung, closing the subject.

"But I can't bear it!" Anika cried. "They could both have been killed!"

"Try not to think of that when you tell him good morning," said Emerald.

Spinel felt the calm pumping into him like freshened water. *Safe.*

:You are safe.: Words in the mind. ESP?

His thin eyelids were oddly heavy. He sensed pale green dimness.

Image: room where aliens (no danger) made themselves clean. Faucets for water: those he understood. Basin, for cleaning—now in his case for food, drink, sleep. Walls lined in what looked like fine green stone but was artificial.

:Plastic,: said Words-in-mind.

Floor covering to ease soft alien feet.

:Carpet.:

He croaked, "ESP?"

:Yes. Keep your eyes closed one minute. I show you.: His light organs caught movement of a red shape.

:Here is what you see when you open your eyes.:

Big red furred land-mammal. Calm red eyes. From both sides of the black snout long red hairs paling toward the tip. *:Called whiskers.:* Black V in the forehead with a white line in it. *:Now, these sharp things are not to harm but to defend you when you cannot help yourself, and add to our armor of shocks for enemies.:* The creature laughed at its own pun, showing great fanged teeth and a rasp tongue that was a weapon in itself, lifted a limb: long claws sprang from its digits.

It waited a moment or so until Spinel had absorbed all this with his nourishment, and said in rumbling Qsaprinli, "Now open your eyes."

Spinel's eyes popped open and out, and found the creature reclining on the edge of the sunken tub. "Well, Old Man, how do you feel?"

"Weak."

"Then you wait here until you feel strong, and you can come out into another room when you like." Emerald got up.

"Push that thing when you want the water to drain out."

Emerald—? How did he know her (her?) name? She had been feeding him information when he was unconscious, he decided, because he knew, unquestionably knew, that Renny had landed on this world (Fthel IV, in the Twelveworlds of Galactic Federation Central); there his cocoon had been hacked out of the boat, which had been turned over to a police division. Renny had produced and authenticated identification concealed in a false tooth and nagged Base authorities to roust out a sleepy and grumbling ESP who testified that, yes, somewhere in the huge mass of solidified foam was a planet's Emperor, a refugee and applicant for membership in GalFed. And she had managed all of this without giving more detail: a tactical masterpiece! Afterward there was a tense wait for a land transport, another Station where he had been pried free and decontaminated, and one more dark and secret journey here.

Dear Lord of the Sea, said Spinel to himself. What adventures have I had without knowing it! But he had had more than enough that he knew of, and all he could think of now, surely, was Aspartil, and Binatrel, and even that reprobate Spinel-beta . . . and yet his mind would wander. . .

Emerald, Emerald, green name for a red—

:Cat,: said Emerald.

And Renny had a mother, who was blue, and Emerald had a man (?) much like herself—

And it was a whole new world!

Renny was putting the best possible face on a grim mood. She was ashamed of allowing herself to kill a man she despised; ashamed of not taking better care of Spinel; worried because she had expected to meet Kinnear when she returned and her grapevine had informed her he was in custody. And she was responsible for a grossly endangered fugitive who looked like an oversized crawfish and behaved like the King in an old melodrama—as well as two damned big bad-tempered cats. Also she owed a small fortune in expenses and was owed nearly as much for Special Services. It seemed

unlikely now that Kinnear could ever scrape this out of the
Miscellaneous pot, and her base pay wasn't enough to keep a
streetsweeping machine in fuel and grease. "Better go walking down Paradise Street," she muttered.

"What?" Anika was setting out a game of solitaire. She
liked traditional cards better than Tarot, particularly because
the Court figures looked more inscrutable to her in their
hieratic formality; she could have divined from them, but her
customers preferred Tarot. "Did you say—"

"I've done as much in the regular line of work for a lot less
money." She sighed. "But if he'd been killed so would his
GalFed application, and his world would be. . ."

"Was it wrong to dump the corpse, then?"

"No. We have no official protection and there'd be even
more unwelcome attention if we had the local police buzzing.
If we tried to reach GalFed now I'm sure the line would be
tapped." She looked about the room. "I'm not sure we aren't
being bugged already. . ."

Emerald came in. "His Imperial Majesty is awake, and he
thinks it is a great world here."

"I'm glad someone thinks so."

"And as for being bugged," Emerald lifted the pendant of
her necklace, "if we are, this is buzzing."

"Is that what it's for? I bet somebody's surely told you to
put it away in a safe."

Emerald grinned. "Yes, some official does make that
suggestion. I doubt anyone does it again. It is hard to steal
from a person like me. And also the gems, though authentic
in structure, are man-made."

"But it's so big. Why are there so many? The fanciest
bug-picker doesn't need all that."

Emerald said with exaggerated dignity, "It is an emblem
to show that I am a civilized being, to be treated so—and as
such no better than these dogtags. The links shaped like stars
are wire-recorders, and those shaped like flowers are mag-
netic tracers, to be stuck where necessary."

"And," Raanung yawned, "the bloody thing is also

meant to remind us that we are to be at the throats of enemies
rather than each other,'' and ducked a whack in the chops
from Emerald's tail.

Spinel was the best-humored of the lot during the rest of
that day. He ventured out of the tub, but spoke mainly to
Renny. He was used to aliens, but still shy of the big fierce
ones. Renny, with some hesitation, told him how he had
saved himself in spite of her carelessness, but this sobered
him only slightly. His debt to her was great, and though he
did not wish to be an embarrassment—and a danger—to
others, he was perfectly single-minded about saving his own
world.

Emerald and Raanung dozed, twitching, woke and ate
with greater enthusiasm; Anika had bought them fresh meat,
but neither she nor Renny had stomach for their own meals.

The clock wound into afternoon and the Ungrukh were
getting bored. Raanung began to pace. ''I want to get out.''

''So do we all,'' Emerald growled. She blamed herself for
pulling Raanung along on this expedition but pushed down
the feeling to keep from adding to the general moodiness.
''We are of no use here.''

''I've heard you're very good at burial duty,'' Renny said,
pokerfaced. ''Spinel would be sick with hysteria if Emerald
hadn't been able to calm him. And so far it's Us: 2 and Them:
0—and you can't say that's nothing.'' But he stayed sulky.

Shadows went on lengthening and tempers shortening.

Anika, glancing from time to time uneasily at the Ungrukh, laid out Tarot spreads in a vague hope of inspiration,
but kept turning up the Fool: he ambled stupidly smiling and
drowsy-eyed, dog nipping at his behind. She gave up.

''Mra'it,'' Raanung said harshly. Of all Ungrukh only
Khreng took the trouble to pronounce his daughter's name
properly. ''It is no use staying here. We have nothing to do.
We take up space and need space ourselves.''

Emerald drew on her own small store of patience. ''Why

do you not stand watch outside? Your nose may find something interesting.''

"Are we to expect and withstand attack every night as if it is timed by some great clock? I am a huntsman, not a watcher by fires.'' He roared, "Where is Kinnear? I do not expect to be dropped in a world of strangers!''

Renny, frightened for once, found herself the focus of four red disks of eyeshine. "What can I say? I just haven't heard!''

"You can tell the truth, because that is not it!''

"Raanung!'' But Emerald herself believed Renny was lying; her nose was fine enough to catch the burst of sweat on the girl's palms and hairline. "Raanung!''

He had leaped up and was out of the house. She dashed after, caught up with his tail and clamped it between her teeth, he swung, claws out, she twisted her head and the claws caught in her necklace: it half choked her until she shook her head free and dropped to the grass. Raanung's fangs bared, his claws reached, she saw the strange thing in his mind, sensed the mind, beyond, sensing her mind, minds doubled and tripled, mind making Raanung the weapon against her, no other needed; changing sulk to fury, ESP stranger she could not get a grip on, Raanung's tail whipped, she fell on her back among the trees in the late dusk, the sweet air, he dropped on her with fangs at her neck, she could not cry out but her mind screamed *Raanung! Father! Mother! Engni!* Teeth in her fur beginning to close over the jugular and

the Hierophant

a man was walking down the street, singing softly in a high tenor and an old language:

Onward, Christian soldiers
Marching as to war. . .

Raanung's ears pricked, his jaws turned rigid. Emerald

hardly realized this. She felt herself in the presence of her
brother Tugrik, and that meant death. She knew nothing of
the song except that it came from no malign mind, and she
used her half-second's respite to drive her whole consciousness at the source of the assault. If her own experience was
limited she had the whole streaming power of her ranks of
ESP foremothers to draw on, and it jetted like a volcanic
firebomb against the attack.

An ordinary mind would have split like a nutshell; this did
not, but it cracked for an instant, flashing a white-hot interior
and a short searing burst of rage, revenge, a chaos of flesh
ripped with knives, pits of strange distorted creatures . . .
and gone.

Raanung loosened his jaws of his own will and with
wrenching effort, and drew away. She told herself dully that
she ought to track down the evil, but she did not know where
it was, or whether it was one or many joined. She wondered
why the street was not full of screaming neighbors; probably
they had been blocked. She looked up and saw that the man
who had been singing was sitting in the middle of the road
shaking his head like a wet dog's. He knew. She felt the
presence of Tugrik again, briefly, and saw that it was not a
sign of death. She stood up and shook her head too, and the
rest of her body with it.

Now it was dark. The street lamps came on softly, like a
string of pearls.

Raanung was lying on his side, panting; his eyes were
inflamed, his nose running, his mind kaleidoscopic. She did
not touch him. He got up and came to her unsteadily, his tail
hanging as if its weight was too much for him. She did not
move. He dipped his head and nuzzled it under her jaw, in the
fur he had tried to rip a moment ago. She licked his neck.

The man in the street got up and dusted his backside,
smoothed down his white hair and came up the walk. He was
tall and lean and walked looselimbed, slightly bent forward
to balance the pack on his back. His grey zip had a silver
badge on the collar and no other ornament. He saw that

Renny and Anika were gaping in the doorway, but looked down at Emerald and Raanung and spread his hands to touch a shoulder of each.

"My name is William Bellingrose and I have been sent by Kinnear because he cannot come yet. You are Emerald and Raanung."

"Yes," Emerald whispered. "For a moment your mind feels . . . like someone I know."

Bellingrose picked up the necklace from the grass. "You don't know me. But you will."

During the twelve days Kinnear spent in custody he managed to lose track of time. He had no clock or window, and the nightly dimming of his room did not always let him sleep. He exercised minimally, moped a great deal, and reread his news-sheets till they lost meaning. He had nothing with which to scratch a tally of his days. Occasionally he became very angry, but the nearest he got to rebellion was to consider smearing liquid soap on the spy-eye in the bath cubicle—a childish thought he put out of his mind almost as soon as it slipped in.

He was sitting moping with his back to the door when he heard it slide open for the first time since the Locksmith's visit. He was so deep in lethargy and frustration, and shame at giving into them, that he did not even esp. He had been expecting a cheap lawyer sooner or later.

"Well now, Dun, would you like me to bring down your tea, or do you prefer to come up and drink it?"

He turned, not to learn who his visitor was, but to set eyes on his grinning friend in turban, dark skin and thick beard, leaning against the doorway with arms folded and ankles crossed in imitation of his own stance.

Laughter bubbled up almost hysterically. "If it's all the same to you I'll come up." :*But what happened?*:

"Come up and find out," said Singh.

"What about the charge?"

"It was dropped."

:That's a good thing. I was guilty.:

Singh gave a cat's grin and said, *:I'm glad you say "was",
because I am your employer again, and you'd better keep
your record clean.:*

The group in the Committee Room included the
Locksmith, another surprise for Kinnear. The Praximif was
in his basic small-elderly-man shape, and managed the quirk
of lips meant to be taken for a smile. Kinnear returned it, but
had none for Bengstrom, a grim woman with a head wrapped
in black braids and the build of a janitorial machine; she was
the Supervisor and superior who had replaced Singh with
Thorndecker. She shifted in her chair and said, "I'm truly
glad to see you," in the subdued roar of a janitorial machine.

"Where's Thorndecker?"

"I'm afraid he's gone."

The Locksmith said, "During the end-thirtyday holiday
when staff here was down to maintenance he cleared out
overnight with his own crew and equipment and a headful of
high security."

Bengstrom said, mildly for her, "You are not here in
official capacity, and no one asked you to speak."

"I want him here," Singh said, "because he found the
evidence that Thorndecker was an imposter."

"Actually," the Locksmith said, "I'm here because Kinnear told me how to find the evidence in your own Archives."

Bengstrom sighed; she was not arrogant or unreasonable.
"I was tricked, and I'm still not sure how it happened. I was
presented with a man who seemed ordinary except that he
was wearing a decontamination suit. He explained that he
had these fears, but they wouldn't affect his work. I accepted
that because otherwise he did seem ordinary, in face and
manner, and—and I know how strange some people can be
around here. I assumed he was an ESP. He never mentioned
it, though there was a code-mark for it in his record—without
the rating."

"But you never checked—or even wondered?"

"Oh, I wondered . . . I had letters supposedly from my superiors, ordering me to appoint him Director of Singh's division—though they hadn't consulted me. He had a superb record and a wad of commendations and references a meter thick. I wondered, I thought of checking. Every time I wondered or thought my mind seemed to turn away. If I pushed too hard at it I felt as if I were going to vomit . . ." She flushed. "I'm making myself sound weak, but I'm going to be called to account, just like anyone else."

"Hypnosis," said the Locksmith. "So much for *my* powers. Even I thought he was just a man with a severe neurosis. Until I looked at the Archives."

The Locksmith, who did not like to stray too far from his terrain or put himself on public record by enquiring at the Archives in person, used his own powers to conscript a clerk who obtained hard copy of records on Qsaprinel, Praximf, and the moon Calidor. He refused to explain how he had winkled a similar document from the Sectoral Registry which Thorndecker, in a spasm of panic, had denied Kinnear. As Kinnear had suspected, the Archives reported discovery of Qsaprinel a hundred and fifty years earlier; the Sector Registry gave a figure of ten. Why did Thorndecker allow such a gap to stand? Probably because he did not dare tamper with an informatic structure as huge as the Archives, and hoped by control to concentrate on the narrow area he had chosen: the pinpoint of Qsaprinel under Narinder Singh, whom he had forced out.

The Locksmith knew a lot about chicanery, but with these documents in hand he learned that a lot he did not know about had been going on in a territory he claimed for his own, and this piqued him very much. He examined his essence for signs of contamination. An ordinary mind contemplating itself is like a person looking into a mirror and presenting the best face. For a Praximif who spends a lifetime doing this it is a different matter. The Locksmith found his mind in its usual order, with the warps he could not correct where expected, the small scars of rectification in their usual places, and the rest straight and true. Then he began to scan.

When he found the greatest disturbance in Bengstrom, in the form of a very powerful but clumsy block, he sent her the documents with an anonymous note, and broke the block. Being a Praximif and naturally self-centered, he made a mistake. He did not pay attention to Thorndecker until it was too late.

"But how in hell could you have let him go?"

"In spite of what he said I never really believed him an ESP, only an accomplished blocker. Of course he would have had ESPs on his personal staff. I had no reason at all to think of him until I felt Praximf was in danger."

"You can't be sure he's not an ESP."

"I don't have the senses, like smell or hearing, in the way you have, except when I need to create them for some purpose. But I do know who is an ESP and who is not."

What the records showed:

During the first fifty years after discovery, GalFed, with permission, made four landfalls on Qsaprinel. The teams surveyed and collected specimens. The Qsaprinli were not hostile, but they did not wish to trade or become members. After some time they realized that though they were able to work quite skillfully with wood, stone, and cast metals, they were missing something: steel. Their kilns were not powerful enough: they were afraid of great heat. They began a small trade in precious metals and gemstones, usually in return for surgical instruments, because medicine, mathematics and philosophy were their basic intellectual arts.

GalFed did not press. During the next twenty-five years there were four more visits: survey stopovers on a world that was a xenobiological laboratory. The study of medicine among the Qsaprinli had quickened and produced sideshoots of anthropology, paleontology and a small cluster of other life-sciences.

The Two Continents of the world dropped down from the
arctic region like ripe fruits on one stem, separated by a
glacial valley with many crevasses. Where the tongue of the
glacier ended below the snow line the swath of scrublands
began; dwarf conifers were barely supported by thin sedi-
ments coating ancient shield rock. The world was a cool one,
and even past the watershed, where the rivers poured their
contents far outward to the desert oceans of landless water, or
inward to the Grand Division, or Gulf, of the subcontinents,
the vegetation became only slightly thicker, changing in
character to evergreens with thick boles and broad leaves, no
taller than their northern cousins; the clearings were covered
with grasses which had risen from the sea and spread north
over the Gulf's wide expanse of sand and shingle. The
continents divided away into bulbar landmasses, and the Gulf
was lined with sandstone compressed by eons of sedimenta-
tion, folding in its layers the fossils that would become the
logbook of its people.

The Qsaprinli were not really Cephalopods, though they
were formed mainly as heads surrounded by limbs, nor
Crustaceans, though they had claws on their hind limbs, their
belly-skin was hornlike, and their heads were rigid, nor
vertebrates, though the cartilage frames that supported them
were stiffened by calcium. For convenience they might be
called reptilian, but what they were was one more form of
The People, like all other sentient beings.

They had come out of the sea, driven by enemies or other
mysterious urges, to the rockpools on the shore. These were a
moderate environment. The waves were low because Qsaprinel had no moon but only tides pulled by the sun. In those
days they did not have the water-skins that let them carry an
environment on their backs and, as in the sea, took nourishment through their pores, tiny life-forms that grew in the
pools and the waters running beneath sand and pebbles. They
fought territorial battles with their electric arms and had no
other enemies except the storms or rock cleavages that
changed the shoreline. Their brains and bodies swelled by the

strange law that works on some creatures of flesh and bone,
but they were animals. Their forelimbs grew fingers to use
for burrowing among pebbles to find water in dry areas; their
bipolar arms developed suckers for climbing the rock walls
that hindered them, their hind legs thickened with muscles
that let them leap from pool to pool.

After a while their kind home became overpopulated,
and family groups began to leave the central delta, exploring
the uplands, which were nearly barren and too dry, and the
sea which, since they had become used to the admixture of
fresh river water, was too salt. They began to spread east and
west into rougher ground. The eastward groups were sharper:
they realized dimly that the broken scarps above let down
more water in that direction. They hopped from pool to pool,
year to year, died and were born with the urge eastward.

They stopped at the foot of the greatest river, and the finest
sedimentary expanse. There were many pools, all populated
with their more primitive cousins, but those were small, and
there was room for everyone. They did not notice that all of
these little cousins had water-skins and hopped freely on the
land, and that this was why they were not overcrowded. All
these things they realized later, from their testaments in
stone.

They settled in. And part of their first cohort were born
with water-skins. Every larva wears an amniotic transparency until birth; these babies had theirs firmly attached to
their backs.

The Qsaprinli, on the verge of sentient intelligence, were
perplexed. If there had been one or two out of every twenty or
forty they might have been forced out, as with most of the
deformed, to shrivel and die. But two out of five? Four out of
nine? And in the next birthing, over half.

Worse still most of these monsters died young. The inner
skin, which had been normal integument, was thin and em-
bryonic: it ruptured easily and led to death by hemorrhage;
the forelimbs were thin and short-clawed, barely supportive.
Fewer than a third grew to maturity. Yet when they did they

reached normal size and spent more time on land, though
with their tender fingers they could pick up only one pebble at
a time, instead of burrowing for water as they had done. But
they needed to burrow less, since they carried so much water
with them.

But they were still animals. Even on the verge of extinction
they did not reason. They remained where the nourishment
was and went on breeding, normal with abnormal, first
shrinking in number, so there was no need for population
battle, occasionally fissioning, then increasing while their
bodies learned to react to new developments. The water-
skins thickened and formed new arterial and valvular systems. They strayed further and further from their pools and
learned to use their pouch flaps to make noises at each other,
and their fingers to make gestures, of warning, affection,
hostility. Their hind legs and polar arms thickened to free
their forelimbs.

And one venturer with evil in his heart, instead of leaping
with charged arms over the rattling scree upon his enemy,
picked up a stone in his small exact fingers and crept up
behind him in the dark to bash his braincase in. *Ecce homo!*

From there it was a short step to picking up stones and
piling them in forts against attack. And civilization got born.

This, as they had pieced it together, was the record given
by the Qsaprinli, over the passing of a hundred years, to
GalFed.

the Wheel of Fortune

Fifty years before Spinel-alpha set out on his great adven-
ture, a brilliant eccentric on Sol III who had made a fortune
inventing subtle and sophisticated new weapons and selling
them regardless of legality to the highest bidder—decided
that the world was too much with him. He had done his best to
contaminate it. He closed out his business and willy-nilly
gathered his clan by blood and marriage, numbering 75, and
applied for GalFed Colonial status. This was refused because

the number of breeding pairs was too small for genetic safety. Without wasting time on argument he searched the Neutral Appendices of the Archives. There were few places attractive to Solthrees that were not already colonized, and he was left with a rather unattractive one: Qsaprinel. On top of the eastern escarpment above the shore where the Qsaprinli had become human there was a valley deep enough to hold good oxygen, thickly lined with sediment and supporting a relatively rich plant growth. GalFed had surveyed it and found nothing wrong with it. They would have colonized it themselves if allowed.

The putative founder presented himself to the Emperor and offered to buy or rent this territory at whatever price was asked. He was an intimidating man. The Spinel of the time wanted neutrality and peace. Nothing more. His people had spread back to the western gulf, were mining rock and hewing forest, and he did not care about that piece of land. His stipulation was that the colonists import no heavy weapons and maintain the population at no more than double its founding level. And that neither party would ever inform GalFed or the rest of Qsaprinel of this agreement; he got on equably with his people and was terrified of disturbance.

The Founder landed a ship with people and machines and named his kingdom Hydesland, after himself. The only two of the 75 persons not related were a married couple, doctor and nurse.

For five or six years of hard work all went well. Hyde was an old man with an artificial heart, and he did not expect to see his population double. He longed only to see the first of his great-grandchildren, and his grand-daughter was pregnant. Three other women became pregnant as she approached term. Hyde's heart worked well, but his kidneys failed, and he took to his bed; all that kept him alive was the fierce will to see that child.

And when it was born his joy was almost savage: his line was laid down forever.

But no one would show it to him.

He raged until his brain was near bursting, and finally his
timid wife gave in. The nurse brought the baby, a grossly
deformed creature near death.

The Founder died reaching for the gun beneath his pillow.

An aberration.

The three babies then in utero were all born deformed; the
doctor battled to keep them alive in the weak hope of finding
some cause. Two died soon after birth; someone discon-
nected the life-support system of the third.

"Thank God we're sterile," said the doctor.

The nurse was called to the cliff-edge where a hiker had
fainted from dizziness. She caught her foot in a tree-root,
dropped, and died on the rocks below. Someone had done
Hyde's work.

The doctor bit on his grief and terror. He was alone. He had
thought to find interesting work and found himself among a
pack of hyenas. No woman dared conceive for a year. He
treated all with his usual care; they were civil. He hated them
all, but he wanted to scream at them to embark and leave, get
off the cursed ground. But they would not radio for help or
advice, or even speak to the Qsaprinli. It seemed to him that
the blood and spirit of Hyde were more poisonous than
whatever was deforming their children.

At the end of the year two women became pregnant. The
doctor began stealing and secreting weapons; there were so
many of them among the sons of Hyde that the few missing
caused only quick and forgotten scuffles.

At parturition Hyde's wife and one unmarried daughter
found the courage to become his volunteer nurses. The two
babies, born within three days of each other, were deformed.
When both were in life support he transported all the women
to safety, laid out his guns as if they were surgical instruments, and waited for the hysterical gang. The radio was a
step away from the infirmary, and while he waited he called
GalFed. He counted on hysteria: cooler heads would kill him
quietly.

Classic hysteria was what he got—armed men waving

torches. He was grateful for their light. The rising dawn was dim. He allowed them one shot. Then, belly-flat on the roof, he picked out the two men he was sure had killed his wife, shot them dead and used stunners on the rest. He lost the lobe of one ear, but the sullen remnant, torches fallen, fires out, dragged off the dead and the unconscious. No one else came after him. The babies were alive. In a week the colonists lifted off, leaving Hydesland scoured of their property.

Two days later GalFed picked him up with the babies. He told his story and, after landing and debriefing, disappeared. Hyde's ship crashed within sight of home on a GalFed mining asteroid.

"The old bastard's name was Henry Thorndecker-Hyde," said Bengstrom.

"And that doctor was really telling the truth?" Kinnear asked.

"According to ESP probes. Thorndecker-Hyde wasn't doing anything strictly illegal—just crazy."

"And . . . the deformed babies?"

"The old man had left plenty of credit back home, as a cushion to fall back on. The estate took the babies and their records away—so there's no description of their deformities, or if they lived or died, or anything. Hyde had built a lot of memorials to himself—charitable foundations for tax shelter—so maybe they were afraid of scandal."

"Yet here's somebody pretty weird calling himself Thorndecker. If it's one of them—but you said there was no description."

Narinder Singh said, "Among all the lies there was a piece of truth. He spoke of a fungus plague. . ."

"XenoBi sent in a team after those babies were born," Bengstrom said. "The Emperor hadn't known much, and he got pretty squeamish after they told him. GalFed did manage to keep it quiet. The fungus grows on a plant indigenous to the eastern region—like the ergot we used to get on corn, or the yeasts on grapes. But it acts like colchicine. I don't know whether it's still used on chemical plant mutation—"

"On cell division after fertilization," Singh said. "My father used it in his gardens."

"Of course!" Kinnear slapped the table. "You can't have a big evolutionary leap in one generation."

"The spores are carried by wind and wash into the river," Bengstrom said. "It gets into everything they eat."

"And the Qsaprinli turned up with monsters, but they managed to live with them, so—"

"After constant exposure during the time they settled in and mated—remember, it's not poisonous like venom, or even contagious—they first bred rather infantile forms, kept some of them alive long enough to reproduce, and through generations of natural selection, nobody knows how many, manufactured or made use of an enzyme already in their systems to break down that particular alkaloid in the spore so they could use it, no matter where it spread. It became necessary to them. It made them human."

"And," said Singh, "it took a lot of finagling by GalFed to get bodies for dissection and find out that much. The enzyme's produced by chemical action when sperm meets egg. Very neat."

"And what happens to . . . mammals?"

"There's so few on Qsaprinel it's hard to tell. XenoBi experimented on various Galactic mammals. They fed them the fungal alkaloid. It settles in the ovaries and testes. The animals carried full term and gave birth to large embryos at third- to half-term development, most with whole tough amniotic sacs. They were put on life-support and the ones that stayed alive longest were the ones with unbroken amnions. None of them matured very much."

"Our hypothetical Thorndecker can't be going about with an amniotic membrane."

"Decontamination suit."

"Oh. And additional prostheses to increase the appearance of normality. But did they do anything with the enzyme?"

"They extracted it and fed it to Group B normal animals along with the alkaloid. Offspring were normal. They synthesized the enzyme—called it *pintrelase* for all the good that'll do, treated Group C normals with the same result and divided the abnormal embryos and fetuses into three carefully matched groups. One for control, one for extract, and one for synthetic, and fed them. Control stayed the same or died, extract and *pintrelase* grew bigger, stronger and smarter, but no more mature. They could survive without the amnion, but not without unbilical support. So XenoBi wrote it up and packed it away in case they ever heard from the Thorndecker-Hyde estate. But they never did."

"Thorndecker obviously knew all about Qsaprinel—but maybe not about the enzyme. Do you think that was what he was after?"

"If he found out about it eventually, yes, that, or revenge, or both."

"Revenge?"

Bengstrom said, "You can see his whole character was infantile, if you're allowed to look at it with a clear head. Selfish, greedy, amoral, boastful—all those faked praises, but skewed with half-truths, like a kid afraid to tell a whole lie for fear he won't be able to keep a straight face." She grinned. "Maybe you can't tell by looking at me, but I had four of them. None of them got bent."

Kinnear laughed. "I can't imagine you letting them." His laugh faded. "But what you say about Hypothetical Thorndecker makes him sound like a chip off the old man up in Hydesland."

"Oh, I guess he had fertile ground."

"What would he do for revenge? Kill all the people? Blow up the world?"

"That's the trouble. We don't know. Not even where he went."

"He might have done better going after my job," said Kinnear.

"He landed two steps higher on the ladder," said Singh. "And he was angling for Supervisor."

"I'm retiring in two years," said Bengstrom, "and if he thought he was going to cheat me out of my pension he was in for a lot more trouble, hypnosis or not."

Kinnear said to Singh, "I'm very glad you're back."

"And I'm glad you're out."

"Has anybody thanked the Locksmith?"

"They will," said the Locksmith, and left without seeming to move.

"And, oh God, I've got to get out to Cinnabar and take care of my own babies before they tear the place apart."

"No, Kinnear," Singh said gently. "You can take your holidays later. You have Sector 492 to co-ordinate, a killer embryo to look for, and a world to care for. When it comes to those cats your cool head gets ridden over by your hot heart. You're needed here, you're no use there. We picked your brains while you weren't looking, and the Locksmith has done it again and picked the man. He's a good one—and he's gone—so get the look off your face!"

"Why you damned—"

But Singh, laughing, had filled the teapot from a whiskey bottle and was holding out the cup.

the Seven of Swords

The Locksmith had gone stalking. He was looking for a peacemaker, and not one with a gun. He concentrated on Solthrees because they were the alien form the Ungrukh knew best. He wanted a Solthree with something of Kinnear and something of Ungruwarkh about him, and he scanned the towers briefly because that was seldom to be found among the earnest shufflers of information they housed.

In one form or other he scoured the Pit of Seventh Heaven, among the serving, staggering, the idle, old spacemen drunk, crazy or coked; children of the powerful, superficial or already withered by experience; mumbling old men and women who had been gifted with beauty and respect and did not know how they had lost them; whores of all sexes and ages in clownish makeup: these were his element. He was waiting for the incongruous to leap out at him.

Backed in a corner stood one man.

The Locksmith watched him.

William Bellingrose was a chaplain of Solthrees in an organization called The AlphOmegan Ecumen—a conglomeration of whatever religions agreed to let him perform the religious ceremonies concerned with birth, marriage and death. At that time the number of Christian, Jewish, Buddhist, Moslem and other groups ceding these rights was many times greater than that of his congregation, covering pit corridors 51 to 60.

He was also something of a GalFed agent, in that during the rare times he was offplanet he gathered information of the kind that any civilian might absorb, about economy, popular opinion, personal treatment, and whatever else he might feel about the place, and reported on them. He always told the truth in matters of fact, and hedged on judgments.

His wife was in a hospital on Fthel IV with premature senility, and did not recognize him. GalFed paid for this; his salary was small. He lived frugally, ate properly, and exercised; he was neither frail nor clumsy, though he looked both, because of his build. He was very tall, his hair and brows were white, his face pink and permanently lined by anxiety.

He unfolded a portable lectern and piled a few worn books on it. Surrounding him were twelve persons. Three wanted religion, four were looking for trouble, the rest curious.

He picked up a small book with a red cover and opened it where he had placed the marker. Before he began to speak, he glanced directly at the Locksmith and his mind said clearly, :*I have heard of you and know of your powers. Please do not use them here, whatever may happen.*:

:*I won't,*: said the Locksmith, and took one step back.

William Bellingrose said, "My text for today is this: 'Lifting a rock only to drop it on one's foot' is a folk saying to describe the behavior of certain fools. . . . This is not a religious saying, but an ideological one, and it was spoken some centuries ago by a very powerful man. He held power over greater numbers of people than any other one man has done in the history of all the worlds I know. What he did was such a mixture of good and evil that it can hardly be considered with justice. But finally he dropped a rock on his own foot.''

He watched the faces, the shifts of limb and body. ''Today it is a good thing that no one has such power. Some still have too much; some have none at all, and feel hurt and helpless. I want power only over my own mind and body, and I do not have all of that.'' He paused for a moment and went on without shift of tone or stance. ''You, there, Jojo, are planning to throw a bag of shit at me when I reach what you consider the pitch of my sermon, as you did some days ago at Chaplain Nobu Shigashi. You hit my sister Nobu-chan and made her weep. That will not happen to me because I am older and more experienced; I will use my lectern as a shield—and believe me, I have washed a lot of shit off this lectern. You notice people are drawing away from you. The bag has already begun to leak, and there is a drop on your shoe. Soon the rock will fall on your foot. Leaving already? Watch out for the Security men, and when you come back another day I will tell you more about power.'' Without missing a beat, he went on, ''Gudger, give me the knife. There's a Security man on the way because he thinks something's been going on here. If he catches it on you you'll get two years with that record, and if you stick anybody with it it's life.'' Half the group melted away, but the beefy Security man stopped Gudger.

''Hey, Gudger, whatcha got up your sleeve today? You all right, Reverend?''

''Chaplain,'' said Bellingrose. ''Everything is quite smooth, Officer.''

''Mind if I search this one?''

''As long as you tell him his rights.''

Security muttered something like a blessing and ran his hands over runty Gudger. ''Clean.'' Then he noticed the knife beside the pile of books on the lectern. ''Hey, I've never seen one of these before. Looks like it cost.''

Bellingrose polished it on his sleeve and turned it in his

hands. "From the Forges of Chlis. It's a souvenir, their specialty."

"Don't blame you for carrying one in this garbage dump."

"Don't you?" asked Bellingrose. "You should."

Security, looking slightly puzzled, left. "Gudger!" Bellingrose called. "Don't go away yet. No, you can't have the knife. I'll keep it with my souvenirs."

"With the bags of shit," Gudger snarled.

Bellingrose laughed gently. "Gudger, go straight home and don't get drunk. I promise you she'll be back inside an hour, and she wasn't doing what you thought . . . now the rest of you I presume are present because you want to hear what I have to say. 'Where two or three are gathered together . . .' Have you had enough, Locksmith?"

"No," said the Locksmith. "But you know where to find me."

the Ace of Cups

The best organized and most efficient tribes on Ungruwarkh have one or two males who are bigger and handsomer than average. They fish, hunt, mate, fight defensively, and engage in the usual tasks. But they do not compete, and never lead. Gentle and good-humored by some genetic quirk, they are tribal stabilizers, and are called Stillers. Ungrukh are as fierce in love and loyalty as they are in hate, yet they do not actually like each other. But no one bristles at a Stiller. Emerald's brother Tugrik had been one until he became maddened by the savage murder of the woman he loved and died in a hopeless attempt to avenge it.

Bellingrose's personality had something of the Stiller in it, and this was why Emerald, near death, had sensed her brother's presence. She realized why Bellingrose had been chosen and was not resentful, but rather pleased that such a quality could be found in other peoples.

Bellingrose, in the now rather crowded living-room, told all he had learned from GalFed, through Emerald, in five

minutes, and gave an even more compressed version to
Renny in ten.

Renny turned a bit pale. If the enzyme had been the object
of that stupid treaty then Hartog had had it in his hand, his
very hand! and smashed it on a wall! She did not say this
aloud, for fear of upsetting Spinel.

But Spinel said sadly, "That terrible man grasped the
enzyme in his hand and smashed the eggs of my children
. . . and there was no need, when it had already been
manufactured. My father-father Spinel was a weak man and a
damned fool to let that colony settle. And so I am afraid was
Meta-Spinel to think he could turn time back by fissioning.
Perhaps if Galactic Federation can find a way to give the drug
to the man Thorndecker he will stop troubling us."

"I'm afraid he can't turn time back either," said Bellingrose. "And perhaps those other Emperors were not stupid
but good-hearted like you, Spinel." And Spinel thought
there was something he recognized in this kind man: a resonance of his wise friend Binatrel.

"Mother, what are you doing?"

Anika was on foot, pulling her shawl around her. "I'm
sick and tired and frightened. I know we've got to make
plans. I think we've got to move away from here, all of us,
because those bastards out there aren't going to keep running
into the thorn tree. But the way I see it I'm the most expendable, and if I leave that box of cards shut up and dark tonight
we'll have the police buzzing around to find out why, so I'm
going to lay out some Tarot, and you can manage without
me."

Renny jumped up, but Emerald was in front of her with
open claws raised. The door slammed. While Renny sat
down glaring, Bellingrose put a finger to his lips and counted
off a minute on his chronometer; the sound of the moped
faded. He gestured to Raanung and Emerald, and they
slipped out.

Renny said through her teeth, "Do you think they can keep
from killing each other long enough to guard her?"

"Yes," said Bellingrose.

Spinel said, "Lady, she has borne much and is over-wrought. I am sorry to have caused you so much trouble. I should not have come. It was terrible arrogance on my part to have forced you with such threats and bravado."

"Don't say that. I don't regret it. There's very few I know as brave as you."

"Oh, please don't praise me so. That will make me vain and ruin my character."

"Don't worry about that," Bellingrose nearly choked on his laughter, "and listen, Renny—as far as enemies go, the headaches Emerald delivered tonight were probably much more disabling than the one you've been suffering."

Nothing disastrous happened.

Emerald and Raanung, perfectly capable of enjoying themselves in the heart of danger, padded through rich night gardens among amazing odors, passed within two meters of a pair of lovers, grinned a share of pleasure, took their own turn in a quiet place in a spice of uncharacteristic silence, had a few hungry thoughts about some of the larger carp in the fishponds . . . always keeping Anika in mind.

Anika opened shop to a group of three couples in a giggling mood. She used the full pack this time, awkward as it was; she sensed some kind of complicated and strained relationship among them beneath all the laughter, and in that situation she did not want to turn up Judgement, Justice, Death and the Devil too often. She handled her clients lightly, let them laugh at her, and charged double. She began to relax a little.

Next came a boy-girl pair, very moony. She got quite light-headed, perhaps in reaction to the day's excitements, unlimbered her sleight-of-hand and dealt them The World, The Sun and The Lovers at half price.

Then there was emptiness and darkness in her mind, an hour to midnight, and she was very tired. She had begun late, and done little. But there was one still waiting.

This was a big ruddy young man with curly red hair and

beard. He was wearing a rust-colored vest and pants and
ivory turtleneck of a thin knitted stuff. His clothes looked
vaguely like the uniform of some kind of private guard. He
sat down and rested his big hands on the table.

Anika scratched her chin and then reached down to scratch
the skin under her knife. Questioner's right hand twitched.

ESP!

She was about to pull down shields when Emerald said
clearly, *:Let me shield you. He is not an ESP but a competent
blocker. He is nervous about you, is all. Carries only a
low-grade stunner.:*

Anika fought down her primary annoyance at being moni-
tored. *:One of them?:*

*:Doubt it. Cautious, defensive, wants to know if he can
trust you. Try to loosen him a bit?:*

Anika watched him shuffling the deck, blond-white brows
drawn over his grey eyes. He shuffled clumsily; his size was
not in fat, and his rawboned hands made the big cards look
small.

"Tell me your question, or ask it silently?"

He handed her the deck, wary. "Am I in the situation I am
looking for?"

She laughed gently. "If you're looking for Anika Gurdja
you are."

Her tone was so light and teasing he could not take offense.
"I think you know what I mean, Madame."

"Just put the cards down." Since he obviously did not care
about Tarot she was more curious than he to see what would
turn up.

Two of Cups.

"What does that mean?"

"The cards should be dealt out before . . . but . . . this is
a Significator implying you are in a situation of cooperation
and partnership. If that is relevant to your question. . ."

He kept his face tight.

"Crossing with . . . Temperance. The acceptance of real-
ity, and below that. . ." The Knight of Pentacles, "you
have been patient and reliable."

"That's right," he said simply. Didn't look like a citizen of Miramar, and obviously didn't get around much.

:Inhibited,: said Emerald.

"And above that . . . The Nine of Swords. Your future is a choice." She folded her hands. "I'm afraid, young sir, we're at an impasse. The snake is eating its tail, and we have come back to your question. You obviously don't want to change your present association," (or you wouldn't be wearing your employer's uniform or asking this question on Company time, *:or travelling in his skimmer,:* Emerald added.) "So perhaps you are thinking of bringing another element into the partnership, and I feel that is a choice you must make for yourself."

He looked surprised. "Don't people ask things like this all the time, and aren't *you* supposed to answer them?"

"Most of the ones who ask usually know what they want to do and come to me to justify it. I think your case is different, and you must trust yourself."

"Suppose you saw death in the cards—say, a knife in the back. Would you tell me?"

"I'd certainly warn you—in a way that would make you cautious, rather than frightened. I carry a knife myself, really a meat-slicer, but I know how to scare off bullies and robbers, of which you are obviously neither. Perhaps you need a business advisor rather than a fortune-teller."

He smiled slightly. "I don't think so."

"Well then, I'm tired and want to close shop. The incomplete reading is free, but if you would like to pay for my time, it should be worth twenty-five keys."

"Oh, of course I'll pay." With bumpkin earnestness he took a small leather pouch from an inside pocket, shook out five tokens, and went out quietly, neat of movement.

Oh well, I buggered up that one.

Anika set about closing. After a few minutes Emerald slipped in. "His name is Morgan and he works for one called Agassiz. I am not sure what Agassiz is, because he has hard blocks around that, but his orders are to look for Thorndecker."

"Good God! Another one!"

"They have no connection with GalFed, but I doubt they mean harm to us."

"But what would this Agassiz want with—"

"He, she or it loves him."

"Oh come on, Emerald! That's weird!"

"I give out only what comes from Morgan."

"They sent out that young lumpkin to—"

"That young lumpkin is not so green a sprout as he looks."

"You said he's inhibited."

"I mean he is being inhibited. The low-grade stunner is all his employer allows, and the young man is a non-ESP fully aware of coming into possibly great danger—very courageous."

"How do they know about us?"

"Perhaps they hang about the port—or just look down the street." Emerald laughed at the expression on Anika's face. "You think you make a mess and learn nothing. Now you do not like what we learn." Raanung settled on the doorstep and started licking dirt off his pads with a sound like a ripsaw.

"I don't know what we're supposed to do about him," Anika said.

"He smells like a good piece of flesh, but I doubt we eat him," Raanung said, "even though he is a scout who is expendable."

"He is not expendable," said Emerald. "From Morgan's feelings about his employer I suspect Agassiz is peaceful. More than peaceful as opposed to Thorndecker. Anti-violent."

Anika shrugged. "Love takes all forms."

"I don't see how we *could* do anything about Agassiz," said Bellingrose, "So we'd better not try." He was packing up the miniature radio with which he had reported to his GalFed contact. "Our directive is to keep Spinel and ourselves alive and safe. We may have to move away, but I don't think we'll be attacked again tonight after the recent piece of fireworks.''

"I don't like running away," Raanung growled.

"Neither does—" Emerald began, and stopped.

"Go ahead! Say it!"

"Neither does your father, and we end by losing someone we love! So I say it, for all the good it does. Now I say it is time to sleep, and I am going! The back hall carpet is better than what we sleep on at home, and that way we free a bed. Good night.''

Raanung grumbled, "If I want someone just like my mother I find her easier in the Hills." But he followed, whiskers sticking out like points on a compass.

"Help!" said Anika feebly.

Bellingrose grinned. "I'm very happy to accept the offer of a bed.''

"Yeah, now that we can afford to pay the rent," for Bellingrose had brought a generous credit voucher, "we can't afford to stay.''

the Hermit

"There's no way out of it. Everyone knows we're here. Even if Thorndecker isn't around his guns are." Renny's headache had eased and she had a good appetite for breakfast.

"I know it's best to get out," Anika said. "Dammit, I like the place.''

"Why must you leave for good?" Raanung asked. "This situation cannot last forever. Is there no way to make people believe the house is still occupied?"

"Automatic lights, recorded conversations, alarms . . . wouldn't stand up to an ESP or hold up long, but it's not half bad," said Renny.

"Yes, it's sensible," Bellingrose said. "But where can we stay together? Especially with Spinel?"

Anika barked with laughter. "There's always the Circus!"

"Ah, we jump through hoops of fire!" cried Emerald.

"What a challenge!"

"Yeah?" said Renny. "What'd happen if the Ringmaster put his head in *your* mouth?" But she knew Anika was serious, and though she might shut up her crystal gazebo for a while and go on vacation, she could never come back to the Refinery after being exposed in the Circus. "And safety in public is not that safe."

"We could fit up a caravan and keep moving," said Bellingrose. "Not from here, where we're known. Maybe from North Key. It'd be terribly cramped, but. . ."

"Yes," Anika said sadly. "Irenyi, my love?"

"I agree . . . but what about Spinel?"

"Hey, Spinel! How do people travel on your world?"

"On wheels, of course," said Spinel. "Like everyone else."

Miramar, like the rest of Cinnabar, got unpleasantly hot in the afternoon, and its citizens shopped in the morning and closed up home and business after the sun reached zenith.

Renny went shopping in a burnoose with a lot of pockets. Though she had the credit voucher she did not want to go on record for the purchase of the small but expensive components she needed in preparing the house for emptiness.

Emerald refrained from offering to go along; she knew she was conspicuous and that even if she were not Renny would refuse on principle. But she suspected that Renny resented the high-handed assumption that she loved risk to the point of going into murderous situations that were often accompanied by the ravage of her self-respect. She was a cool one, but not so cool as men thought. Yet she must somewhere have weighed the choice to sleep with fools and knaves and kill them, even in self-defense. Emerald put on her finger-stalls with their fine-point prosthetic tips, set the trace-receiver— one more medallion—and gave it to Raanung to hang round his neck.

"Where are *you* going, woman?"

"Nowhere yet. If someone catches Renny at the market I

start running." She removed the heavy necklace, unscrewed one of the tracers from the setting of a flower-shaped jewel, and stuck it on the back of her ESP-tag. She dumped the necklace in the equipment bag.

"Maybe you need more than one of those."

"The damned thing weighs me down. If I need more, somebody brings it."

"Somebody, ha."

She went outside to join Spinel, who was crouching in bushes and trying to decide, from his shadowy nest, whether he liked really blue sky. Spinel could speak *lingua* as fast as she pumped it into him, but the effort was too distracting, and her project was to teach him the language he would need as a GalFed member. She was aquiring some Qsaprinli, but she could not speak it even as well as Renny because, though the sounds and syntax were as crude and simple as those of most Ungrukh dialects (excluding the *l* which hardly an Ungrukh could wring a tongue around) she could not perform the delicate hand-signing which gave the language its sophistication. "You are looking at the sky," she told Spinel in *lingua*.

"I know I'm looking at the sky," said Spinel in his own language. "It's still too bright."

"Well, Majesty," she purred, "suppose you close your eyes, absorb it through your light organs, and describe it to me in *lingua*."

Renny was not alone in her burnoose. Most of the population wore them, with little or nothing underneath; Security men sweated in British-Imperialist style khaki shorts and solar topees. The mall resembled an enclave of villas with red tile roofs, and courtyard cafes in shaded corners. Renny was well known at the hardware because she and Anika out of necessity did most of their own minor repairs. As a point of honor she seldom shoplifted here, but she was not in much danger. Even ambassadors had their weaknesses, and if a few items anonymously marked "Merchandise" appeared on the charge a couple of thirtydays later they were usually paid without question or embarrassment. She charged a few small

items and went to collect her moped in the parking range out
back. Her actions were so normal, the performance so ordinary, the situation was beginning to seem unreal to her,
particularly when a neighbor gave her a cheerful good-
morning. The day had become divorced from violence, pain
and fear. She might jump on that moped and ride to nowhere.

"Give me that thing again," said Emerald. "I want one of
the recorders."

The one "Good morning!" that was too hearty and cheerful to be rewarded by her little smile made her lift her head
sharply.

"I don't know you!"

"Your mother does," said the red-bearded young man. He
gripped her hard around the shoulders and said, "If you make
a fuss I will accuse you of terrible things even you might not
have thought of yet."

"I am known here and you are not, Morgan," she said
coldly. "Shout away."

"Ah, Morgan? I heard you were an Imper, Irenyi Gurdja.
You've picked my pockets of several items I paid honest cash
for. I have the receipts. I was watching."

She twisted away, whipped off the burnoose and flung it at
him; underneath she was wearing the thin grey zip she used
for such emergencies. He caught both the garment and the
hand with which it was thrown.

"I only *look* clumsy," he said. "Let's talk it over, love."

Back of her she heard a giggle, and the mutter of her
neighbor, the local gossip. "Time she found somebody—but
I don't think it'll last."

He drew her behind the comfort station, a graceful bun-
galow with lace curtains, where he had parked his moped,
and the shadow for afternoon lovers had not yet lengthened.

Her other arm rose, viciously stiff-fingered; he ducked it
and clasped her not quite like a lover, a hand imprisoned
behind her shoulderblades, his arm around her neck so that

her chin ground into his collar-bone, his heel hooking an ankle.

"I want to talk to you," he said politely.

"Then why are you holding me like this?" She spoke through closed teeth because she could not get her mouth open.

"Perhaps because I like you," as his pounding heart and swelling groin showed, "or maybe I heard how you killed Hartog—talk has gotten around among the free lances—and I'm afraid to let go."

"I have no weapon."

"You don't need one."

"Of course not. Did your lances tell you I'm called the Black Widow in my Division? First the sex and then the death?"

"I don't work with that kind of men and it's not my business, Madame. I'm only trying to keep alive. Agassiz wasn't satisfied with the answers your mother gave him last night."

"She didn't give him any answers! You aren't an ESP!"

"No, but I was wired up and an ESP blocked me first. I was sent to bring in someone, and you aren't my choice, in spite of what I, um, feel. You were the one I was able to get hold of. I would have preferred that old man—but I'm damned glad I didn't get one of the cats."

Irenyi would dearly have loved to be replaced by one of the cats. "For God's sake, what do you want? Either tell me or let go. I hate hurting people, even if you don't believe it, and I'll see Agassiz if he won't harm me or my friends."

"Agassiz would never harm anyone," Morgan said, loosening his hold a little. "But I have to tell you . . . he's forty-four years old, and—and in the shape of an embryo, near three months—if you've ever seen what those look like?—but big, maybe a meter long?" His hold relaxed a little more. She pulled her head away and looked up at him. His eyes were not on her. "He's the cousin of that Thorndecker everybody's after." His eyes met hers with neither revulsion nor desire. "The second embryo . . . The ones who work for him, he treats us very well and—and we wouldn't want to see his feelings hurt." He let go and stood away with his hands empty and out. "I wanted you to hear that and think about it without fighting or running away."

Renny picked up her crumpled burnoose and wrapped it around her arm.

Nobody will know where . . . but I must. Come on, Rosinante. "You've got a pillion on that thing. Let's go."

A moment later Emerald arrived panting and furious after fifteen minutes of hard running. *:Stupid me! I let her go out without a tracer! Now they are heading for the skimmer field and we have only the moped.:*

Raanung said from the house, *:The way he comes and goes so quickly it may not be far to follow.:*

:Then I take the moped.:

:Hell and damnation, no! I am on my way! Anika says that thing has the juice and if you push the wrong pedal you are a flying carpet!:

:Then give Anika the receiver first!:

:Tscha! Any fool thinks of that!:

Emerald spared herself a second's curse at underestimating Raanung's intelligence again. Then she crouched in the growing shadow of the comfort station with her head wrapped in her forearms, doing her best to extract a destination from Morgan before he passed the vanishing point of five km which was the extreme limit of her ESP range. She got a fix on skimmer identification and an approximate area before she lost the pair, and had time to wonder briefly what a flying carpet was when Raanung appeared, as hot and weary as she had been.

The moped was easy to find by smell among the few left. He leaped on, she followed on pillion, he whipped up and polarized the bubble-shield, and gunned it as if he had been born to it. Emerald disliked machines and learned to use them, conscientiously and ploddingly, in order to keep up with developments. Raanung was utterly indifferent to them and they jumped to serve him at a touch. Emerald thought it was damnably unfair, and she was sulky as the devil for neglecting to plant a tracer on Renny.

:What is the difference? The man Morgan says no harm comes to her, and you can find none in him yourself.:

:We have plenty of experience with hypnotism and I believe what I see with a clear head when the blocks are down.:

The eyes of the Ungrukh were still sore from running in full sunlight without the contacts that protected them from suns brighter than their own world's. But the polarized bubble softened the light, as well as concealing from the curious that there were two big red cats slightly overweighing the moped.

Raanung was not nice about sticking to roads. He was a fine tracker; his nose was as good as Emerald's father Khreng's, but he also had a sharp sense of the sun's position and the direction of its shadows (and he was one of the rare Ungrukh who could tell time without depending only on his stomach); this ability had not deserted him on Fthel IV, and here where he could not use his nose, sun-slant and Emerald's ESP sent him through parks, valleys and gardens like a hawk splitting the air.

:This is good!:

:And I am sick! Now we get to eat fresh meat I am about to throw up!:

:Not here, woman! Save it till we get there.:

:Note we have police skimmers coming up and Morgan can fly over the Sound to North Key while we must use the bridge!:

:Is anyone in that tunnel ahead?:

:Maybe two drowned cats.:

:It is an overflow from the Sound we fly over coming in. Tide is not up.: He depolarized the bubble and plunged into the dark. Water plumed from their juiced wheels like wings. Out of the tunnel he swerved west and drove canted on the bank at forty-five degrees until the air dried the blotches of

water on the plasmix surface. Emerald thought she should
have been frightened out of her head, but the fear was
spending itself churning up her belly.

Raanung laughed. "No police now." He slowed long
enough to open the shield for fresh air.

*:That is Morgan's skimmer crossing the Sound now, and
he is not exceeding the speed limit, you may notice.:*

*:You may notice that little black skimmer following him
and speeding to catch up. What is that, now?:*

Emerald glanced up and saw the tiny black thing homing
on Morgan's skimmer like a flea. *:Damn, that is one of our
tail-biting trackers and if I try to warn Morgan he gets hot in
the neck*—: She saw through the trailer's eyes: hand on stick,
hand on gun-mount—

But the glance upward from the jouncing ground had
flicked her endurance over the edge, and she gasped, "Stop
this thing, I must get out, I must—"

In reflex Raanung pulled up short, her nausea welling in
him, her/his mind in the bucket-seat of the trailing buzzer.
Emerald swept the bubble down, leaped out on the bank
under overhanging leaves and heaved into the water with a
terrible belly-spasm.

She spat. "By hell's hot stones, I know why my mother
does not care to travel!"

"Look up," said Raanung dryly. "Somebody else is losing a taste for it."

The black trailer was falling from the sky, popping with
drogue chutes.

"My mind is locked on his. . ."

"Otherwise it is raining air-traffic." The pilot had been
strapped in and was unharmed, but the craft landed with a
firm crunch at the bridgeway entrance, where traffic had
turned aside to avoid it. "That occupies the police."

"And we lose Morgan. We cannot use the bridgeway."

"We don't need to. Now your stomach is empty we take
the shortcut." He pulled the shield to and rushed forward
along the bank.

The bridge was a graceful iron-lace structure in keeping with all the other old-style architecture of the Keys. With attention diverted above, Raanung sent the juiced moped leaping off the embankment onto one of the truss-beams beneath the roadway. It was quite smooth, and a few centimeters wider than the wheel of the moped. Emerald clung with claws, teeth and tail, but her tightly shut eyes did not keep her from seeing through Raanung's, or feeling the ferocious grin on his face.

Once in the skimmer Morgan did not speak to Renny. Perhaps he had a prepared line of conversation and nothing else to say when it was used up. Or he despised her. Or he was not what he seemed, and she was going into one of those situations again. Over the North Key she looked down and saw the same greenery, dotted with the same kind of red-tile roof. The greenery thinned when a bare hilltop showed itself, thickened again into coarser growth without roofs.

She clenched her fists between her knees and watched his hands moving over the grips and switches. Red-gold hairs on his wrists and the backs of his fingers. Human enough. So was Hartog, and the man and woman she had killed in self-defence, other times.

"For God's sake, say something!" she snarled.

He glanced at her and back at the panel. "I don't like this."

"What?"

"Doing this kind of thing."

"Fair enough," she said, and shut up.

Finally she saw something like a roof, but it was green; and the flat spread of a small landing field, also green. He set the skimmer down there and taxied it under a portico roofed with leafy boughs. He opened the door for her and held out the rolled-up burnoose. She made no move to take it. "You'll want this," he said. "It gets cool in the evening."

"I don't expect to stay." Ridiculous words she spoke because they were in character. He shrugged, pulled the moped from its carrying rack and stuffed her robe into its packbag with his own.

She rode pillion with him across the landing field and down a gravel path lined with shrubs. After a minute or two both became aware that there were shadows loping to either side of them, but it was not yet evening and there was only one sun. Morgan slowed and the shadows resolved them-selves into two big red cats. They were muddy, dusty, burr-caught, even their tails were weary, but they were still very fierce. The moped stopped.

Renny began to laugh and the back of Morgan's neck flushed. When his right hand moved she grasped it with her own hard fingers.

"That is no good," said Raanung, and made the ritual fang-and-claw gesture of his father Mundr's warrior days. "One stunner does not equal two Ungrukh."

Morgan's brows drew down and the tip of his nose whitened. "I want to take this woman Irenyi Gurdja to talk to Agassiz. We mean no harm."

"Good," said Emerald. "We also wish to speak to Agas-siz and we know what to expect. I open my mind to Agassiz and *he* knows what to expect."

Morgan pushed a button on his console. "Morgan here. I—"

A small shrill voice said, "Come in, Morgan, and bring Emerald and Raanung with the woman."

"Come along, then," said Morgan, rather dazed.

"But, if you please, let us all walk," Emerald said. "It is not far and I don't want to see another one of those things for a while."

The heavy surrounding walls of stone reminded Renny briefly of Qsaprinel, but these were nearly covered with shrubs and ivy, and inside there was a vast garden of trees, paths and fishponds. A score of men and women moved among them, all wearing plain clothing like Morgan's, in muted colors.

Under one of the trees there was a cradle in the shape of a great scallop shell; it had a framework of instruments over it, and beneath a substructure of working pumps and beeping indicators.

Agassiz was lying in it on pillows; he was swept with the dappled shade, and wearing a green dhoti and nothing else. This covered the umbilicus, thick as a tree-root, that ran into the pumps, but left his legs free. His limbs twitched uncontrollably and his fingers and toes were badly clubbed. His skin was smooth, though it had grown a few of the moles common to a middle-aged man, even one in the shape of an embryo. His life-support equipment seemed usual enough to his visitors, who had either seen or heard of the bottled ESP brains kept alive for hundreds of years.

His face was hard to look at, for a moment, because his eyes were in his temples, his forehead a huge bilobar structure, and his nose a flattened snout shaped like the cut half of a mushroom. Emerald shucked her knife-harness, walked up to him without hesitation, and put her nose over the edge of the shell. One of the men pulled a framework of prisms over the embryo's eyes so that he could see. His uncoordinated hand brushed her whiskers, his lipless mouth opened to show, astonishingly, two rows of tiny teeth. He laughed, a baby's chuckle, and said in his shrill whisper, "Are you my friend, Emerald?"

"I hope so, Agassiz."

He breathed haltingly, with the tremulous squeaks of the newborn, and licked saliva from the corners of his mouth, every movement forced by the tremendous driving will that masked his intelligence. His wavering hand reached for her forehead.

"Do not touch me until I wash, man. I am filthy."

His fingers touched and rested trembling on the black V of her forehead. "I'm not worried about a little dirt, Ungrukh. I need a friend like you."

the Knight of Cups

"Consider, Agassiz," said Emerald. "It costs a pretty pair of keys to feed a pair of Ungrukh." She and Raanung had been sprayed down by Agassiz's gardener and shaken themselves dry in the sun.

"If that's no more than a third of what I pay to feed the twenty-two people I keep here it's fair enough," said Agassiz. Emerald, whose own eyes were too wide apart for close vision, saw those of Agassiz through the prisms in more normal configuration, and it seemed to her that there was a livening sparkle in them.

"Just one minute!" Renny stood hands on hips and brows drawn down like thunderclouds. "No one's asked *me* about an agreement that seems to have been reached long ago." And added, "Keep your smirky face to yourself, Morgan."

Agassiz gurgled and pulled his jerking arms together so that the tips of the fingers touched. "Emerald, tell dem's'l Irenyi how you rescued her and Morgan."

"What do you mean!"

"What is there to tell?" Emerald asked. "I throw up, he falls down. It is an embarrassment."

Someone came to hook a suction tube into the corner of the embryo's mouth. A straight spare man of medium height in his seventies; unlike the others he wore a white coverall, but its white was in an off-tone that did not glare. His harsh granitic features seemed to have been planed by experience rather than age. His left earlobe was missing, and Emerald, too cautious to esp, guessed that this was the original doctor who had rescued the embryos.

When the liquid was drained he removed the tube, and Agassiz said, "I have three doctors, but this one is Doctor."

"Yes," said Emerald. "I believe I know which one that is."

Doctor did not look at her, but pressed buttons on the superstructure; a net of fine soft strands, invisible against the pillows, lifted Agassiz and turned him this way and that as Doctor's long bony fingers massaged him with salves and smoothed the wrinkle marks on his back, checked the loincloth for dryness and comfort. The umbilicus hung down from its folds, a meter of great blue vein wound with the double strand of red arteries and a transparency of amniotic membrane.

While this was going on, Emerald explained. "Because it seems clear now that we can be easily followed wherever we go, I take responsibility and make the decision to stay. It is as good a place as any."

Doctor shook and turned the pillows, lowered Agassiz and left without a word.

"What's the price of it?" Renny asked. She had relaxed to the point of accepting a chair, and Morgan, still sore-headed, had gone about some business of his own.

"Emerald," said Agassiz, "I also have three ESPs and none are as good as you. Let me give you an open mind so I can sleep." Without hesitation he wriggled himself into comfort, closed his eyes and slept. His lids were thick and lashless, but he was lucky in his condition to have any, particularly ones that worked.

"He may be childlike," said Renny, "but he's got a lot of nerve."

"That is quite all right," said Emerald. "When he wakes I give him *my* conditions. The price is this: he wants us to help give Thorndecker the enzyme, because he receives it himself."

"How?"

"Through Doctor, who is the rescuer of Hydesland you hear about from Bellingrose."

"Thorndecker is going to march in like a good little boy and stand in line for his medicine!"

"Once we are all here Thorndecker is coming after us. That happens in any case, but here it is the only way Agassiz can meet him. How we arrange things so that most everyone does not die is why Agassiz needs a friend."

Renny emitted a stream of corrosive expletives. "Is he sane?"

"As sane as such a one can be, and that is a good deal."

"But why?"

"He feels that Thorndecker must have a share of the substance that gives him as much life and awareness as *he* has."

"Thorndecker may have had it already."

"I don't know, but presume not, from the way he is acting in relation to Qsaprinel. Agassiz is no dreamer; he expects no great changes. But he feels about Thorndecker much as Spinel feels about that deformed sib of his. Justice and fairness demand it."

"Demand we get killed! I thought this was supposed to be a hiding-place."

"It is a defending-place, with more provision than moving about in a caravan. The force-field goes on every night, and also that thing on the roof of the house that looks like a tree is a radar antenna."

Raanung said, "We are also near the spit of the land, where we are accessible to all and sundry."

"Sundry is cooling his head in the police station, and all are not here yet."

Renny's eyes were on the move, watching. "And Doctor! He's hardly human, except for that ear."

"He can have that fixed, but I think he keeps it as some kind of badge of honor, to show that he does something worth while—in spite of how Thorndecker turns out . . . oh yes," she rolled in the thick grass, stretching luxuriously and drawing a few stares, "there are some warps here, especially when Agassiz is willing to risk our lives in order to do justice to that evil one."

"How does he keep all these people here, with the kind of loyalty Doctor and Morgan give him? He must have money from the estate, but—"

"I cannot tell without esping deeper than I want to do now, but *he* believes it is by love and trust, because he loves and trusts everyone. That, and even his willingness to risk our lives, are a kind of—of innocence. I don't know the word for it."

"Ingenuousness," said Renny. "God save us from it."

"Agassiz," Emerald addressed the sleeper, "I want to speak to Doctor. When you wake you remember what we say, so nothing is hidden."

She watched Agassiz's fingers moving aimlessly over his chest; they had tiny nails like pearl sequins. After a moment the long thin shadow fell over the Ungrukh.

Doctor said, "You wanted to see me."

"Yes, I am esping Agassiz with his permission, but not anyone else. I hope it is no offense if I ask you a few questions."

"That depends on the questions."

Poker player, Renny thought. Mama will love him.

"Agassiz seems to feel he is near death. Do you know how much longer he has to live?"

"Not exactly, thank God. But he has a child's metabolism and forty-four is a ripe age for him."

Emerald grinned. "Ripe for Ungrukh too. Does Thorndecker have the same kind of life-span?"

"I don't know. He would have had quite a lot longer one with the pintrelase, maybe still if he got it. His development was much further along, over six months, and he looked more normal than Agassiz. But I lost track of him, and I don't know how he was treated."

"And the last question you do not answer if you choose. When Agassiz dies, what becomes of you people?"

"I don't know about the others." Doctor's expression had not changed. He still did not have one. "I get a small allowance to live on. Agassiz's lawyer asked me what I wanted and that was it. I don't need more. My life's work is done."

"Thank you very much," said Emerald, and kept her eyes on his retreating back. "I think we trust him. Forty-four years, plus seven in Hydesland, is a long time. Soon we deal with Agassiz, and then we call home. If no one there wishes to come, we leave here."

"They won't let us go," said Renny.

"They let us go," said Raanung, and shot his claws. "They have more to lose by trying to keep *us*."

"If we leave we are dodging on the move," Emerald said. "I am content to defend from here. Besides, I think I like this Agassiz. He is one of those great-hearted fools, like Spinel."

"That is the first time I hear of you liking a fool," said Raanung.

Shadows swept the lawns; the moist air cooled a little, and someone covered Agassiz with a blue blanket. A machine had finished excavating what was to be a pond for Spinel, in a shaded place, and a first lining had been sprayed. The colors of the flowers dimmed, native species big as birds; they were rivalled by foliage that ranged through all the greens from blue to yellow, and many reds, some the color of Ungrukh.

The three remained in their places, sipping tea from bowl and glass and content to be apart from the others who were shy of them. Agassiz began to stir.

"Soon we get dinner," said Raanung.

"Not before I settle with Agassiz," said Emerald. She poked her head over the shell's rim. "You see I am still here. Do you recall what happens while you are asleep?"

"Yes," Agassiz murmured, eyes opening.

"And now you are awake and quite clear in your head." She moved the prism-frame down. "So I tell you our conditions."

"You look like a hard bargainer, Emerald."

"You judge. I am shielding and blocking now, and this conversation is for you and Raanung and me. I swear friendship and I put my life on it, but I give my life first to Spinel, because that is what I am hired for. In a short time we call him and the others by your CommUnit, but I do not want them here before tomorrow. Now, I trust you and Doctor and Morgan, and there is a day's loss of protection for Spinel, but I must make sure all of this place is safe before I let them in."

Agassiz twisted in alarm. "Whom do you suspect?"

"No one at all right now. I only want to make sure. I want

one day of privileges, until this time tomorrow. Then Spinel is here, and I am sure he is safe with your people. Assuming that he agrees to come, and I think he does."

"What privileges?"

"I want the force-field on the whole time, except to allow my friends through, and guards at the boundaries while they come in. I want your ESPs to stand guard all night. And I want to esp everyone and question whom I choose, with all my care not to alarm or offend. And the freedom of the grounds for us three."

"I think it will be a miracle if you can do all those without alarming or offending, Emerald, but I give them—with an added condition of my own. Any traitor you may find must not be killed."

"I must kill to defend my life. Your traitors are not my business."

"Not even Thorndecker?"

"No, Agassiz."

Renny, coming out of the house grateful for a bath and the loan of clean clothes, ran into Doctor on his way out of the infirmary. His back, if possible, stiffened even more. Tight-assed, she thought. Or, as Anika would have said more charitably, playing it close to the chest. "Excuse me," he said.

Renny could chew up and spit out any bully, but this man was intimidating in a different way. "I hope no one is ill," she murmured.

"Somebody collapsed from heat exhaustion working on the pool today. It happens occasionally."

"I'm sorry."

Something in her tone made him relent a bit. "I don't mean to sound as if I'm blaming you people for that. It wasn't all that hot, and his fever's unusually high, so it may be one of the new tropical bugs that turn up every so often."

"You don't blame us . . . Doctor, I'm an Impervious, and though Emerald probably knows I'm speaking to you she

certainly has no idea of what I mean to say. I don't know if I
can say it so it sounds right either. We know why Agassiz
wants a friend, and we ourselves need as many friends as we
can get. But our job is to protect the Emperor Spinel, and not
at all to come between Agassiz and the people he loves. I
imagine Agassiz loves you best, and he should—''

"In plain words, you think I am jealous." He smiled
slightly, and his face did not crack into a thousand fragments
of granite. "I would hope at my age not to feel anything so
silly."

"Doctor, I can't read minds, thank God, and sometimes I
make mistakes. Emerald likely wants to ask some favors of
you, to help protect Spinel, and I'm sure she'll worry about
offending you. She *is* very young."

"And I am pretty damned old, but I'll do what I can."

The house was a low rambling structure with a steep green
roof, and ivy-covered walls. A trestle-table had been set up in
front of it, and was being laid with cloths and china. It would
be a pleasant place to eat, but Emerald thought it might be
unsettling for those who were eating there to watch a pair of
Ungrukh gulping raw meat out of bowls. *:Feeding time at the
zoo,:* came a faint wisp of thought. She did not attempt to
trace it, but answered, *:I hope somebody has a sense of
humor.:*

Agassiz has a wormy fish or two. . .

She sought out a squat muscular man with warty grey skin
and short spiny hair or hairy spines. His eyes were startlingly
normal blue. Likely he had been engineered for life on a very
strange world and drifted here. "Quattro?"

"ESP-two at your service, lady." He had been leaning on
the excavator and straightened to make the caricature of a
bow, but a goodnatured one. The ESPs wore brighter colors
than the others, not for status but as a constant reminder that
they were not sneaks or skulkers. "Our zoo friend better be
careful or he'll end up with a bloody nose."

"Don't tell that to Agassiz, Quattro, and save the bloody

nose for when we need it. I think you are a better ESP than your rating."

"I'm happy enough with the one I've got now, and," he grinned, "I think we understand each other."

"You know what we want."

"Force-fields, guards, and supper in your room one hour from now."

"Right. We are as tired as hell-be-damned, but I want to look about here first. And, Quattro, this is Spinel." She gave him the image: limbs, water-skin, bipolar arms, pop-eyes and all.

"I've never seen one of them."

"You get to see a lot of him, I hope. Also, put yourself in the head of a possible enemy—I don't mean you—and consider how he can attack."

The Ungrukh found a pair of china soup tureens filled with raw cubed meat waiting for them. "They may find big animals strange," said Raanung, "but they know something about big appetites."

"Mine is not so big after that ride today," Emerald said, but surprised herself by digging in grunting and snorting with as much satisfaction as Raanung.

"This tastes of the freezer but it is better than those damned crumbs in packages." He looked up. "What's the matter?"

Emerald, on haunches, was staring into the half-empty bowl. "Raanung, lay a tongue on this. There is more than the freezer here. It is not right."

"There is nothing wrong with mine." But he leaned to taste it.

She whispered, "I mean to ask Doctor to make sure. . ." Her eyes glazed and closed, and she keeled over.

Anika, Spinel and Bellingrose all agreed to move the next day, but refused Agassiz's offer of transportation; though

there was a scrambler on the CommUnit they did not want
their plans known.

"I'm not sure why we're going," Anika said. "We're
supposed to protect Spinel, not catch Thorndecker, and I
have a feeling there's as much danger in that place as there is
here—if not more."

"Then we won't go," said Bellingrose. "We'll ask for
GalFed protection."

"I know *them,* from my younger days and from Renny.
Before they make up their minds to send it, and if they agree,
until we get it—we could be out of it."

"I would like to meet that Agassiz," Spinel said wistfully.
"He sounds like an interesting one."

"Lord, we're stuck without a choice again," said Anika.
"Maybe we'd better move now."

"No. If Renny says tomorrow she's got a reason. The
stores are still open and I want to get the house set up the way
we planned. But we're sure as hell not going to stay here
overnight. I've got friends in the Circus, and after spending
some time with Emerald and Raanung I don't at all mind
sleeping in straw next to the lions and tigers."

the Page of Swords

Emerald took her night's sleep in the infirmary hooked to
monitors with a ventilator tube in her nose and an i.v. needle
in her arm. By stomach pump she had lost the second meal in
one day. Raanung to save time had hauled her on his back,
and when he returned for the evidence the dishes were gone.

"I can tell from what's missing here," said Doctor. He
was very pale, and scratched his face nervously. The two
other doctors were jittering about, hoping that what worked
for Solthrees would do the same for a cat of the leopard
family. "It's speed barbiturate and time-release neutralizer.
The evidence would run out of her kidneys. Raanung—what
about you?"

"I am a little drowsy, but then I am also very tired."

"I suppose you were expected to fall asleep and find her dead when you woke. The strange taste would have been the neutralizer. The sleep drug hasn't any."

Renny was pacing furiously, eyes blue bruises and arms wrapped tightly around herself. "How do we find out who? Where do we look? She trusts everyone, and everyone is loyal!"

Raanung snarled, "Don't ask me! I know her best, and I must go by what she says. This is my woman and I worry about her first!"

"Quattro?" said Doctor. "What are you doing here?"

The grey-skinned man stood in the doorway. "Why . . . she called me. God!" He stared down at Emerald sprawled across two beds; her tail hung down over an edge, her nostril bulged with the tube, bits of fur had been clipped where needles and monitors were taped.

"Called you? But she's unconscious!"

Quattro turned his palms out. " 'Quattro, I need help,' she says."

"But—"

"Wait," said Renny. "She can esp others while they're sleeping. If she can send now I want to know what she has to say."

"If she wakes too quickly she'll be in danger."

"She doesn't have to. There seems to be some part of her mind that's perfectly aware, and it called for Quattro. Raanung, what do you think?"

"I think Emerald usually gets what she wants."

Renny snorted. "When will she wake?"

"In a few hours, I hope . . . God, I should have kept watch on the drugs."

"I think she means to ask for that," Raanung said. "I don't know why she cannot esp when someone poisons the food."

"Go ahead, Quattro," Renny said.

"I'm scared, but. . ." He squatted beside Emerald's sleeping head and blew gently into her ear. It did not twitch.

"There'll be plenty of twitching when she comes out of it," said Doctor.

"Then tape down her hands, if you want to stay in one piece," Raanung said. "Also her tail. If she does not break something with it she breaks it on something."

"Emerald," Quattro said softly, "I'm here . . . what?" He made a quizzical face. "I know you trust me. Sure." He scratched his head and the spines crackled. "Yes, before you ate . . . you esped nothing . . . but I was guarding and you felt safe . . . huh. I know you trust Agassiz . . . and me, you already told me that . . . and Doctor, and Morgan. So four off twenty-three leaves nineteen, and—you do? I mean, you did!" He rocked back on his heels while the air pushed into Emerald's nose and bubbled out of her mouth.

" 'I count eighteen. . .' God almighty, I am stupid! Doctor!"

Doctor was already out of the room with Quattro following, and Raanung had dashed off in the opposite direction. The other doctors were fussing over Emerald and Renny was left standing with her mouth open until the light broke over her and she whispered, "Goddam, *you've* got an Imper!" to unresponding air.

The little room where the feverish patient had been lying was empty. There was a crumpled sleepsuit on the bed.

"Don't ask," said Doctor. "I knew he was an Imper, but I'm not an ESP and I forgot. Well, he can't get through the force-field."

Quattro said, "As long as he's on the grounds we can—"

"Do what?" Raanung had returned on silent feet. "Before you begin scouring the grounds and scaring the neighbors I suggest you look in his sleeping quarters."

"Why?"

"You have no proof, no evidence. No voiceprints; I bet no foot- or fingerprints or ways to test for them. No one sees or esps him. There is a scent-track to the kitchen, but the dishes are sterile from the machine. We may be sure of him, but I doubt Agassiz permits torture, and even on Ungruwarkh, where we also judge men at times, we do not convict only on the delicacy of a nose.''

Quattro found his man, as Raanung had predicted, in his own bed. His name was Pritchard and he had been with Agassiz for four years. Quattro put a guard on his door, added another to the hall patrol, and went back outside to take up double duty.

Raanung ordered Renny to bed, with a baring of teeth. Emerald began to twitch; he sent away the other doctors, who were dozing in their chairs, and when the twitching became thrashing held down Emerald's hindquarters. Within an hour she was calm. An hour later consciousness bloomed in an angry flare like a fiery rose that snuffed after a few seconds and replaced itself with the crystal globe of her awareness. ''Why do I have all these things stuck in me?''

''You needed them,'' said Doctor shortly. ''I suppose you can get along by yourself now.''

Emerald grinned. ''I am not by myself. I have all of you to help, especially this one, who is very heavy on the legs.''

''And not without scratches either,'' said Raanung.

''Doctor, it is no disgrace that you let a man deceive you by pretending that he is ill.''

''I suppose not, but it isn't something I'd give myself a medal for.''

Quattro came in, yawning. ''I see you made it.''

''We're a tough lot.''

''Yeah. You set me a problem. How the hypothetical enemy would attack Spinel. I guess we don't count his taking out the guardian ESP. He'd have to be an Imper. Spinel's got eyes, or something like them, that can look backward, so a direct attack would come in the dark—but there's too many guards about to try bashing his brains in, or even to use a gun. The attacker would leave himself in the open. . .''

''No, it must be a trap to spring *after* Spinel comes and *he* escapes or believes he is unsuspected. The attacks on me are meant to get rid of a nuisance. The earliest is supposedly a result of Raanung's bad temper—''

"Hah!''

"—and this one from the carelessness or malice of the
kitchen staff.''

"I don't have to deal with those now. The problem is your
Emperor. All I could think of was poison, something in the
pool. But this suspect wouldn't know what would poison
Spinel—though he might figure a good dose of chlorine
could do it. . .''

"Spinel is very sensitive to taste and smell.''

"Yes, I thought he would be—so I asked the electrician to
check the pool fixtures—''

"That is not the kind of thing I think of. I am certainly right
to trust you!''

"What?'' Doctor asked.

"The sealer had been removed from two of the recessed
lights, and if the water had got in . . . we weren't too careful
about guarding that, I guess.'' He sighed. "You're still
giving orders, so what do you want done?''

"Fix the pool so that it is safe,'' Emerald said. "It is not
hard evidence either.''

Quattro rubbed his eyes and yawned again. "Why don't
we just fill it with water and drop him in? It'd solve a few
problems.''

"And cause a few more. Agassiz must send the man away,
even at risk that he is innocent. Quattro, you are making me
yawn. What time is it?''

"A couple of hours to dawn.''

"Then go sleep . . . Doctor, I feel very drowsy again. Is
something wrong?''

"No. You may think you've had all the sleep you'll need
for a year, but a couple of hours of the real thing will do you
good. So take it.''

In spite of his yawns, Quattro's sleepiness had peaked, and
he was determined to see the night through for its remaining
few hours. When the last patrol was changed in the halls he
took over from Morgan.

Morgan was tired and bored, but no more relaxed than Quattro. The attack on Emerald had distressed him, not for her own sake, because he did not particularly like her, but because someone had nearly been murdered on Agassiz's grounds. He realized that the term "sacrilege" was too pretentious for this act, but he felt, in a confused way, that the pattern of his life was shifting out of the order he valued.

Someone in a room along the way had left the door slightly ajar and a dim light shone from the opening; he would have paid no further attention if he had not heard a peculiar sound. He pushed the door open slightly and looked in, prepared to duck back in a hurry. Renny was crouched on the edge of her bed, hands knotted between her knees, shivering. Her teeth were chattering.

She looked up, saw him and said, "Go a-w-way!"

"You sure?"

"N-no."

He slipped in. "What's the matter?"

"Matter? Emerald nearly dead and Spinel nearly and that sonofabitch cracked my head against the wall and—" her voice rose and rose "—filthy Hartog ripped out the egg-sac and smashed it on the wall, on the wall and you grabbed and dragged me and—"

He knelt and clamped his hand on her mouth. "Stop yelling. You'll wake everyone."

She blinked at him in fury, but did not pull at his hand.

"Can you be quiet now?"

She nodded and he took his hand away. "You're looking a bit blue. Maybe you've got—"

"It's a hereditary condition. A bit of what my mother has."

"I thought that was makeup. If I sit beside you will you punch me up?"

"No, silly." He sat beside her and dared put an arm round her shoulders. "But I won't sleep with you."

"I didn't ask. I ask when I want it. What happened with the egg-sac? I never heard anything about that."

She told him.

"I see."

"Do you? Like watching a rape that happens so fast you can't stop—"

"If I didn't understand I might be working for a Hartog instead of an Agassiz."

Her black eyes bored into him. "Why do you work for him? Really, why?"

"He's a good man and he pays well, in that order. The only one I know who's never done evil."

"How could he!"

"Thorndecker did, and he wasn't all that better off. Agassiz had Doctor, but when he was mature enough he could have bought any doctor he wanted. You're thinking Agassiz is too good to be true, especially with my putting on my simpleton act. The gawkiness is an act, and," he grinned, "I admit I enjoy it when people like you find out it *is*—but what I said about loving and serving is true. Agassiz does have a flaw. It's like a big sore spot. He wants *everybody* to love him—and he can't have it. He's got Doctor and Quattro and me. Maybe a couple others. The rest work for him because he's a good man, pays well, and won't let them starve when he dies. Doctor loves him because Agassiz is the baby he saved and grew, and would have done the same for Thorndecker if he could. With Quattro and me, the kind of courage and determination he's got satisfies something in us. Maybe we're not quite sure what it is, so we call it love. I don't know if *you'd* understand *that*."

"Don't be too sure."

"No . . . I did see how you handled Doctor today. But not everybody can, or even should, love Agassiz the way he wants . . . and especially, because his body doesn't know anything at all about sex, he wants the one person he can never have. . ."

"Emerald was right. Sounds too damn much like the Spinels and their fission."

"I'm telling you what I get from Doctor. I don't know if it's right. It sounds reasonable."

Renny had stopped shivering, but still crunched into herself as if she were freezing. She rubbed her neck against Morgan's arm. "How'd that comic opera part get started—separating the two?"

"Not so comic, but it did start like that. Doctor identified them, at the Base hospital. He was sorry later."

"Why?"

"Thorndecker was the direct descendant of Thorndecker-Hyde, through his son, Agassiz from his daughter. The old man had lots of sisters and female descendants. Girls ran in the family. But by family tradition they always kept the name going, and men inherited from the estate directly while the women got trust funds and interest, and whatever man wanted to marry into the family had to change his name to Thorndecker or Hyde, or both. Or get cut out of the money."

"Yeah, I've heard of that kind of thing. It's—"

"Sexist, bigoted, arrogant and everything else those men were. And Agassiz's father was one of the few who wouldn't budge."

"Why'd he move to Qsaprinel?"

"Maybe his wife wanted it, and he gave in that far. After Thorndecker-Hyde's executors collected their babies and took them back to Sol Three they must have done some arguing and decided that because he had the name—his father's name *was* Thorndecker—the estate should go to that heir, to be put toward keeping him alive, I guess, and dumped Agassiz, who was in far worse shape, into a state hospital—"

"Ugh!"

"Right. But the executors did have a bit of, um, if you worked at it you could call it conscience. They arranged for him to have some kind of small allowance. Not enough to keep *him* alive. I learned this in bits and pieces, so I can't vouch for all of it. Things at the hospital got chaotic. They couldn't afford to do everything that was needed for Agassiz, they certainly didn't want to let him die, some of the doctors were interested in him and there was a lot of publicity. And the Administration was screaming they couldn't keep the institution going. Finally they got lawyers and gnawed at Thorndecker's administrators till they'd bitten off a third of the estate. Enough to keep going and put the rest in trust for Agassiz. . .''

"And meanwhile back at the heart of Galactic Empire—"

"Doctor—his name is Per Hansen—he'd been left with nothing. Got odd jobs at Base Hospital. Took his locals and qualified. He was sick of people then, and worked in the labs—''

She slid away from his arm and landed on the pillow. He pulled her feet up to the bed. "Let me guess. He found out about the pintrelase, and—''

"That's something we don't ever ask about," he said firmly.

She was too weary for temperament. "I'm not spying on you, Morgan.''

"We get protective, like you with Spinel—but I don't know and don't want to. All I know is, he got here with the pintrelase and the report. He tried to get it to Thorndecker's people because he thought they had both embryos—but he couldn't get near them. They'd pulled out. But he did find Agassiz, so he gave everything to the hospital and worked there until Agassiz could decide to leave. That's why Agassiz has brains to think with, and speech, and teeth, and can eat a little food through his mouth, and see with his eyes. . .''

"And earn the loyalty of people—''

"The way Spinel's earned yours.''

"Emerald said they were both great-hearted fools.''

"Maybe she's right.'' He brushed away the strands of hair that had gotten plastered to her forehead with cold sweat. "You're not clammy and you're not shaking. Now we go sleep in our little narrow beds.''

Her eyes closed. The tone of her voice half-belied the words: "Don't think you've got on my good side yet, Morgan.''

He stretched, eyes toward the ceiling. "Hartog ever sit down beside you and talk you out of your nerves?''

"You . . ." But he was gone and she was drifting into sleep before she could think of the very last word.

Judgement

In the morning there was a three-cornered affair in the dayroom.

"Kangaroo court," Pritchard sneered. He was a short compact man with a thin tanned face and light brown hair; the small and deadly type Thorndecker seemed to prefer. He was the apex. In another corner Emerald and Raanung were joined by Doctor and Quattro.

"He's right, you know," Agassiz quavered. "You can't show proof." He was the third of the angles.

"Right now I don't care about showing proof," said Emerald. "I know it seems unfair. I am sorry I break my promise to keep this place safe without alarming or offending. But everything I know and sense tells me this man is a danger and if he stays we go no matter who wills what."

"I can see the way it's going," said Pritchard. "I've been judged guilty without proof or defense and there's nothing I can do about it. I'll get out. I wouldn't stay if you begged me."

"I can't ask you to stay, Pritchard." Agassiz's treble verged on tears. "You may collect a half-year's extra pay."

"And I've served you for four years. Remember that!"

"Except for vacations."

Pritchard jerked as if a live wire had touched him. Renny was leaning on the doorway, still a bit blue about the mouth. Her eyes were dangerous. "You've lost weight, Richards. You're looking good." She straightened, hands on hips. "Sorry I couldn't get here earlier. Somehow my door got jammed, and the sound-proofing's too good. But if you need a deposition, I depose that this man, Richards/Pritchard-whatever, was one of Hartog's group on Qsaprinel. I can give you dates you can check against his absences. He also has a red hemangioma, that's a lump of veins, on the back of his left earlobe. I can't see it from here, but—"

"Just what are you going to do about it?"

"Nothing, Richards. While I was getting unstuck I did a little thinking, and I think that fellow following us was meant to kill me so I wouldn't recognize someone."

"Why don't you ask him?"

"That is not possible," Emerald said. "The man is dead, after poisoning himself in the police cell. I also do a little thinking, and that is about Thorndecker. Hartog is dead, after committing an irrational act; a man who might escape runs into a thorn-bush which kills him; a third kills himself. All fail in some way. Thorndecker is skilled at hypnosis, and I wonder if he does not plant a self-destruct order which activates in those who fail."

"Shit," said Pritchard.

"Maybe so, but you fail to kill me, even though you manage to avoid being seen by Irenyi Gurdja until now. Perhaps with warning you take care. And Pritchard, I promise Agassiz that if a traitor is found we do not kill him. Now I go further, perhaps against the wishes of Agassiz, and use my authority before I give it up, with gratitude. Do not try to communicate with Thorndecker or his associates, or even your friends. Go to places you never visit and live with people you do not know. Possibly you stay alive."

Pritchard hesitated fractionally, as if he might be giving up the only sanctuary he had ever known, and left without a word. Renny pulled away from the doorway when he passed, as if his nearness might burn her. He did not look at her.

"And the rest of what I think about Thorndecker is this: I think Pritchard has plenty of opportunities to smuggle out pintrelase for him, and it is not difficult to synthesize for whomever he wants to use it on. If he takes it, all it seems to do is make him more lively and enthusiastic about killing."

No one replied to that. Renny said, "Do you think he'll take your advice?"

"I doubt it, but I must try." Agassiz was breathing tremulously, and Doctor stroked his head. The old man's face was ravaged. Emerald hooked her whiskers over the scallop shell once more. "Agassiz, you are thinking that you let

serpents into your garden when you want friends. But every
garden has a snake or two, and we drive one out. And today I
bring you three new friends who are worth your trust and
love, I promise you."

Morgan said to Emerald, "I found the radio wrapped in his
underwear. I removed a few parts. Why didn't you let me
plant tracers on him?"

"I don't want to know where he is, and I rather not find
another dead one." She grinned. "Even I can be a bit
soft-headed."

"You also promised Agassiz you'd bring him his love-
object," said Renny. "What are you going to do about
Thorndecker now?"

"Whatever I can to stop him. I am afraid to allow him in
the presence of Agassiz for one minute."

the Three of Cups

After identification by Renny, the forcefield was shut off
and a mauve hearse drove slowly through the gates.

When it stopped, Bellingrose slipped from the cab and
raised the back door. Anika was riding shotgun on the coffin,
the largest available and bound in scrolls of brass. Six men
lifted it out and set it on the ground.

"Very tasteful," said Doctor.

"Nothing but the best for our departed," said Bellingrose.

"Do we present it to Agassiz like Cleopatra in her carpet,
or just open it here?"

"I'd sure as hell want to get out of that," said Anika.

So Spinel emerged from folds of pale pink satinette and
approached Agassiz on his own six feet. Under Renny's
direction the carpenter had built him a lectern, and it waited
beside the scallop shell.

Spinel had the liveliest expectations of pleasure in meeting
Agassiz, and he propped himself on the lectern eagerly.
Though he was almost as sensitive to physical appearance as
any Qsaprinil, some of his chauvinism had been tempered by

his love for Beta, and he had learned the Galactic's cos-momorphic sense very quickly; Agassiz's looks registered in a mild and neutral way. "Good day, dear friend!"

"And good day to you, your Majesty," said Agassiz.

"Oh, I am plain Spinel here, Agassiz, and I like it. I am only sorry to use your speech so badly."

"I love your companions and I am delighted to meet you, Spinel. You will learn with me and we will be friends forever."

Emerald's fur stood on end. Agassiz was not far from death. And Spinel. . . ?

She watched the two speaking in the dappled shade, Spinel signing with his hands as though he were speaking in his own language, and Agassiz understanding because she supplemented for him. She had given up her authority and the forcefield was shut off. The fierce heat it had generated eased, and the trees rustled, and the ponds rippled when birds or insects skimmed them. Bellingrose sat quietly and observed his surroundings. Anika, after one look at Quattro, scrubbed off her makeup: here she felt free to be blue. The hearse was repainted in camouflage colors and parked on the landing field for emergency use.

Emerald said to Renny, "I hope I choose the right course for Pritchard. I worry about that."

"I know you don't want revenge on him, Emerald. I don't either. In spite of what he tried to do he didn't manage to make a murderer of himself . . . and I'm certain he would never have led you to Thorndecker."

But Emerald did not feel relieved. She had had only one respite. She had planned to ask before breakfast that all unsealed drugs and opened or thawed food packages be destroyed, and she knew that this would not sit well with Agassiz's people. But Doctor, who had been badly shaken, had already gotten rid of loose drugs, and the kitchen staff, disturbed and embarrassed, had done the same with the food; since they were normally cautious in a hot climate, and proud of a well-run kitchen, there was little to dispose of.

She sought out Raanung, who was enjoying a full-bellied

doze in the shade, punctuated by the occasional belch. She flicked his rump with her tail.

He opened one eye. "You want sex *now?*" He yawned. "Or a rub on that sore belly of yours?"

She snarled, "I want to find Thorndecker. I do not want to roll about in the grass any more."

"You change minds very fast. Now you have a sore head, and soon you make mine sore too. You have no idea how to go about finding Thorndecker. You must know nobody here does. Unless you want to run about chasing your tail, and good luck catching it." He snorted. "Where is the cool mind now?" And fell asleep again.

Emerald crept into a corner of the garden, curled herself under a shrub on grass as green as her name, and sulked.

By the Blue Pit, I am getting like my mother and grandmother!

And how she missed them. Prandra, Tengura with the eternal white-noise of her grumbling mind, Raanung's mother, that thorn-sharp Nga, his sister Nurunda, her twin aunts Ypra and Ygne. . .

:None of the men, Emerald?:

She uncoiled, fangs bared and prehensile tail ready to whip about a neck.

Quattro was standing a few meters away: while she had moved, so had he, and there was the stem of a leaf-bladed throwing-knife in his fingers.

"I *was* only joking, you know," he said evenly. "Answering the questions you haven't asked, I also have privileges in the matter of esping, and yes, I have permission for my knives as I suppose you have for the two you carry, as well as the teeth and claws."

"We both have very good reflexes." She dropped to a crouch and settled her snout at the juncture of her crossed wrists. "One of my knives is on loan from my mother as a talisman. It comes from the Forges of Chlis, but not like the one Bellingrose takes off his nervous customer. It is for gutting and scaling fish, because that is what we mainly eat at home until we grow food animals. In truth it is more use as a crowbar. But your knife is like no other I ever see."

He had returned it to the quivver behind his shoulder. "It's used for throwing at targets in various kinds of exhibitions. People like me find ourselves in strange places."

Emerald blinked and scratched the tip of her nose with her tongue. "I am sorry to react so violently and provoke you. Now I answer your first question. There are men I miss, like my father and my Tribesman Araandru; particularly my son, who does not quite count as a man—and then the dead ones, my brother Tugrik and Raanung's father. Among the women, there are some I do not like much, but I miss the power of their esp and their experience, because they are older. Here I have Raanung, with a good head and the finest nose among the tribes I know, but he does not have the esp, and neither do most of our men."

"Tough on them."

"But I have you. . ." *:Now, Quattro, I want to ask a question without seeing the point of your knife, because I mean no harm. When do you work for Thorndecker?:*

He dropped to his knees, blue-water eyes bulging in a stare against her own, and slapped his thighs with thick warty hands. *:I never worked for him! Never! Never!:*

"I believe you, man. Please don't give me a headache." His shield was firm around them, and his vehemence rebounded within its limits. She did not know what to do or expect, and they waited staring at each other for a moment.

Until he turned away and whispered, "I was . . . I was—why did you ask that?"

:When you say "strange places" it brings up an image you cannot suppress—like and not-like Agassiz. . . : And other pictures she herself had experienced during the attack in the street and would not have described if she could.

His face had turned yellowish and his nose began bleeding suddenly in a freshet. When he turned his head back to avoid dripping and groped for a handkerchief she noticed the pale scars under his jaws below the ears.

:Gill slits. I had the gills sewn up. After. . . :

"Tactless. Ungrukh have no tact. We never become diplomats. Tell me when you feel better."

"When will I feel better?" His voice was stifled by handkerchief and emotion.

"You want Doctor?"

"Nah. For this you lie down and hold your nose." He did
so.

"I know you are better than ESP-two, but it does not occur
to me you have such a good block and reflector when I am
esping you."

"I learned. Yeah, I learned. Never knew my own head
could teach me so much."

"You are better than my grandmother."

"For an amateur. But I always was the best   "

Temperance Reversed

at everything.

The three STs: STrength, STamina, STorage. These lumps
all over me aren't goose-bumps, they're nodes for storing
water, like you get in a frog. People who called me Frog used
to get their heads bust, but I *was* the best frog in the pond. Salt
pond. I take water and salt all day, but at night I sleep in water
with a tube in my nose for air and it makes the membranes
sore so they bleed, but I wouldn't have those gills. And this
undersuit keeps the water in so I won't dry but lets the air in so
I won't stink but absorbs traces of mucus from the water-
pores so I won't drip. The spines on my head are collapsible
antennas. Can you imagine how useful? I'm not—no, I see
you realize I'm not a masochistic whiner. Really? You don't
have them kind on Ungruwarkh? Not your grandmother Tengura? *Now* you see. Bellingrose gave you what led up to
Agassiz and Thorndecker, and what Morgan told Renny led
down to their separation, and I'm not sure exactly what
formed Thorndecker's personality to make it so different
from Agassiz's—but I know what he was like seven years

ago, and what he wanted from me—a slave he thought was as
ugly in body as he was in his own mind. Agassiz doesn't
count, he's an arrested embryo as nature made him and looks
just that, and Spinel is a norm for his type like all the other
types. But nature didn't make me

and my maker—our
makers—made a big fat mistake when they forgot to make us
slaves. You thought it was a colony on some weird planet we
were engineered for, but it was Sol Three, permanent
amphibian—but mainly underwater—force for overseeing
farming installations, that's machines for growing kelp and
gathering seaweed and plankton, along with fish-breeding,
erosion-monitoring, water-testing. No need for wetsuits,
aqualungs, decompression chambers.

The shelf west of
Florida. The project head was a fine Italian scientist who's
maybe glad to be forgotten now, called me Quattro because I
was the fourth successful male. I didn't mind that. He could
have been my father and he wasn't a mean person. Big lab,
big staff, enGeneering in its boom, enough IQ points to
match the electrons in the universe. Men gave sperm, women
gave ova, volunteer wombs because the tanks weren't quite
up to development. But beautifully planned: every chromo-
some put together like a jigsaw to make one of Us, optimum
hundred breeding pairs—hundred and ten, actually . . .
beautiful. When it came to sex they took X chromosomes
from half the men and Y's from the other half and each
woman produced ova for one sex, never both, so it would be
almost impossible for relatives to mate.

All those carefully
picked women who rented the wombs never saw us—not that
any of them would have wanted to keep one.

Oh and the staff
loved us—the way a chemist loves a perfect crystal—little
tadpoles gagging and coughing from water to air, air to
water. They even had the good taste not to give us flippers for
feet, hard to flap around a lab on flippers drawing maps and

dictating into machines . . . I was the only ESP, lucky for them because I'm goodnatured, I dunno why

and we played kid games, some they taught us, some we made up, and as we got older we worked down there and learned the dark, and then up in the light and told what we'd seen—you can't tell I've got a permanent third eyelid, a polarizing membrane, miraculous engineering, but

they forgot, among other things they forgot to make us *dull,* so we wouldn't know it was *normal* to have a pink or brown or black skin, or even the kind of blue Anika can get rid of, thought we wouldn't know why people came to admire and gawk, hell, it was *them* that was being admired, not us, they forgot

there were *men and women* inside the skulls and under the skins and nobody'd ever get to know it unless they dug up our bones when the flesh had rotted off, those weren't plankton farmers produced by all the IQ points they were so proud of, rocking to sleep at night in our underwater nets, with the huge machines going like beating hearts scaring off the big fish

inside the skulls we were an architect, a flutist, an administrator, a chess-player, a doctor, a clerk, a gardener, a space-pilot,

and me, I was a knife-thrower because it was something you did with your feet on the earth and your head up and your back straight fighting against the air and finally

they forgot the kibbutz effect. A whole bunch of kids nearly the same age brought up together in one family, having to cooperate, hold it all in, nobody the same, like Bokhanovsky twins . . . can't get up a lot of sexual interest in each other—and who the hell among us would have wanted kids that looked like *us?* After all those precautions to avoid incest they ended with a two-hundred-fold incest barrier.

Panic. My old man the Director ready to

retire, us nearly twenty, no culmination, no climax. Funds
shrinking, staff drifting, already instruments can do better
than we can, but expensive, and we're still good for countries
and worlds that can't afford the machines. And we must
breed. For them. They had one ESP there, not too bright,
didn't like me at all, tried to hypnotize the brains out of me,
and I don't hypnotize so I played even dumber . . . and
when the mutter-mutter began about artificial insemination,
now or never, I caught it

                and we drifted . . . all of us . . . all
two hundred and seven of us . . . within twenty-four hours
. . . some to the east and some to the west and some the wide
world round . . . I wish I could believe it, never heard from
many, only cared for few . . . some ripped by teeth, some
into the abyss and smoth—

                hell, there goes my nose again—
:*Then rest. Wait.*:
What for? You want to know, you get it. One

                girl, woman,
thing, frightened, didn't know what, a clinger, stuck to me. I
knew I couldn't desert her, knew it in my head because I
didn't have much feeling for her. We swam the bay, had a
couple of knives and a speargun, not much more to fight than
a jellyfish, slept in the marshes by day because we need salt
and by night went through the swamps or hitched rides on
carts loaded with garden refuse and sewage on the way to the
converters. That don't bother you when you've lived in the
muck down there and can sleep your way clean in the morning. There were fish and shore animals to eat with the mixed
veg. We made sure nobody saw us. It didn't matter we had no
clothes—there wasn't much thrilling to see—but nobody
knew what we were.

             Except.

                I don't know how long it was or
where we went, I'd never been out of my own square kilometer about forty meters deep, until a couple of guys in a
skimmer fished us up with a net one midmorning when we

were asleep—and by God that's a shock! because you've got
to get the water out of your trachea and blow the concentrated
brine out of your sinuses when you get in the air, and you
wake up like that—I guess maybe

                         Thorndecker got his first
thrill out of us through the eyes of his ESP watching us
writhing in the net, never pulled us up, left us hanging under
the belly through the bay door grinning like apes for, I dunno,
maybe minutes or hours till they dropped us in a pool in the
middle of a courtyard.

Atrium

            is what Thorndecker called it. Little emperor
wrapped up in embroidered cloth waiting for his next toy.
Forget the bullshit about scared of germs, he's a damn deadly
bacterium, doesn't even need the umbilical system, he'd got
free of that, the doctors the estate let at him gave him
everything in the book—thyroid, pituitrin, androgens,
steroids . . . I wonder what became of those doctors.

                                   Never
really esped him, never wanted to get in his mind, I was
scared of that ESP of his, scared they'd find out how much of
one I was and played dumb. Thorndecker was

                               size of a kid
about two and a half, beard, chestful of hair, muscles like a
weightlifter, man-size set of equipment I wouldn't try to
think if or how he used, "Infant Hercules Syndrome" Doctor
calls it, from all the stuff he'd been treated with, nothing at all
like a dwarf or midget, not like Agassiz except for size. He
had these dickey-suits fitted with prosthetics to give him
proper legs and arms and face-masks because even with the
beard you could see he had baby features. Every time

                                     he got a
new one he'd march around trying it out for the slaves to
admire—because all them around him were slaves, the ones
he paid well, the ones with guns, they thought they admired
him, he made them think so. A fine master must have taught
him hypnosis but if he never got away after Thorndecker'd

scoured out his mind it was no more than he deserved. It
never quite worked on me, but it did take effort to keep my
head half closed off and make him think he'd got halfway
there. Even *she* wasn't really free, but I didn't mind too much
because she'd have gone crazy scared

                              the times when he was
sitting in that throne-chair by the pool with us in it and men
with spear-guns on the rim and said *Fuck*

                              and by God you
don't know how you could do it but the men with the guns and
the girl with her eyes starting to turn up and you've got to
keep her mind blank or she'll—and them grinning *Fuck!*

                                             We
got good food and water, lived in outbuildings, never saw the
inside of the house, a big stucco spread-out place, bigger than
here, maybe the old Thorndecker estate, we didn't mind the
storms . . . she started getting, like, I don't know, she'd
grown into a late puberty, more adult, developed, more like
the ones with the pink, brown, black skins

                                        I told myself
puberty, I knew pregnancy, and it sounds stupid but I began
to love her, she was wakening, thinking, I was playing blank
looking for outs. The property opened on the beach, but there
were docks and boats, men with guns, women for the men—
tough and dumb and counting their blessings when they got to
leave, never saw us, I saw too much of them—and the big
ESP and the little Nero. No outs, no outs, I was sick with fear
and desperation when she went into labor and they drugged
me and took her and I never saw
*(Leave it dark, (Quattro, leave it dark, (ripping with knives,
screaming, distorted (tank in the secret room floating with
preserved (   )))) leave it dark, Quattro!)*

                                        I became
their dog. Something to kick. Fed scraps. Slept in dirty
water. No more clean pool. Not quite a dog for Thorndecker.
He knew, he knew he'd never quite got at me for all my
dragging around. He'd have me kissing his baby toes before I

died. That's why he kept me. Listen, Lady Ungrukh, I know you, and I know you can see that dark where I won't look. He could do something like that. But when the thing happened I woke up. I got sick in that dirty water, I got well in that dirty water, I had the way to block, I learned it fast and I won't go inside, not in me, but I knew how it worked, got under the ESP, took him apart and put him together without shifting him, they're replaceable and I preferred the one I knew, dipped into Thorndecker long enough to watch the maggots squirming

and I began to wear clothes, rags or cast-offs, I didn't care, they had a good laugh at my sudden attack of modesty and it didn't bother me, I worked with the laborers who did small repairs and waited for the hurricane to blow out the big window Thorndecker posed in front of looking at the sea and the pool,

everybody else had stuff that turns to powder, but him, he had to have thick pure real glass, better than you get here but not good enough against that storm, it happened nearly every year and he put the same damn thing in again. It was a long chance I would have waited a lifetime for.

And I got it. Blew out just like a bomb explosion—in the middle of the night, and at dawn they had everybody grubbing in the mud and yelping, it was so sharp, and you can't get a magnet to pick up that stuff. Beautiful. I got three pieces, all I dared, sharp, you could cut your eyes looking at them, and I went down where the laborers were working and used just a little power, fitted them with weighted handles of whatever scraps were around, they weren't beauties but even the Forgemasters of Chlis would have respected their balance, coated the blades with tile-sealer I could peel off and replace. I kept them on my body. Always. I didn't think I'd come out alive, but I wanted to get somebody. I didn't care who.

the Ace of Swords

So the next time the ESP gave me a cross-eyed look I
told him to screw off—I got beat up for it, luckily just my face
because I wouldn't have wanted those pieces of glass
punched in my gut—and I got over it so easy I *knew*
Thorndecker had given up on me. And he wasn't just going to
split my skull, he'd find some way to make it fun—and I was
curious, really curious, because I was just half-nutty enough
then to want to die in an interesting way—as long as I could
take somebody. And I ate scraps with the other slaves because I wasn't afraid of being poisoned, and slept soundly in
the dirty water because it wasn't a fancy enough place to die
in

but five or six nights later I was told to sleep in the pool,
and I said What for? and they said You'll see! Grinning like
apes. I didn't have to esp. I knew their heads. I wrapped
enough cloth around me to hold the three glass knives and lay
down in the bottom like a good boy and had my REM
twitches and my delta rhythms going and waited.

I wanted
as much of that clean water as I could get. After a
while there was a clink in the far corner of the pool and the
ESP yelling, Hey, Quattro, maybe you can use this! and I
heard the skimmer and there was a tremendous flump! It was
a shark, a young sand-tiger, something over two meters, with
a whacking big tail—they must have bought it, I can't see
them catching that—

and they'd thrown a knife in the far
corner of the deep end, the idea being to see if I could get it
before the teeth got me

standing there grinning with their
spearguns and a floodlight on so Thorndecker could watch
through his window without getting a splash. Huh.

I just
slid back and stood up in the shallow end watching it coming

up to butt.me so it could get me under the snout where the
teeth were. But they'd got it disoriented, and I had hold of
its brains, all it needed was a touch so they wouldn't
suspect.

No contest. An anticlimax. I knew they were going
to push me out of the corner and drop in something bloody. I
wanted blood, all right. One of my glass blades was broader
than I like, but I didn't have much choice in the pickings and
figured it would be good enough for close work. I got it out
and just ducked under the teeth and walked down the slope
ripping that fish's belly from dorsal to anal fins. I was a bit
sorry about that. She was a graceful young thing.

When the
thrashing was going on and the pool clouding up with blood I
picked up the knife they'd thrown in and tossed it at the ESP,
not hard, just to glance

and when he started turning this way
and that trying to figure out what hit him between the light
and the dark water I gave him my second glass knife. For
good. I picked up his speargun and took out the light, and
when the second fellow came running I gave him a glass knife
too. I had no more knives left, but I've never been sentimen-
tal about them.

The damn fool in the skimmer lowered to find
out what was happening and opened the bay doors looking
where to aim. I took him with a spear.

Three for two.

I
thought that was fair, but I'm more bloody-minded than
Doctor.

There was an awful mess in that pool but I was out to
sea without even trying to find what Thorndecker was thinking.

"Well. I had the mind of a dim twelve-year-old. My own
species, I mean. But I should have been able to avoid the
whole thing."

Raanung, who had wakened and approached to listen,
said, "I am a warrior and I cannot think how to behave
differently—except to die first of frustration and bad
temper."

Emerald gave him a lick on the snout. "We have chances
for that coming. Quattro, it is strange Agassiz finds you, not
so?"

"It would have been stranger if he hadn't been looking for
someone like me half his life—but it was strange enough. I
was in the sea with the stars up and the phosphorescence
around and my body my own. Only my mind had the abscess
. . ." He stared without seeing at the blood spot on his thigh
staining the bright orange of his zip. "I seemed to know my
way back to the installation, by smell, taste or sonar, and it
was the only place I knew. I didn't know what I'd do there. I
don't think it's possible to make anybody understand the state
of my ignorance. Or my demoralization. In spite of what had
been done to me I thought of myself just then as less valuable
than a rabid dog and believed if I reported Thorndecker I'd
have to tell what I did and be shot down on the spot—so they
had got to me halfway. I was a bit saner when I reached the
Station and found everything dark, and an alarm fence
around it. Even the underwater stuff. Silent as death. And I
felt that way inside, as if I'd been changed from Quattro to
Niente. Kept north, didn't know where else, water by day,
shore by night. Around Naples I picked up Frog. Carnival by
the water. Microcephalic. Failed experiment, maybe . . .
never thought they'd be grubby enough to sell their failures to
. . . Tank of dirty . . . you've never been in a zoo, so I
guess you don't know where to find the ugliest people in the
world. Laughing their heads off in the monkeyhouse. I
thought my heart would go *fft* then, but it didn't, so I waited
till the lights went out, and when I saw they weren't going to
strike the works and move on I sneaked ashore and stole a
couple of knives from the thrower to find out what kind of
places supplied them. I said I was ignorant. Never went near
the idiot in the tank. Nothing to help there and he didn't mind.
I worked north, ducking storms, healing my brains, stole

enough money so I could buy clothes to wear in the open when I had to but I never let anybody get near me. Still didn't know what to do, hardly anybody hires throwers anyway. In all that time I didn't hear one word about Thorndecker. I guess he'd cut his losses, but I didn't know what he was planning.

"When I hit the islands I ran into the *GRAND * PANGALACTIC * TRAVELLING * UNIVERSE *. Big business, one of a chain of shows that went all over with acts from hundreds of worlds, real class. Nobody'd heard of the Frog experiment and when I was taking a chance wandering around like a rube I heard someone say they weren't hiring on no freaks nor geeks neither. I said I wasn't hiring out, I just threw knives in my spare time. It got them on the funnybone, I'm not sure why, but they sent me to one of their alley shows—little independents, like fleas on a dog. I don't know what most of them do but this one ran contraband. They wanted me like a dog wants a flea, but I'd come from Upstairs, and it was a bit rough till I'd convinced them I wasn't narking or clawing up their backs, just wanted to get away. As for pulling my weight they didn't want to share much and I wouldn't touch the hard stuff and risk prison. I'd blow like Thorndecker's window. They gave me samples of a new kind of industrial gem and they kept the deposit for a finder's fee. I didn't care. They thought I'd be caught out for an amateur going through customs and that'd be it. When it came to check-out I just packed the stones one by one in my gills. It hurt a bit, but—they were like the glass knives. No way to tell, It's funny with those guys on the line. They'll look in your ears and up your nose and down your throat and everywhere else—but gills look like open wounds to them and they'll turn their eyes away. They had ESP checkers, so I blocked. No trouble at all. But I decided then to have the gills closed.

"After I dropped out on Fthel Five, delivered and came here I was sitting in a bar drinking fizz and feeling almost good except for what next—and like some kind of smoke-bomb I smelled—you say like and not-like Agassiz? This was like and not-like Thorndecker. I went rigid. I didn't have to look in any mirror to know my face was purple. Before I could think *goodbye* I felt two ESPs trained on me with a CALM DOWN/DON'T MOVE. Who could move? and Doctor walked in and sat down across from me with his hands folded and the Thorndecker-Agassiz story set in his skull like a diamond. And I'm here. My nose is dry.'' He stood up. ''I think you'll enjoy your dinner properly tonight.'' He moved away in his blood-orange to join his fellow ESPs in their bright blue and yellow among the muted colors of the others.

''Now you know something of Thorndecker,'' Raanung said.

''More than I like and less than I need. Where do you think he is?''

''By the way he deploys his troops I suspect South Key, or else he has a base there. It is still very close to here, and I do not see why in all the universe he chooses to stay near Agassiz when he has the pintrelase probably for years and there is no danger in this place.''

''Perhaps if he is here it is Agassiz who is following him,'' said Emerald.

''Agassiz is sitting here over twenty years.''

''And Thorndecker knows about it all that time, you bet, and makes no move against anyone until we come. Great help!''

''You are right and wrong. Yes, he does nothing, and no, it is not true we are no help at all. Anything that diverts his attention from Qsaprinel even a little is good right now—though I don't care for you to eat more poison.''

Emerald said impatiently, ''Nothing is diverting his attention from Qsaprinel. Every attack they do not make on Spinel directly they make against us as a group trying to protect him. Even tracking the skimmer. I'm sure the aim is not at Morgan. All attacks are against Spinel.''

Worst of all, Spinel knew it. He knew that his world would be subjected to greater threats, that his enemies might trick him and trap his allies, subvert his friends, destroy his family. . .

Raanung said, "What is that you have stuck in back of your consciousness?"

"A suspicion or two I don't like to examine too closely myself. Look, supper is ready. Maybe we do enjoy it better tonight."

She and Raanung ate in the open with the others, from the tureens which had been set near the table. The kitchen staff had assured her they would not break easily, and she decided that if the company had gotten used to Agassiz being spoonfed by Doctor they could accept the sight of two big cats bolting red meat and licking its juices from two ornate china bowls decorated, for Emerald, with roses, and for Raanung with cornflowers. The habits of Hills people were sloppy compared with those of the Plains, but Raanung learned quickly, and his neat disposal matched favorably against the sawing and masticating of any Solthree.

She addressed Quattro. *:There is one I feel it is not courteous to esp. One of your ESPs, the girl in yellow whose eyes are red with weeping.:*

A slender little thing with long copper braids and a soft quivering mouth, her upper lip's deep cleft bringing it to a point that emphasized her vulnerability.

:Sylvie Ringgold? She was Pritchard's girl.:

:How strange. Is she with him all the time?:

:Most of the three years she's been here. I've never had her. I avoid the ones who think they want to get it off with a freak.: His tone, in spite of the words, was neutral.

:I presume he never tells her his secrets.:

:Not that I know. The three of us—: he meant to include the third ESP, Ti-Jacques, the man in blue, who was huge, black and quiet, *:—are pretty free with our heads. That doesn't mean we're voyeurs. What do you have in mind?:*

:Whatever I can learn by asking questions. This morning somebody jams Renny's door so she can barely get out in time to identify Pritchard. I wonder if someone hypnotizes his guard. . ..

:Emerald, dear, I won't blame you for not remembering,

*because you had your mind and your belly on other things—
but I was that guard! I took over from Morgan on the last
watch, I can swear to every move he made, because I've
esped him, and I brought Pritchard down with my hand on his
arm the whole time, and he never looked me in the eye!*:

:*I don't blame him. He is a brave man to spend four years
in your company!*:

:*And?*:

:*Morgan spends some time with Renny—*:

:*Leaving the door unlocked the way he found it. He asked
me to look in on her. I told you I could swear.*:

:*Good. That is a relief.*: So the door might have been
jammed when Quattro was bring Pritchard downstairs, and
Renny, overtired, still sleeping. Sylvie . . . If Pritchard had
learned hypnotic control from his master, a few whispered
words: *Sylvie, that woman's dangerous, and in case they try
to blame me*—and a look from those eyes. . .

:*Well? Who's the next suspect?*:

:*We leave the matter as is now, Quattro. I do know the
door is well jammed and needs repairs.*:

:*But I'm not supposed to get too nosy.*:

:*Oh, I have plenty to say. You harbor Pritchard through
four years without suspicion. Agassiz is here twenty years,
and Thorndecker knows of it, and makes no move—not even
against you!—but only against Spinel and our group around
him. And we are here simply on the whim of Agassiz. Is
Thorndecker preserving this place for some purpose? And is
he afraid we are spoilers? Especially now that Spinel and
Agassiz are so fond of each other? I am sure it is hard for you
to have people like us stirring up your lives, Quattro. But do
you wish Agassiz—and yourself—preserved for whatever
reason Thorndecker has?*:

:*Emerald, you have some very strange ideas—and they
may be right—but they're only a theory.*:

:*I know. But a theory is all I have right now.*:

:*Can I help?*:

:*You are always a help, Quattro. Right now, can you bear
to let me see what Thorndecker looks like?*:

He showed her. The word *Silenus* whispered in from some Solthree myth. Small priapic figure incredibly hairy and bearded in rank growth color of rust or dried blood. :*Ha. That is what we look for.*:

:*Good luck.*:

She licked the last drop of juice in the bowl. Then she went to tell the Keeper of Stores to remove the finery from the bed she would share with Raanung and replace it with the oldest rug available. Ungrukh dreams sometimes bit and scratched.

That done, she curled on the bed and nibbled the end of her tail. The full belly should have made her drowsy, but her mind was turbulent with questions darting in all directions . . . She remembered the great energy beings, the Qumedni, who had paid their fearful visit to her world in a time that seemed so long gone now. They had been great spheres of the indescribable, of nothingness, swarming with darts of fire. Surely not the best symbol of what she was contending with, and she shivered a little. She could not think of them as worse than Thorndecker now, and that was ironic.

Raanung came, lay beside her in silence, and slept, a velvet fall. He had grappled with her questions and found no answers either.

Renny was guarding Spinel, who loved his new pool so much he insisted on sleeping in it. The night sky was wheeling with stars, and Renny saw it reflected in the water, and beneath that Spinel's body wheeling with the tiny colored lights of the phosphorescent protozoa and algae that grew and fed under his skin, galaxy in miniature.

Spinel had much to think of:

Dear Lord of the Sea, protect those I love, and protect me for the sake of those I love. . .

It is, I think, five twelves of days and more since I left my home, and perhaps four more to travel straight back—with precious few between. Dear Agassiz, we will not stay with you forever . . . and why did I choose out those twelve of twelve for my absence? Is it because by then Aspartil's egg-sac will have ripened again? May be. If I were a

philosopher I would consider how love—and biology—
influence patriotism. . .

Quattro's sleep was uneasy: he had no peaceful space to
dream in. Bellingrose, half-awake, lingered near the wife he
once had known, now only 60 km away in South Key, where
he dared not risk visiting her, and a universe away in her dead
eyes. Ti-Jacques took over the watch on Spinel, who slept
like a baby. The sleeping body of Agassiz clasped the soul of
a man. Childish as his fixation on Thorndecker seemed, it
was no more than the longing, slightly distorted, of an orphan
or adoptee curious about his family.

And Emerald kept pushing against the being Thorndecker.
How to find him. When to go after him. What to do when she
got him—or he got her.

Beside her Raanung snored dreaming of running down
from the Hills in silence and darkness, the sheath of his knife
slapping his flank, shouldering his brothers and sisters and
following their father Tribesman Mundr. Emerald and their
son Engni had not yet come into his dreams, but she took pity
on him because the world he dreamed in was gone and would
never return. But like him, like her parents, she thought: Life
is simpler on Ungruwarkh. And finally fell asleep.

the whole bloody Pack

The atmosphere surrounding Agassiz, at least in its material aspects, seemed homely and natural for Solthrees, but
was complex when examined, like its other aspects. The
rooms with running water were lined with ceramics and
plastics, and these were always particular marvels to the
Ungrukh, who lived in a hole in a rock. But the floors were
carpentered in parquetry that even Spinel admired, and softened with looped and braided rugs in subtle colors and
patterns where the eye lost itself. The furniture looked delicate but was of tough wicker that managed not to scratch.
Nothing appeared expensive; everything was rich, from the

scroll-patterned doors to the embroidered quilts, to the stop-
pered porcelain ewers of cool spring water. The idealized
dream of an old country house. A dream it would be sad to
waken from.

The dawn rose under thick morbid cloud cover, and
Raanung woke to the smell of meat and rolled himself off the
rug-covered bed with a thump. The Ungrukh brushed each
other down and lightly oiled themselves to face the day.

Anika woke with the presentiment that what she called a
"heavy event" was coming, and thought the hell with it. She
was tired of any kind of event.

But after breakfast a quarrel erupted between the usually
cheerful Hashimoto brothers about whether to set the force-
field against the coming storm to shelter their newly planted
seedlings. Brandishing rakes and hoes, they advised each
other in Japanese, with curses, that there was not enough
room in the garden for both.

Raanung and Emerald had been nearby enjoying the sight
of a phenomenon rare on their world: roiling masses of
overhead clouds darting with claws of lightning and growling
like Ungrukh. The quarrel broke so sharply they simply
gaped, and before they could interfere the first wicked
rainsplats hit the ground, the fight stopped short, and the
combatants ran off together to have the force-field turned on.

In the library, where the light was dim and green, Bellingrose had been trying to persuade Anika to tell his fortune but
she, perhaps fearing he might ridicule her, even with silence,
had declared firmly for gin rummy. They were interrupted by
Emerald and Raanung, shapes darkened, eyes alight.

"What's the matter?" Anika asked.

Emerald said, "I think if not for the storm the Hashimotos
are beating each other's brains out with rake and hoe."

"What the hell for?"

"I don't know. It is like the lightning, so fast."

"Well, I had this stupid feeling—"

"Wait!" Emerald faced the doorway in one snaking twist.

Within three seconds, Ti-Jacques appeared, hands gripping the doorframe and blood in his eye. "Where's Quattro!" Not now the quiet man with the pleasant bass rumble.

Anika snorted. "You're an ESP. You should know."

But Bellingrose said very quietly, "He's having a nice talk with Spinel about the vicissitudes of underwater life. Why?"

"He stole my Hand of Fatima! He's trying to give me the Evil Eye and I'm going to rip that damn frogskin off him!"

Emerald was prepared this time and pulled his eyes toward her quickly. "Ti-Zzacques, why do you not look in your underclothes to see if the chain breaks and your amulet falls in some fold or wrinkle?"

His face went blank. He turned and zipped down his suit, fumbled for a moment and faced them again, zipping with one hand, holding a medallion on a silver chain in the other. There were all kinds of expressions struggling on his face. "It's my i.d.," he muttered. "I gave the Hand to some girl and I don't believe in the Evil Eye." He looked down at her, where she was crouching with jaw on arms. "What's all this? Would it be happening if you weren't here?"

"Perhaps not," she scratched her nose with her tongue, "or perhaps you are now tearing the skin off your friend."

He swallowed and looked away. "I know that. I'm sorry."

When he was gone a sickly green quiet settled on the room.

:Quattro, you esp that?:

:My God, how could I miss it! What are we going to do?:

:If you are esping you know I am beating my head over it.:

The signal on Bellingrose's chronometer beeped. "Radio," he sighed and got up. "What now?"

:But you don't know where he is and what he wants. We've been sitting around ducking pot-shots for the last few days.:

Emerald growled, "And providing food, sleep and sexual comfort to a spy for four years. Remember, Quattro, I allow myself to be led here. I do not push myself in." Anika rolled her eyes and got out the Tarot, but Emerald turned to Raanung and said, "You are strategist. What do you suggest?"

"I already say my piece. What else do you want?"

She snarled, "You are no better than all the rest. I think we are all contaminated by post-hypnotic suggestion, and you, Quattro, must know that best—or are you afraid to use the brains in your stickleback head?" She cut him off to let him stew for a moment. "Raanung, you say Thorndecker is based in South Key. All *I* can think to do is track or search by flyover, and neither of those sounds very useful."

"In that you are right. You cannot get there from here. You need links."

Quattro came in and sat on the floor with his legs crossed. He had lost his ill-humor on the way, and he faced Emerald eye to eye. "And you sent your link out the gate yesterday without a tracer or a radio."

"Pritchard? Tracers and radios can be picked up by others, and if I let others trace him he is dead."

"Very tender-hearted," said Anika.

"Yes. Perhaps it is better that I batter his brains out with an ash-tray." All of the ill humor seemed to be draining into her.

"We still must have links," Raanung said, "and we can do nothing when you go into your Tengura mode and get hot in the head."

She said pointedly, "It is too bad for you if I take after my *mother's* side of the family."

Bellingrose came in. "Tsk. You don't have to bother about that if you know about Spinel."

"Yes. He is just now made a member of Galactic Federation . . . if he gets home in time to establish the claim on his world."

"In the meantime he has jumped out of the pool and is dancing around it. And Agassiz is clapping his hands."

Emerald softened. "Those are dear ones. It is terrible that good news means more danger."

"I told our contact that we have a situation of some urgency, and they will send some help. At least a couple of ESPs."

"That is a thank-you-for-nothing."

"But expensive. Bengtvadi's *Zarandu of Thanamar* is

dumping diplomats here in a day or two and the fare is astronomical. No pun intended, but that's what they're coming on.''

''The superfast cruiser?'' Emerald jumped up.

''Yes.''

''Then they need all the ESPs they can find for themselves and us!''

''But why?''

''Oh man, if you are Thorndecker, what is the best present you can think of giving yourself?''

''He wouldn't dare.''

''Why not? He dares everything else.'' Emerald licked her jaws. ''I don't mind having one of those either. Thorndecker must certainly not get near it.''

''But Pritchard *was* our only link with him, and he's gone,'' said Quattro.

''And Pritchard leaves his room clean,'' Emerald said. ''My bug-picker finds nothing.''

Raanung laughed, hissing. ''Ask Morgan if he still has those pieces he picks out to dismantle the radio.''

''Yes, but they are not bugs.''

''Catch him before he throws them away. They are links from Pritchard.''

''I don't see how.''

''Let's look at them anyway. And find Renny. She is also a link.''

''No, he was a loner,'' said Renny. ''Not one of the fellows.'' She grinned mischievously. ''Like Morgan here. No arm-wrestling. A sipper, not a gulper. He *was* good at hypnosis, and I'm sure Thorndecker valued him for that, but I used to wonder why he was there, otherwise. Always standing back watching. Now I wonder if he wasn't just picking up the money because it was good and also collecting anything he could use against Thorndecker in case there was any funny business.''

''And we never find out,'' Emerald growled. ''A

standstill." She sighed. "Well, Morgan, show us your pieces of rubbish and find us a neat-handed person."

"I'm him. Radioman's assistant. What I don't know we'll ask Antonescu." He squatted beside Emerald and unfolded the cloth square on the floor. "Not much here, I didn't have the time. Chip, part of volume control, power cell. . ."

"What's the copper helix?" Renny asked.

"Should be a choking coil—"

"But it's bent. What was it attached to?"

"I don't know, I was too busy grabbing. It's garbage now."

"If you'd pulled it out like garbage it'd be a mess." She held it to the light and straightened it to look through an end. "Bet it wasn't attached to anything. Just shoved in wherever he could find a space."

"What the hell you doing?"

"Cutting my stupid fingers!" She was pulling, pulling, pulling. The hair-thin wire seemed to stretch to eternity.

"For God's sake, you're ruining—"

"—a piece of garbage to get what's inside." She pulled the cloth from under the components and wrapped it around her hand, set her foot on the wire and went on dragging at it. Finally picked out the tiny plastic capsule and sat back with a breathless "Whoof!"

"The poison for his self-destruct," said Emerald.

"Not our Pritchard. Get the lights up." She calipered the ends in thumb and finger. "Some grainy stuff inside . . . and also something else." She spread out the cloth, blood-spotted from her hand's cuts, and gently pulled the capsule apart over it. A tiny folded paper sat in the middle of the little crystalline pile. "Maybe it's poisonous, so I won't touch it without gloves, but if I know anything at all about Pritchard it's sugar or salt."

Doctor came in, gloved, and took a magnifying glass from his pocket. He isolated a crystal on one fingertip. "I'm no analytical chemist, but it looks like salt. Nice little cube." He applied the tip of his tongue, gingerly. "Tastes like salt." He shrugged and picked up the paper. "Manuscript in a copper cylinder? I wonder if it's too old to open without cracking."

"Pritchard smoked dope, a little. Everything in moderation. Imported fancy papers, and that looks like one. It can't be that old, even if the salt dried it out a bit."

Doctor unfolded it, a minuscule oblong covered with hairlines. "God, look at that writing! It might as well be microdots. I'll put it on the projector."

It was impossible to guess how Pritchard, or another, had written on it, but he knew how to put a lot of material on a small area.

"Family tree," said Doctor. "A skeleton of one, at least. T.-H. = Thorndecker-Hyde. Daughters A, B, C. So much for women. Araminta, Belinda, Corinthia. It's true. The man *was* weird. Son: T.-H. II. m. R. That was Ruth. Of issue, the daughters L. and M. are Leona and Meredith. L. married Agassiz. Son T. I forget who the others married." He added bitterly, "I gave that information to GalFed myself. It's as far as the line went on Qsaprinel. Thorndecker must have put together the rest. That T. son of II should have been Thorndecker-Hyde III, but he scrapped with the family for one of the usual crazy reasons and dropped the Hyde. His descendant T. II is our Thorndecker, and Leona's son A. II is my Agassiz."

There was a silence until Quattro dared break it: "Those other names are getting to look very odd."

The family's branches scraggled and thickened further along. Thin twigs supporting the dead leaves of Thorndecker-Hyde siblings and progeny burst out and careered wildly twisting wherever there was space, some the dead ends of mazes, in angles and mysterious initials. At the bottom they resolved into ten names.

R. Hobbsbaum. M. Owen. S. Wynn. O. & G. Erichsen (siblings). S. Ashe. R. & A. Bendetto (married third cousins once removed). Q. MacVicar. M. Ellis.

Specifically, Doctor's assistant, Dr. Hobbsbaum; Morgan; Sylvie; Olga the cook; Gunnar the carpenter; Ashe the electrician; Rosa, who kept accounts; Antonio, who maintained ordnance, that is, anything not domestic; Queenie, Keeper of Stores in-house, and Mary, a practical nurse who put her hands to whatever else was needed. A little less than half of Agassiz's establishment.

Emerald said in a rasping drawl, "I wonder if those are all he can find, or he chooses those he finds most useful?"

"What do you mean?" Doctor said sharply.

"That is his preserve, not so? A Family. I ask Quattro: why is Thorndecker preserving you so long when he must know you are here? As soon as we come he finds us easily enough. And by mistake Morgan is almost killed bringing Renny. His family: ages of what? Twenty-two to thirty-nine. Getting a bit over-ripe toward the last—for Solthrees. And no children. A great mistake, I think. Prevented by either loyalty to Agassiz or indirect order of Thorndecker. Too bad. Most likely Agassiz finds children very enjoyable—or perhaps Thorndecker is afraid he corrupts them!"

"I still don't—"

Morgan yelled, "You mean we're being kept for some kind of goddam breeding colony?"

"I think she means that," said Quattro.

"But —" He could not seem to get out the words; neither Quattro nor Emerald helped: they did not want to hear them. Morgan had been one of those closest to Agassiz; he was also the youngest of the five males—from Thorndecker's point of view that would mean a prime breeder. He muttered, "It sounds like being a parasite. Feeding off Agassiz. . ."

Doctor depolarized the window and stood looking out with his back toward the rest. Bellingrose seemed about to speak, but it was Raanung who stood up, twitched so that his hairs stood on end, established himself the most massive in the room and by blazing color in sunlight drew eyes toward him. This was also a trick of Mundr's, for the dangerous silences that grew sometimes around a fire. "For a parasite you work at great risk to give service and love to Agassiz. No hypnosis

of Thorndecker's can make you do *that*." With a hunch of
one shoulder he dismissed the matter to oblivion and trotted
to his room for a nap until lunch.

"Some came asking for work," Doctor murmured.
"Some we found, like Quattro . . . what was Pritchard
doing with this?"

"Probably turned it up on one of his sneaking expeditions," said Renny, "and saved it to play both ends against
the middle if things got rough."

Quattro said, "If Thorndecker's been growing a crèche
here, five breeding pairs don't make a great population."

"It's not necessarily complete," said Bellingrose. "I
don't think there's any more candidates here—but he'd got
fairly high up in GalFed and had access to a lot of Colonial
Registries in Solthree sectors. We can't tell how many he
might have tracked down, younger ones. What he's got here
looks like a skeleton working crew."

Doctor stared. "Not for—"

"You need to ask far?"

"Qsaprinel! Why?"

Emerald felt the rough bite of longing for her hole in the
rock on Ungruwarkh, Engni nipping her ear for a ride on her
back. "With that man, for reasons the madder the more
likely. We don't know whether he can live longer than
Agassiz, but he must believe he can. The list suggests he
wants to begin again and complete the work of his ancestor.
He may feel the place belongs to him; he may believe that
Hyde pays the incumbent Spinel for it, though the Qsaprinli
are notoriously indifferent traders. I don't meet the man: I
know the sort of mind. It can convince itself the Qsaprinli
know all about the fungus and its effects without telling of
them—so he wants revenge. It is no surprise to me if his
guardians infect him with resentment over having to pay
estate money to Agassiz. He gets back at that by having
Agassiz care for his 'crèche'—and they are surely cared for
safe away from the rough crews Thorndecker fancies. He
may even think the pintrelase is deliberately kept from
him—perhaps by you, Doctor—until it is too late to do much

good. Worst, there is always someone to love Agassiz for himself, all his life, because no matter how terrible the conditions in that hospital the people there care for him, and you, Doctor, come to make him loving and worthy of love. I do not think Thorndecker has anything like that.''

Doctor whispered, ''I would have done the same. I wanted. . .''

''There is no changing that. You can also look at the man from a slightly different angle. The classic dangerous criminal: a rationalizing criminal psychotic. Qsaprinel is not much exploited, but it has many valuable things: the jewels that so many love, though to the Qsaprinli they are—are—yes, William? As marbles to a child? I take your word. There are metals they do not refine because they fear great heat, and who knows what treasure in those vast seas. There are themselves: they can work in many conditions on different worlds without special equipment. Slaves. *You* know, Quattro. And a living source of pintrelase for the colonists. And if Thorndecker works at it he can find a way to neutralize the electrical effects.'' She scratched behind her ear with her hind foot like a giant house-cat. ''So I keep asking myself how to find the man and discover I am a storehouse of ignorance. If we can move he can move. I cannot esp him, Raanung cannot smell him. He knows where we are, and if he can take the *Zarandu* he does not need a base. It is possible he never has a permanent base in the Keys. He can stay in a rented property, or with some associate. GalFed is looking for him, he is attacking steadily, the *Zarandu* is coming. Add the list of names to that—and his operation is at a crux. I think pretty soon he comes to collect the rent—and return to Qsaprinel. If Spinel cannot reach Qsaprinel as a GalFed representative Thorndecker is safe. At least for a while. He can intimidate the Qsaprinli into sheltering him, while they are still neutral, and consolidate his plans. So he must not have the *Zarandu*. That is not to say he cannot find something else.''

Quattro's voice was cold. ''From what I can pick out among all the words Thorndecker's going to come here and

gather up his family—and maybe kill the rest of us—and you
have nothing to say about that!''

''Quattro, Ungrukh are well known to be very poor plan-
ners, and we draw up tactics in the climax of whatever event
comes. I can say *I* like to have the *Zarandu*, and that is as far
as I can see now. For the rest, I am a damned fool to come
here for the sake of either Kinnear *or* Agassiz, but that does
not mean I don't intend to fight.'' She stood. ''Now let us
spoil lunch for everyone by telling them what to expect.''

''Surely you wouldn't tell them all!'' Doctor cried.

''Surely there are some who must get out. A person unwilling to stay is a potential enemy, and a person who cannot act
because of fear is an impediment. It is a sin to leave people in
danger and tell them nothing, and I doubt Agassiz wants to
direct people under such conditions.''

''If I tell him it will break his heart.'' The stone planes had
shifted, the face had aged greatly in so few days.

Emerald said very gently, ''Doctor, forgive me, but Agassiz knows. It is *his* family, I cannot keep that hidden—and he
needs no more Pritchards. He is also quite alive and in good
health.''

the Ten of Swords

Renny turned at the door and saw Morgan alone, still
sitting motionless, hands clamped together, eyes staring. She
turned back and knelt beside him.

''Morgan . . .'' She peeled his hands apart finger by
finger and found between them the scrunched copper tangle
that had been the helix. She threw it into the disposal. ''I
might have jammed your door,'' he said, ''Even if Quattro
says not.''

''I don't think you did, but if Pritchard had gotten at me
with one of those looks I might have done it myself.''

''When I came here I thought I'd found an identity,'' he
said. ''I mean, as somebody with a purpose and a function.
That Owen wasn't my father. He was the pimp who hung
around long enough to bring me up. He was a bastard, but I

guess he was better than the others.'' He looked at her. ''You understand.''

''How can I avoid it? My mother, for all her looks, was born in the Kentucky hills. She was one of the Black Griggses who didn't get on too well with the Red Griggses. I guess they were different shades of blue. When she got out and was travelling with the Circus in that part of Hungary that used to be called Transylvania she fell in love with the ringmaster. Gurdja. She never knew what he was, he made himself a background like Dracula. She was young and a bit dumb and married him, but I don't know if he was my father. He was a sweet guy but he went after everything. I mean—well, everything. She kicked him out to keep him away from me, even though she still loved him. Hell, I must be one of the few people here who knows who my mother is. Let's go and have lunch, Morgan.''

The strangest atmosphere about lunch was not the waves of fear that rose, fell and eddied about the company, but the very faint sense of relief that allowed everyone to eat heartily. The truth was bare, stark and terrible, but present to be examined and dealt with. No one had yet asked to leave, but Emerald expected—even hoped—they would after they had absorbed the shock. Their feelings prompted her to examine her own mind with the same kind of rigor as the Locksmith had done with his. She seemed to be in order.

''Thorndecker must have some super ESPs,'' said Quattro.

''So has Agassiz. Why do *you* feel relief, Quattro?''

''Once you've been scared enough to go crazy, and you didn't, you can't go much further.''

''And these others?''

''Emerald, everyone here has been getting up with the birds and going to bed with the crickets for years. They haven't resented it much, but it's been a hell of a dull life.''

''These last few days are not enough?''

''They haven't had much part of it, most of them. I don't think there's any kind of contamination right now.'' He added rather bitterly, "Thorndecker doesn't need it."

She said for his mind alone, *:He does for the ten,:* and left him with the thought.

When she had told Agassiz of the "family" he had been harboring, he said *:I knew nothing and did my best. What can I regret now, Emerald? The ones I am sorry for are Doctor and Spinel. Doctor gave me his life and mine. Even if my death would have freed him I had no physical ability to bring it about.:*

:Your life gives Doctor his.:

:Maybe. But I have no control. I ask for what I think can be given, and I give whatever I have. Those ten aren't under my orders. They have always been free of me. I am fearfully sorry for Spinel because he holds life and death for so many, and I am sure he suffers, knowing it. While Thorndecker's "family" is only an idea to me; they are people I love. Oh Emerald, it may seem shameful, but I have such terrible pity for Thorndecker. All I could give was so little and I have received so much. Emerald! I am so thankful that a meaningless cipher like me should have been given so much! Don't let that pitiful terrible thing harm the others!:

"Spinel."

"Yes, Emerald." He had raised his snout above the water and was taking a holiday from learning *lingua* by speaking in his own language. "I am perfectly ready to fight and quite looking forward to it."

"Good." But he was not going to fight; she did not tell him that. The time for frankness had been temporarily suspended. There were pieces of a plan in her mind that would make a whole if she allowed them to join, but she dared not. Everything she did must seem to be on the moment. Except for one part.

:Raanung.: She reached him on the deepest level, one Quattro had and could have used if he had not been scared off years before.

:Hah?: He too was allowing himself a luxury, a series of slurps as he licked his bowl.

:What do you think of target practice?:

:The targets?:

:Us.:

:Not much. I presume you know what we are doing?:

:I hope I know, when we do it.:

:Any kill?:

:Maybe you get to use the teeth and claws. I prefer not.:

:When?:

:Solthree sleep-time.:

:Then I take my nap early.:

It was still strange to her that, as an Ungrukh of a warrior tribe, he did not need to ask, argue, discuss, debate, as her own tribal members would. It was only a blessing that, like all Ungrukh men, finally, he trusted his woman's esp. Enough debacles had proven the case.

She knew that she was also capable of engineering a great debacle. And so did he. Ungrukh are prime realists. This quality gives them the little humility they have.

Emerald, waiting, listened to conversations. There was worry, but no feeling of urgency.

"What have we got for weapons? Knives, stunners . . . not even a bomb-shelter."

"A shelter can be a trap. Explosives thrown in."

"There's the forcefield—but I'd bet it could be broken."

"Esp power. How could we equal. . . ?"

There was no sense of family among the Chosen. Aside from the sibling pair and the married pair they had nothing in common except their work for Agassiz, and had never previously met. The relationships were so distant that they provoked nothing but mild perplexity and annoyance at having been singled out for dubious honors. There were no signs of avoidance in anyone; even the level of resentment at having their lives disrupted by the Ungrukh and Spinel neither rose nor fell. Those presences had perhaps delayed the inevitable direct confrontation with Thorndecker for a few days.

It was then Emerald realized that the turgidity of the atmosphere was not now some residue of hypnotic control emanating from Thorndecker; it came unconsciously from Agassiz. He had simply made his people too comfortable in the peaceful garden. And she dared not say so directly.

"Suppose we put it on the line. You think we ought to make a secret ballot and find out how many want to go?"

"What's the use of secrets? And where'd we go? Either be picked off or infected with some arrangement to self-destruct?"

Emerald said, "All these years you live here with feelings of safety. Maybe you examine those and see if they are not influencing you to your disadvantage?"

Quattro was watching her. His mind felt slightly askew until he realized the subtlety of what she was trying to say. "We don't need ballots," he said. "I don't think it matters *who* particularly wants to go or stay, or whether they're afraid of being considered cowards. *I've* known enough fear. Some *should* go, if only to try and obstruct Thorndecker. So why don't the ones who want to leave just get up and go, without any ill-feeling from anyone else?"

The Hashimoto brothers grinned in unison, and the elder said, "You see we are trembling like leaves out of fear. We have no black belts in anything. But we would like to see the garden saved with the people. And plants do need care."

No one moved, and there was nothing more for Emerald to do or say. "Agassiz is well served."

The little voice piped from the scallop: "I realize that. But I have no medals to give out."

"If you had it'd be better to wait and see what we can do for ourselves," Ti-Jacques said. He turned to Emerald. "If Ungrukh are so poor in time-sense and planning, I suppose you have no idea when Thorndecker will make his move."

"I believe it depends when the *Zarandu* comes in, and what happens with it. It is due in roughly a day and a half. I think I can give you one clear day. You ask the gods for anything else you want."

"Spinel and you are the ones Thorndecker is sure to kill, if he can. Why don't *you* try getting out?"

"We also have a commitment to Agassiz."

Agassiz's wealth had made a garden of a rough tract of land on an isolated spit in a world where important diplomats were well guarded, and a man who hated violence could live in peace. So there were no weapons to gather, and no plans to make.

Anika said to Bellingrose, "Willie, why don't you go visit your wife while you still have the chance?"

"In the hearse, Anika? I hope I'll be able to visit her one day soon. Meantime I'll take my chances here." He too had his commitment, and Emerald dared not move him, because he had no part in her personal plan.

She lay in the shade and gave Spinel the urge to spend the afternoon close by Agassiz. The Emperor, who had known the embryo for only a day, and already loved him as dearly as his best friend and more than his sib, would not be with him much longer.

She rubbed herself on a tree's bark and dislodged the insects which had made themselves a home in her comfortable fur. It was not quite so comfortable to her in this place: a thick coat tailored for the cold plains; her nose dripped and her pads were always slippery with sweat. She set discomfort aside with an effort, and tried to put together all she had scoured from the skull-pits around her.

The *Zarandu* had no set arrival time, beyond a probable landing on a certain day: the warped time it traveled in at such speed was adjusted to the conditions of the space it passed through. It did not land on the Keys but in the big port in the center of the continent. It was not a Solthree ship, and she did not know what Bengtvadi were like, nor was she sure where they came from. Because of Spinel Bellingrose had arranged for the Solthree contingent on guard at the port, and she knew through him who the contact was. That contact was intended as a watchdog, but she intended to use it differently.

The other dafum she added was that Agassiz's skimmer

was capable of far greater speed and altitude than had been used. Although the crew behaved with circumspection by order of Agassiz, he always bought nothing but the best.

That was enough to sum up—for the moment. Within the last few hours she had put on her Hills identity, the one she had adopted living with Raanung's Tribe, when he was his father's son.

She went into the house, where the coolness was a step closer to comfort, intending to join Raanung, and on the way passed the open door of the room where Renny was lying on her bed, hands folded above her head, eyes open.

Emerald paused. Anika had made a friend of Bellingrose, and Spinel and Agassiz were together. Renny had done what she could for Morgan: the rest he must fight out for himself.

"Emerald?" The sharp black eyes turned toward her.

On impulse she slipped in and slid the door shut. She spoke in her quietest voice, at mid-pitch where it had least resonance. "I am shielding as hard as I can but I cannot keep it up long, and I need to save the strength. I want to tell you one half of what I plan to do. Then I block you so you cannot tell anyone else. Are you willing to listen on those terms?"

Renny sat up with a quick breath. "Go ahead."

Emerald told her. "You can help me."

"I'll come along."

"No. Your experience is needed here too, and the dangers are equal. Even Raanung and I are one too many, but I need his nose and his strength. You have ability and stamina but we need esp too, and I dare not use an Imper."

"But . . . Emerald, if they find you gone—they won't believe you're coming back. Not from my telling them."

"I leave them a message they believe. Trust me. Now: you know everything Bellingrose does, and more. I want to check codes, distances, times. Also the working of the machine. Raanung uses them at home, but this one seems more complicated."

Renny gave her the information, tersely. "But—it's so—"

"Everything is. Now I hope you don't mind that I block

you. I can do that with an Imper, if you look at me."

"I don't mind, but I don't need a block. You know I'd never tell."

"I don't want you talking in your sleep."

"I won't sleep."

"Oh yes. You sleep."

Renny, on an unimaginable impulse of her own, took Emerald's head between her hands and kissed her.

"Renny," Emerald said sadly, "I do not much care for this work, and I think in your soul you feel the same. Perhaps my-mother," she meant Nga, "can bring herself to be proud for me, but I am not very."

:Raanung.:

"Aargh!"

:I am glad to find you awake. My belly tells me it is near suppertime, but I also have a chronometer Renny is kind enough to give me. You take it tonight and I wear the heavy stuff.:

:There is a chronometer in the skimmer.:

:We are not using the skimmer all of the time.:

:Telling that woman is a risk.:

:Everything is. Sending Spinel away from us is the one I like least—but once it is done that one is not on our backs.:

:Spinel is until we get him on the skimmer, and he makes one damn heavy load.:

:Maybe we can ask him to lose a little water.:

:Just try asking!:

:I know. But I am afraid to make him do it by hypnosis. I know nothing about his nervous system and I dare not tamper with his water balance.:

Spinel sulked. :But I want to stay and fight!:

:I understand. But do not thrash about, Spinel. Too many know already what we are planning. We must separate Thorndecker's objectives. Agassiz holds himself responsible for twenty-odd, and a few may die. You he surely means to kill, and you are responsible for a million or more who may *be enslaved and thousands who are certain to die.:*

*:Alas! You are right. I may reach home too late, or die
without a chance of battle. But I am still Emperor, and I must
do what I can.:*

the Tower reversed

Emerald had planned to eat lightly, in preparation for the
excitement ahead, but there was no need to remind herself;
she was frightened half out of her skin. The plan was so frail,
and yet so necessary. The choices were so few. She was
positive that Thorndecker would make a swoop to gather his
Colony, that he intended to preserve them, that he might
simply ignore Agassiz and not care if a few of the others
escaped. But as she had spoken in all certainty, he could not
leave Spinel alive.

Fthel IV's day of twenty-eight hours standard was a
damned long day by Ungrukh measure, and even fifteen
degrees south of the equator the evenings dragged.

Hours of darkness, thirteen; sunset approximately 2200,
morning 0700. Solthree sleep-time average 2630. Tonight
everyone would feel drowsier than usual half an hour earlier.
Long day or not, nine hours was a tight enough squeeze for
what the Ungrukh planned. Every time Emerald thought of it
she found more gaps and traps.

She and Raanung slept again. Solthrees sometimes caught
up their sleep rhythm with an hour's nap during the day. They
all knew that cats slept whenever they felt like it. Moments
when her sleep lightened to a doze she caught the flow of
loving and earnest conversation between Spinel and Agassiz,
and her heart grew heavier with the burden of a guilt not yet
earned.

Both woke to the *ping!* of the chronometer's alarm.
Raanung padded down the hall and out; Emerald stopped at
Quattro's door, and slid it open very gently. As with Spinel's
water balance, she wanted to leave his sleep pattern alone.
The less tampering the better.

He lay underwater in his basin, breathing evenly with slight bubbling from the tube in his nostril; a thread of blood drifted from its edge. She unclasped her mother's knife, wound the harness around it, and placed it by the basin's rim. She gave him a thought for when he came to touch it, and left as quietly as she had come.

Renny was on guard outdoors; she had easy access to first watch because everyone else was a bit sleepy. When she saw Spinel emerging from the pool and Raanung from the house she ran to help move the coffin from the hearse to the skimmer. This container had more style than substance, and was not as heavy as it looked, but the lining was firm and would likely protect Spinel from the jolts Emerald expected.

Outworlders who looked at Qsaprinli and saw only bulging water-skins and slow movements could not help thinking that they must slosh about a lot inside; they forgot about the many breakwaters and valves that controlled the liquid, and that Qsaprinli did not feel much need to move fast. Spinel, now, had dropped about fifteen kilos of water and was moving, though not so quickly as a vertebrate, at a good pace. He looked rather shrunken, but assured Emerald that he would bear up well if he got into water at destination.

Renny did not know if she would see him again, and looked at him steadily. The faint glitter of his armlets in the starlight was eclipsed by his phosphorescence. She whispered to Emerald, "I've greased everything that moves—I hope," and knelt to take the small claw hand she had held for hours a long double thirtyday ago. "Goodbye, Spinel."

He dared not speak because he could not whisper, but tried to tell with his eyes what he owed her for putting her life at his disposal. Emerald did not try to interpret for him. He boarded the skimmer and climbed into the coffin. He disliked being closed in, but since he was self-contained, had no claustrophobia.

Emerald stood and rested padded hands on Renny's shoulders. "Breakfast oh-eight hours," she hissed, with a tickle of whiskers, and slipped through the hatch. Raanung lowered his head in guest-friendship and followed. The door locked

home. The skimmer moved from shelter to landing-field with
scarcely a hum.

Renny pulled off her shoes and ran into the house, to the
controls room. She counted ten seconds and shut off the
force-field and the radar which automatically took over from
it; counted to five and turned them back on. Then she went
outside, put her shoes on and stood by the pool. A few
crickets chirped and the water rippled with the fall of a dry
leaf.

Raanung kept the skimmer low and sedate over the city and
the outlying hills. The radar picked up a few blips and
Emerald scanned. "One man of business bringing samples of
unbreakable clay pipes. One party-goer who is better to stay
where he is partying and sleep it off. One drug-runner carrying the stuff smokers use in the pipes, I suppose, and
whoop!—followed by police. If they get too close maybe he
jumps out and flies with his own wings."

"This is too damned slow. We leave no margin for the
usual disasters."

"No one ever does. We cannot afford them. Ugh! I think
we have someone following. Now you can have your
speed."

But Raanung swung steeply and began returning eastward
at the same pace.

"What in the Blue Pit are you doing, man?"

"Look there. The fire. Someone crashes in the barrens
northeast. Probably your party-goer. I am taking bearings on
him and putting in an anonymous call to the police while you
esp the tracker. It is probably the last thing he expects."

:Spinel, are you all right back there?:

:No. I am stupid with fright.:

:There is nothing to be afraid of yet.:

The maneuver took no more than five minutes, and
Raanung was able to turn once more. "*Now* we drink the
juice. What do you pick up?"

"The usual thug type. There must be an army of them."

"Nothing else?"

"The hint of a location. I am not sure. We try that later. Get on with it, big man!"

"You are the one who gets sick."

"That is one time. Forewarned is to take a pill—and I am sorry we have none for Spinel." The skimmer, banking, accelerated steeply and sharply. "I still don't like it."

"No sign of tracker. Perhaps flying low."

"I'm not worrying about him now. It's radio time." Renny had packed the equipment for her, and Raanung fed her back the procedures she had stored in him. She put on finger-prostheses, pressed buttons and flicked switches.

Scramblers on, she called Bellingrose's contact. Port Central's codes brought her a guarded, "Yes? Identify please."

"Am I speaking to Horatius?"

"No, sir. He is on other duties and cannot be reached. But I am authorized to speak for him."

"It's madame, Madame. Evangel's Green wants to speak to him. Now can you reach him?"

"No, Madame."

She said to Raanung, "Hell's blazes, in the firepot again. Here is the unforeseen that you foresee. What am I to do?"

"Find out whether this person is worth speaking to," said Raanung.

"Listen, Horatius's Madame, do you know Evangel's Green?"

"I know Evangel, Ma'am, but neither of us has spoken to a Green."

Emerald was not quite desperate enough to identify fully, but she was reaching the point. :Any sign of tracker?:

:No, but it does not mean he is not about and shielding. This is one time you plan too secret and too far ahead.:

:Thank you for nothing. If I cannot find a more comfortable place to put my tail I think I wind it well around my throat and solve all problems.:

:Like for instance?:

She snarled, "Listen, speaker-for-Horatius, this is an emergency and you better find your big man or a bigger one I can speak to pretty damn fast!"

"If you can't give your message to me, I'm sorry, but— oh, just a mom—"

:*HELLO?*:

That was not radio, but *esp,* and it nearly cracked both of the Ungrukhs' skulls. Emerald pulled out her earplug and rubbed her head. "What—"

:*HELLO, GREEN AND CO.! DO YOU MIND ANOTHER LADY HERE? THIS IS—excuse me! I sometimes get a bit enthusiastic over long distances. This is Sector Co-ordinator Threyha of Khagodis, and I picked you up because I noticed this poor woman sweating here. I hope you don't mind my intruding, but without your naming any names I think we can identify each other quite easily. Are you willing?*:

Emerald settled her mike and said faintly, "Yes, Co-ordinator." She knew Khagodi could esp great distances, but had never expected to make contact with one.

:*Threyha's better, if you can pronounce it. I've never decided quite how, because we hear but can't speak. Now: who rescued my Uncle Lokh from shame and imprisonment on the world called Yirl?*:

"That one I know well enough! My mother and father."

:*Right! Now are you willing to speak to me?*:

"Certainly, Threyha, but I think you are waking up half the continent."

:*No, dear. I may beam loud but I beam true, and only you and Co. are receiving a word from me. I swear it.*:

Emerald wiped her sweating pads on her fur and breathed deep relief. Raanung said, "Luck does sometimes help fools like us," and for once she had no sharp answer.

This was how Emerald and Raanung came to meet a Khagodi, all three meters and 600 kilos of her, iridescent scales, topaz eyes and pearl claws. They were content to deliver Spinel in her presence. It was a great presence, and they had met greater, but this was an ally, for a change, who did not make them feel small. She was an incongruous one, for her narrow head and slender arms and hands topped a huge torso supported by tremendous legs and tail. She and her helpers were nearly all they saw of Port Central; though they debarked for a moment they did not leave the field.

Out of caution, Threyha would not let them open the coffin, and it was as difficult for them as for Renny to say goodbye to Spinel.

:*Hurry, my friends. He has done well, but he needs water badly.*:

"I know." :*Spinel, this is a damned poor way to take leave of you, but we hope to meet you again in your proper place.*:

:*Dear Emerald and Raanung, I hope to thank you some time in a proper way. Now go quickly. You are already in too much danger for my sake.*: She sensed him, cramped, holding his Seal in one hand and his casket of supplies in the other, and even so he did not lack dignity.

There was nothing more to do than thank Threyha and leave. Emerald had directed her to see that Spinel and his accreditation reached Qsaprinel. She did not know how that was to be done, and she did not want to know. Nor did she ask or esp to find out whether the *Zarandu* had arrived. No Khagodi had ever been known to betray and she could not think of any shelter safer for Spinel than Threyha's guardianship.

"I suppose you don't mind being an ESP like that one, ha?"

"I am good enough for me," said Emerald. They were high over the land and she had time to look at the stars and feel as if she were swimming among them. "She has too great a power to envy. And I don't think you want one like that for your woman!"

He grunted. "One-forty-three is not bad for time. We are home by four if no one shoots us down first, and then—"

"—comes what Solthrees call the wild-goose-chase. I am not sure what that is exactly, but it sounds right."

"It sounds like something to eat."

"I hope it is nothing to kill."

"Or be killed. It is good to think of one's own health once
in a while."

About that time Quattro awoke with a bad dream. He
rarely had any other kind. He realized at once that Spinel
and the Ungrukh were gone, sat up quickly and touched the
light-switch.

He immediately saw the knife on the edge of the basin.
Reached out slowly to grasp it.

A voice in his mind said clearly: *We are removing Spinel.
If we are not back by breakfast time keep the knife with love
from Emerald and Raanung, but do not try to throw it.*

It was nearly time to take over guard duty from Renny. He
rolled out of the water, towelled and dressed, all the while
holding the knife. He was trying to put his thoughts in order.
He felt as if he were still dreaming, and if he let go the knife
the Ungrukh would die. He buckled on the harness; it was
uncomfortable, and the knife, which only an Ungrukh could
handle properly, was a monstrosity. "They damn well better
come back," he muttered.

Renny was as frightened now as Emerald had been; she
might have run away if not for the presence of Anika and
Bellingrose. She could not believe anyone would accept her
story, and she felt surrounded by enemies who were at the
same time frightened blameless people whose lives must be
saved.

She went quietly along the upstairs hall under the dim
yellowish lightstrip, expecting as customary to tap Quattro's
door as a sign that she was going off duty. The door slid open
before she reached it, and he stepped out. From the set of his
face she saw that he knew; the light turned his eyes sea-water
green.

One hand was on his thigh, over his knife. She took a step
back, opened her hands and held them out, almost caught
herself saying *please!*

He grinned and moved his hand away to show Emerald's

borrowed knife, and she noticed the thin harness over his shoulder and round the thorax. "It's all right," he said. "I got the message. Breakfast at eight. Sleep well."

She stood shivering while he passed and descended. Her shoulders slumped, she bit a thumb-knuckle and went on. An arm stopped her. "The natives are restless," said Morgan. She looked up at him in sleepsuit, red-bursting hair ruffled. "I was thinking of hot chocolate . . . and then I thought—but. . ."

She was finding herself wordless, lately. He dropped his arm to let her by and kept the regret out of his eyes.

She reached up and tangled her fingers in his beard, very gently. He let himself be drawn into his own room.

Quattro kept his mind to himself and looked out at the pale streak of phosphorescence across the lawn, puzzled for a moment until he realized that Spinel had let off his water as he moved away from the pool and left a ghostly track.

Raanung parked the skimmer at the Miramar port's field, from which it could be called back by remote. Emerald, fully rigged in jewels and tags, was warned by the guard, as before, against going about with valuables, and purred, as before, that she did not expect to be accosted. Grinning and shooting her claws for emphasis. Raanung heaved the moped out of the stowage compartment, and they sailed away at a pace calculated to let Emerald keep hold of her stomach. It was 0355. There was no hurry.

"Now where's the wild goose?"

"Keep to main streets first and around Anika's house where we spend no more than fifteen minutes smelling out whatever may be interesting."

"Any ESP Thorndecker sends is sure to know the house is empty as soon as he reaches it."

"First he must break in and ensure we are not inside and shielding," said Emerald.

"And the police find a broken house and tramp about leaving a whole dog's breakfast of scent."

"Give that one credit for knowing how to get in and out of a house without leaving a sign."

"Supposing *in* but not *out?*"

"Why am I wearing this damned piece of junk? One or two pickups on the walls tell us if even a heart is beating inside."

But the house was silent, as if shut up for the night, and no heart beat within.

Except for the Solthree leopard no one tracks as silently as Ungrukh. Raanung found three unfamiliar scents he stored for further use; his cat's eyes, unaided, found no sign of break-in. He did not need the fifteen minutes.

"Now what? We are not going to find those smells doing cross-town tracking to and fro."

"No. During that incident of ours so fortunately broken up by Bellingrose I get a sense of attack from the southeast. Do not snort, please. It is not a big town here, and I also get the same sense from the one following us tonight. And one flash of a round house." She opened her mind to him for examination.

He squeezed his eyes shut. "That is not quite round. It is made of many straight pieces. Angles. It is strange. I think we have another madman about."

"Probably here they call him eccentric."

"There are still too many houses for us to run around picking it out."

"Why bother? There is a Security Station across the road, nicely lighted. If it is so easy to identify someone there knows of it."

"Why not just esp?"

"I like to show how innocent we are."

"And we are leaving a damned big track."

"There is no secrecy in this district any more. I doubt the house is occupied, but I want to see if it can tell us anything."

Raanung growled, "It can say, 'I am a trap.' "

"That is why I warn of the kill," Emerald said, "and why I leave two free hours for us to put heads together and get out of it."

"Then stuff yourself with sickness pills, woman, because we may have one hell of a fast ride home."

"Come now and let us ask at the station."

Raanung hunched a shoulder. "I am glad of your simple faith in us."

The sleepy deskman had seen almost everything, but never a pair of Ungrukh, though he had heard rumors of their presence.

Emerald, cool grand lady crimson and flashing green facets, identified herself and Raanung fully. "First we stay for a while with that Mrs. Gurdja, who reads the cards, and then there is a," she picked a name out of the air, "Mr. Rhee, who invites us to stay with him. But we must leave for a while, and now we are back late we cannot find the address of the house he is renting."

"I'm sorry, Ma'am, but I've never heard of him, and if you don't know where you are I don't see how I can help."

"We know where *we* are. We don't know where *he* is. But he does say the house is very odd, something like round, with angles."

"Oh that! Old Wardman. Queer as a clockwork orange—excuse me, Ma'am. Lives alone in the big gazebo with a couple of robots to clean and cook. But he left word a thirtyday ago he was taking off for a while and we go by to check his automatic lighting every couple of nights. Never let on he was renting. Nobody's supposed to do that without permission."

"Perhaps there is some good reason." Emerald flipped her GalFed ESP tag. "But I am not esping without permission, so if you please, where is that gazebo?"

"Three streets east and third house down from the second street south, Ma'am," said Security, with a certain resigned air, as if he dealt with big red ESP cats in emeralds every day.

"It is clever of them to use Security as a lookout," Emerald said.

"What in Hell's Pit is a clockwork orange?"

"There is no visual connotation in his mind. It is only another term for eccentric."

"Now he knows there are two more of them around the place."

The Wardman house was hard to miss, but it did not look like Anika's gazebo. The structure was raised half a meter above ground, though it was a good fifteen meters in diameter, and supported by a great many decorative wrought-iron legs terminating in ball-and-claw feet. There were many angles to it; seven or eight were visible from one side. It shone very brightly, but not from windows: there were none in the outside wall; a recessed light was fitted under the pagoda-slanted roof in each plane.

"I think that roof is open at the center . . . maybe there is a courtyard." *Atrium,* Quattro had said. Thorndecker liked an atrium. "I don't much care to meet the mind that creates that house."

Raanung stopped the moped squarely in front of the big stucco mansion. Every second plane was decorated by a black wrought-iron trellis growing with vines. A wide stone path led to a short flight of steps with railings of still more wrought-iron, and double black doors with huge brass knobs. The grounds were large, though nothing like those of Agassiz, for they were bordered by neighboring estates.

"Now, big man, what next?"

"You tell me. What do you esp?"

"Nothing from here. Empty, or white-noise."

"Or shielding. Same procedure as Anika's place."

"No, man. Here comes Security in his funny hat and not so funny gun."

"Up the front walk, then, nice kittycats."

By the time they reached the front door Security had biked past with the flick of a light at them. His mind registered what he had been told to watch for, found nothing suspicious and settled to its usual placid hum.

"Now—" Emerald began.

The doors opened.

The Ungrukh as one leaped over the railing to the grass.

The doors opened slow and wide to nothing but a brightly lit hall furnished with an oval mirror and a marble table.

Emerald said, "So? What do you think?"

"I think of a Solthree saying about curiosity killing cats. As for the doors, foot pressure, electric eye, tripwire, anything. How about home?"

"You have a lot to say about the kill."

Raanung grunted. "Not when doors open by themselves in so-called empty houses."

" 'I am a trap,' says the house. I want to know what the trap says."

"Then go through those doors."

"I don't deal with a trap on its own terms. Those trees look good and thick."

"When do you ever climb a tree?"

"I climb plenty of lava hills that are steeper and harder. In your territory. See how few footfalls it takes to reach that second tree, in case there are underground alarms."

Emerald was right, in that the tree's bark was kinder than the scoriated lava she was used to climbing. When they were settled in the first fork she sniffed and said, "There is a smell here as if—"

"—we are not the first to bury a corpse in a back garden."

"Any body we know?"

"No," said Raanung. "It is too far gone. And too shallow. Very shoddy piece of work. But I think you need not worry about meeting the mind that creates the house."

"Any of those from around Anika's place?"

"Not underground. I have one scent, but not fresh."

"Then come higher. I want to find out what is inside the roof."

"Not from that branch. Unlike lava, it bends."

A few steps further would have dumped her head first. She followed Raanung higher. The wood creaked, and she wondered what her ancestors had found so fine about trees.

.The inside of the roof was unremarkable: an area with

table, chairs and umbrellas where people might enjoy sun and
air; no forcefield, radar, or sign of trap. The floor and wall
were a bowl of concrete broken by an archway with steps
leading downward. Raanung crept the tree-limb foot before
foot: at its bowing-point, he bunched and leaped. The moment his feet touched surface the archway lit.

"Ho!" said Raanung. He and Emerald faced each other.
"There is another stairway here this side of the wall. You can
see its light on me. Are alarms ringing at the Station?"

Emerald esped. "No alarms. It is either a convenience for
those who drop in by hovercraft at night—or a trap for the
curious like us."

"Or maybe both, depending on circumstance. Onward or
back?"

In answer she landed beside him. Without moving her feet
she turned to peer at the second stairway. It was marbled,
graceful, and curved out of sight. "The one thing we do not
do is separate."

"I agree, but I am worried about what pressure points are
on this floor."

She gave a glancing blow to one of the chairlegs with her
tail. The chair slid. "This seems to be a chair. And I'm not
spending the whole two hours testing the roof."

"We are making enough noise to bring up the household."

"I prefer them up here. We can go down the wall faster.
But no one is coming and the concrete is too thick for my
pickups. Let's take the far stairway. This one looks too bright
and inviting."

They went down stalking, to one side out of the direct glare
of lights, not touching the wall. At base they faced a brightly
lit hall like the one they had seen through the open doors, but
higher up. The light made them squint a bit. The brightness
plus emptiness were eerier than the stark plains of Ungruwarkh.

"Now I smell something that is familiar but not
quite," said Raanung. "Keep low and jump to that place
where the wall is blank."

As they landed Emerald heard a screech of metal and

whipped about. Beside the archway they had come through there was a kind of ridged marble stand, and on it a metal figure in the shape of a Solthree. Or rather a casing, because it was faceless and she could see through the joints that it was hollow, or nearly, Both arms had descended and its metal gloves were holding a rod with a short chain attached, and a spiked ball hanging from that. A few hairs from the tip of Raanung's tail floated down from it.

"My nose is right," said Raanung. "It is metal and oil I smell. I presume that is something for Solthree warriors to use."

"*I* presume an upright Solthree gets a smashed head coming past that."

"Then it is good to behave like Ungrukh in the land of Solthrees. Not so?"

"It may be a challenge for you, but if the whole place is full of traps like this I think I give up and go home."

"This is your plan, woman, and I am not using those stairs again. I am sure there are more traps, but not many. The trapper is not expecting the police, or an army, or thieves."

"No. Us. I am beginning to suspect that is why the tracker allows us a vision of this place."

To Emerald's horror, Raanung crossed the hall, snaked out his tail and yanked hard at the weapon in the hands of the armored figure. It came with difficulty because it had been cemented in, and the pedestal rocked but did not fall.

"What do you want that dreadful thing for?"

"A souvenir." He picked up the stem in his jaws, careful to keep the spikes well away from his flesh. *:Also, it is made of wood and leather in the handle, and useful for testing whatever may be electrified.:*

They crept along the angled hall, avoiding light fixtures and keeping out of the way of the lightstrip in the ceiling. Once Raanung threw his flail at a closed door and it came away sparking and left a black burst on the enamel. And once through an open doorway, and nothing happened except that the walls lit up with pictures of Solthrees of all ages engaged in strange activities with each other and with animals.

"Whatever is that?" Raanung asked.

"I believe something to do with copulation," said Emerald. "In unusual ways. It is something like Quattro's experience with Thorndecker."

"Wardman and Thorndecker seem to have something in common, then. I wonder why Thorndecker kills him."

"You are not sure it is Wardman."

"I am. His smell here is related to the one outside, even though that is far gone."

"Then I suppose there is some kind of bargain and some kind of quarrel."

Raanung pulled the weapon away with his tail, and they passed by. Without the compass on Renny's chronometer they would have been completely disoriented among the angles, but they did know what they were looking for: a staircase leading to ground level. Emerald had concluded that the only information available from the house was that it wanted to kill two Ungrukh.

Another closed door; this one had a panel of buttons beside it. "This looks like an elevator," said Emerald, "and I am having nothing to do with *that*." Just beyond, another lighted archway beckoned in the wall. "There is the stairway, I see the bannister. Which one of us takes the first step?"

Another beautiful marble staircase, this one had a broad bannister of magnificent wood. Raanung dropped his flail and sniffed about carefully without touching anything. "I cannot vouch for the steps, but that railing is certainly wood." He picked up the flail in his teeth again, jumped to the bannister's railing and walked down with great dignity and no hurry.

But the Ungrukh, eyes down, did not notice until they had reached bottom that there was no hallway to either side. The stairs led directly through an oval doorway into a huge room.

It was much stranger than the small room with lewd pictures. Its structure followed that of the rest of the house: its walls had seventeen angles. There was no rug; the floor was grained as beautifully as the railing; the round table in the center was bare wood; it was circled with twelve upholstered dining-chairs. Fitting against two of the wall's planes was a sideboard with a trellis of flowers painted above it. The planes to either side, and alternately all the way around were set with great oval mirrors framed in marble carved with curious and grotesque shapes. Many Ungrukh stared back at the two true ones in the rainbow of crystal facets from the chandelier above the table. The planes between the mirrors opened to staircases leading up or down.

"I don't see the openings to those when we are upstairs," said Emerald.

"I feel no currents coming from them," Raanung said. "They are pictures of staircases." A *whishh* behind them; they twisted their heads. Double doors had shut their entrance, and these too had a staircase painted on them.

Raanung sighed. "Now you find out what the trap really has to say."

"There is some kind of white flash when they close. Is that electric?"

"No. Metal. Those doors are knives. They fit on the bevel, very fine, and likely slice very well too."

"I think this man is worse than Thorndecker while he lives."

"And that one makes good use of the toy when he dies. This little plaything with the spikes is not much use here. There may be other doors, but they are not opening for us."

The lights of the chandelier faded; the room was dark for a moment, and then three blinding beams shot from the ceiling, and when the Ungrukh had blinked the stars from their eyes they found a man standing on the table.

Raanung roared, and Emerald said, "Hush. That is not a real person but a projection of one, like in the picture cubes."

She was terrified, but not quite to witlessness. She recognized at once the mannekin of Quattro's nightmares: a meter in height, infantile features grotesquely decked with a thick auburn beard, baby-blue eyes. And he was dressed in clothing of a kind they had never seen before: a wide-brimmed hat and suit of red velvet, almost their own color, with white lace at sleeve-ends and throat; embossed leather boots and a belt with a tiny sword hanging from it.

The mannekin bowed and leered. The trap was about to speak.

"Good evening, guests!" The voice was deep—artificially deepened, probably—and boomed from the walls. "Now of course although you can see me I can't see you and don't know whom I am addressing—but may I guess that you are the red cats? Not only because you are so venturesome but because you have been trying to save Spinel." He simpered. "Did you really believe that I was planning to take the *Zarandu?* Or think I had no other fast cruiser available from all the worlds outside the Federation? Or that you could actually save Spinel? It may sound foolish to you that I am asking so many questions I will get no answers for, but I can guess at them. And, guest or guests, if you have managed to come so far to learn I can tell you one thing. Your friend, the Emperor of Fools, is dead. As you will be. You have been an invigorating challenge, friends, but you have played enough."

He swept off his cartwheel hat in a little bow that should have been ridiculous but was sinister and terrifying, and disappeared.

The beams blackened; the lights of the chandelier flashed.

Raanung growled low in his throat, but Emerald's paws dripped sweat, and her nose began to run.

Raanung asked, "Can that be true?"

"Tue or not, he means to break us." Her voice quavered, and for a moment she hated herself for weakness. Then she gave a great roaring shriek of rage and frustration. It made even Raanung jump, for she had never behaved so.

"Woman! Woman!"

"I am not afraid, big man. Only angry. I do not break yet."

There was a creaking and clicking below them.

"There are traps in the floor now!" Emerald cried.

"No. The room is turning."

"That is stupid. Is he killing us with dizziness?"

"No. Look at the doors!"

There were four trompe-l'oeil doors, all knife-edged, opening and shutting in irregular rhythms. Raanung glanced about swiftly and said, "Get under the table and look at the floor. The lights and mirrors are dizzy-making."

Emerald crouched with him under the table, but she did not need the shelter. The great darkness in her mind at the thought of a dead Spinel was enough to blind her.

"My love, push that out of your mind for now. I want us to stay alive."

The spin quickened a little, but soon reached its limit. The structure was very great; its motor could only bear so much. And the movement was calculated mainly to upset the balance of anyone trying to reach the doors.

"It is good you take those pills."

But they were moving quite slowly in the center, and turning did not upset Emerald. She shook darkness from her head. "Which is the door, and how to get through?"

"One door has straight vertical edges. Another slants. The third is wavy from top to bottom and the fourth zigzags. They all look very sharp. I believe I know a way through. But which doors?"

"Those who love and use toys like these seem to go on the principle that simple things are for the simple-minded. Choose the worst doors."

Raanung knocked over a heavy chair and sent it skittering toward the wall. It screeched over the floor and the studs of its upholstery scored the wood. Emerald did the same with another. Her mind was so full of black fury it did not even register her body's balance against speed and spin when she followed. The chair was resting on back and seat edge, the legs were in her hands, and as the zigzag door opened she shoved it in, and Raanung did the same with the other chair and the wavy door.

The knives sheared the beautiful handmade tapestry, and tried to bite through the iron-hard wood. Then the room bellowed as though its teeth had been pulled. There was a great ratchet-sound of gears stripping, the floor shuddered and canted two degrees, three of the mirrors shattered in a burst of glass and marble fragments, the chandelier fell half down and hung in a tangle of wires, dripping crystal tears that rang on the table.

Under the floor the machine muttered *clockwork! clockwork! clockwork!* and gave one last shudder before it stopped and died. Raanung's theory, hardly articulated, that the irregular openings of the doors depended on eccentric gears meshing into the rest of the mechanism, appeared to have been correct.

But Raanung, peering through his conquered door, was snarling. "Hell and damnation! This stairway goes *up!*"

"But mine goes down," said Emerald. Raanung picked up his spiked flail, which had fetched up by a wall, and flung it through the zigzag door. It bounced down a short straight flight and landed in a bright hall. He took the steps in one bound.

"There are the front doors, and they are still open!"

the suit of Swords

Emerald followed. Gratefully she sniffed the damp night air, a bare ten meters away.

whrrrtck! whrrrtck!

A *thing* was skimming down the hall, whirring, whirling, swinging a tentacle at walls and ceiling.

"Robot," Emerald snarled. "I forget the robots."

It was, or had been, a domestic robot. At the end of its tentacle there was not a suction inlet but a knife. It was as tall as Thorndecker and had antennas and faceted sensor lenses. It paused before the open doors, swinging its tentacle as a blind man might probe the air with a stick. "It must be aiming at us, or why the knife?"

"I don't know how it smells us out," Raanung said.

"Any thermostat is sensitive to temperature. Why not this?" She kicked the flail toward Raanung. "Go down the other way. I have an idea for this one."

"Don't be a fool, woman! Station says there are more robots than one."

"This is the only one after us. I doubt the kitchen robot is mobile and I don't intend to find out. Get going!"

He backed, handle in teeth, away from the open door, the inviting door.

Emerald stood square in the staircase entrance. For once she wished she had kept her mother's knife. Its blunt strength would have conquered any fine blade.

The machine paused, clicked, aimed its tentacle at her. Skewers sprang from a band in its middle, and the band spun.

She backed growling up the stairs, the machine followed, humming. Wheeled, it stopped before the first step, but the tentacle reached. She grabbed it below the blade as one might grip a poison snake beneath the jaws, and bent it backward, gripping with hands, tail, fangs, pushing the knife away. She pulled, dragging the stretching coil up the stairs while the machine hummed and spun, slicing air. The moment it dropped treads to climb the stairs Raanung appeared, flail in hands wrapped with tail, and slammed it.

He battered again and again at sensors and antennas, and even after it whined and stilled and the tentacle went limp he beat and beat it into ploughshares.

Emerald cast the tentacle away and cried, "Stop! stop! We are going mad as our enemies!"

He looked at her, eyes red-lit and bloodshot besides. He was panting. "Well," he said. "It is a kill of sorts."

"We have three minutes of seven and cutting fine."

"It is a wonder there are no alarms and police."

"Obviously this house does not want police."

There were no more robots, no more traps. They passed through the doorway and down the steps. They heard the doors shutting politely behind them and did not glance back. Emerald said, "You look ridiculous with that thing in your teeth."

:*You do not think so back there, woman. As long as it is a saver of lives and takes none, Agassiz may wish to hang it on his wall.*:

Emerald did not think so, but was too worn with fatigue and despair to argue. The dawn was rising gently with soft winds, and there was some thin cloud, color of rainbow, over the horizon. It appeared on Ungruwarkh sometimes, rarer than rainbows, and she thought of Ungruwarkh, home, and of Spinel and his home.

"Thorndecker is a liar," said Raanung.

"He is not lying to himself, this time, I feel it. But I hope he is wrong." What piled hurt on hurt was that a Khagodi, of the most powerful organic ESP species in the Galaxy, of a people with an ethic carved in granite, might have let Spinel die.

Raanung followed his original unorthodox shortcut back to Agassiz and his garden, and Emerald did not even fear the bridgeway trestle.

the Devil reversed

Morgan lay in bed, hand propped on elbow, and watched Renny. She was squatting in a corner, smoking one of her mother's violent cigarettes; she had showered, and her hair, now straight and very black, gleamed under a lamp above her shoulder; its light cast her half into shadow, like a moon.

He had wondered if she would make love like an Ungrukh, or as one engaged in the last act of life, but she had behaved simply as a loving woman.

She said, "Are you disappointed?"

He startled at having his thoughts divined by an Imper. "Why do you ask?"

"It seemed to me you were attracted because you thought I was savage." She butted the cigarette in the ashtray and looked away. "Many men are. They approach me—figuratively—with a whip and a chair. Some . . . like to be hurt."

He said, a bit sharply, "If I wanted that I'd wrestle with an Ungrukh. What's bothering you?" He added, more gently, "I don't mean about Emerald and Raanung—and your Emperor. Quattro just told us about them. But what?"

"Most of the ones I go with are rabid dogs. On my own time, often I just say the hell with it, even when I want. . ." She looked him in the eye. "Why did you want me?"

He regarded her gravely and then burst into laughter. "You're extraordinary! No, I don't mean it as an insult! I've been around ESPs for a long time, and I'm not one, so I get, like the Ungrukh males, a sense of—I'd better not say smell! I just thought I saw something behind your eyes, even when I was tracking you in the Plaza. If you'd been fierce—the way you can be—I wouldn't have minded, but I'd have been a bit disappointed. Now I'm giving myself a gold star because I was right!"

Renny laughed. "And my mother thought you were a bumpkin!"

"Hah. You know why I ran away from home? I found out my 'father' the pimp thought I was a good investment."

"God. And did you beat him up?"

"No. He was bigger than me, then. And he was a sorry dog, not a rabid one."

"Well, I'm coming back to bed with you now, Morgan. But—fair warning—I want sleep."

The breakfast table was set outside in the fair fresh morning, and two minutes before the hour the company sat down to eat. They did not speak much, and for that reason heard, beyond the clinking of china and silver, the coughing of the moped. Quattro and the younger Hashimoto ran down to the gate. Emerald and Raanung dismounted with gratitude, the latter fetched his weapon out of the carryall, and they followed as the others wheeled in the machine.

They were greeted by feelings of relief mixed with perplexity.

But Quattro said, "Why are you shielding so hard, Emerald?"

She looked at him and opened her soul.

There was a cry of anguish from Agassiz. While Anika was explaining to Renny, Emerald, weary beyond belief, dragged herself half-stumbling to the big scallop and touched the embryo's hand with her nose. "We do our best for him, man. There is no proof he is dead. We are only sorry to keep secrets from you."

"I don't blame you for that, Emerald, but—" He wept.

Emerald looked up at Doctor. There was no jealousy in him now. Even through unremitting trouble he had been grateful that Agassiz had found the kindred spirit he himself could never be. Emerald, in bringing Spinel, had given Agassiz almost the finest gift of his life.

Raanung came bearing his gift in his teeth and dropped it beside the shell. "Agassiz, I know you hate weapons, and I respect your feelings, but this one is of value to us because it saves our lives without taking a life in return."

"Thank you, Raanung. I will value it because I love you and Emerald."

Bellingrose picked it up gingerly. "It's an ancient Solthree weapon, called a morningstar."

"That is too beautiful a name for such a nasty thing," said Emerald.

Bellingrose's mouth quirked. "Sometimes it was called a holy-water sprinkler."

"I know nothing of such matters, but I do know that breakfast is getting cold for everyone, and I want to eat before I fall dead from weariness."

"Emerald, I can radio and find out what happened."

"No, man, that way you risk letting Thorndecker know *we* are alive, and it is better to let him believe we are all three dead."

Raanung said, "William, you are a Solthree who knows much about strange people. Why is that house so insane?"

"From what we know of Thorndecker I'd say it was normal, for him, but I suspect your dotty Wardman was a high-ranking criminal—or official *and* criminal—who liked to terrorize his underlings. I'd like to see the faces of the police when they find out. Unless they know more than they let on."

"No. They are merely stupid." Emerald dug her snout in the bowl and paused. Security *could* be stupid. Was it possi-

EMPEROR, SWORDS, PENTACLES   175

ble that at the Port they were no match for Thorndecker even
with the help of Threyha? Had that high-minded creature kept
on trying to protect him? She dared not ask—and did not
know how to reach Threyha if she did.

Quattro hunkered beside her and put the Chlisi knife near
the dish. "I hope Spinel—"

"So do I, but that cannot matter to you. The mad house
tells me something, in my own person, of your experience.
What Thorndecker can do. What he plans.

"Quattro, as many of you as possible *must* get out. I doubt
that you can move Agassiz, and Doctor does not leave him. I
don't think Thorndecker kills them: he makes too big a meal
on their misery. But he has scores to settle with you, and you
are useful only as long as he needs you to guard the chosen.
But *they* are the great worry in this easy place. It is a good
womb for Agassiz, but they cannot spend their lives in a
womb. They do not know what it means to be slaves and
suffer unending abuse. When I am sick with poison I think
there are a few here who are sorry not to be rid of me
altogether even if they do not admit it to themselves. We
visitors spoil the order of things, but it is an order that cannot
last—and that is a feeling I have from the moment I come
here."

"I know," said Quattro. "What are *you* going to do?"

"Disobey my own strictures and stay to do what I can for
Agassiz. I owe that to Spinel. Raanung does what he thinks
best. We have a son at home, and there are hundreds of
thousands of women there much like me to—"

Raanung, snarling, raised bloody jaws. "After your
mother and father and grandmother and uncles and aunts
finish with me those women are in a great hurry to make love
to my scattered bones! Why in Hell's Pit do I choose you?"

"Answer for yourself," said Emerald with great dignity.
"But Quattro, you know I must try to save my friends."

"I agree. I'm staying too. I want to stamp that lump of
poison into the ground."

"You must care for the others first."

"Understood. Damned if I know how I'm going to manage

it. But just let me ask one more thing: what in God's name is
the Blue Pit of Hell you're always swearing by? You never
give any image.''

"That? Oh, it is a gas jet from a fissure in a volcanic cone.
It burns blue when it catches fire and long ago we think it
comes from the Dead World. We are not so superstitious
now, but it is still good for swearing on.''

Sylvie made the first move. She did not try to conceal it
and no one tried to stop it. She came out of the house with a
backpack, wearing a hooded zip in the same kind of near-
invisible shadow-grey as Renny's. The others glanced at her,
but did not speak; they did not know what to say. She had
taken no other lovers since Pritchard had come, and though
her association with him had stained her faintly, in retros-
pect, she herself had always behaved honestly and in good
conscience. She would betray no one.

She went without pause to the scallop and said, "Agassiz,
I am leaving.''

"You are right to do so,'' said Agassiz. "Go in safety.''

Renny's eyes narrowed. In the indifference of the others,
who were simply worried and bewildered, she interpreted
revulsion. She hooked her legs over the bench. "I don't think
my mother will mind if I offer you the moped. It'll be safer,
as long as you're alone.''

Sylvie looked for contempt or irony and found none.
"Thanks.''

Then Emerald had the horrid thought. Whether it came
from lack of sleep, or the fearful experience she had been
through, or was actually good reasoning—she could not tell.
But it seemed ugly enough to shield immediately before it
came to the expressive part of her mind.

Renny was saying, "That machine has a couple of quirks
I'd better just show you.''

Emerald leaped over her feeding bowl and planted herself
between the two Solthree women. "No!''

They gaped at her, Sylvie with her pale vulnerable face,

Renny with nostrils flared. "What in hell's the matter with you?"

"Renny, it is not right for her to go by machine on open roads where someone can track her, or someone else believes this happens."

"I don't know what you're talking about. She's an ESP—like *you*. She knows how to dodge."

"I am not worrying about esp. There are other kinds of threats. Sylvie, you are thinking that I accuse you of jamming the door and being untrustworthy. That is not so. Whoever jams that door is under hypnosis and not responsible. I don't care about it, and I do *not* put you in the category of Pritchard. But I must give you the same advice. Stay away from roads. Go hidden to places you do not know, where no one knows you. Believe me, I tell you this to save your life."

"You have no right to tell me how to save my life," Sylvie said in a small cold voice.

"No. But I do like people to stay alive."

"Come on, Emerald," Quattro said, "I don't know what you're making all the fuss about at a time like this."

"No? Then I say the ugly thing and get the burning coals dumped on my head." She opened her mind. "Sylvie, do not go to Pritchard. I beg you."

Sylvie flushed. "You don't know anyth—"

"I don't know. I make guesses and presumptions. Your face gives me suspicions. At some unguarded moment Pritchard tells you where he may hide, and puts a block on you so you cannot tell. There is nothing wrong with that. It saves him and is no harm to others. After all, I myself let him go. But if you go to him now, when he is an Imper and cannot see your mind, he may believe that Thorndecker orders you to betray him, which is not true, or that someone follows you to find him, which is possible. Thorndecker can let you live, but Pritchard cannot, and he is quite ready to kill and run."

Sylvie was half-crying, and she pulled off a grey wisp of glove to scrub at her eyes. "That's a lie! You're a filthy thing, filthy!" In her eagerness to defend Pritchard she used words harsher than she meant.

Emerald remained gentle and careful. "I want only to save your life."

"I don't care!" The thought hovered: *I still love him.*

Quattro sighed. "Sylvie, he did give you a thick lip a couple of times. Nobody could avoid noticing that."

"He'd never—he'd never try to kill me!"

"Oh hell, I can't see a man like Pritchard being so impulsive," Renny said.

Bellingrose said mildly, "Maybe Hartog was something like that before he met you." He was the only one in the world who could have said that, and it was Renny's turn to become red in the face.

Sylvie had regained her composure. "I'm sorry for what I said. But you shamed me."

"Not by intention. Please be free to go in whatever manner you wish."

"I don't need the moped. I can get along without it."

Emerald and Renny exchanged glances. Anika sighed and got up to put an arm about the slender grey shoulders. "I'm not an ESP or an Imper and have nothing to do with anything, so before anything else blows up let me give you the moped and show you its cranky habits. Come on, girl."

Before either of them could take a step, a landcar roared up to the gate, stopped briefly for its riders to hurl out a heavy object, and raced away with a diminishing shriek.

The Ungrukh, who were the swiftest, reached the gates first, dragged them open, and pulled in Spinel's coffin.

It was so battered the lid was loose and had only to be knocked away. The body was there, a spike in its braincase. The waterskin was drained almost empty, and crinkled like dead leaves. The eyes were sunken.

Renny and Anika ran to it at once, followed by Bellingrose. Anika burst into tears and turned for comfort to Bellingrose; but Renny snarled deep in her throat, like an Ungrukh. The morning sun slanted on green, and the sky was pure cobalt blue. The garden had never looked more beautiful. Agassiz was silent in shock.

If any there thought it was good that the great crawfish was dead, Emerald did not vilify them. She and Raanung sat to either side of the body like red stone lions without a word or thought.

Only Quattro noticed something strange in this tableau. He stood silently and kept his mind as blank as those of the Ungrukh.

The body said, :*That was very clever of you.*:

"We shield very hard," Emerald said. "Your deliverers are far away."

:*I had not counted on the Ungrukh sense of smell.*:

"Before, we are not even sure that you are alive, but we know Spinel's smell, and you are not he, though we don't know what you are."

:*I will show you. I hate to do this in public, but circumstances. . . :*

The spike in the braincase slowly pushed itself out and fell aside, but after that no one could have described exactly what happened. The Qsaprinli limbs drew into the body, the form became globular and blurry, veiled itself in a mist of vapor, rose in foaming protoplasm dimly seen, bubbling in vacuoles and glittering with crystals through a cage of collagen threads and nerve fibers, grew new head and limbs, darkened—

—and it was Bellingrose who recognized.

"Hello, Locksmith," he said.

"Good day, Bellingrose. That was the damned hardest form I ever took." The little man in dark lenses and black zip sat on the lawn in the lotus position. "I'm sorry to have given you so much anguish, but you can understand why. And I assure you that Spinel is very much alive."

"The joy of Agassiz is worth this moment," Emerald said. But it was her joy that rose like a fountain. She had not delivered the Emperor to his death, and a Khagodi's word was unbreakable. She added shyly, "Can Threyha's mind reach me here? I wish to thank her again."

The Locksmith's mouth twitched a little. "I'm afraid the curve of the world limits her, and even so her attention turns like a lighthouse, very slowly. You are lucky to have caught the beam when you did."

Doctor wheeled the scallop so that Agassiz and the Locksmith could appraise each other. Though the embryo rejoiced, he was a bit pale and subdued. "My debts are growing so complicated I ought to hire a book-keeper of deeds. Tell me, Locksmith, have two stranger creatures ever met?"

The Locksmith gave his little smile again. "Many times, Agassiz. There is nothing strange about you to me. You are a man among your people. The Ungrukh and I are out of our places."

"I am happy that Spinel is alive, but I am afraid there is a terrible story."

"Not a cheerful one. We were certain that Thorndecker would try to raid the *Zarandu*, if only because we intend to use it against him. It arrived a little earlier than expected, and Spinel close after, very convenient for raiding, but we had Threyha's help, and hid Spinel while I made my transformation—"

Emerald snorted. "How do you manage him?"

"With great difficulty. He was enraged because we wouldn't let him fight, so I had to put him very deeply asleep. But the raid was more savage than we expected. Thorndecker has a very powerful ESP whom even I know nothing about except that it is not a Qumedon, a Lyhhrt, or even another Khagodi. When I am in better shape I would like to meet that one, and so would Threyha. Two of our Security died believing they were defending Spinel. But we kept the *Zarandu*, and gave them a dead Emperor."

"Thorndecker—or his image—says he has access to other fast cruisers."

"Yes, and to other criminal minds, many of whom are saner than Wardman and more dangerous than his house. *Zarandu* is aging, but still top of the line, and he would have liked to have it in spite of his bravado."

The Locksmith removed his dark glasses and absorbed

them somehow, because he did not put them away. There was a loosening of breath among those who had been watching him; his mystery was discomfiting, and his pale normal eyes lessened it. He turned to Sylvie. "You ought to know that Pritchard was traced by Thorndecker's people, and warned away by us, so his old hiding places are empty. We believe he is safe, but we prefer not to know where."

She turned away. Previously she had been the focus of more attention than she wanted; now she did not know what to do any more than the others. It was Quattro who stood his ground and asked the questions. "Locksmith, I think you got yourself delivered here for more than one reason. We're grateful for good news—but you've said you have plans for using the *Zarandu*. Are we included in them?"

The Locksmith said evenly, "We have a score of plans: no two alike, and they depend on the willingness of their participants—you and others."

Raanung purred, "Maybe you give us an example?"

"Not before I say this: Kinnear and I have made an agreement, and the reason he made it with *me* is because my world's sun is the nearest to Qsaprinel's, and Thorndecker is using my moon as a base. I have a stake in whatever we do, so you will find our oath as good as Threyha's. I am not using any hypnosis whatever on an ally unless that ally requests it. No one will be forced into danger. There is plenty of danger in all of the plans, and Emerald was right when she said an unwilling person is as good as an enemy. But as one example—for those who are willing—some will scatter, and perhaps we won't know for years whether they're safe; Agassiz will not be moved but protected here as well as possible. Some will ride the *Zarandu*, along with Spinel and Kinnear—and some will travel to Qsaprinel with Thorndecker: and I will be one of those."

the High Priestess reversed

Thorndecker orbited in his shuttle, masked from radar, shielded from hot light and cold dark. He swung gently in his cushioned hammock, a net cocoon, sucking on a bulb of

eggnog with rum and milk in it and clasping one of his tiny
feet with his free hand. The shuttle was on auto, and he had
no one with him but the ESP, who was drifting with one claw
hooked in a handhold on the wall.

Thorndecker enjoyed being alone, sometimes, and loved
weightlessness. He was as aware that it was womblike as he
was that there was much in his character that was infantile.
He had absorbed these actualities. And every gravity was his
enemy: his boots were heavily built up not for vanity but
because his feet were too small to balance his overgrown
head, muscles and genitals.

Now he was weightless, sucking his brand of honeydew
and playing with his toes, and he thought pleasing thoughts.
Radio had told him the *Zarandu* was loading for takeoff, but
with Spinel and the cats gone he did not worry about that. He
was waiting for news of his own fast cruiser, a powerful new
model he had obtained with money and guile, which could
land anywhere in space and dock with his own vehicles. This
would come within a few hours and then would be time for
the Ingathering. His mind rested briefly on dead Spinel and
mangled cats; at greater length he considered Colony and
Empire: earnings owed him. His doctors had promised him
ten more of his earthly years, and they would be enough. In
his mind's eye, in images given him by his ESPs, he saw a
decayed Agassiz, who had been his toy, and a ravaged
Doctor, who had deserted him. He gave a little time to one
more toy, Quattro: the one person in the universe who had
retarded his aims by pure will and in battle, and by his kind of
reasoning, the one he respected most. He could have retaken
Quattro many times; instead he had planted him in a garden
and watched him grow. This gave him pleasure. The being he
would destroy now was more powerful, a new toy, a greater
pleasure. He laughed, let go of his foot, and rubbed his
stomach with the little hand to bring up the bubble.

The ESP was a being named Esne, of a neutral species
called Encid, and it had this in common with the Praximfi and
Qumedni in that there was no way of completely describing
it. It lacked the concepts to describe itself. It knew where its

home world was, but not how to tell where. It did not know what sex it was or if it were any, though it brought forth progeny parthenogenetically, and for convenience was called *she;* "she" exchanged genetic material with her sisters in a way she could not communicate at times when it seemed appropriate.

The species had no mouth, ears, or digestive processes. The Encid was a brain, about 25 cm in diameter, completely surrounded by something like a placenta, whose vessels fed it; these permeated a heavy protective membrane beyond which was a densely packed centimeter of humus containing symbiotes, both animal and vegetable, and held together by a "skull", a network of cartilage. Its interstices supported the roots of the Encid exterior, a dense growth of feathery blue-black leaves whose thickness, never greater than a couple of centimeters, varied among individuals, or sometimes according to climate, for the Encid lived in rain forests.

There were four or five simple eyes dotted about its surface; the optic tracts led directly to the brain, but the muscles allowed each eye to turn laterally in a half-circle, so it did not matter to any one Encid which direction she was looking from, and none of the eyes saw very sharply. This sphere rested on a horny standard, half its diameter in length, which branched into six feet like chicken-claws, with resting-pads and sharp pincers.

Esne did not communicate many thoughts. She was a telepathic amplifier of great capacity; her intelligence had never been tested. She was more adaptable than Spinel to strange life-forms that could be ingested, far less adaptable than the Locksmith to society. She did not know what society was. On their world Encid lived alone and used their esp to find information about food and water sources from others. She would kill for food and water, and in self-defense. She would use esp to help Thorndecker kill, because he had had her rescued from a wrecked derelict loaded with specimens; Praximfi had antipathy to intruders who might interfere with their religious practices: Encid had no comparable defenses and so used the power of their esp to protect their privacy, as

several shiploads of half-insane xenobiologists could testify.
Esne knew in an abstract way, like words in a strange language, that Thorndecker might never free her or send her
home, but the knowledge was self-encapsulated, and had no
direct meaning. But he had saved her, and therefore she was
loyal; he, on his part, loved the grotesque, and for him she
was the ultimate. He was probably the only Solthree in the
universe who enjoyed the company of an Encid.

YOU ARE SECURE, said the computer, and Thorndecker
grinned. The code told him that the cruiser was his, and the
Encid who was his drifted from the wall with a ruffle of
feather-leaves and grasped his wrist with careful pads.

"Shuttle to Keys rendezvous," Thorndecker told his
cradling vessel; one last step before he began the final voyage
to the land of his birth.

There was a silence after the Locksmith spoke, but
Emerald knew that the membrane of apathy had dissolved:
the spell was broken.

She dropped her head in relief, and fell asleep on the spot.

the Nine of Wands

In the Imperial Tower of Qsaprinel under the co-Regency
everyone expected factional splitting. It was usual.

There had been a great deal of jealousy among the Royals
when Meta-Spinel took his brother-in-law's first cousin
twice removed as a second concubine. There was no great
passion involved. Meta-Spinel was making a gesture toward
reviving an old custom; in some ways he was as difficult to
understand as his fission-product Spinel-beta would be. The
character and family of the concubine were impeccable; the
Emperor rarely had congress with her, and never when her
egg-sac was ripe: she was not much older than his daughter
Dunenli. Perhaps he merely wanted, in his loneliness, an ally
in the continual battle-triangle with his Empress and his first
concubine.

There was as much consternation when Spinel-alpha took

that concubine, Aspartil, for Empress. He was not disturbed. He reminded the court that he was one half of Meta-Spinel, and claiming one third of his wives. He assured them that he intended to take his future children out of succession. Seventeen heirs-in-line were enough.

But Spinel-beta was sexually jealous, as well as envious of power. He had brooded and waited for opportunity, with near-disastrous results.

Aspartil, after Spinel's departure, waited and watched very carefully. A member of the Council had died of old age, and there was a vacancy. How she wished Dunenli—half a year from maturation—were of age!—because her only ally on the Council was the wildly undependable Dowager Empress.

"I want Binatrel to fill that space on the Council," she told Spinel-beta.

"He is a servant," said Beta.

"He is Spinel's friend, and he was a member of the Royal Guard until you forced him out."

"He seems to be serving closely enough as your personal guard," said Spinel-beta with a touch of malice. Binatrel's father had been Meta-Spinel's closest friend; Binatrel, born three years before fission, had almost inevitably fallen into friendship with Spinel-alpha: this made him Beta's enemy.

"You have made a close counsellor of Lord Beletrel," Aspartil said calmly, "as well as Lady Petranyl." This last remark was particularly embarrassing to Beta. He would have been glad to get free of that Lady; she was the very loyal sister of the First Concubine, who was in a perfect snit because she had been knocked completely off the power-ladder. Beta's body shifted into the position of poor-cripple-being-picked-on. It looked like pose, but was not: he felt that way about himself.

"Beta, please let us give up sparring and work peacefully. Dunenli has attached herself to me by no choice of mine. I love that old Dowager mother of hers but she is full of greed and resentment, and I want protection from it for Dunenli." Sometimes she wondered with shame if Spinel had not left to get out of all these situations, and if he really wanted to come back.

She got her way but, to avoid rumor, conferred with Binatrel only in the presence of others: Dunenli, heirs, Guard members, even the Dowager. Dunenli, as Spinel had judged, was shrewd and sensible. She shared all important discussions but either Aspartil or Binatrel was always with her when she spoke to Spinel-beta.

"I can't bear him," she told Aspartil. "When he's at his friendliest he disturbs me most. I was never afraid of my father—and there is half my father. His deformities don't bother me; I only feel regret for them—but he *is* half my father—and he frightens me." Her little clawed hands moved in gestures of futility.

"He is technically parental because you have half his hereditary material," Binatrel said, "but with his different brain structure and personality, probably not legally so."

"That is not what she is getting at, Binatrel. My dear, what you are afraid of would make him a fool *and* a criminal." Dunenli's eyes popped in embarrassment. "There is no way he could get power by making himself your consort because that has been illegal for hundreds of years. He does want power, but to get it by ingratiating himself—and he simply doesn't know how because he has never tried before."

Dunenli asked quaveringly, "How can you be sure?"

"I know it when I see it," said Aspartil. "If that was all we had to worry about we would be safe."

"When—and I mean when—those aliens come back with bigger ships and weapons, then he will be a real enemy," Binatrel said.

"I hope now he has had enough of them. I know *I* have."

Dunenli said, "I wish we had a proper radio, like those the Galactic Federation people have. Then we might have word of the Emperor."

"Then our enemies might listen too," said Aspartil. "But I also wish we had it, and we do not, so it is better not to think of it." But she did, long and often, as the days passed by six and twelve.

Spinel-beta was both annoyed and hurt. Of course he hated his sib's allies, but he had determined to make some peace with them as long as he had no advantage—yet the harder he tried the more his words came out wrongwise. He was avid for power, but he did not hate Dunenli: he had played with her and the other heirs when they were little children and he their father. And he repelled her!

He knew that this was not because of his deformities. Whatever he felt, everyone else had learned to live with them. He concluded that Dunenli's guardians had turned her against him. He could not speak to them without resentment hampering both sides, but he believed that if only he could speak to her alone he *must* be able to find words—because she had been his and Spinel's child—to win her over.

He was not ready to give up on aliens entirely, but he would be exceedingly wary. His plan to gain power by alliance had rebounded as if his own electric shocks were turned against him: he was left terrified, helpless, and horribly in the wrong. An Empress had been harmed, an alien killed. And the treaty had been poison: the alien woman taught a strict lesson. So much for trusting strangers. Yet . . . *I* am an alien! his spirit cried. He could not stand his own body and did not even like those he called friends. Days of bitter water went by for him.

"What I am afraid of," Aspartil forced the words out, "is that they may be here already. The world is huge to us, but easy for them to get about on, and if they can travel the void they must be able to do so underwater." She was standing on the ramp with Binatrel and several of the guards, propped against the southern balustrade and watching the sea's nearest wavelets catch fire from the setting sun.

"I have increased the guard on the sluices," Binatrel said. "Aliens may get about under water, but I don't think they like to live there."

"That was a good idea, Binatrel."

But he did not thank her for this compliment. He had swivelled one eye backward to watch Dunenli, an exemplar

of patience, taking a walk with her mother. Aspartil did not
miss this glance nor the one returned by Dunenli. Further
along, as in a procession, came Spinel-beta trailed by a pair
of cronies, trying to pick up some precious pebble of information along the way.

Aspartil said, "My Councillor, would you like to have the
young lady?"

"I have already asked her, my lady—"

"Ah, how bold!—but don't become bashful now! Danger
has made us all bolder, and about time."

"But she won't have me, even at maturation, unless the
Emperor comes back."   .

"*I* know Spinel would be delighted, and we might persuade her to retract the condition—but let it stand for now."

A stone—no precious pebble, but grit in the eye! Spinel-
beta fumed till he felt his hearts would crack like stones.
Binatrel and Dunenli! How could he have missed this? And
the bold creatures had spoken neither to him *nor* Aspartil—
and she did not care! Was pleased! *Spinel would be delighted*
. . . His waters tasted like poison and stung like fire.

He spent the night and most of the next day in a bath of
soothing herbs. There were no Council meetings; the day was
quiet; the winds hardly disturbed the vaporous air, and the
mild tide, even at its height, did not touch the Tower's stones.

He was calmer now; he rehearsed what he would say:
reasonable persuasions, a soft voice to ask for what he
wanted: a word at the lectern of power. What could he beg
more than not to be shoved aside? It was ironic that as
co-Regent he had a greater power in name than when he had
been the power behind the name; but he was forced to share
it, and to agree that the measures Aspartil—and even
Binatrel—put forward often and urgently were more sensible
than those of his old toadies. But he had lost most of the
deference of those who knew where power lay. He would
never regain it all, but he was convinced that if Dunenli
would only listen he might lay a foundation for a lifetime of
lasting respect.

He had decided against approaching her at night in case he might be taken for some skulker; he waited for the late-afternoon taking-of-waters. As he climbed the ramp he could hear the little children frolicking and spurting water at each other in their huge basin, sometimes screaming or being rebuked by their nurses for unauthorized use of their mild electric shocks. Occasionally some of their elders would use this time to make love, but with the Great Tower threatened by siege the air of tension lay heavy over it and there were few playful roilings behind the doors.

Doors closed behind the Dowager, the Concubine, the Empress; Dunenli and Binatrel separated with a last touching of hands and the Royal heir went inside her suite followed by her attendant, and a guard took his place outside.

He moved respectfully aside as Spinel-beta tapped at that door. It opened a crack and light broke from the windowed room into the dusky hall.

"Who is calling?" the attendant asked.

"Who's there?" Dunenli's voice cried, and the echoes of their voices followed those of closing doors around the ramps to the highest arch.

"It is the Regent, and if you please, I would like to speak to her Highness."

"Is that Spinel-beta? Are you alone?"

Spinel-beta recognized the fear in her voice, and forced himself to keep the exasperation out of his own. "My dear, I am alone except for your guard and your lady. I don't want to intrude on your privacy. Would you come to the door and speak to me for a few moments?"

"No, no! I don't want to speak to you! Stay away from me! Tatri, close the door!"

Beta stared in astonishment at the closed door. "But Dunenli! Child! To speak a civil word to me? Dunenli!"

Dunenli was at the door now, beating savage arms against it. "Get away, away! Can't you understand? I hate you!"

Spinel-beta backed away, appalled. "Hate me? Me?" He stood like a rock with all of her emotions raining down on him. The guard, frightened, summoned Binatrel; at the same

time Aspartil, hearing the noise, came from her rooms next
door, dripping.

"Beta, let me take care of that young woman, and you
speak to Binatrel."

But Spinel-beta crouched staring at them, furious eyes
bulging. "She hates me—and after all I have tried—you have
turned her against me!"

"Oh no, Beta! You have simply never learned how to
try—and I have told her that many times."

"I knew she did not care for me—but so much hate? and
fear?" It seemed to him he recognized terrible things in their
eyes. "Dear Lord of the Sea! She really believes I would hurt
and shame her! And I was Meta-Spinel and she my child and I
carried her in my pouch in silence until she was ready to walk
in freedom! How could it have come to this?"

"Beta . . . dear Beta, you have not been without fault,
but you do not deserve this. I will take care of Dunenli, and
you must let Binatrel help you. We surely would not want to
wake the howling Dowager."

"No! I don't care about that stupid stream of filth! I have
always been alone, and alone is how I stay! Now it is your
turn to keep away from me!"

"Majesty—"

"Binatrel, I am charged and will shock you if you come
near me—and if you should die it will be no loss!" He turned
and scuttled down the ramp with quite astonishing speed.

"That fool!" said Aspartil.

"I'll see he does not harm himself," Binatrel said.

"That is not the one I meant," said Aspartil. She slammed
the door with her own heavy shock-arm. "Dunenli, this is
Aspartil and you will let me in at once!"

Dunenli was cowering by the window. "Don't let him near
me! If he comes in I will run away, I swear."

"You don't have to run away. He has already done that,
and he is a fool too. Dunenli, whatever has made you behave
so? The Emperor insisted that you were intelligent and sensible, and until this moment I agreed with him."

"You don't understand!"

"Dearest, I want to. Spinel-beta is not a very good man, but in this case he was probably only trying to wheedle some assurance from you that you would not cast him aside completely when you took the throne."

"I don't want the throne any more, and I don't want this place! I want Binatrel to take me away from all of it!"

Aspartil watched her for a moment; then she removed her amber armlets, set them on the floor, and raised her left polar arm in the giving-of-trust. "I suspect our mischievous Beta is not the only cause of the outburst. Please hold my arm for a little while and tell me what is in your thought."

Dunenli crept slowly around the pool to take the extended arm of Aspartil in her hands. "O Aspartil, it is so mixed together! I have to be patient with my mother's raging and whining, you and Binatrel are always so busy with plans I am afraid will not help us, the Council is always arguing and pushing, Beta twisting this way and that for more power. Inatrili," she meant the First Concubine, "snarls at me whenever she sees me, everyone says there is to be a war and—and difficult as my father was, all the worst part seems to have drained into Beta and the best gone away with Spinel. And—oh, I am so ashamed—Beta is so obviously disagreeable I have heaped everything on him, so unjust and irrational, when it was aimed at everyone. . ."

"And at me too," Aspartil said gently. "But Dunenli, I have not been unfaithful to Spinel, nor am I a rival for Binatrel. I suggested he ask for you before I learned he had already done so, and after my hope for Spinel's safety my dearest wish is for you to be joined with Binatrel."

"I believe that, and I am so sorry. . ."

"And you see me playing at being Empress and perhaps you think I enjoy it—and Dunenli, there is some truth to it. I understand now why Spinel enjoyed the taste of it before he left. But I have Beta and the others to remind me that a taste is medicine and a path of it is poison. And when Spinel and I put the amber rings on your arms I hope you will realize it too."

"Forgive me, Aspartil. I will apologize to Beta, if he will listen, and try to be more agreeable."

"And cautious," said Aspartil dryly. "There is nothing irrational in that."

Spinel-beta had disappeared before Binatrel could reach him. It seemed as if he had evaporated. Binatrel called on his closest friends among the guard, and they searched the Tower carefully but quietly to avoid alarm. Without result. The puzzle was that he had managed to vanish so completely after only a moment to himself. There was no one on the ramps, in or out; or on the shore. There was the great wide sea, but adjustment to an environment so salty would have taken time. Binatrel did not think Beta was suicidal; he was more likely to sulk somewhere until his rage bubbled itself away. Still, Binatrel was ready to call out Divers and send them into the shore waters when something else occurred to him.

The Tower had many windings and eccentricities, most well known to its inhabitants, like the "secret" passage between the chambers of Emperor and Empress. They were secrets only to children who played games of chase and hiding in them, and since most were quite safe, adults generally knew what their children were up to and did not worry about them. Binatrel considered his own childhood, which was not so very far into the past. He went back to Dunenli's door, looked down the ramp in the direction where he had last seen Beta hurrying, and followed.

About two hundred and fifty degrees around, almost one whole floor below and not far above ground level there was a small archway. This led to a number of adjoining storerooms, a chamber with an old broken hoist for lifting heavy materials to the upper floors, and at the very end one small room, now empty, which had once been used to store old lecterns fit only for scrap lumber. A huge stone block forming part of the corner in this room had shifted and cracked by a collapse in the sandstone foundation, leaving a gaping fissure. The crack opened slantwise into the winding caverns of fresh water pumped into the Tower. The caverns were also partly dammed by the sluice-gates to the sea, and the waters swirled dangerously. This had been a true secret, and the children of

Binatrel's day, when his father was a Councillor, had used to
crawl through and swim in the plunging maelstroms. When
one of the children got seriously injured the game had been
stopped, and the fissure closed up. But because Qsaprinli
stonework was as fine as its woodwork, even then it had been
a matter of pride not to use mortar in the Tower. Workmen
dug out the crumbled stone and replaced it with a hard one
small enough to set in, filled the spaces with pebbles, and
evened the floor out with a wooden slab. No one knew how
long the opening existed; perhaps Meta-Spinel had slid
through it as a child. And perhaps Spinel-beta was sitting in
this deserted place, sulking in the dark. Binatrel called for an
oil lamp and prepared to risk Beta's anger for the sake of his
safety.

He was astonished to find, instead of a snappish Beta, the
room half-lit by a greenish glow from the faulted corner, the
wooden slab pushed aside, and the opening emptied of stone
and pebbles.

"Lord of the Sea," his Guardsman said, "has the man
done something as foolish as this?"

"I don't know. I would never have thought he was strong
enough—but there is something strange and dangerous happening." He handed back the lamp and immediately began to
slide backward down the opening.

"My Lord, wait until I call the others!"

"Call the others, but I can't wait!"

Spinel-beta *had* intended to crouch moping in the dark
forgotten chamber. He had chosen it because the opening to
this particular oubliette was almost invisible in the dim hall,
and he did not want to be caught up with and placated. He had
not even intended to go into the farthest room because it was
so dark and neglected, but had been fuming away his rage on
the platform of the old hoist when he heard a peculiar scrap-
ing, and on investigating was even more shocked than Binatrel to find the slab pushed away and, by the light that was let
through, the dust on the floor disturbed by footprints: *alien
footprints*. It was wisdom to report this immediately, but his

mixture of anger and perplexity sent him slithering down the
fissure in the old familiar way of the child Meta-Spinel. He
had an easier time of it than Binatrel would, for his body was
smaller, and because of what he called the "constant nag-
ging" of Spinel-alpha he had kept up exercises even more
strenuous than those of the military, so was quite fit.

For a moment, as his body hit the waters below after their
long slide, he felt the delicious sense of freedom he had
known as a true child. The caverns boomed and eddied in a
strange light, turned greenish by the thin layer of glistening
mold on the roofs. He breasted the whirlpools with powerful
kicks, and was reaching for a stone bracket to pull himself up
on, when his foot caught something that should not have been
there. Half-supported by the shelf, he pulled at it, and was
horrified to find himself grasping the polar arm of a dead
Qsaprinil, a guardswoman with a spear driven though her
body.

Evidently she had been patrolling the sluice-gates
when. . .

Alien footprints.

He had forgotten he was so close on the back of the alien.
Was this the invasion at last? No, for then there would have
been great forces with heavier weapons. This was a scout
who had been interrupted and, not knowing how these currents behaved, believed the body would merely be carried out
to sea. He let go the arm, and could not bear to watch the body
whirling and sinking. Pulled himself back on the scree border
and rolled his eyes anxiously, but there were so many twisting places to hide in . . . yet the alien knew of his presence,
he was sure.

And was assured when the upright figure stepped from
behind a rock pillar on the shore across the underground
river, speargun aimed.

But Beta, small and twisted, was not an easy target. He
leaped into the water, knowing by instinct and practice ways
to move that countered the swallow and gulp of the currents,
and raised protuberant eyes hardly different from the bubbles

on the surface. The water was not roiled enough to make him invisible to the man in mask and tanks, and the aim lowered.

Beta prepared to dive, until he heard the rattle and splash behind him, and the spear rose. He dared not turn, nor was the light bright enough to register much on his primitive-eyes, but he knew that the one behind him, if under aim, must be a Qsaprinil.

His polar arms were already charged by fear and anger; exercise and training in the martial arts gave him one more weapon. Almost without thinking he diverted volumes of water to the proximal sinuses behind his charging areas, raised his arms, contracted muscles that sent twin streams of water across the charging areas and converging on the spear-man. The alien leaped convulsively—his teeth cracked to-gether so loudly they could be heard above the roar of waters—and fell forward, head submerged.

There was another rattle and clatter of Qsaprinli behind him, but Spinel-beta turned, intent only on discovering whom he had saved.

Binatrel!

What a terrible, stupid embarrassment! He could not re-fuse the arm extended to help pull him ashore, but all his resentment flooded back, though his charge had dissipated. Now the fool would think he had done some idiotic good deed to set himself to rights with Dunenli!

"Your Majesty, you have saved my life!"

"Be good enough not to thank me. I hardly knew what I was doing."

Binatrel said gently and firmly, "That makes no difference whatever."

"There is a dead guardswoman down there, killed by a spear. Her body must be brought up, so that she can be honored—and we must have *that* one, to examine. Make sure you find his speargun."

"We can't bring them up through that opening," said one of the guard.

"No, you fool, we will go round by the sea."

For once Binatrel was content that Beta was his old snappish self. The latter, unharmed, struck out through the sluice-gates and round about to the shore, leaving the others to follow.

"I said they might already be here." Aspartil, not squeamish, stared at the body stretched out on the shore. "He must have been reconnoitering alone, or others would have come to help him, and he was certainly not an ESP, or he would have not been surprised when Binatrel appeared."

"He could have been sacrificed to make it appear he was alone," said Binatrel.

"What shall we do with this body then, your Majesty?"

"Leave him in the sea," said Beta, "but not weighted, so it will seem he was caught in a whirlpool and battered against rocks. I am sure he will be searched for."

"Those bones in his head are broken, but not the mask he is wearing to see through."

"Those are called *teeth* and are used to grind what aliens take in for food. They cracked during his convulsion. I hate to do such a thing even to this one, but we must tear and beat the body to make it look truly battered. The speargun would have sunk and been lost, so we may keep that and see if we can reproduce it; it is not very complicated."

"It is good that he did not come at night."

Aspartil said, "We don't know he did not come at night, or what he discovered then. These men with their silent flying machines can make themselves invisible at night, and we have no defense against them. But we will have to find their base. I can't believe they do all their reconnaissance from orbit."

Beta, unmindful of emotions past, had one thought: the alien. The man was not one he recognized from the group who had come earlier, or those who had come at other times, though he could not tell very many apart, and might have been mistaken. But this man must still be connected with the expedition from Calidor—and all of them surely knew about *him*: the one with the twisted body so easily identified, who had controlled the Emperor's power. Even if Qsaprinli looked alike to all Solthrees they must recognize *him*. The man with the speargun must have recognized *him,* the old ally of Calidor. And he had been ready to kill.

The men of Calidor were his enemies, with no hope otherwise. Enemies.

"We can evacuate to the sea, but no matter how far we readapt we will still need some fresh water," said Aspartil. "It would be very difficult to organize ourselves. In the forests we would have to keep near water systems and set up a supply line: that leaves us visible. If we hide in the mines we get no standing water with life-forms. And however we travel those wood-burning wagons are ridiculous compared to what our enemies have. I am sorry all those Emperors did not accept some GalFed technology when it was offered them."

Spinel-beta said, "Whatever technology the Calidorians offered, I am afraid we would not have been left alive to make use of it."

"Our society worked very well when we did not need to do battle," Binatrel said. "Once we begin piling up *things* it will be hard to give them up."

"There is an enemy on this world," Aspartil said, "and if we have no better defense than we have now we are committing suicide."

Spinel-beta snorted. "At the moment the only alien weapon we have is one speargun. I might as well speak to the Ironworkers and see if it can be reproduced."

"No, Regent," said the Master of Forges, "begging your Majesty's pardon. We might manage the spears and the tubing, but we don't have the equipment to make these steel springs which are both strong and flexible. Also, the aliens have their digits on heavily muscled arms; our hands are on the weakest limbs, and lack strength to pull the trigger repeatedly. In addition, the mechanism is driven by explosives and would recoil badly."

"But we must have something!" Beta cried. "What about our catapults?"

"You know your history better than I, Regent. They took six days to construct, six men to operate, and twelve to move. They have not been used for hundreds of standard years, since the Great War."

"Five hundred and thirty-one years," said Beta resignedly.

"And as for this spear, it looks like a good weapon for close fighting, but to be thrown it still needs alien strength. We might make some lighter ones of wood."

"Presuming they have an orbiting ship, like the ones who came before," Binatrel said, "they may have underwater shuttles, but life in them would be as awkward as we would find it under water. Perhaps a large raft, something more complicated than the kind we use to cross the bays. . ."

"No, no!" cried Aspartil. "That is all too clumsy. I am no strategist, but if I were commander I still say I would have a land base in a place I could survive in—a place my enemies do not need or use, from which I could send out my forces."

"What do we have then?" Binatrel asked. "Ice, rock, hilly forest where we are uncomfortable even when we are so much more adaptable than they—"

"But they are already working off Calidor, which by all reports is a barren moon," said Spinel-beta.

"That is a base from which they may establish other bases," said Binatrel. "Not one they can use to send a single reconnoiterer. But where? Dear Lord of the Sea, we do not know all of our own land, but we have all the maps Galactic Federation sent copies of, in case we wished to join them one day. Why do we not find someone to read them for us?"

"And who would that be?" Aspartil asked tartly.

the Hierophant reversed

In the little observatory, a short distance away, lived the ancient astronomer. Qsaprinli science had detoured around him, but by night, he still peered with weak eyes through his primitive telescope at the misty stars, though he had forgotten their names.

"Forgive me, your Majesties, but I could never read the alien documents, nor could I now, even if my eyes were good enough. I had a young assistant once, but he retired, I don't know where."

"But the maps exist, do they not?" Beta snarled.

"Oh indeed, by the Basin of Heaven, they do, along with the translations my—"

"Your assistant made translations?"

"Of course. What would it be worth keeping them for, otherwise?"

Binatrel and Aspartil dragged the long chest up the narrow winding ramp from the cellar. Awkward but not heavy, it was made of thin metal well waterproofed and filled with rolls of charts: the GalFed ones, of fine material as fresh as the day they had been sealed, and the Qsaprinli translations, of rough beaten papyrus, just possible to unroll without cracking. The assistant, with his reed pens and home-made inks, had faithfully, albeit waveringly, copied every line of the continental chart, reproducing in translation the co-ordinates and remarks of the original, but had neglected the segmented whole-globe map which showed merely that except for a few protruding rocks there were no land masses other than the Two Continents.

"This at least I remember," said the old man, "if you would just hold down the corners, please . . . here is the eastern escarpment, with its cascades, and our ancestors lived in the tide-pools at the foot of it. The only place where Solthrees might live in any comfort is this valley to the north of the scarp's peak. It is mainly grassy, and has some soil where they thought they could grow crops. You can see the indication of its depth. GalFed asked permission to buy that piece of land and offer it to colonists, but Spinel the Fourteenth—or was it the Sixteenth?—"

"Refused because he did not want interlopers," said Beta,

"and quite rightly."

Aspartil gave him a sidelong glance, which he did not notice. "I wonder why we never considered living there."

"Well, you see, with the depth and greenery the air was denser, and we would have had to adjust to that; then there was the Great River running down from the mountains in the north, and it divided among the ridges above the eastern rim. One branch ran over the rim and became the cascades that freshened the tide-pools below, and the other ran through the valley to the ocean, cutting passages through the southern and eastern cliffs—it is all on the map, Majesty, as you can see. There was no standing water to grow the life-forms we feed on, and in those days I doubt we had the means of damming such a heavy flow."

"When was it last surveyed?" Binatrel asked.

"No more than forty-five or fifty years ago . . . the cascades had shrunk, as I recall, and so had the pools below—we could make the shore livable if we needed the space. We did not climb the escarpment because it is slow going, and too hard to reach and use. The western land is very humped. Even if the polar ice has retreated and shrunk the river the rainfall would keep it flowing and still make it a hard place for us to live."

"But not for aliens," said Aspartil. Perfect for aliens.

"We threw it away! Simply threw it away!" Beta fumed. "We could have cut our way through and built a fortress on the heights any time these last years."

Aspartil said, "It is hard of access, difficult to live in, and we have no weapons. That is no fortress for us. We must find out if it is a base for aliens. And in the meantime fill up that dangerous opening right here with stones, pebbles, *and* plenty of cement—no matter how the Stonemasters' Guild pops their eyes."

the Page of Cups

Palander was an uncle and foster-father of Aspartil's, and as fiercely against the exercise of power as Meta-Spinel had been—and Beta still was—for it. When he heard that Aspartil had been chosen as Second Concubine he went into a great rage and set out to vent it on Meta-Spinel—in words—without regard to consequences. But he had to wait his turn with the other suppliants, and among these was an assassin. Palander, without harm to anyone, forestalled him: he did not care for that kind of power seizure either.

Meta-Spinel, without knowing his feelings, offered Palander a ransom's worth of reward, which he refused. Aspartil's pleading persuaded him to absorb his bile, and he asked for work in the mines, where the pay was good. His children were grown, and when his wife died he quit work and used his savings to build a boat and weave a sail; morning to evening, and sometimes nights, he trolled the shore with nets to gather flotsam for drying, grinding and fertilizing the saplings planted in reforestation areas. All his life he had worked for others. Now the old curmudgeon was his own man.

His relationship with Aspartil continued loyal and loving, and it seemed logical, even to Beta, that Aspartil would choose Palander for the most dangerous task on land or sea: to scout for the base.

He was tough: because he had trained himself to go without changing water for great lengths of time his waterskin was ineradicably folded and opaque, almost as strong as his horn belly which was hard as Qsaprinli wood.

The Council allowed three days for the aliens to search for their lost reconnoiterer; they did not want Palander running into armed parties. When summoned he had asked to be told as little as possible; having heard all the gossip he knew what was going on and how to keep his thoughts to himself. Aspartil simply told him to examine the escarpment and the valley to see if they were suitable for colonizing; he replied, "Certainly, your Highnesses," with his usual acerbity, and left before they could offer to pay him. When he came back he would ask for what he wanted, if he could decide what that would be.

At evening he set out without giving notice, trimming his
sail to the southeast wind. He washed and put out his net with
the usual practised hand and floated steadily through the
night clothed in the swirling mist. The takings were not very
good in the east, but he did not want them; when the net was
filled enough to slow him he emptied it and went on.

The winds were good; by sunrise he had completed a
quarter of his sail and made his first significant catch. A small
empty container of a bright blue material neither wood nor
metal. Both color and matter were strange to Qsaprinel. It
was in swifter current than his usual harvest of weeds and
small decaying corpses and he would not have seen it so far
away if it had not glittered in a sun ray pushing through a
cloud rift. He flattened himself to the planking as if resting
and let the sail shift to idle his way outward and scoop the
object from starboard. He turned it this way and that, then
made a gesture of throwing it back in the sea; it landed in his
locker. He reset the sail and kept away from the shore; his net
caught much less. There was nothing suspicious in this behavior: he knew many a troller paid by the day who took a
pleasant nap in the shadow of the sail without doing much
work. But he was uneasy: aliens must have been camping on
the escarpment quite a while for their jetsam to come so far;
people who threw their trash over the cliffs had too good a
view of the sea to suit him. He would have to take to the land.

He veered northeast toward a cove he knew and on this
course found two other strange objects. One was an oblong
slab of sawn wood, a table or door suitable for aliens. The
water had not rotted it, but it was very grey and cracked by
weathering, how old he could not tell. This he left alone. The
other was a foamy white block, much smaller, with strange
hollows. He stared at it and thought hard while it bumped
against the raft, before he picked it up and stowed it away. It
did not seem to be good for anything—*unless it had been
used to pack something that fitted the hollows*. Enough of
collecting; he hid the two objects in the rotten mess in the
bottom of his locker. It stank most satisfactorily; he doubted
many would want to come near it.

At the cove he dragged his anchor rope over the pebbly beach because he could not pull the squatty boat ashore, and hitched to a tree growing in a clump of reeds. After a few minutes he found a good pool in which to change water, but did not turn back from it; the moonless tides were low, and he had left nothing worth stealing, except the craft. He valued it highly, but the rope, which he had twined himself, was as strong as a chain, his knot gripping as a lock.

An hour's climb through reed, scrub and forest, brought him hails from foresters he had not seen in many years: he was a hard person to forget. Another couple of hours climbing to the northeast brought him to a mining storage depot, where he found more old acquaintances. They did not mind that he answered their greetings with grunts: they knew him. He got a lift on one of the old chuffing flatbeds along a stony road to a mine he had worked in as a much younger man. It was near evening. The workers here were as young as he had been then, and did not know him, except from old stories. He jumped off when the wagon could go no further, and set off due east, by the way no one took, toward the lost valley. Twice during the night he slept for an hour; the land was beginning to ripple. There was a brief and violent storm; he kept to the open, admired the lightning and refreshed himself in a rain-pool before it drained off. He went on this way, day and night again, by ever stonier and more broken land, and by next morning arrived within a day of the valley.

A piece of technology which would have helped immeasurably was a fine small telescope Qsaprinel had acquired in trade, the only one of its kind. It was better than the old astronomer's, but hard to carry and impossible to hide. Aspartil had urged it on him but he refused; if the enemy found such an instrument on him he would be dead. His eyes were good enough.

His first introduction to the Colony was its noise. The sun burned off the mist at this altitude and the ground was nearly dry on the floor of stone and scrub. The noise almost dis-

tracted him from the poles. But the western light was back of
him, he saw clearly, and the appearance of the poles kept him
from hurrying to find the source of the noise. He stopped to
watch; his body, dark and crinkled, blended with the terrain.

The poles were set on the crests of the escarpment and
obviously marked boundaries. The nearest was what Palander would call twelve dranels away, a Solthree about fifteen
meters, and they were somewhat further apart from each
other. They were made likely of some dull metal, and on top
of each was a thing that turned back and forth. It looked like
an eye, and Palander caught a star of light from the late sun on
a moving lens. The Empress's spy knew little of technology,
but he did infer that someone in the Colony saw what those
eyes saw.

He changed plans. He had intended to wait out the night in
hiding for surveillance by day, but he was afraid of those
eyes, and suspected that they could see at night. The distracting noise might stop with darkness, but the watching would
go on.

The spy-eyes did not sweep the area at the same speeds and
directions; this was not strange to him: any Qsaprinil's eyes
could turn like that, but not so far apart. Perhaps there were
blind spots in their survey: a small mistake he could profit
from. He waited for the two nearest lenses to turn apart, but
dared not wait long, because the sun was on the horizon and
he had yet to see the Colony.

He slid sideways in the shadows until he was at a greater
vantage point between two scanners. They might also be
sensitive to heat, but they would not get much from him.

Now. He found what he judged to be the blind spot and
scuttled to the peak of the rim, knowing he must take in all at
one intense look.

In the valley was a cluster of buildings, not made of stone
but of wood and other materials he did not know, some
perhaps of cement. The noisy machine was a great metal
thing that operated by itself, rolling to crunch gravel before it
and lay out smooth road behind it among the buildings. There
were men with guns, a couple of twelves, perhaps,

guarding—or threatening?—workers supervising other rock crunchers; animals, smaller than aliens, larger than native mammals, with four limbs and tails. The buildings were of different sizes and he was ignorant of their uses, but they seemed finished, and he judged that the roads would complete the Colony; no vessel was landed at the moment, but the armed men already suggested a base. There was no free water in sight: it would be channeled or piped, and that would suggest permanence. He was grateful, at least, not to see a single Qsaprinil among the workers; no local slaves—yet.

Spying done, he pulled back quickly. The lenses were apart, but he did not know whether there were ESPs among the aliens.

As he reached the shelter of a bush one of the four-legged creatures leaped at him; it was making loud noises which had been drowned by the machines. The big land mammal had savage teeth and a collar of metal spikes, all capable of ripping even his tough skin. He flipped on his back with terrific speed, and it landed on his horn belly with a harmless thump; though Palander's eyes were pressed back against the ground he did not need sight to wrap his electric arms around it.

He did not kill it—no use leaving evidence—but left it stunned. In a little while it would drag itself back to its mates. The moment Palander pushed it away the noise of the machines stopped and he scrambled off. He was not quite sure whether he had been lucky: an ESP, even if it had missed him, might probe that creature . . . then he reasoned: why waste precious ESPs on a building project? With ESPs there was no need for spy-eyes and guard animals.

The Colony was nearly finished. Dangerous things would happen soon. More aliens would come, with guns *and* ESPs—and Palander had hills to climb and seas to sail. Why should that young snip of a niece choose an old body like him to go far and slow?

Because she knew he would find the way.

He travelled all night, turning south, by a different way.

He had avoided the most easterly Station because he wanted secrecy; now he wanted to spread knowledge.

In the morning he heard the sound of a machine again, but this was one of the old chuffers. A land without imports or fossil fuels was left with wood-chips.

Palander kneeled on the cleared track in the way of the vehicle, and when the impatient forester stopped, called, "Young one!"

"What is it, old man? You are in my way!"

"Have you heard of a bad-tempered old fellow called Palander, used to be known in these parts?"

"I've heard tell of him, that I have, man. Why?"

"And how great a liar he was and how many troubles he caused?"

"I've heard he caused a great deal of trouble to himself times he told truths nobody wanted to hear! Now what?"

"Good. I am that man and I am on a most urgent errand for my niece."

"The Empress? What do you want of me, Palander?"

"Have you heard of the alien visitors?"

"Of course. Who has not? Do you want me to help you fight them?"

"No, no! Don't set your waters boiling! Go as quickly as you can to the Double Rapids Station and tell them to relay a radio message to Aspartil in my name. Say: *Colony base complete*. She will understand and must know sooner than I can reach her. You and your helpers will be rewarded."

"Our enemies may overhear."

"The frequency is low, the language poorly understood. We will take the risk."

Palander stopped at the Station long enough to change water and went on his way without rest. By evening and morning and evening again he found his craft where he had left it. The smell of his locker was too much even for him, and he cleaned it out, discarding the artifacts because it was too late for them to matter. Then he unhitched and gave his sail to the winds and himself to fate.

"Complete!" cried Aspartil. "I was right. Lord of the Sea protect him!"

"The attack will come here—and soon," said Binatrel. "The messenger tells me there were rewards promised in your name by Palander. It seems four persons were involved."

"Oh, give them what they want!" Aspartil dropped from her stand, pulled off one of her armlets and sent it spinning. "Wood for houses, jewels for show, service in this household if they are fools enough to want it. I doubt they will have much time to enjoy it."

Spinel-beta slipped away. The only extremes of emotion he cared about were his own. The fear-desire of aliens was still most complicated and painful. They had tried to kill *him*, the only one who had ever welcomed them. He found himself drawn down, downward to those vaults where soldiers stood guard with fragile spears by half-closed sluices; many more of them now, and changed often. Beta did not even look at them. Their loyalty was not his and he was fated not to belong with aliens. He was alone. He crawled to a rock ledge where he would not be noticed, eyes half-closed and sunk.

The shift had not finished when one of the thick double panels of the wooden seagate exploded, tossing up six or seven men, and a troop of aliens in diving gear stormed the opening. They were firing not spears but flame guns, and the flames did not drown in water but clung and ate the flesh of screaming victims.

Beta crouched unseen and paralyzed. His eyes popped. An attack in daylight! A few aliens were contemptuous of his whole world!

And the defenders had no weapons except the light spears they drove and guided with tiny hands along their shock arms. Beta could not think. His captains called their men to rally, but defense was a hideous joke. The flames over and under the waters and the horrible cries of the wounded drove the caverns into a savage turbulence flickering with orange and yellow light.

A shape rose before him, and Beta saw a grinning face and a gun. Hands curled into small knotted fists, eyes shrunk and slitted, Beta waited for torment and death.

> *the Diviner, sighing, waits for death too*
> *and turns up the Nine of Wands*

These things had not happened when the Locksmith arrived in Agassiz's garden. Before that, in a time difficult to measure by the way it curves among worlds and suns, Dunbar Macpherson Kinnear, co-ordinating Sector 492, began to track his persecutor Thorndecker, the enemy he had never seen. He had the blessing of Bengstrom, a Supervisor of Directors, the encouragement of Narinder Singh, a Director of Sector Co-ordinators, the competence of sub-Director Ptrilititi, and a fair supply of funds; but he did not have what he needed. Because Narinder Singh's division covered Sectors 491-5 with a total of 487 worlds.

"Dun, for the twentieth time, I have not got personnel to spare! Qsaprinel's certification has not come in—"

"But we expect—"

"I know we expect. I am certain, sure, positive! But Qsaprinel is not yet a member whichever way you turn it and our best gen tells us Thorndecker is still on Fthel IV—and that is near, while Qsaprinel is far. Dun, what can I do? I have wars sputtering among half my worlds, another third snarling and crouched to spring, three hundred and seventy-six requests for peacekeeping forces and two hundred and thirty-eight for Observers. I can't fill half of either! Your sector is the most peaceful we have right now—I pray it stays that way—*and Qsaprinel is not a member!*"

"But still—"

"I know you are right, but I can do nothing. The Locksmith would be a treasure to me, but he is attached to you because of that stupid Praximf that does not even want him. And we have put ourselves out to keep your Cats safe. It is little enough, but there is no more. You may have to hire mercenaries the way Thorndecker does."

Kinnear was taken aback. GalFed hiring mercenaries? Why not? They had paid plenty of slimy informants. But those were not warriors. The thought came unbidden: There are thousands around here sitting on their butts. . .

:And they are not warriors either.:

"Maybe we could suit up Bengstrom and send her out as a tank."

Narinder Singh laughed. "She'd probably enjoy it."

Warriors. Why not say soldiers? Soldiers were like police and civil servants, who played a lot of concertos on electronic data processors. Warriors were primitive, tribal defenders of territory on Ungruwarkh, Qsaprinel, Xirifor. . .

Kinnear had a very large staff and they were not warriors. They were clerks, as he was a clerk, a thin-haired middle-aged man who exercised to keep strong and fit.

He found staff with light workloads and dumped on them. Drove them here and there, digging out every aspect of Thorndecker's history, unearthing every root-hair to its source. He thought of Qsaprinel, where hundreds of thousands of intelligent beings had nothing but their own bodies for weapons. Like Ungruwarkh.

He got reports from IV: his Cats, his spies, his Emperor were alive, repelling attacks he could not prevent.

"I believe I can do something," said the Locksmith.

"Like what?"

"Go to Fthel IV, to begin. After that, we can try to plan, perhaps."

A curious trail developed on Sol III; the Thorndecker dynasty had its origin there, and Kinnear was rewarded by his local contacts. The great mansion in Florida, south of Naples, which had been locked and left deserted, was broken into by vandals. They regretted it, because they found the sub-cellar vault far from empty, and when the police caught them they were gibbering. No one knew what to do with the evidence. It was photographed and destroyed.

An old man in a drunk tank not far away claimed to be the

former assistant of a famous scientist who made what he called "fish-men." A farm laborer heard of this on the local news and said, "Say, I seen one of them in a carnival," and called the station in time to get his face on a screen.

Though the place with the alarm-fence belonged to the Feds even they could not hush it up then. But it was a three-days' wonder. The Human Rights Court had taken care of it long ago, and there was plenty of other news, as always.

Kinnear gave little thought to this strange trace until Bellingrose reported the presence and story of Quattro. "Two hundred of those—whatsits—aquamen?—and all disappeared? dead? Just what we could use on that water-world. Some luck."

"I think . . . I know of some like them." Uivingra was a Xirifer woman, a hairless grey-blue hominid, usually uncomfortable in the plastic body-skin she wore to wet the huge branching gills growing from elbow to hip. Like most Xirifri she was a low-range ESP but there was nothing low about her intelligence. It was too restless for her tribal world, and though Kinnear was grateful for her services he felt guilty, because her world needed her more than he. But with her drive and passion she had suffocated there as she would have shrivelled naked in dry air.

"Uivingra! What did you say?"

"Well, I've seen—oh, maybe twenty of them."

"Where in hell did you see twenty!"

"I don't know how they got there, but they turned up at our Embassy on Four and we hired them as guards and performers for the pearl-diving exhibitions . . . I don't know any more about them, but they look—they look exactly like the—the ones in the holos."

"Your world's out of our division. . ."

"My people keep reminding me. But this is between you and me, ahi?" The words teased a bit, and Kinnear grinned because she, with her purple gills and the two teats centered one above the other on her belly, was as sexless to him as he in his pink hairy skin was to her.

"How do they work out?"

"The Frogs? Honest and capable. No other ESPs."

"Frogs . . . we need people. Underwater people would be so . . . you're not alienated from the Xirifri—"

"My brother and my man are in the Embassy."

"Maybe we could persuade the Embassy to hire guards elsewhere for a while, or expand the pearl market with their overstocks." The giant oysters and their great blue baroque pearls were part of Xirifor's raison d'être as a GalFed member. The arrangement was no great source of pride to GalFed, but it had saved a world from death by tribal warfare, disease and invasion. "I'll see if Singh can get Bengstrom onto that. Your man and your brother are too close. The Tribes wouldn't like it—but hell, nepotism must be good for something."

Uivingra could not smile because her mouth was an almost rigid tube with a leathery tongue, but her eye-membranes flickered. "We are not all stupid over there, Kinnear. I have many exogamous mating connections. I think your problem is in recruiting your fishmen."

"It is. I'm not worried about the Xirifri."

"Perhaps Quattro could do it for you."

"From what I've heard I suspect I'm going to need them to handle him."

Kinnear stared at the hard copy for a moment before he threw it in the disposal: XENOBI READY TO GO WHERE YOU WANT AND DO WHAT YOU NEED.

Good! Fine! Pipe all three of them aboard. He sighed. The Locksmith, meaning well, had fished out his only friends. And . . . three more were three more. He answered: CHOOSE YOUR POISON.

The Locksmith did not offer any of the people with whom he usually did business; he didn't trust them. And he knew Kinnear was going to do his own funny business in his own way.

"Singh, when the *Zarandu* lands she's dumping how many embassy crews from our division—fifteen or eighteen?"

"Nineteen."

"And how many embassies scared shitless of terrorists?"

"Four. How many of the rest are you planning to strip the guards from?"

"No stripping. When there's fifteen guards per twelve embassy members, we liberate three. Leaves them one to one. And we pay."

"The ratio's more likely twelve to ten. You'll get twenty-five at most—and Dun, I'll have to tell Bengstrom."

"I know."

"There's no more to spare for you."

"That too."

Elaborately casual: "You haven't mentioned a ship for yourself."

"Because you know. The *Zarandu*. We have freighting privileges. We'll do the real work with two crew lifeboats and a pilot's emergency that are as fast as anything slower than light. All legitimate: their ships are being refitted and I got there fastest with the most credit."

"They won't hold many."

"You keep telling me I can't have many—and don't worry, I won't ask for more." He paused. "If there's an emergency at Port Central on Four when *Zarandu* comes in, I'll have to free my men if they ask for reinforcements."

"Ask *you?*"

"Because I'm going. I have holiday time coming and you'll have to jug me to stop me. Stop pretending you didn't know. I'm not changing my mind. Ptrilititi can take care of my work with an eyestalk and two tentacles."

"You should realize by now my left hand doesn't *always* want to know—and be careful what you say about your job. What about an emergency with the *Zarandu?*"

"If Thorndecker *is* still on Four, he'll want it—and I'd rather have him there than heading for Qsaprinel."

"I have some connections for you," said Uivingra. "No questions."

"Good. Have the pictures transmitted holo in all their

grisly glory. For the Frogs—um, I presume they don't mind being called that?''

"No. It bothered them when they were young, but now they seem rather proud of it.''

"I guess they had no choice. Also, have them told everything within your clearance.''

Singh was scratching in his beard.

I never knew we had freighting privileges on *Zarandu* . . . hm, it seems we do now—but I don't think I'll mention that to Bengstrom for a while.

THREYHA 523 TO KINNEAR 492: THE BIG SQUATS WILL PASS CERTIFICATION WITHIN SIX HOURS. SCRAMBLE.

The screen blanked. Kinnear scrambled and put a button in his ear. A robot voice said: Confirmed. Your. Skyhook. On. The. Big. Z. Four. Days. Standard. *beep* Ferry. Departs. One-point-five. Hours. *beep* Now. You. Owe. Me. One. Lover. Boy. *beep* Wipe. *beep*.

Kinnear pushed the wipe, removed the button and took from his shelf a small bag containing depilatory, tooth cleaner and a change of underwear.

"Ptrilitititi, give me a voucher for as much as you can, refer messages to Evangel's Green on Four, and wish me happy holidays.''

Ptrilitititi lifted one eye on a stem. :*Can I put your vacation pay in the pot, dear?*:

"If necessary.''

He sat on the dock in the sun with his knees pulled up and his arms wrapped around them. He had let a Xirifer summon the divers by the esp they were used to; it was lunch hour, with few tourists about, and they rose from the water one by one, stopping to honk the gouts of brine from their noses. The water here was saltier than their original world's.

Quattro, he had heard, was squat and muscular, but these

differed in build as any Solthrees might: tall, short, broad,
narrow. Some were thin but none fat. One had slightly
negroid features, and one a very Semitic nose. There were
eight women, thirteen men. Women, slightly smaller and
with more surface to the kilo, might have perished sooner in
the wide oceans, if all had escaped that way. He had esped
them—to a limit. No children; they would not have children
like themselves. (If allowed, Quattro would have loved his
child, but.) Uivingra had been right. There were no bent
ones; few conflicts.

They were independent and practical: he would pay for
services rendered, but the Xirifri paid by the hour; no reason
to waste money meeting him at the Port. But they sat without
restlessness, glistening in the sun, some paddling feet in the
water. Frogs and Xirifri liked cold water. Here it was tepid,
the air just bearable. Kinnear, in light clothing, was flushed
with heat and hurry, conscious again how pink he was among
grey and blue-grey.

The nearest man spoke. Hooknose. His name was Fouad.
"We saw the pictures and heard the story. You want us to
chase your toy mastermind. I suppose he's big in the crime
area, and I know Quattro's had it tough. We liked him well
enough, but that's no reason we should die for you. You
should know, you're the ESP. Except for Quattro we don't
care much for ESPs."

"You're insulting your employers," Kinnear said mildly.
"I wanted to put the proposition and let you think of it for a
while."

"We thought about it when we heard about it."

"And you all agree?"

"Yeah," in rough chorus.

"As I should know? I asked a friend of mine who knows
you what you were like and she said: honest and capable. I
esped for that and she's right. Also if you had children.
Nothing else. I want you because I need fighters. There aren't
many I can get and you're tough. You've survived. The
business is a nothing by Galactic standards. No medals, no
speeches. The world in question is mostly under water and its

people look like big crabs—and *they* don't care much for
Solthrees. But there's a million and a half of them and they
are people. They work and love and argue. Everybody agrees
about that. GalFed does.

"But you—you were lab animals, and lately you've been
freaks and exhibits, like the pinhead in the carnival tank. You
may work and love and argue, but the ones who come to
watch you think: *freaks*. You don't need esp to know that."

The eyes burned at him, brown, black, blue, grey: the
chessplayer, the mathematician, the flutist. They were capable of killing. Yes.

"I don't think there's anything noble about fighting. It's a
filthy thing sometimes *people* have to do or be killed. GalFed
doesn't send forces out to fight often, but when they do they
send *people*. You've been around all kinds. You should
know."

After a moment's silence, the woman near Fouad, Settima, said, "If we did this I suppose you'd have your big ESP
Quattro in charge of everything."

Kinnear grinned at the display of misplaced jealousy.
"Quattro's been scarred to the bone and I don't think he'd
want to look at a Frogman right now. I need to use him
because of his esp, but you'd have to convince him to work
with *you*."

He unfolded himself and stood. "You change your mind,
tell the fellow who brought me. You have three hours." He
turned.

"Hey, man!" One at the dock's end had risen to his knees.
Esteban. "Do we get arms or is this bare-knuckle?"

Kinnear faced them again. "Stunners to spearguns to flamers. Anything you can handle. There's no time to train you
and no big stuff. You just have to remember we're a *defensive
force helping by request,* not going in for a shoot-out."

"You don't know if there'll be an attack."

"Oh, there'll be an attack—may already have been. The
moon of the neighboring sun has a base aimed dead on, and
they've made a sortie already. Otherwise I wouldn't be
here."

Hopefully: "Outfits?" Their clothes were rough and they dove only in loinstraps, even women, whose almost prepubic buds were hardly noticeable.

"You'll get all that at Port Central. I couldn't bring twenty-one suits in assorted sizes."

Fouad said, "Give us an hour to knock off. Where's your ride?"

"I'll come round by water in the skimmer. It'll hold all of you."

"Had us figured, hah? Maybe you've been doing more esping than you say."

Kinnear shook his head. "I had hope. Honest and capable is all I wanted to know. The rest is none of my business."

The pearl divers watched Kinnear's diminishing figure and did not move. He had told one lie. He had esped further, perhaps unconsciously, and they gave him the benefit of the doubt, because the thought had strayed from him under the ferocity of their combined gaze. He had acknowledged the lawyer, the doctor, the architect, the chessplayer. His warriors.

"And he'd still let us die," Settima said.

"Yeah," said Esteban. "As people."

Kinnear and his group had half a world to cross, and by the time they reached Port Central there was a mess of blood being scoured by machines, but only two men had died. Neither of his. His relief was tempered by shame.

:*No need. It is their line of business*,: said Threyha from her sector office, where workmen were trying not to tread on her tail while they repaired shattered panels. :*Your Emperor Spinel is safe. I will show you what he looks like but not where he is right now.*:

:*I didn't even know he was coming. How*—:

She told him. :*That young Emerald is quite the lady, and her man is not utterly unworthy. I would have liked to meet their parents.*:

:Forgive me, but I hope you don't have to. There's another one I owe you.:

:No, that was taken care of by Khreng and Prandra some years back, if you remember Uncle Lokh.:

:Yes . . . has the Locksmith been here?:

:He is, but he is busy with plans and will come when he chooses. As for the Majestic One, he needs rest and a chance to get over his bad temper at not being allowed to do battle.:

:He can have it. Well, thanks are in order, Threyha. They're not enough, but they're in order.:

:No fuss, Kinnear. Now I have my own territory to deal with and get these idiots to finish repairs.:

:Threyha, dear,: Kinnear said gently, :you might try giving them a little room by moving out of the office for a while.:

The silent conversation had been let into the minds of the divers, Kinnear's mark of trust.

"The business is much bigger than you were telling us about," Fouad said.

Kinnear said wearily, "I take care of whatever happens connected with my sector. It doesn't mean that's all there is."

"That big lizard looks as if she could take care of a few things."

"She has. Her *sector* is way out of my division and six times the size."

"And she took time—"

"To help a friend. A Khagodi is the best you can get. Maybe one day you'll want to come in deeper and find out. In the meantime go up two levels in the third tube from the left over there and get processed. I have work to do and you'll get whatever else you need upside."

He was tired and hungry, with little prospect of sleep. He got a cubicle assigned to himself, ordered a meal of the usual Staff-Caff muck, and ate it while he read hard copy of fifty-year-old reports from GalFed expeditions to Qsaprinel. Then he reviewed his guards, the twenty-four he had

weaseled out. A marginal lot; he suspected the Frogs were
much better.

And Spinel. One more high-speed learning experience.

"Spinel, I have no time to introduce myself properly or
welcome you in the royal manner you deserve. I am Kinnear,
an old friend of the Ungrukh, and that will have to do. You
are now as acknowledged Emperor the representative of
Galactic Federation's newest member, the world Qsaprinel. I
know how you feel about not being allowed to fight here, but
you must save your strength to fight on your world, and we
are sworn to help you."

Spinel was rarely bad-tempered and had calmed quickly.
"I understand that. I have thanked many already; some I have
promised to thank when—if—we are safe, and I will do the
same for you."

"Agreed. I understand how you use your shocks—but for
effective   defense   you   need   something   quicker—
projectiles."

"Guns, in short," said Spinel dryly. One more gift
Threyha had given him was a high-speed sleep-course in
lingua. "You don't have to be euphemistic with me. But
most of the things you have available are too hot, heavy and
explosive. Our hands are too small and weak for them: they
have stiff triggers and recoils that might break our water-
skins."

"Even if you could use them you'd need training, and
we're in a hurry. You don't need *very* powerful weapons—
just enough to give you some extra help and time. You've got
plenty of forces. . ." He considered. "Underwater . . .
why *not* spearguns? There's so much fishing here the planet's
full of them. Not the ones with explosives and kickback.
Simple ones that even the children use—excuse me, I'm not
demeaning you: they really do work. All you'd need to learn
is to be sure to point them at the enemy."

"Whatever we can get will be good."

"What I want is in the tens of thousands—and yesterday.
We'll see."

Kinnear demanded spearguns in a stentorian voice and used a much softer one putting in a call to Clothier. The machine's feelings were easily hurt.

"Including myself, forty-seven field suits, hominid. One of the grey men is not present, and you'll have to obtain an approximate description from the others."

"Conditions?"

"Equator of mainly ocean world. Averages: 10°C on land, humidity 62%, precipitation per standard thirtyday 2.2 cm, general mist and cloud, sun usually visible one or two hours at zenith."

"I suggest hypoallergenic taklon-zaxwul mix, bureau-crat-grey for low visibility, moss-green identifying stripe down outer arm; assuming sexual and eliminating arrangements similar for all, two-way zipper with inner placket running inside left leg and around groin area to allow foldback, then forward up midline to neck; no collar, one zip pocket right breast, usual sector insigne over left, same green."

"Also for the grey men two sets each longjohns thermal design but light, absorbent and ventilative, 44 sets together."

"Required?"

"One standard day."

"Then I must be busy. Good day, Kinnear."

"Go in good order, Clothier."

the World reversed

In Agassiz's garden the noon meal was a heavier one than usual because there would be no long trestle tables set out for dinner. The Locksmith sat unchanged on the lawn, silent, pulled into himself. The mild autumn was coming; to Emerald and, she sensed, to some others, the garden seemed to be withering; few spoke. There was less fear than psychic pain at the cutting short of a way of life that ought to have changed slowly and naturally.

When the table was cleared the Hashimotos quietly went

on with their gardening, snipping, planting, setting, but the rest gathered around the Locksmith, sitting to chew grassblades or blink at the flickering sun.

The Locksmith opened his eyes. "Those who are travelling on the *Zarandu* must leave as soon as possible. The Bengtvadi call the ship a fast cruiser, but it's really a fast carrier, a freighter. They're too proud to admit they had to modify it for financial reasons. It's still very fast and the best we can get; Thorndecker may have something faster.

"Everyone has had pintrelase, whether or not they're going to Qsaprinel, in case Spinel brought any of the fungus on him. The enzyme's been harmless for forty years and I doubt it will hurt anyone now. One small deceit I would like to practice: I swore I wouldn't hypnotize anyone without permission, and I keep to that, but I want to install blocks to keep any ESP from learning Spinel and the Ungrukh are alive. Any objections?"

None.

"I hate to say so, but there may be other, um, unsympathetic people after Thorndecker. The way he's thrown his wealth around I think he's run out of it. The business with Wardman's house suggests he's allowed himself to go deeply into debt, and he's counting on his cleverness to juggle his way out of it. He's not quite desperate yet. But, though I have never been a creditor, I have dealt with a few. Wardman was one, and we all know what happened to him. There are probably others, and they won't like us much either."

Emerald said, "What you imply is: the more confident Thorndecker is, the better it is for everyone."

"From his point of view, yes, I'm afraid so."

"When the carousel stops its circles, the axis is: your plans require the family of ten, so that Thorndecker can reach what he considers a safe place—quickly."

The Locksmith said hastily, "They don't have to be the actual family—just a body count—excuse me, that is a poor expression. I mean any ten on whom I can superimpose personalities. Thorndecker doesn't seem to care about individuals. But Sylvie, I am sorry, but you are too afraid to go."

Sylvie had been looking down at her hands, clenched in her lap. She got up and went into the house.

After a moment of awkward silence, Morgan said, "How much danger is Agassiz in?"

"Oh, dear man, don't worry about me!"

"I can't tell," the Locksmith said. "Thorndecker may ignore him—or he may be jealous and malicious."

Renny said, "Whoever goes is bound to draw poison away from both Agassiz and Spinel." She wrapped her arms around her knees. "Why not let me be your Sylvie?"

"Goddammit," Anika growled, "look at you!" Renny: steel-tight, black-haired, dark-skinned with touches of blue.

She grinned. "Got a make-up box, haven't you, Mama? A couple of freckles will go a long way. Some bleach, a headscarf, a little illusion . . . as for danger, Thorndecker may be a treat compared to Hartog."

"Danger to the family is the least worry," the Locksmith said. "Family is what Thorndecker wants most."

"I *am* family," said Morgan. "If it'll be more help than harm to Agassiz, I'll go."

Doctor Hobbsbaum said quietly, "I'm willing to go, but we'll be helpless if we're tangled in the fighting."

"I will be with you to help as much as I can," said the Locksmith, "but I can't swear to protect you perfectly. There is no overtime pay."

"Take me!" cried Agassiz. "I ought to die for some good reason."

"There is no good reason that you die for Thorndecker," said Emerald.

Quattro said grimly, "I'll certainly go."

"You certainly do not," said Emerald, "go through everything again twenty times worse."

"He hasn't touched me all these years."

Raanung growled, "On Ungruwarkh we also throw back little fish."

Quattro automatically reached over his shoulder for a knife and the Locksmith looked him in the eye. "Kinnear wants you on the *Zarandu*—if you can manage enough self-

discipline. You will get to Qsaprinel by a different route."
To the rest, "We have three. I don't want Ti-Jacques or the
Hashimotos because they are too hard to disguise, and—"

"I go along to give Thorndecker a toy if he needs one,"
said Raanung.

Emerald screeched, "What do you think you are doing?
Maybe Thorndecker likes the big kittycat? And flames and
spears bounce off your big head?"

"You, I suppose, are invulnerable?"

"No! I stay with Agassiz as I swear for the sake of
Spinel!"

"But I release you, Emerald!"

"I stay! I stay!"

Raanung shot his claws and lashed his tail. "No you do
not, you stupid woman!"

"This wise one who is needed by Spinel as a warrior wants
to be a plaything of Thorndecker!" They circled, gnashing
and snarling. And on and on.

Anika groaned. "Oh for God's sake, Willie, can't you
stop this dumb stuff? It's what you were hired for!"

Bellingrose said calmly, "They won't hurt each other.
They're trying to save each other. Time will take care of it.
There isn't much left."

Quattro, unwilling to wait, gave Raanung a swift kick in
the rump. When both Ungrukh whirled against him he grinned and held his hands up. "None of *us* is going with
Thorndecker. Give the others a chance to work it out."

And it worked itself out simply. The rest of the family
volunteered. Doctor vetoed Mary, the practical nurse, because of a circulatory problem; Agassiz dissuaded Rosa and
Antonio: they had put off childbearing plans so long he found
the burden of their loyalty too great. The three would move to
Port Central and vanish. Three other hardy souls took their
places.

The Hashimotos were firm in their own decision: Naoki,
the younger, had a woman in town who had become pregnant:
a happy accident at a nervous time; Ti-Jacques, Doctor, and the other doctor, Cerrito, had set their lives in this

place. Agassiz refused to say more about the disposition of his household.

"And the rest will disperse from the Port too," said the Locksmith. "Anika?"

Before she could answer there was a heavy thump in the direction of the sea, and all held their breath except the Locksmith, who, having none to hold, said, "Don't be alarmed. That's only the ferry bringing the wagons."

"Wagons?"

"A little carnival that helps us out sometimes. They'll be staying with the Circus a while, but first they'll give us some transportation."

In a few moments three bright wagons drew up before the gate. They lacked a calliope but a clown and several tumblers emerged to do handsprings on the lawn. Anika clapped her hands.

"Nothing like comic relief," Renny muttered.

"Just let Agassiz enjoy them."

The clown poked his bulb nose at Agassiz and leered. "Want a job?"

Agassiz giggled. "If you need a baby."

The clown touched his hand gently and said, "Another time, chum. Now who needs the paint here? Anika, you want a touchup?"

"Hey, Petrovski! What's with you these twenty years?"

"Clowning around." He pulled a thick brush out of his pocket. "Where do I start?"

"No joke, Boris. I want you to give Willie here a blue job."

"Anika!"

"Darling, we're not only unneeded here, we are in the way. You and I are going to spend a few days at the Circus as a rhapsody in blue, and then sit it out at my house until everything's over. There's not many grudges against us and we'll just lay low."

Boris said, "If you really want that, Anushka, it's not what I do. Hey Paco, bring the makeup kit."

"You'll lose your job, Anika," said Bellingrose.

"That'll be forgotten—I'll even read the cards for you."

"If that's a proposition it's the oddest one I ever got."

Paco regarded Renny doubtfully. "I dunno what I'm going to do with you."

"Don't say what you're thinking, Morgan. Sweetie, you've got a red string mop and a can of white paint, haven't you?"

"We got a proper wig and makeup, young lady."

"I don't think you're really carny, Paco, but I'm not shy. Just shave my head and paint me sickly white. The young woman I'm supposed to look like is in the kitchen."

Petrovski said, "Those red folk of yours who look like cats—"

"We are cats!"

"—are going to stick out like a bloody thumb."

Bellingrose said, "There are black leopards on Sol Three."

"Just about extinct. It's a crime transporting them."

"More danger leaving them red," said Quattro.

Raanung roared and Petrovski winced. "It'll wash off with water quick enough, don't you worry. Hey Stranglo, now we need a tarp. Locksmith, can't you squeeze out a little more money for this job?"

"I'll take it up with the authorities."

"Shit."

Raanung grimly submitted to being sprayed black.

"Red eyes? Yeesh. Just keep him in the shadows. Now let's have the lady."

"Hey, Emerald!"

But there was no Emerald. Deep red, glittering green, white-tipped whiskers and all. Gone, disappeared.

The Locksmith, who had taught himself emotion, learned a new one. Much earlier he had been given fear and anger by his captors, and many other feelings had grown out of his association with aliens: now he knew panic.

Emerald had slipped away. The power of his esp did not break through whatever kind of shield she was using. It was not her customary one, and he sensed that there was one, from somewhere, but not from where.

Raanung had opened his mouth to growl, and Quattro said, "Shut up. I get white noise."

Raanung swallowed his bile. "That is Tengura's shield." The deep-grained family sulkiness that hid itself in an extreme of privacy walled about by the powerful white-noise field of disorganized memories, sights, sounds cemented in inextricable confusion. Tengura's mother had been a powerful therapist, her daughter Prandra an adventurer. Tengura, barred from such achievements by early blindness, had created her own: her grand-daughter had learned it earlier than her daughter—and the Locksmith simply did not know enough about the mammalian mind to force a way through it.

"She's not in the house or grounds," Ti-Jacques said.

"She can climb over anything here," Raanung said. "I track her."

Bellingrose's chronometer pinged.

"No," said the Locksmith. "The signal says Thorndecker's shuttle is on the way. Forgive me, Raanung."

Raanung stopped in mid-leap, the red eyes in his blackened fur dulled, his tail sagged. He turned and trotted slowly toward the wagons, as if his mind were engaged in a terrible battle with the Locksmith.

"Better tie him down," said Quattro. "Otherwise I'm not staying around when he comes out of that." He stopped by the great scallop, took the little hand of Agassiz and bent to kiss the damp pink forehead without a word, and climbed into the bright wagon.

"Why did she leave? Why can't I reach her?" The Locksmith's wounded vanity insulted the injury of danger.

"Whatever her reasons, they may do us some good," said Bellingrose, "and as for why you, Locksmith—they are Solthrees, and you meditators don't have the ragbag Solthree mind."

"Willie, I'm supposed to be the sensitive. I just wonder how you can be sure."

"I'm not," said Bellingrose. He took Anika's hand, pulled her up, and led her to the wagon. Agassiz had had many greetings and farewells: neither he nor Anika could think of suitable ones now. But Anika pulled away from Bellingrose and ran back to hug Renny, as if she had just realized that there was a daughter in that stranger.

"If I cry I'll ruin this muck," Renny said.

"I'll do everything necessary in that line," said Anika, and left.

The ten, family and substitutes, waited in the shade of one tree, as if it would protect them. Sylvie came out of the house as quietly as she had done the first time and boarded a wagon, while Rosa and Antonio lined up behind her with Mary, to be given a hand up by the clown and his helpers.

Then the three dropped flat as boards and at the same time six of the ten fell.

Boris yelped, "What the hell—"

Everyone on legs ran to pull the fallen three into the wagon. "What in God's name is that? I can't budge them!"

Anika shoved her head out of a window. "Quattro and Sylvie are down too."

"They're not dead," said the Locksmith. "Boris and you lot—" he gestured to the substitutes, "—get into the wagons! Get going! Hurry!"

"Renny!" Anika screamed. "Renny!"

Renny was on her knees, looking round her at Morgan and the other five lying every which way. She smiled, shook her head, and lay down among them.

Cerrito, Doctor and Ti-Jacques placed themselves around Agassiz's cradle as if to shelter him; the Hashimotos squatted beside their garden tools.

"Ren—" The false-blue hand of Bellingrose pulled Anika back, the door closed, the windows were barred and shuttered, the lead wagon gunned its motor and rolled, pulling the others creaking behind it. Their sounds diminished.

Ti-Jacques said, "Locksmith, what's happening?"

"I don't know." He stepped backward until he came to

rest against one of the dwarf trees, pushed into it until it absorbed him; the trunk thickened, new moss rose up on its raw bark like a green wave.

He was brooding. He had considered himself a match for any ESP of Thorndecker's, and now he wondered. Yet Raanung, now released, was stirring and Emerald still sending her weird signal. So Thorndecker did not yet know they were alive. Esp could not reach an Impervious like Renny. The one logical answer was that Pritchard, a very powerful hypnotist, had performed one last post-hypnotic task—maybe long ago and often reinforced—for Thorndecker. Quattro had sworn that Pritchard had not laid an eye on him—but Pritchard would have made sure that Quattro would forget it when he did. But he could have worked on Renny—and she had been left untouched. Perhaps he had something else in mind for her . . . But it came to a puzzle without solution, and he let go.

Agassiz spoke in a calm voice to his doctors and Ti-Jacques. "Move away, please. Give me the light and let me think."

Because my dark brother is coming at last.

the Queen of Swords reversed

Why must I do such a stupid thing? Emerald asked herself. She was crouched among bushes outside Agassiz's grounds.

Because I do not wish to be painted black. No, that is not it, idiot! It is because I am a defender and not a war-maker. Running with my man beside that bloody Mundr and Nga in my own Hills is a great thrill for a childish one in those times—and those times are not even over when I come out to strange worlds only to fight. But I am here to fight for the weaponless if the Locksmith can do no more than hold Thorndecker's ESP. You must admit, Locksmith, that without Raanung to track me you cannot find me. Now I drop the noisy shield and use my own. It is not quite so strong, but I must save strength.

:Are you still there, Emerald?:

:Cannot find me yet, Locksmith? Tsk. I know the risks and I come when I am needed.:

:You will not see me when you come. Perhaps not ever again.:

:Then I bless you and wish you well.:

Emerald took the necklace from her neck, wrenched apart all its pieces, and buried them. It was a beautiful thing of its own kind, but not a decoration to wear for meeting Thorndecker. Then she lay licking and spitting the dirt from her claws, ears up and turning for the first hum of the shuttle.

In half an hour it was hovering over the lonely tract. At its first sound Renny twitched once, in terror, and forced herself to lie still.

The shuttle cast the shadow of a roc. The bay door opened, a ladder fell, and three armed figures descended. Thorndecker, in a medium-sized and wine-colored dickey-suit, was let down in a basket seat. Esne was gripping his arm with falcon claws; he swung gently for a few moments. First he glanced at the tumbled figures, seven in one group, three in the other; then turned his attention to those who were awake.

Doctor was resting on a sun cot; Dr. Cerrito feeding crushed apricots from a porcelain dish to Agassiz, Ti-Jacques lying on the grass leaning on one elbow and making unpleasant sounds whistling with a grassblade. The Hashimotos sat cross-legged beside a freshly-clipped hedge, smoking.

All jumped at Thorndecker's first words, an amplified roar: *"What have you done with Quattro?"* He pulled on the lowering rope, came down and climbed out of the basket. Cerrito wiped Agassiz's chin, set the dish and spoon aside, and stood with folded arms. Doctor rose and sat. The Hashimotos did not move, but Ti-Jacques spat his grassblade and picked himself up.

"Our best to see he got away," he said evenly. "We were bound to try."

Thorndecker looked him over through the transparent

mask and give up on him as a little fish. "There is another powerful ESP here. Esne feels it."

"Esne?"

He extended his arm. "This!" The Encid's leaves fluttered, the eyes burned like dark emeralds.

Cerrito said, "Mister Thorndecker, we don't know." Truthfully: he had forgotten which tree the Locksmith had absorbed, did not know if he was still there, and had no contact with Emerald.

"Captain, Doctor."

"Captain Thorndecker, we still don't know."

"Whatever is hidden will turn up in time," said Thorndecker. He raised an arm to his helpers. "Drop the nets and load the ten here."

He turned back to the doctors. "Bring Agassiz to me."

The uncoordinated arms and legs waved from the scallop; the voice came true and clear. "You have the legs, cousin. You come to me."

Doctor trembled, but Thorndecker tipped his head and laughed. The amplification boomed among the trees. He took the ten rather stiff paces that brought him peering over the edge of the shell and raised his mask. "And I thought you were afraid of me all these years, Agassiz."

Cerrito adjusted the prisms and the distorted faces examined each other. Neither of these persons would ever call the other ugly. "Henry, if any ESP has reported that to you, that person is a liar. If you have made yourself believe it you have deceived yourself. I searched for you many years to tell you I loved you. Lately my love for you has shrunk and withered, but it is not quite dead. Yet."

Thorndecker spat on him.

Doctor stood, mask-face baleful. A gun motioned him back.

"I can't spit and I don't hate anyone," said Agassiz. "I suppose that puts me at a disadvantage."

"And everyone loves you, I suppose?"

"No, Henry, but I love you more than anyone else does. The blessings you get from others are empty words."

Doctor came forward slowly, under the guns, to wipe the spittle from Agassiz's cheek.

"You, Doctor! I think you chose the wrong one."

"I wanted both. I was left with one."

"You attacked my family!"

"If you don't know by now what really happened when you were born your ESPs *are* liars. Don't expect me to kneel and beg on account of saving your life."

"I would be more likely to kill you for saving it." Esne climbed his arm higher.

"You are also alive to make the choice," said Doctor quietly.

The Locksmith, treed more firmly than he wished, knew what was coming, and doubted he could stop it without giving himself away. *:Emerald, pay attention and don't answer. This strange ESP suspects my presence and may pick you up by mistake. It's stimulating Thorndecker to provoke our reaction with threats of violence. I must work to get out of this tree, which seemed such a good idea, but my faculties are overextended. Emerald, you must not react! Whatever you intend, don't show yourself! Get away, go to Port Central where you'll be safe!:* Though his shield was there to protect her he was not sure she was still in range. The message might be going to the void.

Emerald absorbed it in three seconds. She had not moved and did not yet know what she was going to do. At this point she dared not move. Whether the forcefield was on or off there were a great many more wild things outside than in Agassiz's cultured garden. Caterpillars were crawling her sides, ants exploring her ears and nostrils, gnats jittering before her eyes. She was afraid to disturb the balance even by sweeping herself with her tail, nor would she empty her bladder in a place she could not move from. There were twigs to crack with every step. For the first time she felt unease at being on such a life-rich world, so many tiny quanta of sensation pulsing about her. She had to push her mind into the garden.

"I needn't make such choices at the moment," Thorndecker was saying. Esne, perched on his shoulder, was dragging it down; he took her by the horny standard and set her on the grass. She moved like an insect, quartering the area in a six-clawed zigzag. Seven of the Family had been loaded; one of the last three was the false Sylvie. Esne stopped beside her.

The Locksmith reproached himself for not taking time to hypnotize Renny, who was wholly conscious. Eyeless, he picked up an image from Ti-Jacques to whom Esne, dark blue-green without wings or "head", still resembled a pecking chicken. As a tree he found it torturous trying to maintain on an Imper the impression of an ordinary penetrable brain, unconscious but autonomously functioning.

You meditators don't have the Solthree mind. Bellingrose was right. Esne, sensing wrongness, raised one claw and raked it across Renny's cheek.

Even Thorndecker's crew jumped. Renny merely took one slightly deeper breath. Another one of those situations. A welt reddened on her cheek but did not bleed; her makeup remained undisturbed. Emerald's skin writhed uncontrollably, and she lost her insect contingent temporarily but did not move.

Thorndecker said, "Get away from that, Esne, and let them load." The last three were hoisted to the hovering shuttle. "Now we need one more net." He leaned over the scallop again and said softly, "Now where is the other ESP?"

"My ESPs are Ti-Jacques, Quattro and Sylvie. You have taken Sylvie, Quattro is gone, and Ti-Jacques is, I think, standing somewhere near you. Which did you want?"

"The one who nearly cracked the brain of my poor Esne on the street of your Mrs. Gurdja. That may have been the cat, and she is dead, but Esne tells me there *is* another ESP here." He unzipped his suit halfway and drew out the little sword Emerald had seen on the holo and considered a toy. Guns were trained on Ti-Jacques the moment he thought of mov-

ing. "Ti-Jacques lets you know this is a sharp thing."
Thorndecker slid the point a centimeter into the baby crease
under Agassiz's chin.

"Poke as you will, Henry. I don't speak under the threat of
weapons."

To Emerald the physical point accentuated the logical one
Raanung had tried to convince her of: she was doing Agassiz
no favor by staying with him. Indecision evaporated: she
began to consider how best to fall into a trap.

Esne resumed her drunkard's walk and reached the bole of
the Locksmith's tree. She scratched around its base. A wind
had come up, and by engineered coincidence a low-growing
twig gave her a slap that knocked her off balance. She jumped
up, hopping with rage, eyes spinning, and began to claw at
the moss and the bark underneath. Thorndecker's dagger
pushed a little deeper.

Emerald sighed. The ESPs were swamped with white
noise.

Esne jumped. Thorndecker cried, "We have it!" He put
his sword away and did not see the tears running from the
corners of his cousin's eyes.

Emerald broadcast to the universe, exposing and concealing her presence at the same time, running with all speed in a
sine-wave, under bush, up tree, branch-hopping, along
shore, through forest and clearing, red on green,
checkerboard-shadowed; a catch to be netted only when the
Locksmith had freed himself and enough time had been
wasted to make Thorndecker curse.

Darkness came between her and the sun; she did not pause
to identify it. Dead leaves fell on her, thorns scratched and
broke in her skin, dry conifer needles pricked between her
toes. One stunner bolt numbed her ear. Another the base of
her tail: she could not lift it. She plunged deeper into thickets.

"Drive her into the clearing so you can net her!"

Her left hind leg went numb and she ran three-footed,
slipping on rotted berries.

"You stupid bastards, we're running late! Get her or I'll
kill you!"

Emerald slowed and pushed her way, hopping three-footed and taking her time, toward the sunbright clearing and the man with the gun. She shook off the rubbish, and crouched, eyes slitted against light, while the shadow approached with a crewman clinging to the ladder, net tucked under his arm. For the second time in her life she flung back her head and howled in pure rage. (*Getting more like your mother all the time,* says Raanung. Ho!)

The sound ricocheted off the shuttle's belly and the man on the ladder jerked and nearly fell off.

"Shut her up, damn you!"

One more bolt skimmed the crown of her skull, the net dropped and she fell into blackness.

The ladder was pulled up with its burdens, the bay doors were sealed. The shuttle accelerated with a diminishing whine.

During the immeasurable nothingness that followed, one thought penetrated.

:*Thank you, Emerald. I am here, and I will stay with you,:* said the Locksmith.

Doctor collapsed noiselessly, clutching his chest in the useless involuntary gesture and clenching his teeth to keep silence.

Without a word the Hashimotos ran for the garden shed and Ti-Jacques to Stores. They came back with an old slatted gate, he spread blankets and carefully lifted Doctor on it.

Cerrito, wiping down Agassiz with a warm damp cloth, did not look at them.

:*He's still alive, but we got to get to the hospital. Tell the old man the truth but give us a head start.:*

"Cerrito, that's a motor starting!"

"Yes, Agassiz."

"Leaving here, but it's not ours!"

"Spinel's hearse. Doctor's had a heart attack, and—"

"He's dead!"

"No, he—"

"Tell me the truth!"

"Give me a chance. Ti-Jacques says not, but he has to get
to the hospital—and he said to tell you the truth."

"Cerrito . . . Emerald is gone . . . the others. . ."

"The Locksmith will protect them."

"Can he? Spinel, Quattro, Morgan, my friends . . .
all. . ."

"I am here. Ti-Jacques and the Hashimotos will be back
soon to stay with you, and Doctor, when he is well."

"If he lives." Agassiz's voice was deadly level. "He saw
that one would have killed me. That is why he may die.
Murderer. I kept them all too long, Cerrito. I am a selfish
man, a fool and a sinner."

"Let us all be such sinners. But I don't think Thorndecker
would have killed you." He raised the sling and turned
Agassiz to wash his sweated back.

Face against the netting, Agassiz said, "Oh yes, he would.
If I were that man with that mind I would. You may think I
know nothing of the world, and perhaps not much of the
flesh, but I know the devil. I am the son of a Thorndecker."

Temperance

At Port Central there was a skyscraper euphemistically
called the Guest House and containing hundreds of tiny
whitewalled chambers for important persons waiting between flights. Some were tanks of liquid, or of gas, or of
liquid-and-gas combinations. Others were tubs of rocks, soil,
vegetation, or mud. Quattro was sitting at table in a Solthree-
type room eating the kind of meal that went with it. He was
similarly indifferent.

He had wakened on the skimmer and knew what happened, but his mind was still turbulent with fear for Agassiz,
Doctor, Morgan, Renny; even Emerald. Shame for Sylvie;
regret for the loss of the few women who had treated him with
spontaneous tenderness. Everyone he might not see again.
And resentment toward the Locksmith who had broken the

pattern of life the way a thumb would press a globe of mercury to droplets.

The buzzer sounded and he yelled, "Come in!" The door slid and the tall man with the bland face stood in its frame.

Kinnear disregarded color, warts, spines, and saw the short muscular aggressive man. Mediterranean type. Very carefully, he did not esp.

And neither did Quattro.

"Hullo. I'm Kinnear."

"I heard about you. Where's my knives?"

"In the safe." He slid the door closed behind him, leaned against the wall and crossed arms and ankles. "Why wasn't your busy-light on? I didn't know you were eating."

Quattro washed down a salt pill and rolled the table away. "Doesn't matter. I'm through. You hear anything?"

"Thorndecker took away everybody he thought he wanted—except you. Doctor had a heart attack; he's fair. Agassiz is stronger than most would suppose, and he's well, and so are the rest with him. Nobody keeps track of the Locksmith."

"And . . . Emerald?"

"Thorndecker got her. She made him hunt her, to draw attention from Renny and the Locksmith, and waste time. She managed it. I don't know if it was what she was planning when she took off, but that's usual for Ungrukh. She got knocked around a bit."

"God. And that ESP of Thorndecker's?"

"Ti-Jacques said he couldn't describe it except to say it looked like a black chicken with no head, leaves for feathers, and one leg like a tripod. I've never heard of anything like that." He rolled the table back toward Quattro. "Finish up."

"What for?"

"You won't be eating again for a while."

Quattro sat still for a moment; his eyes widened. He shoved the table at Kinnear hard enough to knock him down.

Kinnear, prepared, stopped it easily with his big hands, mopped spilled water with a napkin, and picked up a spoon from the floor. "I didn't come here to harm you, Quattro, nor will you harm me."

"You will *not* open my gills! I goddam fucking *won't* breathe water again!"

"You may not be able to. But the herpetologist says if the capillaries haven't died and there's no infection or abscess, he doesn't expect atrophy and they should work quite well."

"A reptile specialist!"

"Threyha uses him when she needs help here, so I wouldn't get insulted. He couldn't do the surgery, of course, but he says he'd like to look in."

"No!"

"Quattro, you've had plenty of chances to leave Agassiz but were loyal enough to stay. When you were told you'd help best coming on the *Zarandu*, you came of your own will. Of course you won't be forced to have surgery. You can walk away from this place like Sylvie did, and we'd keep you safe, too, until there was no threat. If you want to work with us you work under our conditions—and the first of those is to get your gills open. We really need an underwater ESP. We have fast-healing and you'll recover aboard."

"Just in time to get killed!"

"Same chance I'm taking."

Quattro folded his arms and his mind.

Kinnear said quietly, "You must have foreseen this possibility, Quattro. Otherwise you'd have had them cut out."

"I couldn't afford it!" A lie. Agassiz would have afforded him anything. But the gills were part of the self that had defied Thorndecker.

Kinnear said nothing more and slipped out.

Left hanging, unspoken by mind or mouth, was the fact that Emerald had given herself for Quattro, as much as for the others, or more. She had had a sickening taste of Thorndecker's madness in Wardman's house, and now would get more than a bellyful.

Quattro pulled up the table with a savage jerk and stabbed the leftovers.

No trouble with Raanung. After a wash down to his own color, a good meal and a sound sleep, he was ready for anything. Except Emerald in danger. He was used to pushing down fear, and would not stay in one small room.

He spent some time looking at the *Zarandu*. Having seen many marvels in a short life he was not overwhelmed, but a good machine was something he respected.

Zarandu was not an impressive ship. It had been fitted with more powerful engines, but was not even as big as the GalFed Surveyor the Ungrukh used on permanent loan. It was nevertheless the biggest ship allowed to make landfall on Fthel IV. What made it unusual was the webwork of metal and plasmetal that extended in supports and loading docks about it; it seemed a small-bodied insect in a forest of legs. For hours ships had been rising by elevators to take their places in the docks. The ones at lowest level would help lift-off by firing their engines, and pay lower freight rates for the use of their fuel. None of Kinnear's boats was powerful enough to do this. Once in orbit *Zarandu* hooked on to cargo waiting to be towed, and blinked out into fast mode. Now the ship was homeward bound for periodic inspection and Kinnear, far from saving money, had dug into his small pot of gold bribing the Bengtvadi to exchange a few light pieces of freight for one: XenoBi's little Surveyor.

He joined Raanung. "You like that? It's no beauty."

"You know by now beauty means little to us. I think you are making a joke, Kinnear. It works well, everyone tells me." He was silent, and Kinnear, without esping, sensed an unusual shyness and embarrassment emanating from him.

"What's the matter?"

"Nothing . . . but . . . you see, you have everything well organized. Your guards look very fine in their new clothes and the underwater ones seem to know what to do, and Spinel has his purpose and I am satisfied for him. But I . . . am like no one, and do not feel useful. I don't see what help I can be to you, Kinnear."

Kinnear esped briefly to see if Raanung was indulging in

humor or irony, but both knew this was no time for it. "Oh
. . . I imagine we'll find something for you to do."

Kinnear, with Raanung and the guards, would travel on
their boats, locked to *Zarandu,* and go into stasis and then
deep-sleep during the one orbit. The Frogmen, because of
lower metabolism, would go under on land slowly and travel
on the ship in a honeycomb of water-filled cells, Quattro
delivered out of the recovery-room to save time. Spinel
would be with them; the herpetologist did not know what to
find wrong with him; he did need room, and would be
immobilized in a borrowed Khagodi tank by a synthetic gel
whose organic equivalent protected reptilian eggs.

The aquamen reluctantly packed away the new clothing
that would do them no good in water and settled like larvae
into long cold sleep.

Raanung and the conscriptees waited in an embarkation
lounge. They were extremely hungry, like all passengers
going superfast, a form of travel hard on the digestion.
Raanung was hungriest, because he needed the most food.
His consciousness of smells was unusually sensitive, and
among all these fleshy creatures he found himself with un-
seemly thoughts. There were no ESPs here, and perhaps his
expression kept the others at a distance from him.

He forced his thoughts from food and set himself to distin-
guishing individual scents in an abstract way, an occupation
he had begun very young growing up among the savage
hunters of an impoverished tribe. Raanung was bemused by
Spinel's Qsaprinli revulsion against the smells of Solthree
and other mammals: no smell had ever offended him. He
crouched in a corner and concentrated on the homogeneous
mixtures of twenty-odd people, separating out and grouping
components by the microgram from the swirl of air about
him.

"I'm glad that cat's asleep."

"I dunno if he's asleep. I'm just glad he's lying down with
his eyes shut."

"And his mouth."

Solthrees forgot that he also had sharp ears. He returned his attention to his nose . . . one tiny stream of invisible particles. . .

He yawned, rose, shook himself, ambled close to the wall . . . lost it . . . picked it up, stopped. Thornscratch in the memory. Where? Chaos! Lights flashing! Shattering of mirrors! . . . Wardman's house.

I must be wrong.

Yet he had never forgotten a scent and never mistaken one.

The man in the corner, sitting on a hassock to watch a screen, not some trivial program on it, but a broadcast showing preparations for the launch, the topmost array of ships being pulled up into lock position on the *Zarandu*. Big stolid man, square-faced, eyes not moving from the screen. Not one of Thorndecker's small deadly ones.

He watched the squared-off features. Like all Ungrukh males on a world where nearly every female was telepathic he had the third necessary skill: interpreting facial expressions.

Nothing here. Yet. . .

Pressing the wall, he crept to the door, careful not to seem to be stalking, so practised hardly anyone noticed him moving.

He slid the door open a crack and said very quietly to the uniformed guard, "I must get out for a short while." There was just enough hubbub in the room to cover his voice.

He saw the expression clearly enough in her eyes: fear of the savage beast. But she did sense his urgency and kept her voice low. "You are not to leave here once you are inside. Kinnear's orders."

"I have to see Kinnear in a great hurry. You are aiming a weapon at me. At least allow me to step outside." While she hesitated he added, "You see my tag. I am the highest ranking accredited GalFed employee in this company. That must give me some authority."

She moved back a step and he eased out. "But *I* have no authority to send you," she said dryly, "and no guards to spare for escort."

"Send word and he comes."

"I doubt it, but I can ask that much." She told her helmet
mike, "Parsons from Mbulu, buzz Kinnear and say the
red-haired gentleman has an urgent matter for him." After a
moment she blinked and jerked her thumb: "You got it."
Then he raced.

Kinnear was standing in the doorway of his cubicle.

"I need you down there!" Raanung snarled.

"I have some things to clear up before I handle it down
there." He dit-dahed the terminal. "I know which one you
mean but I haven't got their names by memory yet. I'll pull
the file."

Pictures flashed. "That one."

"Issachar Hands, local gun, one of two escorting Senator
J.T. Silver, aka Long John, when on Fthel Four—explains
why you could have smelled him at Wardman's house while
Long John only got here two days ago. Spying's probably
part of the work Hands does. Doesn't name Wardman as a
reference, but if you say so he was there. *I* trust your nose.
Admits to several small misdemeanors. Translate: couple of
big felonies that never got caught out." He sighed. "Beggars
like me aren't choosers." He strummed the terminal again.

TO FILES FROM KINNEAR CO-ORD 492. ANY-
THING WITHIN A-3 CLEARANCE ON (1) JOHN TEN-
NYSON SILVER, SENATOR JOINT/NORAMERI-
COUNCIL SOL III; (2) WINSTON HORTON WARD-
MAN, WARDROBOTIC DOMESTICS; (3) ISSACHAR
HANDS, MIRAMAR LOCAL #FJ79AC866MEGAM2/09;
(4) AND INTERCONNECTIONS. END.

Fifteen seconds.

KINNEAR 492: (1) SILVER OWNS 25% ALLOWABLE
LIMIT SHARES SONOTEK RADIO, LENT TO (3) LATE
WARDMAN CO. CREDIT EQUIVALENT OF 20%
STOCK NO RECORDED TRANSFER=(4); HANDS (3)
CONNECTION UNKNOWN=(0). END.

"Not quite," said Kinnear. "Go back to the lounge and
give any excuse you need. In fifteen minutes I'll look in to

rally the troops and see what I get from Hands. Don't worry. We have a couple of hours.''

On his way Raanung was not surprised to see a jolly hamfaced and white-haired man, addressed affectionately as Long John, saying goodbye to friends bound for vacation.

Kinnear was not surprised to find him still there a few minutes later. He dared not probe him; there were other ESPs about. In the Secure lounge he made General-to-troops sounds: *have to bear up with hunger, you've been through this before, take a little water, no more than 250 ml,* and underneath to Raanung: :*Terrific locking job somebody did on him, but he's got a bugger of a toothache in a lower right molar, can't hide that, never complained at the Physical— guess they didn't look very far—oh . . . Sonotek Radio makes those beautiful micros . . . that's the hand in the glove—I mean the radio in the tooth. X-ray'd show it as a replacement. I see. He's to pick up information for Wardman's consortium. But what? They'd probably know all about Qsaprinel by now.*:

:*Not all. It is a whole world. He leads them to the place on it. I bet Thorndecker does not give it away for a gift.*:

:*Hands won't pick it up till he gets there. And micros are fine, but they can't reach here from there.*:

:*But they can relay by spacelight in some innocent code, not so?*:

:*Raanung, hunger must be getting to me. Guess I'd better pull Hands out.*:

:*No. Let him go.*:

:*That's a dangerous one to leave loose.*:

:*It is the reason I want us to have him now. It is much more dangerous to tell others—like Silver, who realizes he is not with us—how much we know. He cannot disappear yet. I take care of him.*:

:*He may have smuggled a gun. A flamer wouldn't pass the scanners but there are plenty of deadly little plastics.*:

:*I take care of him.*: After a moment, Raanung added, :*Kinnear, if that one makes a promise in all honesty to serve us instead of the others, for pay, do you accept him in spite of his rascality?:*

:Of course. We still need them all.:

Cabins allotted to hominids on the *Zarandu* were large enough for one biped to stand between the door and the couch. When Hands touched the light-switch in his cabin he found Raanung making himself comfortable on the cushions.

"Close the door please. Perhaps you think of turning the light off and neither of us sees in complete darkness, but my nose is very sensitive." Bluff. In a closed cabin full of Hands's scent even Raanung could not have placed him exactly.

Hands left the light on and the door open. "What the hell are you here for?"

"I pick up your scent at Wardman's house."

"Oh sure. What's that supposed to mean?"

"It is a house Thorndecker means for me to die in, but I don't believe you have anything to do with that. Neither do I believe you plant Wardman in the garden."

The door slammed shut. "My God, how—"

"But you and your friends want repayment and revenge. That is not good for Qsaprinel and my friends, and *I* do not want it. We prefer you do not send messages on your fine little Sonotek giving information about us."

"You weren't supposed to be an ESP!"

"I am not. I am a good nose, a good brain, and a few sharp implements." He grinned.

"What do you expect to do with them?"

"Nothing, I hope. We want your service—and your loyalty. If you swear to give them honestly we welcome you. And restore whatever pay you lose from other parties."

"That's garbage, I don't believe it."

"You must believe. For a person like me it is easier to fight than to lie."

"Then say I believe. But you're wasting breath. If I wanted anything to do with that kind of set-up I wouldn't deal with *you.*"

Very quietly, "Why not, Hands?"

"Ever look at yourself in the mirror? I don't make deals with animals."

In Wardman's house there had been many mirrors—and many pictures; perhaps of Hands, or even Silver, for blackmail. . .

Pot calls kettle, say Solthrees.

Raanung clearly understood what was going on. He said, treading coals, "How you make deals is your choice, Hands." No choice. GalFed could not spend as much money as Long John.

"Now get out of here or I'll call emergency."

"My regrets, Hands. I go. Please let me pass."

Hands seemed oddly surprised by his willingness.

"There's no goddam room here." But there was, just. "Christ, this place stinks! I want a wash while there's time." He did not move aside; his left hand hooked the ziploop at his neck while his right one rose. Raanung watched the blocky shape barring the doorway and saw: *Damn thing turned savage on me and I had to.*

"Thought just because you got those teeth and claws—"

Raanung, sadly, waited for the hand to draw the gun from the zipper opening. Then he moved. His long tail whipped out to hook Hands between the cords of his nape and pull him forward so that one padded forepaw could slap the side of his neck. It broke with a crunch. Hands fell sitting against the door.

Raanung flicked the intercom with the tip of his tail and roared, "Get Kinnear!"

In a few moments the door was pulled aside with difficulty and Hands dropped half out, head lolling, gun in hand.

Kinnear looked at Raanung's sulky face. "The damned thing turned savage on you and you had to. But you could have let me in on it, you idiot! You were nearly killed!"

"I don't plan this! I must give him a choice and try to save him. I *am* a warrior and sometimes a killer—but this is the first sentient one I kill who is not of my species, and it is sickening."

"I'm afraid where we're going they'll all be, Raanung—but you have a choice too. There's still time to—"

"Of course I am coming! Why do you think I risk my life at all? But I expect to go against enemies, and this one calls himself an ally."

"Maybe he had his own loyalties—especially to money. But if he'd killed you I'd have had to . . . take care of him. He was too dangerous to keep, and there's no way in law I could ever have proven—oh hell, let's get on with it."

A small hominid with a big head crept under Kinnear's arm to examine the body. He was the average Solthree's image of the classic extraterrestrial: smooth blue hairless skin marbled with yellow, recognizable pugnosed face, plain white tunic to the knee.

"Doctor Xaver from Bengtvad," said Kinnear.

The doctor raised his head and twittered.

"And good wishes to you too," said Raanung. "What is this all about, Kinnear?"

"We're just going to get the radio before we dump the body. If it's better than the micros we use we'll order a lot at very good prices from Long John. As long as you're a killer and a thief a little blackmail can't make your hands much dirtier."

Quattro touched the surface tension of consciousness, and was first aware of a sore nose and an unholy big tube in it carrying his bubbling breath. Good. Maybe he had not been operated on. Then he felt strange around the neck and his hand found a stiff plastic network hugging him under the jaw. Some claw or tentacle plucked his fingers away but they crept up again and discovered something lumpy on one side and then the other. Operation. Shit. He tried to speak, but he was underwater.

:What is he saying?: Wub-wub watery sound.

:He is cursing.: ESP. Damn right I'm cursing. *:He wants to know what the lumps are.:* Yeah. *:Those are bandages over the electrodes, and the netting is to keep you from*

disturbing them. Your gills are in excellent condition and the electrodes will help them heal faster.:
   :He does seem to curse a lot.:
   :Those aggressive Mother-of-Worlders always do.:
   :Just gibberish now.:
   :No, it probably has some meaning in his culture. He says, "When's Frankenstein going to pull the switch?":

When a needle pricked he woke gratefully from the most horrible dream of his life. The plunge into the black cavern he had skirted so precariously for seven years, where even Emerald would not try to explore. The full obscene panorama. Then he discovered that his body was constricted in some kind of fetal knot. The bandages were gone, the netting and electrodes in place. But he could not stretch, walls closed on him. Panic hit in an electric wave as if the switch had been pulled. He tried to tug at the electrodes, but his grasp was too weak, like a baby's, like Agassiz's. His eyes opened to darkness, he squirmed and thrashed.
   :Out of it at last, thank God! Hey Quattro, there's a bunch here who want to get some peace around here, Froggy!:
   :Wha—who?: His body lost panic, remained tense. *:Fouad?:*
   :Mind gone blank, peeper? Now you spilled the garbage let the rest of us go under.:
   :Esteban! Is that you?:
   :Shut up. Talk later.:
   :Settima! Where did you come from?:
   :Leave it alone!:
   :Give him a break, you warts, he's had enough. Take it easy, Quattro. You'll get the whole story when the sun comes up.:

Carlotta, Samson, Fritzi, Monica . . . Sesto . . . Nicklaus . . . Sheva. . .
   Sleep.
   Evaporating one of Kinnear's problems.

The Lovers

Bellingrose went to bed early, Anika late. It seemed his nights crept up earlier and earlier on him, like the autumn season.

Anika sat up in her parlor, laying Tarot. The cards she sometimes found amusing, sometimes despised, had become symbols of Renny, whom she loved best, of the Cats she had come to love, of Kinnear, oldest of her friends.

Whatever she thought of Tarot, she took clients seriously. Alone, her own client, she laid the deck to think upon. *Emperor* first, for signature. Spinel, with whom the horror had begun. Not quite: reverse him, you have Beta, his fission-twin, another beginner, a parallel. She turned the *King of Swords,* reversed, just bloody Hartog, bringing violence. *Page of Wands,* faithful retainer and messenger bring news of—don't look at *The Empress,* turn to. . .

Justice: Oh Mama I couldn't help myself and his head went up in fire and split—

Hartog and now Thorndecker—I kicked out Gurdja to keep her safe, God damn you!

Cutting too close. She decked and boxed the cards. Palmed the tears away.

Bellingrose. Candles and stained glass. To bed with the chickens. Milksop. No. He's brave. But now he's afraid of . . . of me. Has he never had a woman since his wife—and it's not boys or German shepherds or . . . me. But looks at me. Wants to know how I tick. Because I'm rough and crude but not the same way as the bunch he preaches to. Just curious.

The cards boxed. No more to do. Sleep. Not a bad idea. Then what am I doing outside his door . . . and opening it? But he'll be asleep, and if not. . .

She scoured her mind for rationalizations to herself, excuses to him.

Not asleep. He was lying curved on one side, away from her. When the door opened he wrenched about, white hair ruffled, eyes clear as water. "What do you want?" Almost a snarl. "Why are you here?"

She was sweating. "I don't know . . . you've been so quiet—"

"Leave me alone! Please! Go away!"

"Oh Willie, not from that tone of voice!"

He pulled the sheet over his bare shoulder. She had not thought to buy nightclothes for him; he didn't seem to care.

"Anika, will you please go?"

His knees were drawn up, he was pulled into himself, trembling.

She knew all that was necessary. And he did not want her. Yet she could not bear that voice. She sat on the hassock, shaking, like him. "Will—I'm sorry you don't want me." A terrible thing to say—she, big loud Anika, couldn't swallow it and leave it alone!

He twisted about, his voice almost a howl: "I want you! I'm trying not to, God damn it!" He turned away again. "Laugh, laugh. Milk-and-water Bellingrose, can't get three of God's creatures to listen to the word of any god, let alone twelve. Can't—I just can't do what anybody, everybody does. Have to get rid of it like Onan—and he was a sinner— because it's hers. And she doesn't know my name. A laughing matter."

Anika said soberly, "Willie, I wouldn't laugh at you if your face was blue."

"Right now it's too damned red."

She stood. "Tomorrow we'll take the chance and go see her. Or just you."

"No. I want you to come."

"I'll be back in a minute then."

"What for? D'you think now you can—"

"My love, I jiggle the cards sometimes—but not lives."

She came back with a bottle and two glasses. "Local plonk, but it's nice and smooth. There's a fair ride tomorrow, and we'll both need the sleep."

He drank too fast. He was not used to liquor and fell asleep as soon as he emptied the glass. Sipping, she watched him in the dim light from the hall, and when she had finished, dropped her caftan and slid into bed beside him in her cotton nightdress, wrapped her arm around his waist and her body around his. He wouldn't wake too early with that dose.

New position, Anika? For such a skinny one, he's got a nice warm butt. She drifted.

In the night it rained gently and the first of the autumn mists settled. Winter was usually three thirtydays of temperatures five degrees cooler on average, but sometimes autumn began with a kind of one-shot hot-cold day that was stuffy and yet raw. Anika handled the moped with Bellingrose on pillion, through mist and damp. He was shivering, and she insisted on stopping to buy him a jacket even though she did not believe he shivered from cold. She was wearing an old hooded pullover of Renny's and had painted herself a neutral face. She was a background: she would not compromise Bellingrose—with hospital staff, with whatever was left of his wife's spirit.

She did not want to go. She was not afraid of seeing the woman, but of the hope and desire in the man's eyes. He had not seen his wife in half a year. She was not jealous: what hurt was that he had thought she might laugh at him.

The Hospital was in keeping with the Refinery: a graceful rambling mansion on beautiful grounds, its only incongruity the presence of Security for ailing VIPs and the ivy-twined antenna on the roof. Indoors were thick carpets and leaded windows. Even the shadows were luxurious.

The door to the room was open, and Bellingrose stood for a moment watching the nurse feed his wife. She was sitting in a chair by the window, pale blue silk dressing-gown, pale fleecy blanket on her knees, hands folded in lap.

"Chew it, dear," the nurse said gently. "It's just toast. You like toast. Not the raisin? Spit it out, love, that's right." The slow tongue pushed the raisin over the lip and it dropped to the spitpan. "Now here's your William to see you, Francie, and we'll eat some more later."

Bellingrose approached; Anika pulled back. The woman in the chair was his analogue, slim, pale-eyed, her thick white hair dutch-cut.

"Francie," he whispered.

She looked at him. The nurse moved away like a shadow.

He dropped to his knees before the chair, grasping her hands. He laid his head in her lap and placed the flaccid hands about his neck, where they must have rested often.

Anika, waiting in the hall, was about to leave, when the woman raised her head and said in a high voice, "You!" Her skin was fresh and fair, its lifelines smoothed.

"Yes?" The sound came half-smothered.

"I don't know you either." Her eyes were smashed diamonds. "Who is this man?" She pulled her hands away.

Anika took a deep breath. "Your husband William, Mrs. Bellingrose."

"I don't know what you mean."

Bellingrose made an indescribable sound. Anika jammed her hands in her pockets and strode to the waiting room where she collapsed in a deep chair. In a few moments he came and found her. "Thank you for coming with me." There was no irony in his voice.

Judgement reversed

The mist had cleared but the flagstones were wet and the bushes scattered droplets when the wind shook them. She walked head down, hands in pockets and he followed. The day was warming but she did not want to pull back the hood because she had not painted her neck. She asked the stones, "You want to eat at home or go out tonight?"

No answer. She turned and found him lost in pain. "Willie. . ." She repeated the question.

"Doesn't matter."

From the corner of her eye she saw a stir in the ivy at the antenna's base; she looked full on, and a man emerged with his eye squinting behind the sight of a flame-gun aimed at them.

She pointed, shrieking, "Willie! Watch out for God's sake!"

He pushed her to the ground and dropped to cover her as the fire burst over them.

Pressed flat, nostrils full of burning, breathless, she heard the *slap!* of an obsolete but still deadly Security rifle, the body skittering down the roof-tiles and falling dead as a grain sack on the flags.

She did not quite faint, but she did not, in mercy, see the weight that was pulled from her, though the blood and burned flakes coating her were not her own.

In an alcove nurses washed her down, dabbed her scratches and stuck her with antibiotics. Security recognized her by the blue skin.

"The killer had no i.d. You have any ideas?"

"No." Dead word.

"I knew Bellingrose—a chaplain on Five doing some GalFed work here."

"The job was finished—for us."

"Well, we'll print him and you can look at the body—"

"No!"

"Of the *killer*. Checking will take a couple of hours. It's too far from home so you can rest here."

"I don't feel like doing anything anywhere."

"Just take this," said the nurse briskly.

Security turned up the light in the cold tank. "He'd been printed for passports and visas, no criminal record. But the passports were issued in two names."

"Pritchard and Richards? Mean the same. Maybe neither was his real name.

"You never said you'd met him."

"No, nor seen him, except in the mind of an ESP."

His clothes had been good, but become worn from his scrambles, and tight from the times when he had nothing to do but sit and eat. His face, its tan faded, was sickly pale, pudgy, and needed a shave. No longer the neatbodied killer. Nothing but a slackfaced dead man. But he was recognizable, as she had seen him in the images given by Quattro and Emerald.

"Anything else you know about him?"

"He was probably doing odd jobs for a few people on your

list, but his regular employment the last four years was with a man living in North Key. Agassiz.''

"You mean the freak?''

Anika lifted and regarded her blue hands, turning them from palm to back, until Security's face had had time to grow very red. "The man in North Key, Agassiz,'' she said, "employed him until he was proven to be—untrustworthy. Then he got kicked out. Anything else you'll have to ask GalFed. Like—like Bellingrose I'm only a part-timer, with a C-3 clearance, and if we learn anything higher by chance we're not cleared to give it. You have my file.''

Security's voice hardened. "I don't want to be pushing up your clearance, but maybe you can give me an idea why this happened?'' For a moment her eyes were murderous. "I'm sorry. I shouldn't have said that—at least not that way. I knew all about Bellingrose and his wife—I've been here as long as she has—and he used to drop into my office for a cup of tea. . .''

Her eyes were full of tears. "This little flea never saw or knew about either of us. And he'd been hiding out. I just don't know why.''

She pulled at the damp wool around her neck, and suddenly she knew why, and went cold.

Renny had taken a couple of these sweaters along on assignment last time, and come home with a distaste for them. Anika, a few centimeters taller, slightly bigger-boned, but lean, with the same walk and gestures. . .

Security, whose name was Arthur Fortescue-Holmes, touched her shoulder and said, "Anika, *I'm* not your enemy. I'll try to leave you alone, but if I have to ask more questions—you'll be around?''

"The rest of my life,'' said Anika.

> *the Diviner pushes thought away and*
> *with blank eyes turns up*
> *The Chariot reversed*

XenoBi's little Surveyor, last to be picked up by the *Zarandu*, was the first to be unhitched when she came out of unspace. The cruiser was now nearer Qsaprinel than Calidor, and XenoBi were grateful to be free of the docking process.

Told to choose their task, they had decided to cripple the Calidor base. They were smarting from the previous attack and its consequences. Kinnear approved: if they succeeded they would pull a big thorn; if not they knew the risks. Probably most of the moon's forces had joined Thorndecker. Maybe not. . .

Linden Eames was a stocky woman with short fair hair turning ashy; she had been a nurse, was divorced, calm by nature. Ned Watts, jockey-shaped, jittered with small-man syndrome; he did not keep count of marriages, liaisons and children. Philpott was bony and weedy; his sexuality seemed to have been subsumed by XenoBi, because nobody had ever seen evidence of it. The three were so sensitive about having widely divergent points of view that they went out of their way to cooperate.

The classes of small ship most costly to GalFed were the Surveyors and lifeboats; both were heavily reinforced: the first because they got a lot of wear, the second because they were designed to survive explosive disasters. All needed much food and fuel, and two modes of controls: simplified and professional. They were often handled by personnel without formal training. Philpott's place was in the cockpit but he would not call himself a pilot, though he took much supplementary instruction. The others also had doubled careers: Watts maintained supplies—like fragmentation bombs—and Linden took care of health & welfare.

Watts said, "They've probably got more radar bases now."

"We have two days to worry about it," said Linden. The world was very small in the viewer, the moon invisible.

"Criminals can afford those things," Philpott said.

"It would have been nice to afford better controls on this crate," said Watts. "And a couple of cannon."

"I'd like to see the kind of welcome we'd get from Praximf wearing cannons," said Linden.

"We're not going there."

"I think I'd rather . . . I wonder if we'll ever go back again."

"I'll be happy not having to go back to Calidor," said Philpott. "Dropping frags! Ugh."

"It's better than being shot at."

"Will there be a choice?"

The automatic course had been fed into the computer, the team well drilled: *Straight in low gives you a chance to duck radar, beep tells you strap in. Retros fire, five seconds to check and correct, beep if you're on. Ten to frag the field and station, beep if you're empty, fire up and around home-free to Qsaprinel and, luck.* Simple.

"It's so simple it's simple-minded," said Watts.

"We stuck it to ourselves," said Linden. "Let's make a vow against agonizing reappraisals."

During the two days the team grew increasingly aware of approaching a cold dark sphere waiting like a squatting toad to flick its tongue at their insect ship.

It was Linden who had named it *Red Rover* after an old childhood game: *Red Rover, Red Rover, let Linden come over. . .*

Launching herself at the linked-arm row of the opposing team. And always breaking through—they did not call her "beef-to-the-heels" for nothing—and once leaving a broken arm in her wake. There was less trouble than she expected, over that, but she never played again.

After two days Standard *Red Rover* came round the sunlit backside of Calidor, radar receptors whining.

"Under the radar my ass!" Watts snarled. "Whup! They're after us, right on our tail! They haven't even set out yet, just waiting! They probably picked us up by *Zarandu's* radio."

"Maybe," said Philpott calmly. "But that little blip there isn't a troop carrier. It's a fighter or shuttle, no bigger than *Rover.* Their guard crew."

"We can swing around without dumping and pick up speed," said Linden.

Philpott could be stubborn. "They may want to keep the base, but *I* don't want them to. Strap in."

"Have some sense!" Watts cried. "They'll be armed, man, and if we fire the retros and slow down they can blast us *and* our frags."

"I think he's right, Philp."

"You think! If they're chasing us they got guns and maneuverability and we're stuck in a klutz!"

"Then what do you want to do?"

"Praximf," Linden said. "Head inward. Use the tangential speed for that. We can warn them down there and they can hide us. It's time they got it straight about what's going on."

"They may not have a Listener on radio—and whatever speed we have won't be enough."

"It'll have to be enough. Don't worry about radio. They're going to get a nasty surprise anyway."

The first missile burst barely missed them, and settled the discussion. Philpott reached for the switches that would make them responsible for themselves. The second missile buckled the viewport and skinned the outer hull. The crew jolted in their harness; Philpott found that one of his canines had gone through his lower lip, and licked blood off his chin. "They're at six o'clock, fifty km and gaining."

Linden found her teeth chattering for the first time in her life. "We can always go EVA and zap them with our stunners."

No laughs.

"We've got the frags," said Watts.

Philpott snorted. "Are we supposed to stand in the bay belly and lob them out?"

"No. Drop about half of them in the disposal and let them go out with the exhaust."

"Are you crazy?" Linden yelled. "We'll blow ourselves up!"

"Not with impact bombs. They won't burn. If we slip them in the tubes nicely they shouldn't hit too hard going down but the casings and adhesives will catch fire. Those fellows might keep a little distance when they see red-hot things coming at them, even if they cool fast and don't hit. We might just have a *little* luck.''

No argument. Watts unbuckled and went hand over hand down the firepole to the hold. Fifteen minutes later there were thirty-odd sinister clang-clangs to the rear. The tubes, not designed to expel fragmentation bombs, had likely been dented, but there were no explosions.

''They hit hard enough to suit me,'' said Linden.

''We're keeping distance,'' Philpott said. ''This damn lip hurts.''

''How long now?''

''Ten hours approach, three landing.''

''We're bringing killers to Praximf,'' Watts said to Linden. ''Anybody thought of that?''

''I like to think we're bringing help.''

''I know bloody well we're running for it.''

The moon was behind them, the sun at one shoulder; the world grew bigger in the screen.

Praximf never seemed quite to obey the laws of nature. This was one reason for XenoBi's enthusiasm about it. Sometimes the globe was completely obscured by cloud, and sometimes what was seen from space did not coincide with what was found on land. The continents tended to slither, if they were indeed land-masses, and the temperature went cold at the equator and hot at the poles when the inhabitants wanted it that way. Seas changed from marsh to abyss at a yawn. Yet XenoBi did not believe that Praximf slid out completely from the fences of theory that contained species and worlds like those of the Crystalloids and the Qumedni. All would be disclosed in the fullness of time—or maybe not. Their diamond-sharp awareness that the population might be controlling their observations did not bother them; they were grateful for any wonders disclosed, and reported them exactly as they found them.

Now the world was a great white pearl of cloud.

"Calidor won't land before we do. They'll want to know where we are."

"So would I," said Philpott. "The radar's gone. I think it got sheared off, and the indicators are loopy. I've set the flight path, but we'll be going blind through that creepy white stuff."

"No, look . . . there's an opening!"

"My God!"

A nacreous cavern of mauve and blue had opened in the pearl. It did not break straight through but curved about into mystery.

"What are we supposed to do with that?"

Linden said, "I—I think we better go in the way they want us to."

"Want us to?"

"I say what I think."

"One more orbit. We could try for a swing back out to Calidor."

But as they passed the shadow-limb into darkness they could see the enemy in a tiny sun-sparkle behind them, gnatlike yet steady and inescapable.

"*They're* not letting go."

Another grinding hour and the *Rover* passed the limb of light, descending; a few moments later the cloud-cavern had revolved to take them in. It was not quite nothingness: a well of clarity faintly rippling with cylindrical vapor-walls.

"I don't believe the radar's gone," said Philpott, "or that it's even worth deploying the vanes. I think the Praximfi are bringing us down—I don't know how or why, and I don't think I'll ask."

"I goddam wish they'd plug this wormhole for that bloody ship," said Watts.

"They do have *some* curiosity," said Linden.

One more unearthly hour. "This is getting me," said Watts. "We should have been through this glop half an hour ago."

"The dials aren't registering atmosphere."

"Then what is this stuff?"

Linden said, "Maybe it's Praximfi."

"That doesn't sound quite rational."

"When were they ever rational?"

"We've always gone through an atmosphere."

"Because they knew we expected one."

"Now that really is—"

"There's the opening," said Linden.

"Godalmighty!" The retros fired none too soon. Flying blind, they had not known they were so close to planetfall, near enough to see that they had overshot the usual landing area near the equatorial sea. This was not a field, but a site at established coordinates cleared for them at notice by the Praximfi. This time they did not know whether there had been notice because they could not tell if their signals had gone out. "Calidor must be right on our tail by now," Watts said. "Have they cleared a place down there?"

Philpott was zooming on it. "Yeah. There's something in it."

"It's them! They got here first after all!"

Philpott said nothing.

"Godammit, Philp!"

"I think it's a ship. It looks like a squashed fly." He sucked his sore lip. "I'm getting readings and I seem to have my controls to hand. One swing around the pole."

A half-hour later they found a clearing expanded from the field occupied by the broken ship, like a bubble growing from its side. *Rover* landed on a faintly quivering surface. What had cleared away was as always a matter of question. It seemed like closely packed desert growth, flat-slabbed cactus or other succulents: grey-green, green, green-yellow, yellow, yellow-orange, orange, swirling and rather sickly colors. The cleared area looked like midbrown loose-grained soil, and when the team emerged from the *Rover* for the fourth time in fifteen years, they stepped on the same dampish ground, circled by the growth in its rippling colors.

But desert cacti stood still under the sun, and these lifeforms under their dim sky shifted with every blink or twitch

of eyelid, every movement of eyeball, so that they appeared
to move jerkily, as by strobe light, every third of a second.
XenoBi, for all their loyalty to Praximf, found the phenomenon one to endure rather than become used to. But they could
ignore it when they stared at the broken unmoving ship. They
leaned against their seared hull, weary and unsure of themselves as they had never been before.

It was Linden who, in trust, opened up her faceplate and
breathed air. She unshipped her helmet, lifted it off and
shook her hair out. She wore no regulation uniform and her
suit, like much of her clothing, was puce, sometimes called
puke by her associates; a color she could wear well only
because it looked good with her complexion. A wave of the
same color lapped toward her among the twisting growths as
in mild enquiry, or empathy; she suspected it was a mere
tropism. The men in their slate suits took off their helmets
and said nothing. Ordinarily the team would have waited in
place for a designated Speaker to form him/her/it/self and tell
them whatever it was willing they should learn of whatever
they wanted to know. Now they stepped forward as one to
inspect the Calidorian wreck. The cactoid forms moved
closer but none stood in their way. Though the ship's body
was only moderately crumpled its ports and bays had burst
outward in huge metal flowers. Six or seven bodies, sexless
in death, hung out of them; a few more lay clear on the
ground. Their faces were purple with exploded veins and
they and the wreckage were draped with drying strands of
something white and semi-liquid like melted soap, and other
fibers with swellings like ganglion lumps.

Maybe these clouds are Praximfi.

That's irrational.

Sacrifices.

"They came smashing through the cloud," said Philpott.

"And smothered," Watts said. "No atmosphere for
them."

"Could the Praximfi use their esp that far?" Linden wondered. "I don't think singly, but maybe together—"

"We cannot touch the moon but we can reach a ship's

orbit.'' The voice began behind them and moved alongside. If the Locksmith was the caricature of a Solthree this Speaker was a caricature of the Locksmith. XenoBi would never know a Praximif's true shape.

Linden, retrieving boldness, said, ''We thank you for saving us. I think I know the answer to my question, but I must ask. You esped these persons and knew they meant to kill us. But was it really their aim to use Praximf for a base?''

''Yes,'' said the translucent Speaker. ''As we know now, conditions on the moon are harsh and they presumed this place would be more . . . comfortable.''

The crowd of cactoid Praximfi shot upward by half a meter in a second and bowed in all directions, rippling with color. There was more than a suggestion of savage and ironic laughter in the silent display, and it unnerved XenoBi. The Speaker said quietly, ''Selfnamed Locksmith did not lie,'' and the beings shrank and pulled half their lengths into the ground. He looked at the wreck and the bodies: the land sank and drew them under, pulling seamlessly together, like mercury, above. The team shuddered as one and dared not look behind to see if their ship existed.

The Speaker said, ''I am sorry we cannot repair your vessel, but it was sound enough to bring you here and it will take you to the Locksmith.''

''You really want us to go back to him?''

The Speaker did not seem to have heard. ''Things have not been peaceful here with ships falling from the sky. But perhaps we need less peace. We shall discover.''

Linden pushed on. ''The Locksmith wanted to die on his home world, but you must know we are not here because of that.''

''We know. You wished to destroy our enemies because of your love for him. We cannot understand your way of thinking completely, but we realize how important your feelings are to you, and how he has formed them in himself: they must have some value.'' He bent to pick up a handful of soil. ''He was the first aboriginal being to leave this world, and there is none other like him. I do not know whether there should be.

Yet, his spirit does belong here. Now he is in danger and may die before he comes.'' He offered his handful to her and instinctively she reached inside her suit for a film specimen-bag, and he emptied the grains into it. It seemed to her to be pulsing with life, an uncomfortable handful but a precious one. "But you have a good hope of reaching him, and when he receives this he will know that wherever he dies he will be home. That we have given acceptance, and you have brought it to him.''

On the way out *Red Rover* picked up a frantic message from Calidor, reaching for their lost ship. The two remaining crewmen on watch had plenty of food and water but were stranded without escape from their desert base. Ammo was running out. What the hell was going on?

XenoBi sent out a call on the police band to the nearest spacelight relay. They passed by on their way to Qsaprinel and did not frag the base. One day GalFed might be invited in. One day those curious and cantankerous Praximfi might wish to reach out. . .

Qsaprinel:
Spinel-beta crouches on the rock in the cavern of sluices facing the grin of

Death

—all he can see of it through the breathing-mask—above the poised flamer. There is a *thunk!* hardly to be heard over the noise, and the grin freezes, the head sinks, the flamer drops unfired.

Beta perceived this dimly, then, eyes popping, crept forward flat to the rock. The sagging body was pierced by two spears, one alien.

Two hailing figures rose in the swirl of waters and men, one a lieutenant in the guard—the other Spinel-alpha, the

Emperor, Imperial armlets on his arms, speargun triumphant in his hand.

Spinel-beta knew what to think and thought it: he was glad at last to see his sib alive and in good health.

Then shock: the Emperor was not only alive, he had *returned*, bringing troops and weapons! And a battle which had been waged in the manner of all battles, bloody, messy, disorganized, was diminishing as its areas were sliced away with surgical precision, until the attack had ebbed.

But the surgeons were not all Qsaprinli. Some were alien, Solthrees—if they were such—of a kind Beta had never seen before, grey men and women with lumpy skins, filter-cups covering what seemed to be gills under their jaws, and protective shields over the places where their legs joined.

"Spinel-beta, your Highness," a chunky grey man kicked the dead pink one from the rock ledge, "please order your unhurt forces to gather the flamers where they have fallen and bring them to us Solthrees. We will give you spearguns. The others are too dangerous for you to use."

Spinel-beta had much to absorb in a short time. The man was ordering him to give orders, speaking Qsaprinli, roughly but easily understood because he was supplementing it with mental imagery. He was an ESP. Beta glanced at Spinel.

:*Do it, Beta.:* No triumph in his mind, using Quattro as conduit through the noise. He was grim. :*The Empress and our family have been captured. The Tower is conquered.:*

The cavern grew quieter. The dead were soundless. The wounded, native or alien, whimpered; prisoners muttered curses. Authority called out orders.

Beta obeyed as in a dream, but no more spearguns were needed. The attackers, surprised from the rear by fifteen grey men, had lost half their number, the Qsaprinli defence nearly half, the Solthree fish-men only one. But the surviving Qsaprinli were bewildered, and thrashed about aimlessly.

"Guards! Sluicekeepers! Do as the aquamen tell you!" Spinel cried.

"Just call us Frogs!" one raucous voice yelled.

"Shut up, dummy," said Quattro. "They don't know
what a frog is. Just keep the flamers out of their hands."

"Hurry!" Spinel was calling. "I want the Tower
searched."

"I want to know what has been going on," said Beta.

But Spinel directed temporary repairs, and other survivors
carried the wounded up ramps to the Great Hall on the ground
floor. That done, the battlers collapsed exhausted.

"Not even a doctor among us," said Spinel bitterly.

"I'll have one flown from the city," Quattro said, reaching for his hand-radio.

"It will take the rest of the day to search this horrible place
and the time will be wasted."

"There are some live ones here. Your people have been
taken hostage. Thorndecker won't kill them right away."

"Right away!" He and Quattro looked each other in the
eye. Quattro's underwater eyes were perhaps closer related to
Spinel's than to those of ordinary Solthrees. Their characters
were equally frank. Spinel looked away.

"Somebody alive three levels up."

To climb those three levels was to pass the bodies of
servants and their children who had lived in the Tower for
years, and on the third ramp the live one was a child with a
mangled shock arm who croaked for its parents.

"God," Fouad said. He had come with Quattro to carry an
extra gun.

Spinel said, "The valves are closed around the wounds.
Trenli, take him down to wait for the doctor."

Beta, remembering past ambitions, had said nothing of the
dead who had given the Spinels their loyalty and lives. Now
he croaked, "There's a noise—"

"Fourth ramp. Concussion," Quattro said.

But Spinel was bounding upward. "Binatrel! Binatrel!"

Binatrel moved feebly in the dim hall. "I think-think my
brain-case is dented." The quivering pouch-flap rattled his
voice. "I am not quite sure where. . ."

"Just a bang and a lump," said Quattro.

"Binatrel! Do you know me?"

"Of course, your Majesty," Binatrel said faintly.

"It is Spinel! Only Spinel! I am sick to death of Majesty if it cannot save my people."

"Not so fast," said Quattro sharply. "There's still a lot of live ones and you've got to save them first."

Spinel comforted the wounded while pools were filled and Beta got his story: hard work for Quattro, compressing it to the point where Thorndecker, having reached Qsaprinel, sent out the amphibian boat which approached in hiding underwater. "I don't think he just got here. This raid was planned too tight. After settling in the valley he sent his shuttle to make a quick snatch while the sub took out the sluices. He made sure you couldn't trap them the way you did before. They even smashed your radio."

"But you can reach the city with your own."

"Yes, this little thing works much like yours. We've sent warnings and we'll be distributing weapons. Thorndecker didn't bother with citizens. He knew they were helpless."

"With this water-ship—they can attack again!"

Quattro grinned without humor. "I sent out six Frogs with flamers. The lock doors were open, they'd been expecting a quick strike and home free. There were eight crew, but any one of us is worth two—or three—of them. I hope one or two are left. We need somebody to steer the thing."

"But how do you come to be here now, when—"

"That was chance. We'd only just come. We never expected to reach here fast as Thorndecker, and we had to travel further in our own shuttles—they're only lifeboats. We were going to land Spinel here so he could see you and his—his—"

"I know. Go on."

"I have pretty good esp. Picked up on the situation. Instead of landing we dropped in."

"What is happening here! What is going on!" The great squawk echoed through the hall.

"Palander," Beta said dully.

"I have burned my sail with the wind to reach you and all I find is ruin!" The old hardgrained figure hopped among the dead and wounded. "By the Great Lord of the Sea and the Winds His Messengers—"

"Palander—" Beta was too drained for greetings, "—this person with me is Quattro, our friend and helper. He is also a reader-of-minds and he will tell you." He turned away and stared moodily at the wounded moving slow and dull-eyed in their basins.

Wearily, Quattro explained again. But the old troller was a veteran of mines and forests where men and women grew tough from work rather than courses of exercise, and tempers flared under savage conditions; he found no conflict hard to understand.

He barely glanced at the Spinels. "How will you bring back my niece and all the others from those monsters?"

Quattro sighed. "Palander, I only just came here. I'm damned if I know." He frowned. "We have the sub in hand now, but one of my crew has a shattered elbow." And sighed again.

"Our doctor will not know how to treat that."

"He may. Qsaprinli have more limbs and joints than we do. If not, he'd better learn fast."

"I see you are undermanned. And if you had plans you would not want to tell me them—no, I realize it is not because you don't trust me, but someone who is no friend might read your mind."

Quattro stared with respect at the quickest-minded of Qsaprinli. "I wish we did have plans."

"Well, you are a great improvement over that other reader-of-minds who was so neatly disposed of by the young woman who works with you—she does work with you, does she not?—you are certainly two of a kind in your ways though her mind could not be read. Can a person capable as you have ways of keeping your mind from being read—even perhaps preventing the minds around you from being read?"

"It's a possibility."

"Then if I can think of useful plans will you grant me that defence?"

"I grant it now, Palander."

Palander did not realize that he had been awarded a privilege Quattro gave so seldom and unwillingly it was on the order of a royal honor. If he had known, he would not have been impressed. "I presume your Commander has hidden himself, but you have reported by radio. Your signals may be intercepted."

"While we use your bands and talk in your language we won't attract much attention. We've already sent the enemy a false message of victory from the sub." He looked about and shook his head. "When I see this mess I wonder if it wasn't a victory."

"Nonsense, man. There are still very many alive."

"I know, I've said it myself."

"Now you must do something more very quickly. I have seen that valley where the base is—but probably you have taken what you need from my memory already."

"Are you sure you're not a reader-of-minds, Palander?"

"I am as old as we come in this world and I have a little good sense in judging men. Do you know anything more of that valley?"

"I know a man who lived in the Colony when it was first built long ago. It has changed somewhat, but not very much."

"No. The best way to attack it is still very difficult."

"Not difficult, Palander. Impossible."

"Rubbish. I have been sitting in my boat thinking of it for three days. There is no easy way—except for your boats of air, which would be brought down. But it can be done by scaling with nets—the things Qsaprinel-by-the-sea has plenty of."

"But you must fasten nets from the top of the scarp."

Palander lifted a shock arm. "What do you think we have these suckers for?"

"On that rough surface?"

"It is rough where the waters fall. Anyone can tell that looking from sea level. But though the scarp was pushed out of the crust by inner fires and collisions, the shear walls are not worn down so much by tides as those of planets with moons—or so my teacher told me at world's beginning when I was a schoolboy."

"I didn't think they'd teach you plate tectonics."

"We were not too proud to learn from Galactic Federation even if we did not want to live with them then." He snorted. "Now you are going to tell me there will be lookouts up on the rim, but I think they will be a bit laggard because no one expects surface attack from the water, and the growth of trees and vegetation make an overhang which should hide climbers, and—" Quattro hunkered to eye level; his brain was buzzing, and he felt as Kinnear had done confronting Ungrukh for the first time; "—if we have one who can hide our minds or teach us to do it, we can climb—maybe slowly—so others can scramble up—and down—swiftly."

"That doesn't get rid of the lookouts."

"We need only a diversion. A simple matter. I will go away for a little while and think about it."

"Do that, Palander. I am terribly tired, and there's still a great deal to do."

"Allow me to swim to the submersible, if it is that thing floating out at sea's edge and bring back your wounded comrade, so that—she?—will not have to move in the water. I think you are short of conveyors too."

"We are, and I'm grateful for your help."

"I do not need thanks, Undercommander, until I have done something worth while."

Kinnear arrived at that moment with the Qsaprinli physician; he had demoted himself to pilot because there was no other capable of handling the rescue capsule, one third of his fleet. The doctor began directing the classification and treatment of wounded. "It could have been worse," Kinnear said. His face was long.

"Everybody's been telling everybody else that. It was

enough. In half an hour I'm going to introduce you to Aspartil's Uncle Palander, who's as old as the universe and pricklier than the heads of all the Frogmen put together."

"If he's that remarkable I'll be glad of his help."

"Just don't thank him or he'll burn you to a cinder."

"I think I've spent half my life on Qsaprinel's problems. I'd better talk to the Spinels now."

Both sibs were extremely distraught about the capture of their family; Kinnear shared their concern and also had his own people to worry about. He took what information he needed with care not to distract them further. He was the only pinkskin in the company and felt some of the emotions he had had long ago on Ungruwarkh. He was used to the feeling now, and kept out of the way, taking a draught from his oxygen tank every once in a while, until enough calm had settled for plans to be discussed.

If a shattered elbow could be called lucky, it was lucky that Settima had been flung against a bulkhead instead of being shot with a flamer. The doctor palpated the limb while she tried to keep from shrieking through her teeth. The skin was unbroken and most of the bone pieces approximately in place. Quattro had studied medicine informally under Agassiz's three doctors for seven years; he and the Qsaprinli doctor agreed that, with no time to invent a system of traction for another species, the arm ought to be immobilized in the most comfortable position that could be determined until there was someone available to treat it better. Qsaprinel was a world without cloth, and if Quattro had had access to adhesives or foam casts they could not have been used on underwater skin. But the doctor produced a fine-textured version of fishermen's netting, and did what Quattro would have praised as an admirable piece of work if Settima had been able to appreciate it. All he could do was offer a heavy painkiller.

She said through chattering teeth, "Now I can't risk a flamer, can you teach me to throw a knife lefthanded?"

268   PHYLLIS GOTLIEB

"And stretch your muscles so your bones get pulled apart? Not yet. You'll have to fight with your head."

"By butting? I'd rather use my feet and—"

"I know. But among the music, chess and architecture you happen to be radio, and that's what I need."

He turned away to avoid a sarcastic reply. But she cried out in a voice edged with panic, "Quattro, you're not going to leave me here!"

The note of weakness hit him painfully, and he was exhausted. He said with care, "Not where there's no kitchens or latrines. I said we needed you."

Perhaps he had left his mind open once too often, too wide. She snarled, "God damn you, I'm no bloody whiner!"

"God forgive me, Settima, I meant nothing insulting! Doctor's got a basin with good water for you and you'd better drop in and sleep while you can." He felt obliged to keep access to her mind for strategic reasons and this depressed him. The remnant of Quattro's people, an experimental species unvalued and wasted, had regathered by chance and become a community without territory or inheritance, with no common culture, goal, or belief. The ratio of eight females to thirteen males gave no advantage to the women. Esteban turned to Settima only when he had a falling-out with Nicklaus. Throwing a bone. Fritz had been killed and it would make no difference. Now there were twenty separate souls. Quattro corrected himself: twenty-one.

"Kitchens and latrines." Quattro's remark had drifted into Binatrel's mind. "Undercommander, the Emperor wishes to keep the prisoners alive and unharmed, and that is all very well. We can find places to put them, we can let them foul a basin or two for the latrines, and we can provide water—but kitchens we have not got."

"My group was in a hurry. We grabbed enough food for one meal here, and Kinnear's running tight too. I did notice a crate of food concentrates Hartog's crew must have left behind in the upper chamber when they took off. There may be more lying about in odd places—so your prisoners can eat, but they'll have to eat thin until we can get this business settled.''

"Commander—" Spinel began.

"Just Kinnear."

"Kinnear, I have given directions to rouse my people and have them gather and fasten the nets we will need, and they will work all night at that. But. . ."

Kinnear, knowing what to expect, waited.

"I do not like to think of myself as a coward—or have others think so—for I have fought—"

"No one can possibly call you a coward."

"That is kind of you to say, Kinnear, but anyone who wishes can call me a coward. Ingenuous as I am I have always known that. Still, I have promised my people that I would return and take up my place as their Emperor. I have done that, and though my Tower has been ravaged and my soul with it, both are standing firm, and I am still the Emperor—even if only for a short while. My soul wants to do battle to save Aspartil and my family, and my brain tells me that over a million of my people are more important to this world than even Aspartil. With my help they must learn defence. I realize that if the enemy knows I am alive the ones I love will be in much greater danger, and it will not diminish when I send all the others I value—Binatrel, Beta, Palander—to fight. But I believe that I must stay in my house with what is left of my guard—in plain sight among my people—and govern.''

His eyes begged. His armlets glittered in the firelight. He was making a decision far more painful than the one to travel in a tiny craft through unimaginable spaces.

It put a great burden on Kinnear. The Qsaprinli had been given much help, but, braced by the courage and determination which had wakened in Spinel by Hartog's outrage of Aspartil; fortified by their own efforts to think for themselves, fight back massive attack, plan attacks of their own; taking all into account, the Qsaprinli had made a great for-

ward leap on their own hind legs . . . and left GalFed in a
bind. The Qsaprinli rescue plan, and the other half of Kinnear's mission: to rescue his own people, were two quite
different actions.

Yet he said, "Spinel, your Majesty, you *are* the Emperor,
and this is your Empire."

By late evening the Great Hall was quiet and dim. A few
sconces had been lit but windows shuttered so that no light
would show a presence in the Tower. The dead had been
hauled away to be mourned briefly before they were weighted and sunk. Palander and the Spinels co-ordinated information. The Frogs worked on the sluices.

"Your plans are ingenious, but terribly risky," Spinel told
Palander.

"Of course, your Highness. They correspond to the situation."

"Even if I were intelligent as you I doubt if I could think of
better ones," Spinel said mournfully.

"There is nothing wrong with your brains, Emperor. I
have had more information and a good quiet time to think in.
If you approve my proposal for a distraction we must act at
once."

"Yes . . . I suppose so."

"And I would like your sib to come with me and lend
authority to the orders we must give. I will do my best to keep
him from exposure to great risk."

"Risk!" Beta sputtered. "It is a wonder I am alive! In the
light of your feelings about me do you really want me with
you, Palander?"

"Yes, your Grace. You are brave and quick-thinking."

"I really wish I were so brave."

"Binatrel would say so, and—and feelings do change with
time. What do you say, your Majesty?"

"Go," said Spinel.

"Kinnear."

"Yes, Palander."

''We don't want to know where your ships are hidden, but when you return could you leave Beta and me within half a day's footway to the valley? Beta is not heavy, and if we both lose a little water I doubt we will overburden your craft.''

Kinnear stared. ''I hope your plan is as effective as it is wild. Work out the distance and be ready in one Local hour.''

Quattro shook his head. ''Wild is the word. The whole damn thing is going to be a fireworks exhibit.''

''Yeah. We're stuck with helping it work, and if it works it'll help Qsaprinli.'' He pulled a rough hand-drawn map from his pocket. ''The Ungrukh are used to stone cliffs, but net-climbing is out for Solthrees without training—either our Family or my so-called Military. Look: the valley's a rough triangle with the base at top and the apex—more of a semicircle—to the south. Palander thinks he can make a rush from the north, and it's going to have to be sustained over a big area of fields and tillage—''

''While my Frogs and Qsaprinli are scrambling up from the south over the scarp—''

''So the only way for me to come is through the forest and over the western hogsback, while, if the Qsaprinli get away, Thorndecker can jump into his shuttle and take off.''

''You'll have to take out the shuttle.''

''Easier said than done. Let's say it's done. North to south Qsaprinli are going over cliffs, Thorndecker and Co. are trying to escape from east to west—''

''Where you'll be waiting for them.''

''And what if Thorndecker goes off his head and decides to flame all my people first? Our people. The people you lived with. The Tower raid was an act of mad egotism. It doesn't do him any good and it makes things bloody for us.''

''That's what he likes,'' said Quattro.

He found himself staring at Settima's bath, which contained nothing but water. He had a moment of fear until he scanned: she was monitoring the radio in the pilot capsule on the beach.

:I didn't say you had to start right away, goddammit!:
:Do you want the message or not? I think it's nonsense.:
:An offworld message? With our signal?:
:It says: TO CRAB NEBULA.:
:That's us.:
:WE'LL GO NO MORE A-ROVING/ SO LATE INTO THE NIGHT/ BUT AGAIN THE HEART IS LOVING/ AND THE MOON AT LAST IS BRIGHT.:
:That's all?: Kinnear asked. *:They haven't improved Byron but the loving heart probably has to do with Praximf and the Locksmith, and it appears Calidor's been cleaned out.:*
:You mean it isn't nonsense?:
:It's not exactly clear—but it's not Thorndecker's fist and XenoBi do know me. How or why they went to Praximf is a mystery but it's not bad news, for a change.:
:Now thank me for being on hand.:
:Thank you, dear,: said Quattro. *:The message would have been recorded and waiting. Just get into the bath.:*

He watched her coming in. She was neatbodied, her face broad, with slavic cheekbones, and a deep skull to support it. Not at all deflated, she managed a genuine grin while she sank into the water.

Kinnear, waiting for his passengers, leaned against the capsule with arms folded and ankles crossed as he always did when he was pummeling his brains.

Quattro said, "At least you've got some experience from being in Security. I've never given orders and I feel my age has doubled in the last ten hours."

"You don't look a day older. Right now I'm a Civil Service man, a nameless drudge called Commander."

"Yeah."

"Here's a real puzzle. Thorndecker's got that fast ship of his orbiting far up over the ocean on the world's backside. They couldn't have missed us coming in, but they've kept complete silence, unless they've got some kind of radio or signal so advanced that we can't pick it up."

"I don't believe that."

"No, it's not a Qumedni-type thing; it belongs to our plane of existence. But I was pretty sure he didn't intend to leave—at least to go any great distance—when he settled in. He's put everything he owned into the expedition, if not more."

"So it probably doesn't belong to him. He's paid for the ride but not the ship."

"And its owners may not want to start fighting for him. But it's waiting for something."

"Merchandise?"

"Maybe. Samples, anyway. Jewels and wood and— maybe he's not gone completely crazy yet, taking the Qsaprinli royals. Samples. . ."

"Slaves, as Emerald said."

"Thorndecker the showoff, paying his dues with the Royal Family. The coup. Still, I don't think that ship will move against us. It can't land and if it lades from here it will be criminally liable now the world's in GalFed. If I got the XenoBi message right Thorndecker can't bring in any more troops, we've got the sub . . . and if we can only crimp the shuttle. . ."

"But how much does he know about *us?*"

"He's got to wonder something when the sub hasn't come back. We'd better send a message about technical delays, and you've got to get moving by morning with those nets. Here come my hitch-hikers. Let's not bother wishing each other luck. Let's just bloody well get to work."

the Knight of Swords, alone

By GalFed Standard Time Qsaprinel's day measured 27 hours, 11 minutes, 9.2 seconds. GalFed had previously calibrated the day into 24 slightly stretched hours for convenience. Qsaprinli did not need all these hours. They had simple cogged clocks marking off 8 daylight divisions and 4 night ones for work-time, hospital care and guard duty. Kinnear used GalFed time and in an hour and a half of this

had departed his passengers and reached his "base" in a
clearing north of the valley, and hypnoformed his craft
alongside the two other boats, so that temporarily the vegetation there had thickened. An hour was spent in debate which
reached a foregone conclusion. Raanung concluded it by
insisting on setting out alone to cripple Thorndecker's shuttle. "I travel fastest and least noticed. You cannot hypnoform
a running object, nor does radar pick it up on the ground. If
the Locksmith is alive and present he covers me, if not I am in
no more danger than Emerald. Besides, the atmosphere is
thinner here, like Ungruwarkh, it is good to have a run in the
fresh air." Forty km was a good run even for a Hillsman.
"You get signals when the timers are set, and I find a place to
hide. I am sure you trust me."

"I do," said Kinnear.

"Then I see you in good time." He had eaten all the food
that could be spared for him and digested it with a nap; he
bounded out of the smothering, over-ventilated space for a
good run in the fresh air.

His pupils dilated, his skin rippled, his tail curled upward;
he moved, shoulder-blades pumping, in a steady lope, knife
in its harness, plastic and detonators in his pouch. Among the
hazy stars he had Praximf's sun for his timepiece; he did not
want his wrist bound by a chronometer. He clove mists that
eddied briefly along his flanks, sometimes a drop of conden-
sation from the low branch of a semisucculent tree dripped on
him and he twitched it off. Sometimes he scented small
animals, but they did not run in fear because none on this
world recognized the smell of Predatory Cat.

He ran uphill over stones and downhill through rank grass
with the savage joy of the marauding Hillsman, fear for
Emerald compressed to a small knot in his belly, and the skin
of Civilization, if only for a few hours, grown very thin. As
compass points he had the shoulder of the eastern scarp to his
left and the rush of the most easterly branch of the Great River
to his right. Among aliens here only he and the Frogmen
found the thin air refreshing; he would have preferred it
dryer.

Occasionally he smelled Qsaprinli: they were lonely foresters who, having no comfortable basins, slept in huts on
wetted grass-piles so that the wind could not dry them out.
Many were not over-nice about housekeeping and their grass
reeked of rot and mold, but their own animal smell, their
reptile smell, reminded him of the Khagodi, and was com-
forting.

Presently the River veered southeast; soon he must cross it.

At the shore he stopped to rest and felt some small creatures exploring his fur; a dose of cold water would discourage
them. He unhooked the pouch and held it in his jaws. It was
waterproofed but he considered the risks of teeth and saliva
lesser than drenching and rock-ripping. The waters chattered
over pebbles and roared over rocks, but though broad they
were more noise than depth and came no higher than his
shoulders. He did not much like swimming, particularly
athwart the current, and his jaws ached from stretching.
When he came out he shook himself and replaced the pouch,
but did not rest again. He judged he had come halfway in less
than half the allotted time, but the ground ahead was rougher.

The noise of the River faded, and the escarpment angled
away, but he kept his direction by the arc of the star and,
when he heard the first faint hiss of the River's central
branch, was satisfied. From here he had only to follow it
through the Valley. His tail lowered and straightened, his
pistons shimmered, he was very fine and whole in his skin.

He crossed a roadway and passed a heavy-timbered bridge
that was no use to him; he would have been glad to see one
earlier. Past the bridge the ground became so rough and
humping that he found no more signs of Qsaprinli, and he
understood Kinnear's respect for Palander, who had none of
the big cat's range and youth.

The mists were thicker to the ground, and his nocturnal
eyes had to watch for traps where the roiling water sliced
gorges through softer stone and forced him to climb em-
bankments. But the River was straight. He and the water ran
together, it rattled, whispered, foamed over rock-piles, but it
was no companion. It had nothing to say to him. It led him

over a strange world to a valley of destruction.

His sense of freedom and wholeness changed by degrees
into loneliness. He remembered the corridors of Wardman's
malevolent house, how he had kept close to the walls. Now
he wanted Emerald, to distract from the River's nonsense by
speaking sense, no matter how sharp or ironic, no matter how
he resented her withdrawal out of stupid loyalty. He himself
was bound by loyalty.

Eventually he crouched among thorny bushes and looked
down into the Valley as far as mist would allow. The sky was
dark.

This place, which he knew only from a rough map, showed
nothing to mark a divide except the rim past which the ground
sloped downward and did not seem to rise again. There were
no fences and no guards this far out. Perhaps there was a
wind-drift of heavier air, or he imagined one. The vegetation
did not change much, and tilled fields were several kilometers away. He slipped over the crest and went to ground in
stalking mode. Then jerked in a startle of fear. There was a
blip! in his mind as if a bubble, reversing time, had popped
from nothingness into being. He wound his tail around his
rump and took one cautious step. No physical change, in
body or surroundings. An esp shield. Not Emerald, yet not
unfamiliar. The Locksmith.

He stood for a moment, waiting for communication. Nothing. This must be all the Locksmith dared. He inferred a
message: I am in occupied terrain and must make myself
invisible.

That was no problem. The leopard, tawny and spotted by
day, scours villages unseen by night and ravages where he
chooses. Raanung, incommunicado, could maintain invisi-
bility by night. Praximf's sun was above the mist, over the
eastern horizon: it gave him time to complete his work. He
ran, trusting the frail bubble, along the River, through mist,
among trees in their starshade, soon past fields and outbuildings, smelling those few who now guarded the limits and saw
no moving shape, heard no twig crack. Into the scrub along
the riverbank, downward always to the deeper air where his

breathing rasped a little, watching for those poles with eyes, described by Palander.

He could not see in darkness as well as Palander in day-light, but he saw those eyes before they saw him. He could slip between just as neatly and more quickly—unless they were heat-sensitive. With this thought he had the feeling that the skin of his bubble had been tweaked.

Either the Locksmith was trying to warn him, or someone had twigged to the shield, or both. He cast about for a dip in the bank where he could slip down easily, found one, and returned his attention to the spy-eyes. He slithered forward until he could measure their turns. When the two nearest completed their stereoscopic cycle he rolled down the dip in the bank and soaked himself in water, watching until they were near the apogee of their wall-eyed stance, then ran like a demon between them, dripping cold water. Not until he was half a kilometer past them did he pause to shake out his fur. His heart was thudding and his blood stinging with reactive heat. Here he was passing tillage and the small dark houses of Solthrees. These were unguarded and therefore held nothing of value. According to Doctor, Thorndecker-Hyde had planted his house in view of the sea, not far from the southern rim, and he thought Thorndecker II would do the same. He knew that within his film of protection he was pitifully unprepared for squads of men with flamers and perhaps electrified fences. He did not pity himself. He had great experience packed in his few years, and those who held Emerald bound and powerless were just as unprepared for one more bigger cat, this one unbound, half again as heavy as a leopard, just as savage, and hundreds of times more intelli-gent.

He drove forward until he saw lights and heard strange noises. Passed among robot farm machines, cold and still, and sheds storing implements whose smells of wood, oil and metal distracted from other scents. He did not want to catch the scents of his friends, for fear they might enrage him: in rage he would be useless. Crouching at last in the shadow of some house or barracks where he could see all. Too much.

There was an open place, covered with fine grass, fronting
the largest house, which might be Thorndecker's. He could
not see the shuttle, which should have bulked against the sky,
but he could see that in this lawn a pit had been dug and filled
with water. Qsaprinli were inside it, crammed every which
way, and around them, dissipating the mist, a circle of
burning sconces mounted on standards with armed guards
between.

The Qsaprinli squirmed and thrashed, and if their snouts
reached above the surface they made feeble noises. Some
were quite small, and if one tried to creep out of the pit it was
nudged back in by the foot of a guard. The family were not
being   harmed—Thorndecker   would   not   spoil   his
merchandise—but they were in torment.

Raanung had known only one Qsaprinil, and that was
Spinel; the two had seldom spoken to each other, but
Raanung knew that a Qsaprinil must draw air into the pouch
to speak because the lungs were not near the cradling area.
The drawing of air was so practised that it was unnoticeable.
But these Qsaprinli, crying out in fear and anguish, drew air
in painful rasps, croaking and whimpering until they were
pushed down by their struggling fellows. They were impossible to count, but Raanung judged there were over twenty.
He did not wonder why Thorndecker had not simply laded
them into the ship behind the world. He remembered Quattro's story, and knew. The flames and whimpers were hor-
ridly hypnotic.

He felt something shifting in the bushes beside him, without sound or leaf-stir. His hair rose. He smelt nothing familiar, nothing animal, but his senses were confused. Yet there
was a presence. He forced calm on himself and thought
clearly: *Locksmith's world decides to accept him.* He
watched the guards. Not one turned to flame him. His claws,
unconsciously extended, pulled in. He turned his head very
slowly to the east and saw the Praximf's star had disappeared
and the sky was blank in its area. Any fool should have
known the shuttle would be hypnoformed.

He backed slowly and ran westward along the freshly

planted shrubbery behind the buildings. When he came to the area between the house-group and the scarp rim he could see the stars again. There was a guard on that part of the slope, reclining with eyes on the flames. He seemed a little stupefied and perhaps had taken some drug out of boredom. His eyes did not catch the shadow of Raanung climbing the scarp north of him, over, and passing beneath; he gripped the steeply sloped crags with the splayed hind feet of Ungrukh.

He was acquainted with hypnoforming, but he had never found an object disguised in a cleared area, and nearly transparent. The shuttle had occluded the faraway star, which was not very bright, but he could see the fires and guards through it as if it were a blurring lens. Even its landing field, a patch of wild grass, had no marks.

He had brought with him only the vaguest image of the shuttle. He was confident that the Locksmith could give him a better one, and he got it. As well, the warped outline and the mist-drift showed some configuration of the nose and half-retracted wings, and not far behind those would be the lateral exhausts. His aim was to mar, not destroy or hurt anyone. From a screen of shrubbery, he surveyed: the man on the rim was nearly asleep, the one at the sea-watch looking at the struggling Qsaprinli. The Locksmith might be holding them. He crawled into the darkness between ship and rim. Something—the Locksmith?—advised him not to paw about the flank for fear of alarms. He was relieved not to find forcefields or fences, but both for this place would have been prohibitively expensive. He stalked the ship's flank, sniffing, and when he felt heat and smelt fuel, extended a hand gingerly. It disappeared—an eerie feeling—into a warm opening. Probably there would be others higher up, but he dared not climb or reach. He pulled a block of plastic from his pouch, pressed a detonator into it and flicked the timer, pushed it against the upper surface of the invisible cylinder where it would explode into the other exhausts and ripple the flank.

He picked up a few familiar scents, one labelled *dog*. The dogs would be asleep, or they would have smelled him.

There were faint currents of friends, a few micrograms of
Emerald that tightened the knot in his gut and shot pangs from
it. He slid under the shuttle's belly, past the runners, and
repeated the process. This was most dangerous, because he
could be seen. But the men nearest him, some forty meters
away, had their backs to him, and those facing were distracted by firelight and their prisoners. When the detonators
switched on they each caused a millisecond burst of static
over a wavelength prepared for them on Kinnear's radio.
Then Raanung was really on his own. He crept back under the
boat and into darkness northward, then over the ridge of the
scarp walking in silence down the cold stone slope; trotted
north four or five km along the shingle, found a crevice big
enough to shelter him, and crouched there. His nose began to
run and he felt his temperature rising, from the drenchings.
He was going to be uncomfortable for a while. He would not
think of Emerald, and didn't know where his next meal was
coming from. Nevertheless he slept.

Strength

   The Locksmith, though unconfined, was a captive of conscience. The experience was wearing. Protecting Raanung so
well that even Emerald did not suspect his presence was a
small effort; one on quite another scale to keep Sylvie's
personality continuously superimposed over Renny.

   Thorndecker's Family were being held in two small buildings, each with a dim skylight, a heavy door, a sink and a
lavatory. They were not separated by sex; Thorndecker did
not worry about privacy. Emerald woke hungrily in a
storeroom, alone, with limbs firmly haltered, surrounded by
paint, tiles and concrete blocks, none useful for escape. Once
in a while some person with a flamer in one hand opened the
door long enough to shove in a food bowl with the other.
There was one bucket for water, another for excreting, and
the food was Solthree concentrates. Thorndecker had not
prepared for Ungrukh.

She scanned to find the others unharmed and in various states of apprehension, and Renny through their eyes. She sent the others nothing but the message that she was alive; she was horrified to discover the pit full of Qsaprinli. She touched Thorndecker and Esne lightly to orient herself: there was nothing to say to them.

Renny was worst off. Maintaining herself as a pale timid ESP with red hair was not the difficulty. She had wakened with the discovery of a severe allergy to the wig's adhesive, felt her scalp streaked with swollen running welts that itched and stung, and dared not touch it. Even the Locksmith could not have helped her.

It was the morning after the Tower raid when Thorndecker marched his Family (and dragged Emerald) out to observe Qsaprinel's Royals. The large southernmost house, set on a two-step carpeted dais, had a roof of Roman tiles much like Wardman's. Before its entrance was a massive high-backed wooden chair with a low seat. It was deeply carved; in its velvet cushions Thorndecker sat at ease. Esne perched on one armrest; an ESP-two stood beside her to help with translation. He was a captive, as Quattro had been, but without comparable resources. Renny did not look at them. She almost forgot about her scalp when she saw the Qsaprinli.

Thorndecker straightened. He was wearing a richly embroidered linen robe and did not seem uncomfortable in the cool air, though his thinly-clothed Family were. His tiny bare feet dangled a few centimeters from the carpet. Thorndecker's Empire had all the characteristics of any raw new colony, except the spirit. The citizens were armed, the slaves overpowered. The day was grey and moist.

He said, "This is the Royal Family of Qsaprinel, in a pit, except for the Emperor and his sib, who are dead." His voice was shrill, but so clear and precise the whimpers from the pit did not blur it. "I brought them—and you—here at great risk and expense. *They* will be sent away to be sold as slaves—" the shuttle was visible, and ready, "—and *you* are expected to appreciate the trouble I have taken for you. Any who wish

to come forward and thank me for restoring your rightful
inheritance will find me appreciative.'' His eternally staring
eyes rested on each in turn.

:Noon,: said the Locksmith to Emerald alone.

No one stepped forward. This was not quite disconcerting
to Thorndecker. His people had long been under the influence of Agassiz; he had interfered little. But he had persuaded himself of a trace of appreciation.

''So.'' He pursed his mouth. ''Perhaps you are still partly
controlled by this feline ESP. I admit I did not expect to find
this one.'' He turned his attention to Emerald, who blinked.
''Quattro was the one I wanted, and it is a great disappointment to have lost him. A great disappointment. Oh, I wanted
him! But I can bear that, yes, and this one is much stronger.
Even Esne would admit it.'' He raised his little hand to ruffle
the blueblack plumage. The emerald eyes spun. ''And this
cat will give us every bit as much entertainment. When we
are finished there will be no more influence and I will ask
again.'' Emerald did nothing. Any move would have increased his rage. Even nothing was enraging, because a
guard raised a foot to kick her, and pulled it back on some
unspoken order.

The inevitable unforeseen happened. Aspartil, desperately
searching for help, identified the woman who, as Binatrel
had told her, killed her attacker. Healthy adult Qsaprinli are
hard to differentiate: they wear no clothing, have few expressions, little fat, and a narrow range of brown-grey coloring.
They learn early to recognize each other by manner of
movement, temperament, communication. Those who
learned to identify Solthrees disregarded clothing and complexion and used their own standards, adding the two basic to
Solthrees: body and facial configuration. Aspartil ducked
into the water, hoping the jolt of recognition had gone un-
noticed. It might have done, because Thorndecker had not
bothered probing his merchandise. But her tremor had jolted
Lady Petranyl's memory too, and, chronically unable to use
her brains except where they would do the most harm she

cried out, "That is the woman who was here before! Help us, please help us!"

While eyes turned to Renny one of the smaller Qsaprinli crawled out of the pool and scurried away, driven by a terrified child's urge to run. An unthinking captor shot a spear through it. It wailed, writhing horribly, and died.

Thorndecker flicked a glance. A woman near the killer opened a flamer on him. He died with one shriek. Thorndecker wanted all of his merchandise. The child had been one of First Concubine Inatrili's last brood, decanted a few days after Meta-Spinel's fission. Inatrili's scream was not as loud as the dying man's but went on much longer. There were no words to it.

"Stop that noise!" Thorndecker snarled in a rat's squeal. The Qsaprinli understood the meaning if not the language. Inatrili subsided, whimpering, "Bring the child to me. Someone."

Aspartil clambered out of the pit. If the murderer were not already dead she would have hugged him with her bipolar arms and died satisfied. No one tried to stop her. She broke the spear by twisting one of the shocks around it, carefully lifted off the body and returned it to the pit. She knew the child was dead; so did its mother. But Inatrili blurred that knowledge in her mind and clasped the limp body to her belly.

"Soon you will be travelling away from us and you will not have to worry about such unfortunate accidents. Now be quiet. I am tired of your noise and have allowed it to go on far too long." The ESP aide translated, but the Qsaprinli were already silent.

"Bring Gurdja here." One of the men, grinning, grabbed Renny by the arm with one hand and with the other ripped off the wig and tossed it aside. Its interior was streaked with blood and pus and she needed no esp to learn of the sores crawling among the fine black down of new growth. She clamped her mouth shut and let herself be pulled to the steps and shoved down. Emerald growled.

:Shut up,: said the Locksmith. *:He hates you most.:*

Thorndecker hardly blinked at Renny. He caressed his
Encid. "You were right all along, Esne, and I was mistaken.
My apologies." Esne preened under the caress, but knew
nothing of apologies. A servant in hopsacking and rough
sandals had cut a branch and whittled a half-meter stake with
a sharp end. Thorndecker accepted and admired it. "Very
simple and effective."

Emerald was thinking: *Noon,* the Locksmith had said. She
knew that noon was the sun at zenith, and something crucial
would happen then. But the sun, barely visible, was too far
from that place.

Thorndecker was surveying the nine true members of his
Family. "That little Sylvie who seemed so timid," he
sighed, "actually ran off. But I have others waiting to be
brought to me . . . You. Morgan Owen. You nearly became
the pimp's little whore." He giggled. "Don't you consider
yourself lucky? Come here."

His watchdog was careful not to prod him and Morgan
obeyed. Thorndecker locked eyes on him. "That is a traitor
lying there, and you have another opportunity to express
appreciation." He lifted the stake. "You are a good strong
young fellow. We will find you a mallet and you will drive
this stake through her heels and hang her by it on that branch
there until she smothers in her own blood." He brought the
rounds of his eyes to bear on Morgan.

Morgan said, "No."

The Locksmith was protecting him. Perhaps. Emerald did
not dare touch him.

Thorndecker blinked. "It is true you took her to bed, but
you are forgiven because you did not realize how valuable
you are to me." His eyes burned blue flames.

Morgan looked down at Renny, who had turned her head
away and wrapped her arms around it. "No. I won't do
that."

The eyes narrowed and shifted to Emerald. She heard one
step before a gun butt thumped her in the kidneys. She
howled. She did not have any of Renny's notions about pride.

"Hold her, Esne," said Thorndecker, and to Morgan, "Come up here and kneel where I can reach you."

Morgan knelt. The little hand stretched out and hooked a finger in the loop of Morgan's zip. It began to pull down.

"There was much red hair in the family, I have heard," Thorndecker said. "The hair on your chest is almost as dark as mine." He rubbed it between his fingers and pulled the zip down a little further. Morgan looked at the hand as he might watch a cobra's eyes. There was a tiny ring on one finger, worked into the shape of a buckle, with a minuscule ruby alongside. A thing people who knew nothing of babies might choose as a gift. "I do truly care for you," said Thorndecker. The zip went down and the fingers kneaded a fold of flesh. The men and women standing about were grinning, some openly laughing. Morgan flushed and kept his face expressionless.

Emerald wondered if the Locksmith, that volume of changeable liquid and fiber, really understood what a person might think or feel. She risked a probe into Thorndecker's crazy mirror-house of a mind and was astonished, not at the resistance, which she had expected, but at the reflection darting into a corner of her own mind: *Engni, not long past weaning, clawed and kneaded at the awn hair of her belly in search of her shrunken teats. . . .*

Thorndecker, for once, was telling the exact truth. He loved Morgan, the most familial looking of his kin, was trying to express it, was so warped he must make it appear obscene. And why should he not be a hopelessly twisted analogue of Agassiz?

The hand moved from the flesh to pull the loop a little further. "You know I care. You know. Now do what I ask."

Perhaps the Locksmith had gotten the message. Perhaps Morgan did: he was a Thorndecker. His face returned to its normal color. He said quietly, "I believe you." Very gently he removed the hand from his flesh and his clothing and pulled up the zip. "But I can't do a thing like that even for all your love."

Thorndecker gave a high squealing shriek and shoved the

blunt end of the stake into Morgan's chest so that he
staggered. "Get out of my sight!" He pointed the stake and
screamed again, "There is another ESP here! You! Come
here with a knife and skin the truth out of this damned cat!"

Morgan pulled Renny away and no one noticed. A shadow
approached Emerald once more. From far away the dogs
started yelping and then stopped. She had one last glimpse of
the sun.

:The sun is high, Locksmith!:

No answer. Lost, lost! She opened jaws to howl and bit on
a thrust stick gagging her and tied behind her head.

There was a red blur running, leaping, ducking, twisting,
roaring.

:No, Raanung! No! Get away, away!:

But he was wild, he might have been a living demon.
Before he was half-noticed he was crouched before
Thorndecker taking a rasping lick of his feet. He grinned and
snarled, "O great Master! Now you know we are alive whom
you believe dead, listen one moment before you kill us
again!" He had become the old savage fool his father Mundr
had been and he did not care. His nose was wet, his eyeballs
pure red, fever-heat beat from his body. Thorndecker seemed
paralyzed. Emerald took the last desperate strength of her
fury over all she had endured, rolled it into a white fireball
and flung it at Esne.

The effect shocked her. Esne's own strength seemed to
implode. She keeled over and fell off the chair arm in one
swooping curve, landing with a thump on the dais.
Thorndecker hardly noticed with Raanung's fangs and claws
facing him and fierce tongue-rasp on his feet. His forces
blinked themselves out of a trance and raised weapons.
Emerald tried uselessly to hold the slippery glass of his mind.

"Let me speak now and do as you like!" The weapons did
not fire. "Yes, there is one more ESP you are trying to catch!
He is called the Locksmith. He comes from Praximf. You
know the moon of that world, not so? His people are very
powerful. He is very powerful and he does not like you at all.

But he does not have to fear for his world now, because your base on his moon is gone. You do not have to worry about your submersible, because Quattro owns it. Nor boast about your Tower of stone, Master, for Spinel owns it!''

Thorndecker found voice. "Lies! Lies!" he screamed. "You are going to die like her! And you!" to his shrinking family, "you! None of you are real or true or worthy of me! me! All of you will die! Let out the dogs!"

The eight dogs which had been guarding the work site and were trained to sniff out Qsaprinli came baying and yapping, great Alsatians with spiked collars, to snap about the trembling captives in the pit.

"Give over!" Raanung growled. "You are breaking!"

"Lies!" Thorndecker shrieked. "Kill these damned cats first and then those ten and give all in the pit to the dogs!"

The assistant ESP cried, "Sir! Sir!"

Emerald was quick enough this time to freeze the woman who was lifting her flamer toward the helpless man. :*Get away, man! Hide!*:

"Kill!"

To the north someone yelled, "Fire!"

"Yes, fire!" Thorndecker screamed. And froze.

The clump of bushes beside his house grew turbulent with crackling, and a man rushed out of them, waving a handgun and roaring. A big redfaced man with a shock of white hair, red traces in it, he was thinned a little with age, but had been a bull in his time, a leader of men. His denims, stained with earth and blood, had once been fine as silk, its buttons were smoked pearl.

"Stop this nonsense, you damned fools! What is this place! What have you made of my land! Where are my sons, my daughters, my grandchildren! What have you done with them!" He waved his old gun at Thorndecker, who shrank. "What are you and your toy soldiers doing with my chair, my house, my world? What ugly beasts have you dragged here to foul *my* land with? Get out of here! Take your trash and your thugs and your beasts! This world belongs to *me*, Henry

Thorndecker-Hyde!'' The diamond in his massive gold ring
blazed, and his eyes burned with it. "Get out, you filth, get
out!''

Thorndecker fainted.

"Fire!''

Servants, slaves, whatever Thorndecker called those who
did his work, poured out of the buildings in the north,
screaming.

"By Firemaster, it *is* a fire!'' Raanung snarled. He pulled
out his knife and slashed Emerald's bonds; their guards were
watching six great clumsy flatbeds loaded with burning logs,
twigs, chips, roaring down the northern slope, piloted by
Qsaprinli who must have been as brave as three times their
number in Ungrukh.

The troops with spears and flamers aimed them to kill
where they could, but their fire was returned from the scarp's
edge, swarming with Qsaprinli and Solthrees who looked
much like Quattro, Quattro among them. They lowered
weapons and ran for the shuttle; when they were a few meters
away there was a *crump!* and then another *crump!* The
exhausts exploded in metal blossoms.

There was no lack of bravery in them, though none worried
about Thorndecker. They turned westward, firing as they
ran—right into Kinnear's bureaucrat-greys with flamers.

The Qsaprinli in the pit, besieged by dogs, were not
helpless. They had pushed the youngest to the bottom, and
though none were as skilled as Beta at squirting electrified
streams, all had done it as playful children, and in non-lethal
sport in youth. Aspartil, Dunenli, the Dowager, Lady Petranyl and Lord Beletrel had stunned five of the dogs and sent
them howling. But Inatrili, in overpowering rage, had killed
the one she aimed at. It lay with twisted body and smashed
teeth.

Emerald squinted at the sun and found it in a plumb line
overhead. And eventually there was another mess of dead
and wounded, Kinnear standing in the middle of it all, saying, "My God, we did it.''

Thorndecker was still unconscious, his baby's rosebud

mouth twisted in the dark beard. The old man had disappeared, and on the ground in his place lay a little hairless one
in a black zipsuit, hands folded on his chest; straight, cold,
pale as a stone carving on a bier.

Emerald asked herself if the Locksmith were dead, and if
he had created an illusion, rather than changing shape. Then
she remembered: "Esne! Find her! Her scent is on the carpet!" The strange creature had regained consciousness and
run off, and the Ungrukh were off and running too.

The trail was short. Esne was in a corner of the very
toolshed Emerald had been kept in. Her eyes spun wildly and
she was doing a crazy jigging dance on her six-clawed foot.
She was not trying to control anyone and no one was using
her as a channel. Emerald moved closer, curious but cautious; Esne, in absolute terror, took this as an attack and
crouched with madly-waving feather-leaves.

"What *is* the matter with that creature?" Raanung asked.

"Look."

Esne was trying to hide three small objects behind her.
Emerald at first thought they were excrements, but the smell
was of humus, Esne's flesh. They were bound about by some
fiber glistening like silk, and each contained a spark of life.

"That creature is a mother," said Emerald.

Raanung snorted. "Some mother."

The Encid was shooting small thought like needles that
stung for a moment: *Home. Rain forest. Capture. Ship.
Wreck. Rescue by That One. Promise of Home.*

"I understand," Emerald said. *"That One* promises you
home and he is a liar. You know it. *I* cannot promise to send
you home, but I try. I am not lying and you know that too."
She closed the door on Esne and said to Raanung, "Don't let
me forget her."

"She is a murderer."

"A murderer's weapon. Not admirable, but unjustly used
. . . and wants to go home. Everyone wants to go home."
She sighed.

A gravel voice assailed her. "What are you, creature?
Why are you here?"

"I am Emerald, Palander, and I think you know of me."

"Indeed, and at last I know you as well. You are one of those we must thank."

"Ha." Emerald grinned. "And now the Solthree stink does not seem so bad to your people, maybe?"

"What are you trying to tell an old troller of rotten sea-weed, woman?"

Qsaprinli doctors were repeating the scene in the palace hall, dragging off the dead, sorting out and trying to succor the wounded of several species and conflicting loyalties. Quattro had lost a few spines he did not miss; Sesto was dead, as were two of Kinnear's conscripts, one Qsaprinil, four of Thorndecker's men and two of his slaves. Three times as many were wounded. Renny was grateful to have her head anointed, then went off and hid herself. Raanung's fever was brought down by antibiotics and left behind a snivelling cold which he shrugged off contemptuously.

Thorndecker was still unconscious, and the Locksmith lay unmoving before him. Exhibits.

Quattro, Kinnear, and Spinel-beta regarded them. "The Locksmith's not dead," Kinnear said. "If he was he'd be a puddle and a couple of lumps."

:Thank you for those kind words, Kinnear. I am exhausted.:

"Good job you did on Babyface here. Managed to bring him down without insulting his body."

:Whatever Emerald may think, I do have feelings . . . I did that for the sake of Doctor and Agassiz. And of course with Emerald's help in knocking off Esne.:

"So: what shall we do with the baby scorpion?"

Quattro's hate had burned off. "Wrap him up and put him away. I'm tired of blood, blood ties, blood spilt. Blood."

"And keep his eyes covered," Kinnear said. "I still don't trust hypnotists—excusing your presence, Locksmith."

The dogs were rounded up, despiked, and shut in their kennel; Thorndecker's forces put under guard in their own barracks. One of that sullen crew, passing Emerald, spat at her. Emerald ducked in time and grinned up at him. "I do not spit at you, man. You better know your Thorndecker is mad enough to make you people kill each other after you finish with us."

Palander and Spinel-beta helped beat out the grass-fires they had caused. The flatbeds would have to be rebuilt; their battered engines survived. Quattro and the other Frogs pulled the Qsaprinli out of the pit and sent them sliding on their bellies down the nets where the amphibian waited on the surface of the water to take them home. Inatrili remained crouching by the pool while Aspartil gently tried to draw her away. She would not move but stayed clutching the ground, looking up at Quattro with her huge eyes. Quattro sighed and dropped into the pool to fetch the child's body. It was drained and light. He crawled down the net one-armed holding it on his back and delivered it to her as she boarded.

Fleetingly Kinnear wished he had the use of the shuttle. He needed carriers. But if it were whole his enemies would have escaped in it, and if he had taken it into space the mother-ship had the right to claim it. His radio beeped.

CRAB NEBULA?

He pulled his mike spool. "Come in, XenoBi. What's up?"

"You in *control?*" Watts's voice.

"Yes. Don't I sound like it?"

"A bit pale. Listen, that big mother over the ocean just bleeped out. We wondered if it knew something we didn't."

"Maybe it was something you told them."

"Locksmith there?"

"Not too lively yet. Got a message?"

"Yeah. Tell him we have a piece of real estate for him. He'll know."

"Good. You got room for a couple passengers?"

"If we can dump the rest of the frags in the ocean."

"Probably. I'll check, and set a course for you to land."

The Locksmith got back a little of his strength and went in

search of Esne. He reappeared carrying her precious eggs, she dancing in his wake.

Kinnear gaped. "Dear God, don't tell me that's your friend!"

The Locksmith's eyes crinkled, his mouth twitched. "Why not? I respect a good ESP."

Kinnear shook his head and groaned.

"Listen, Kinnear: she is helpless. He promised to send her home when even she can't tell where home is. Emerald promised to try to find home for her. I can give her mine." He looked down at her with an eye both fond and cynical.

"And you don't think that's straining things a bit?"

"She reproduces rarely, and I have a big world. She does not need much space for her miniature rain forest. She cannot override our combined powers, and she can't change shape—but we can try hers. Perhaps even I—"

"Locksmith!" Kinnear said desperately, "all I ask is, please, don't do it *here!*"

Spinel stood at a lectern in his Great Hall, with Aspartil beside him, and said to all who had managed to crowd in:

"Friends, we own our own world again because of the many heroes with us: Irenyi Gurdja, Kinnear, Quattro, the Locksmith, Emerald and Raanung, the XenoBi team, the Aquamen, all our other helpers from Galactic Federation. And my Empress, Spinel-beta, Palander, Binatrel, all our family and many more of our citizens. I thank all to whom I promised thanks, they know who they are, and also those who did not know what courage they had within themselves. I cannot thank properly Anika Gurdja and my dear Agassiz who risked their lives to give me shelter, but I long to see them again. Renny will speak for me to the one, and Morgan to the other.

"You notice I am not quite the jolly and rather fatuous person I was before I left—but people, I never was. I behaved so because I knew no other way to keep peace. Now I have travelled far and become a killer I have earned the right to choose how I will keep peace. Consider that, for you have

behaved much like myself. With all our arguments and skirmishes we have been a fairly contented people. Now we must
determine how many terrible things we need to do—to keep
peace. That may take a few skirmishes yet. People, I am not
claiming wisdom. I want your help, as always, because the
problems are so great. That jolly fellow who amused you so is
not entirely gone—I rather like him myself—and he will
return at times, but not often, or for long. I have lived too
deeply now.''

the Pack displayed

By degrees, hop, jump, and stumble, the voyagers found
their ways home.

Magician and Priestess reversed: XenoBi
went into orbit around Praximf, bearing the Locksmith with
his precious soil and Esne with her precious eggs. By the time
one orbit was completed they were gone. XenoBi did not land
on Praximf again, then or ever. They knew when they had
had enough.

The Page of Cups: Kinnear settled in at Hydesland with the conscripted troops to guard all of the prisoners,
including the ones from the Tower. There was plenty of food
and no more violence. Kinnear saw to it. Three of the dogs
died of distemper, but the rest became pets of a sort, if not a
pleasant sort. Palander, having enjoyed his taste of adven-
ture, stayed on for a short while until someone managed to
bring his boat around for him. He wanted a sail home, the
only reward he asked for, and it was given gladly. He took a
liking to Kinnear and gave him much advice, mostly sensible. Kinnear, who loved so many sentient species, had the
old familiar wrench when Palander, without goodbye, cast
off for home, and he was in space when the boat was found
adrift with Palander, peacefully dead of age, lying in the
shadow of his sail.

Of the Ace of Cups: The Family, Renny,
the Frog Squad, the Ungrukh, collected Thorndecker and
sorted themselves into the lifeboats. During waking hours it

was left to the Ungrukh to supervise Thorndecker. No one
else would. When not in deepsleep he was too far gone in his
mind to care.

Renny had the miseries: she was looking blue, literally.
Emerald met her in a companionway where passing was
difficult, stood in her way and looked her in the eye.

"You want to say something about it, woman?"

Renny snarled. "What?"

"Morgan."

"It's none of—oh God, to hell with it. He's just turned
away. He thinks I'm ugly, with this damn scabby head."

"Is that so? And if he comes to you with open arms?"

Renny hesitated. Honesty won. "I guess I'd think he was
just trying to hide his distaste."

"The poor man is double-damned. You must be some risk
to care about."

"But—"

"Do you pity him? Despise him?"

"Of course not! What for?"

"For not striking out at Thorndecker."

"I thought he was very brave."

"*He* believes you despise him, when he knows
Thorndecker is only trying to express love in the obscene way
which is all he can. That is impossible for Morgan to explain.
And he is another stubborn one."

"I don't know what to do then."

"Does it occur to you to treat him decently and have
patience?" She grinned slyly. "We never meet each other
after today, Renny, so I risk making you angry at me. He says
he asks for it when he wants it, not so? You can be sure he
wants it again."

Renny's face turned a purple worthy of her Mama before
she burst into laughter. "You are a one-hundred-percent
dirty-minded bitch, Emerald, but I'm not going to be angry
with you!"

"Call me anything else you please, woman, but not by the
name of a dog!"

Justice personified and Priestess: Anika

was laying Tarot: Emperor, Empress, Swords and Pentacles, when the figure slipped in. She knew who it was: Renny, head covered in crisp curls, looking a bit boyish, a bit like that fellow who was probably her father; rather sweet, hadn't given his temperament to her. "Bellingrose is dead."

"Yes. You knew he never belonged to you. Mama, why didn't you ever find another one?"

"I found other ones. You staying on with GalFed?"

"Not to get screwed by every pirate from here to the Rim."

"I never blamed you because I left Gurdja. Not for you to break yourself—"

"For God's sake, Ma, that's—"

"Pop-psych? maybe partly true. Gurdja was a bad one and I was stupid. Then scared, turned off. . ."

"Tarot makes you see the worst. Like police and doctors. Or GalFed."

"That's pop-psych too. I don't always see the worst. Not in Agassiz." She smiled. "Don't fidget, girl. Give us a kiss, make a cup of tea and sit down. You've time."

"Time! I've more than enough time."

"Just enough."

"For what?"

"To answer the call I got yesterday, from North Key. I had a hunch, yah? so I bought another moped. Classy job. You can have the old one. But get working first. I need sane company and I want my tea."

The Hermit: Doctor was resting on a couch. Agassiz was looking a bit smaller in his scallop, but otherwise unchanged. He was cooing, gurgling and trying to play pat-a-cake with the naked oriental baby sitting on his chest.

"He is too heavy for you, Agassiz," said an unfamiliar young woman.

"Nonsense, Michiko. We suit each other perfectly. Renny, Michiko is Naoki Hashimoto's wife, and the cherub is Shin-go, their son. True Self, son of Straight Tree."

"One true self deserves another," said Renny.

Agassiz laughed and clapped his hands. Doctor jerked up, blinking, smiled at Renny and lay back asleep. Ti-Jacques came and smiled too. "You've been through the wars."

"Not the only one." There were a few lines in his face, a trace of grey in his hair. Perhaps they had been there before and she had not noticed. Now she did. Doctor, once old, was now aged. "Agassiz is better than I could have hoped."

"The baby helped. But we never know how much time."

"What will you do?"

"Morgan and me, we'll stay on as stewards, for now. After, we'll offer our services to any purchaser. We aren't worried."

A shadow fell on her, hands took her shoulders, the big powerful hands so vulnerable in the raw boniness of their knuckles, the redgold hair on their backs. "No promises!" she mock-growled.

The sun dappled the lawn, the new leaves of spring rustled, gaudy insects skimmed the ripples of the pools. The voice breathed on her neck: "We aren't worried."

The Ace of Swords: Journeying from Fthel IV to Fthel V, Quattro continued to tend Settima. They were wary, these inner-wounded, made no commitments. He stopped esping her. He planned to join GalFed if it would have him, as did the other nine Frogs who had come to like him. The rest would go back to pearl-diving. Settima could have done as she pleased, but it pleased her to be with Quattro, in a guarded way, at knives' ends as it were. She was no clinger, she treated no one with careless tenderness. When Palander had told Quattro he was much like Renny he was right; so was Settima. Any common ground they shared would be thorny, but full of life.

The Queen and Knight of Swords, the King and Queen of Pentacles: Emerald and Raanung jumped the steps of their gangway and sniffed the dusty dry air of their world. Khreng, Prandra and Nga were waiting. The rest of Ugruwarkh had become a little blasé about interworld travel.

The family exchanged the usual ritual bites, cuffs and

rasping licks, and Prandra rolled toward Emerald a good-sized ball of fur which dug itself under her belly and refused to budge.

"You look little older," said Emerald. "I think *our* ages are twice what we start with."

"Living around here makes you old enough," said Prandra.

"How does it go with you, Mother?" Raanung asked.

"Tengura is dead," said Nga, "so we lose a mother and friend. But the Hills Tribe organizes itself once again and I sit in its circle with your brothers and sisters."

"Good. What else is new, my-father?"

Khreng was taken aback for a moment at the change of subject. "Oh. Doctors come to take your cousin Embri's scarred face apart and put it together again, so now she is a fine-looking woman, if still bad-tempered. I go about the Tribes doing Good Works, your-mother is putting together the concept of a Mind which may be the right one, and may not—" snort from Prandra, "—and we have our last pair of Observers, one Zaf, a Yefni, and a Solthree named—"

"Jacob?"

"Ephraim. He says that is the grandson of the Jacob in one of their holy books, but it is still hard to pronounce. We call him Etrem. And you, do you go on to greater adventures?"

"We have enough," said Emerald. "We stay home."

Khreng looked long at Raanung, and said carefully, "In the Hills, my-son?" Eyes away from Nga.

"Son, a warrior does not hide under his mother's belly." Raanung stretched his tail to poke at the fuzz-ball, and looked up, around the Plains and at Khreng. "My-father, home is here."

Emperor and Empress: Spinel rested on his balustrade with Aspartil and Dunenli, gazing toward his city. "Dunenli, I think within a year I will abdicate in your favor and sit on Council with Aspartil and Beta and the rest. We will act as regents for a short while and then within a term agreed on by all, you may abdicate, if *you* agree."

"That is a relief," said Dunenli. "I am not greedy for power, and neither is Binatrel."

"Now perhaps we can work our way through most of the heirs-in-line so that all can have some power—and one day we may even become a republic. It seems a sound idea. Don't you think so, Aspartil?"

She did not answer, and he, brain spinning with new ideas, did not notice. "And when we come to increase trade we must make sure we have increased industry so we do not merely give away raw materials." Now he noticed. "Really, Aspartil, I need your help in making these decisions." But her hands did not gesture, and her eyes were far away.

Dunenli said, "Spinel, I believe they must be *moving!*"

Spinel forgot plans. "O Aspartil, is that so? Oh, give them to me, give them to me!" His delight sent the nutritive juices flowing in his cradle-pouch, and he crouched with snout opened and flap peeled back while she poured in her brood of tiny wrigglers.

From then on, Spinel would spend many half-days as a silent Emperor, but none had ever been so happy, nor would be.

The Fool: In the future, Bengstrom would retire, Narinder Singh replace her, Ptrilitititi replace him and then become homesick and move to a division that contained her own world. Kinnear would become Director, his last job before retiring, having reached his exact level of competence, and contentedly so.

At the moment he was standing with Narinder Singh on the red-lit balcony of the Forensic Hospital, looking down into one of the row of lighted cubicles. Thick glass walls cut sound; a silver mesh of white-noise cut esp.

Kinnear and Singh leaned on the rail and watched Thorndecker standing on the bed in green hospital suit and weighted boots, addressing phantoms with speech and gesture. An orderly poked his head into the glass bubble in the door to watch for a moment, then drew away.

"That's hard to believe," said Singh.

"No, the doctors bent the rules and let me at him for a minute or two. He is asking forgiveness of every single person he has killed, caused to die, or otherwise harmed, from year one and right down through Qsaprinel. Because of

the injustices done him as a child he will eventually be
forgiven by each one—but it will take quite a long while.
Then, if he's still alive, he will have peace.''

"That's not our Thorndecker! It sounds like a set-up.''

"The doctors agree. But they don't know who to
blame—or bless—and nobody wants to ask.''

*The Knight of
Wands:* That day was the last of a Thirty, and by 0430
following Kinnear had replayed all his holo cubes, read his
ponderous essayists, and drunk his allotted whiskey—all
undamaged in transit. He closed his door behind him and
went along and down the passages of his hive. At this hour
Seventh Heaven was thinly peopled and the most noise was
made by the robot cleaner, washing, drying, polishing, pok-
ing sleepers out of doorways to scrub their corners. One of
them was approaching when he reached the Qsaprinel door.
He switched it off.

There was a jolt of quiet, a few heads turned his way, but
he still looked Security and no one bothered him. The door
was unchanged: the bells and the gryphon handle remained,
the gold letters were bright, the wood unscratched by vandals. Like a hex, Kinnear thought, and smiled. He did not try
to open the door. Behind it there might be a dark empty room,
or spaceless nothingness, or a concrete wall. He shook the
little bell to hear it whisper like a pearl, pulled it and heard the
light peal of the bigger one.

He was satisfied and did not wait, but flicked the robot's
switches, except for the one that pestered the wretches of the
corners, and went up home to bed.

> *the Diviner loosens the knife in her
> boot, smooths her hair, and rests her hand
> on the carved ivory box to wait for
> a seeker, a madman, a lover. . .*

BESTSELLING

Science Fiction
and
Fantasy